THE

ANTIDOTE

THE ANTIDOTE

WILLIAM J. EYER
LAWRENCE E. JERALDS

A&L Enterprises
Ava, IL

The Scripture quotations in this publication are from the King James Version of the Bible.

This is a fictional work. The names, characters, places, and incidents (other than Biblical references) used herein are from the imagination of the authors or are used fictitiously and are not to be construed as actual. Any similarity to actual events, items, organizations, locales, or persons, living or dead, is completely coincidental.

The Antidote by William J. Eyer
                    Lawrence E. Jeralds

ISBN-13: **978-0-9745359-6-8**
Copyright © 2008 by William J. Eyer &
                    Lawrence E. Jeralds
Copyright © 2013 by A&L Enterprises

Cover Art by **Jarrett Eyer**
Edited by **Ann B. Jeralds**

Published by:
A&L Enterprises
1531 Highway 151
Ava, IL 62907

Printed in the United States of America by
BookMasters, Inc.

DEDICATION and ACKNOWLEDGEMENT

DEDICATION:

Jan Eyer- In the acknowledgments for their book, Split The Eastern Sky, Bill and Larry wrote this, "...we thank You Jesus for the inspiration that started this project and carried it and us to this point in our lives; we can't wait to enjoy our place in Your Kingdom." My husband, Bill, is now doing just that! He is standing before the Throne of God, singing and praising God with all the angels that he wrote about! Bill always gave God the credit for all his books; but now instead of writing it in the acknowledgments of this book, The Antidote and the first to be published since his death, he can do it in person! How Awesome!

We wish to dedicate **the Antidote** to **Jesus** our **Lord** and to the following people:

Larry- My wife, Ann, and my son, Joseph, for their time allowance and understanding. To Bill for his faith and compulsion to spread the Gospel.

Lastly to our fans who we hope this work gives much enjoyment and inspiration.

....

ACKNOWLEDGMENTS:

We, once again, wish to thank our Publisher, A&L Enterprises and especially one of our Editors, Ann. Ann's eye for detail is so vital to the quality of the work.

We wish to thank Joe Tanner for his enthusiasm in our efforts to spread God's word in an entertaining format.

Finally, we thank You **Jesus** for the inspiration and the opportunity to produce a testament to your great love for all mankind.

TABLE OF CONTENTS

CHAPTER ONE

KAPRE'S PROMOTION

The mighty Angel stood seven feet tall. His muscles rippled under the white ankle length robe bordered with gold at the collar, sleeve cuff and the hem. He swung his crystal blade and two more Demons fell to their fate puffing out of existence; sent back to their Master for punishment, torture and to once again begin the task of clawing their way up the ladder of success at the expense of their fellow demons. They would do anything for the hope of serving in Satan's army just to be defeated once again, and start the heartbreaking, endless process over and over again.

When at rest the giant sword appeared transparent as crystal ice, yet stronger than hardened steel. Now, however, it was filled with the mighty presence of God; a fierce light shining forth in all directions, reflecting off of the blond hair of the Angel and filling the hideous den of General Detestation, chasing the quivering demons who unsuccessfully sought the darkness that was no more. It was all they could do to blindly slither out of Logos' way.

The count was already at one hundred and climbing as General Detestation threw one soldier after another to their deaths as he tried to flee from the wrath of the Nostrum. There were only twelve angels in the mighty organization known as the Nostrum. The very name brought fear to demons and reverence to angels. Each of the twelve served God directly, working on His

1

most pressing business. They were mightier than any other angel or demon and they were, so far, unbeatable in battle, as General Detestation was finding out first hand.

The two ethereal beings had been fighting fiercely but each had now fallen to one knee not two feet from one another. Those evil red eyes of General Detestation stared deep into the ever victorious, piercing blue eyes of Logos. Detestation panted acidic, sulfurous breath into the face of Logos as they knelt nose to nose, both trying to rest enough to finish this contest. The battle had been a long one, and the two were evenly matched in size and ability, but Logos saw the move coming before Detestation even raised his sword to faint to the right then bringing it sideways, trying to slice Logos in half. Logos blocked with the clang of blade against blade. Sparks flew and the cowering demons watching from a short distance had to run for their lives as the two mighty Captains fought their last battle together. Tonight one of them had to die! Logos slid his blade along the blood red blade of Detestation and as they pushed against each other and rose slowly to their feet; Logos kicked out with his right foot causing Detestation to stumble taking two steps backward trying to recover. To Detestation's surprise and horror, suddenly Logos screamed his battle cry, "For My Lord GOD Almighty!" as his bright, pure white blade sliced effortlessly through Detestation directly to his heart. He stood frozen for what seemed an eternity, years of effort flashed before his eyes. He knew what horrors awaited his failure and tears formed in his eyes. The mighty demon of Satan, Detestation, cried one last desperate, "Nooo!" as he puffed out of existence, losing everything he had fought so hard to gain. His long reign of terror was over, as was disease; a cure had been found at last. The earth year 2099 was just passing as the large and final puff of reddish brown smoke filled the now empty chamber, all other demons having wisely fled the premises.

Logos, dropped his sword, collapsed to his knees in exhaustion, and ignored the blood oozing from the open wound in his chest. Never had he fought so hard, or found it so difficult to defeat a foe. He decided that he was badly in need of a vacation, perhaps even retirement. *'The cabin'*, the thought brought a smile to his face and he ignored his wounds while he prayed his prayer of thanksgiving.

TWO DAYS LATER:

As I sit here in this cabin, nestled in the beautiful Rocky Mountains, I have time to appreciate all that God has given me. At the completion of my last assignment, at that moment when Detestation puffed out of existence, I knew! I went to the Lord Jesus and asked that I be reassigned, "After all!" I said, "I've been in the Nostrum for over two thousand years! I believe I'm ready for lighter duty!"

Jesus smiled at me. He stood six feet, two inches tall, looking mightier than ever. His body was large but all muscle, His facial features that of a rugged outdoorsman, skin tanned by the sun and absent of wrinkles. I had seen him in his weaker state when he had walked the earth as a man. He looked much the same except that the wounds on his hands, side and feet had healed, leaving pale white scars on each. The hair of

His head came half way to His shoulders, while his beard was neatly trimmed. Both were white with a slightly golden sheen to it and his face as well as his deep brown eyes emitted His true Nature.

Jesus said, "I understand! Your fatigue is great and not just from your wounds." When Jesus touched me immediately my wounds healed and the pain was gone. He continued, "It's your very being that is fatigued, Logos! Go to the cabin and write down for me what has happened to you over the last ninety-nine years. Tell me what happened to bring this battle to its violent conclusion. Also in your report to me, please include the reasons you think this angel, you have named, should be allowed the distinction of becoming a member of, The Nostrum! There are more experienced and worthy angels around than Kapre! He's only had one charge and he'll be losing him tonight."

The Lord paused, smiled, and then finished, "I see by your expression that you are impressed with Kapre. All right! Write down his story! Convince me as you've obviously convinced yourself that Kapre has what it takes to be Nostrum and I'll consider your request. Now go Logos, with my blessing. You've been very faithful to me over the years and I do have much more for you to do!" Jesus vanished to handle some other pressing matter and I retired to the peaceful mountain cabin to carry out my new assignment.

*   *   *

Later that night at a not-so-secret research facility in the desert called The Antidote Research Facility, the defensive gates were opened for the first time to the public. A crowd of one million people was expected to assemble around the facility to hear from a man who the world had grown to love. A man who had lived a public life that was second to none and a private life that would have shocked the world, had it become known, which it had not, nor would it ever. The five-mile area immediately surrounding the research facility was filling up with dignitaries from around the world, including the current president of the United States, Jennifer Saxon. She had been asked to MC the festivities and had happily accepted. Further out the beloved citizens of the world gathered in the vast desert, which went on for miles and could easily accommodate a million people and even more. Security was a nightmare; port-a-potties lined the sand streets every so many yards. Mobile diners and venders of all types were feeding the multitudes and selling their wares.

The atmosphere was festive and electric with possibilities. The news media was out in force and the speech would be carried live via satellite throughout the world. Never had an item of this magnitude been presented cooperatively to the human race. Many had tried to stop it but had been unsuccessful. Many had tried to buy it but it was not for sale. Justin Schaefer Johnson had insisted on giving it freely to the human race and had arranged that no one government could monopolize it, hide it, or abuse it in any way. In the end he had won the agreement of the United Nations and calmed the fears of the medical professionals around the world. This was too big to keep hidden from suffering humanity, too important to squabble over lost wages or jobs, too fantastic not to give all the credit to the God who made it possible.

A hush came over the large crowd, starting closest to the facility and moving outward throughout the entire crowd till all that could be heard was the wind blowing by the microphones on the stage. The stage was about four foot off the ground and at the end closest to the facility a ramp ran from the stage floor down to the double doors of the facility. Large outdoor movie screens had been erected throughout the area so the crowd would be able to see the man when he came out to address them.

It had been rumored that he had not been out of the facility for fifty-three years, ever since he left the White House after two prosperous terms in office as President of the United States. President Johnson was ninety-nine years old and reportedly just as alert as when he was a young Senator conquering the Middle East. No one human had grown in reputation as a hero and now as an almost mythical creature of divine proportions since Jesus Christ.

Suddenly the dark stage was smothered in light as one set of flood lights after another were switched on. President Saxon walked onto the platform at a slow dignified pace. Her long chestnut hair, streaked throughout with gray, was tousled by the cool evening breeze as she stood center stage before the podium. She had been in office for a year now and her citizens loved her as the grandmother that she was and as their leader. At sixty-two she was still a beautiful woman and she had already proven that she could handle the reins of a government in flux. The United States stood at the gates of a new world order and would soon throw open those gates and share its treasures with the rest of humanity. President Saxon would more than likely have a leading role in this new government and the world trusted her. She had run for office as a Christian but had proven that she could live in harmony with the other religions of the world. Peace would soon follow in light of the discovery that they were unveiling this evening, of this she was sure.

It was, therefore, with confidence and pride that she began her introduction of this evening's star, "Good evening fellow citizens of the world. It is my pleasure to introduce to you this evening, a man who has undoubtedly accomplished more in one lifetime than many people could even hope to lay claim to in their collective lives. I, of course, speak of President Justin Schaefer Johnson."

The audience exploded in applause that lasted for several minutes before it slowly fell silent once again. She continued with a smile, "President Johnson would of course make no such boast so I make it for him." Laughter rippled through the crowd. President Johnson is up for the Nobel Peace Prize, which should come as no surprise after it is disclosed, what he has accomplished through his research.

"President Johnson was a genius from birth, a Senator at thirty and President of the United States by thirty-eight. Since then he has devoted his life to research which brings us to our purpose for being here this evening. Let me present to you - President Justin Schaefer Johnson!" this last she yelled out and waved a hand toward the double doors of the facility to her right, the crowds left. There was thunderous applause, but after several minutes, when nothing happened, silence once again fell upon the desert evening.

Just as President Saxon was deciding that perhaps she should speak again, the double doors whined open and the crowd could hear the buzz of the small motor that powered the wheelchair that carried President Justin Schaefer Johnson. His head was uncovered and bald except for one patch of thin white hair, which stood straight up on top of his head. He leaned forward in the chair as if concentrating all of his effort and energy on the ramp in front of him. He maneuvered the chair quickly up the ramp and drove right to the microphone. He was dressed in a tuxedo which seemed to shock many people who must have expected a doctor's white lab coat and small spectacles balanced precariously on the tip of his nose. He raised his head for the first time and turned his deep green eyes on the crowd before him.

When he spoke, his voice was deeper and steadier than the technicians had expected and they hurriedly turned the volume down a notch, "Hello, my name is President Justin Johnson. . ." thunderous applause ensued and a standing ovation.

When it was quiet again he continued, "I'm sorry I'm late but I had to change the batteries in my chair, my watch, my radio, and my pacemaker. . ." (The crowd roared at his good humor). "You think I jest, but when you get to be my age, if it wasn't for electricity to jump start me and batteries to maintain me, well I'd just be an old man imprisoned in his bed." more laughter and applause.

The old man smiled and said, "Jennifer here told

me that she and I were going on a date, so I dressed up. What she failed to tell me. . ." Here he stopped and stared at the crowd, then continued in a whispered, conspiratorial tone, ". . .was that you all were invited." (The crowd went wild with love for this man.)

He slapped his hand on the microphone and laughed as technicians threw off their headphones, "Enough of this nonsense! You didn't come to listen to an old fool tell bad jokes." Over the protests from the crowd he said, "Oh, yes, I know they're bad because I was just a boy when they were brought out of storage. That means they're older than I am and that's old. Now you youngsters listen up! I only have the strength to tell this to you one time. I've been tinkering in my lab for over fifty years now and I've come across a little discovery that I like to call 'The Antidote.'

"I won't try to explain how it works except to say that it perfects your own body's immune system in such a way that it speeds healing from both injuries and illness. It won't make you immortal by any means, so be careful when you bungee jump or orbital skydive, but it will help you live longer, happier lives." standing ovation and long applause, again.

"Without giving too much away just yet, it will take only one injection of this technology into your brain and one simple surgical procedure and within minutes your body's immune system will clean your entire body of any illness that might be present and it will keep all others away in the future." (A gasp from the crowd.)

"I have sent this technology to scientists all over the world and they concur that it works and have agreed to help me distribute it with the agreed cooperation of the leading world governments. For that we have Jennifer to thank." He made a sweeping movement toward President Jennifer Saxon. (More applause, whistles, and cheers.)

"As many of you know, I, like President Saxon, am a Christian and I must give all the glory and praise for this discovery to my Lord and Savior Jesus Christ. He gave me the brains, the determination, the forgiveness from the cross which made this discovery possible." Justin raised his old, shaky hands to the sky and yelled, "Praise and honor be to my Lord and Savior, Jesus Christ. . ."

On the backside of one of the large screens, to the far side and not visible to the platform, a man was strapped into position. He raised the high-powered rifle and looked through the scope. Indicators pointed from all directions to the center of the scope's sight and centered in that sight was President Justin Schaefer Johnson. The sniper's breathing was smooth and even. The ever-increasing pressure that he now applied to the trigger was patient and ever so smooth. The sniper whispered to himself, "Good night Mr. President."

The silenced explosion released the hollow-point bullet at super high velocity and it raced toward its intended target; the heart of President Justin Schaefer Johnson.

LOGOS AT MOUNTAIN CABIN:

As he proceeded with his assigned task Logos wrote: I must warn you, Lord, that I'm much better with my sword than I am with the pen, but I'll do my best to convey to you what has happened.

I was given this assignment just over ninety-nine years ago. Capt. Detestation was beginning to spread his terror upon the earth. He used natural disasters, wars, and even disease, to bring pain, suffering, and death to the humans of the earth! I was assigned to watch him closely and to stop him from going too far. It was shortly after being handed this assignment that I first met Kapre. I'll admit, Lord, that I was very impressed with Kapre from our very first meeting, ninety-nine years ago, today! I barely knew him or his charge at that time. It was the earth year 2000 and Kapre's charge was about to be born...

Kapre was finally being promoted from search and rescue, to Guardian Angel! That is if he could pass The TEST! Capt. Tutor stood before him with a look of pride as he handed Kapre his new sword. It was in an ornate sheath, which was covered with jewels, and intricate carvings of many famous battles. As Kapre pulled the sword from the sheath, he heard the mighty ring of the special material, which sounded like God's voice ringing through Heaven. A ripple of excitement dripped down Kapre's spine as the sword cleared the sheath. The engravings on the blade told of courageous battles that he himself had fought while in search and rescue. He turned the blade over, and though this side was shiny, and reflected heaven's light, it was free from any engravings. He looked questioningly at his instructor.

Capt. Tutor laughed, slapped Kapre on the back and said, "That side is reserved for the engravings of your new battles boy! Eventually the entire sword will be covered with your own battles and there will be many!"

That statement brought both excitement and a moment of doubt.

Tutor was short for an angel, only five foot six inches tall, but stout and strong. His white robe was trimmed in red and fluttered in the breeze as he watched his student with interest. He saw the doubt and in an inflated voice said, "None of that boy! You're about to become the guardian of the most precious of God's possessions, a human soul! There's no room for questioning or doubt, only loving and courageous service to our Lord!"

Kapre bowed low and whispered, "My apologies mighty teacher!" Kapre was six feet tall and thin. His strength wasn't apparent just to look at him but he used what he had wisely and his skill had improved satisfactorily over his years of training.

Tutor smiled and said, "No harm boy, now prepare yourself for the final test! He approaches!"

Kapre strapped on his new sheath but kept the sword in his right hand, at the ready. He began to tremble as the streets of heaven shook with the presence of the Nostrum. Michael the Archangel stepped toward Kapre and it was all Kapre could do not to faint dead away. He had heard the stories of the mighty Nostrum! He knew, as all angels knew, that Michael was the General of the Nostrum and the mightiest warrior in all creation! Michael, like Logos, was every bit of seven feet tall, of large frame and his muscles rippled as he walked. He put forth such energy at his approach that the air before him became charged with God's powerful presence.

Kapre hadn't realized when Tutor told him of The TEST for promotion that it was to be administered by the mighty Michael, himself!

Kapre, not knowing the nature of The TEST, and fearing Michael's approach began to back up.

"Hold your ground boy!" Tutor yelled, "You can't be a Guardian if you run, no matter what the odds!"

Kapre took a deep breath, took up his warrior stance and surprised himself by not waiting on Michael; motivated by sheer terror he flew with all his might at the surprised if undaunted Michael.

At the instant Kapre reached Michael there was a great flash of blinding light. Kapre looked around and found himself in what seemed to be a mountain cabin somewhere on Earth. Kapre also felt very different than his usual pain-free self and upon further examination found he was in a human body with its usual aches and pains.

Kapre had heard of The TEST during various exchanges with other angels, but no one seemed to know the details of the actual process or at least they wouldn't say. Since he was being promoted to Guardian angel and would be involved in many battle situations, Kapre was sure he would be involved in a spiritual battle of some type. Now here he was in a human body and not quite sure if it was still The TEST or if something else had occurred.

Kapre took inventory of himself and his surroundings to gauge his situation. He was dressed in winter mountain climbing attire and was disappointed to find that the new sword he had been presented was missing. The survey of the cabin had revealed food, extra clothing, plenty of firewood and running water.

Kapre was sitting in a large rocker by a big picture window and was struck by the beauty of the forest outside. Evergreens as far as the eye could see. He could see the green of their needles through the snow that was beginning to accumulate on their branches. Snow! It was falling heavily now and he was in awe at the beauty of God's nature. His thoughts were dimming as he thought about The TEST to see if he had the necessary attributes for a Guardian angel. Kapre knew he was presented a sword as a gift to accompany his advancement to Guardian angel, but now here in human form he was wondering if it was real or had it just been a dream. Kapre was in that dreamy state between dreams and wakefulness. His thoughts were clearing and his numb right hand reminded him to move it and to massage it back to life. He suddenly remembered he was in a mountain cabin with two friends on a late fall hunting trip. Of course, if he told the friends about the angel dream, he would never hear the end of it, so he decided to keep it to himself. It had been so real . . ."Oh well, back to reality, what was I doing?"

Yes, this was the annual trip that he, his best friend in college Phillip and Michael, his boss from work, had taken for the past eleven years. "What was that smell, bacon?"

*　　*　　*

"You know, he almost caught me off guard," Michael said as he winked at Capt. Tutor, "I don't think I remember one ever coming that close before".

Capt. Tutor nodded, "Kapre has been a challenge from the start, but those same traits make him the right one for the job of Guardian angel, especially for this charge."

Michael said, "Well I better get down there, he still has to pass The TEST to make the rank, remember he must make these decisions on his own, and since that is not the nature of an angel, it could be the REAL test". With that Michael vanished leaving Capt. Tutor and the rest of Nostrum to watch from above. They all knew what Michael meant by 'on his own'; angels always knew God's will and acted to fulfill His will without question. Kapre, however was now human, really human, and would have to act from instinct, from the center of his own being. This was the true test of all God's creations.

*   *   *

As Kapre was about to get up from the rocker to discover where the bacon smell was coming from, he heard a voice from the loft saying, "Is that coffee ready yet? I always get extra hungry on these trips; almost as hungry as I was every day in college. Kapre, you seem to always have things going before anyone else is even up".

It was then Kapre noticed eggs and bacon in the big iron skillet on the old wood stove and smelled the distinct odor of biscuits baking. Then he remembered he always drew the cooking duty on these trips and Phil and Michael took on the cleanup chores. Kapre checked the clock on the far wall now showing 5:30 a.m., the trio was about to take on a grand breakfast and then head out for a full day of elk hunting. Among the three of them they

15

had only brought home two trophies in the past eleven years, but of course, that wasn't the real reason for the trip anyway. They all returned to their daily lives refreshed in mind and spirit ready for new challenges. Kapre was embarrassed that he fallen asleep while cooking. He yelled back, "It's almost finished better get down here." He whispered under his breath, "And give thanks nothing burnt while I snoozed."

Phil, climbed down the short ladder from the loft, as he said, "Michael up yet?"

Kapre said, "Yes, he went out to feed the horses, said he'd be back in about 10 minutes."

Just then the door opened and Michael entered the cabin letting in a blast of cold air along with some fresh snow.

He stomped his feet, and joyfully yelled, "First snow of the season! What a glorious day!"

Michael was a tall man of 6' 5", muscular, but lean. He was a man of about 55 years, his hair was already white, and his features rugged, yet intelligent. His dark green eyes sparkled with boyish glee at the new snow.

Kapre rekindled the stove fire that had been disturbed by the gust of wind let in by Michael's entrance. The dream forgotten, Kapre tended to the breakfast while Phillip poured himself and Michael a cup of coffee, noticing that Kapre already had one. Phillip was a younger man of about 35 years, was shorter than Michael, a mere 5' 11". He was on the plumper side, but not really what is thought of as fat. He had a rounded face with red cheeks, a salt and pepper beard, and was teased a lot about being Santa Claus in disguise. Phillip was a happy man and looked it. He was fun to be around and it was no accident that he sold toys for a living. He owned a 'Toys R Us' franchise and he couldn't be happier or richer. He is lucky enough to have a beautiful and loving wife, complete with a newborn baby boy. To prove it he had brought a box of cigars and a chest full of pictures. He had attempted to stay home from the trip this year but his wife would not hear of it, "My mother will help out here, you get out of here and enjoy yourself" she had said when the annual call came. "I'm smart enough to remember that you always come back from these trips a new man and I do not plan to break a healthy tradition, baby or no baby." Philip smiled as he thought of his wife and son then was abruptly brought back to reality when a cold, wet, snowball was shoved down the back of his shirt.

"Yeow!" he yelled as he jumped up and pulled his shirt out of his pants in an attempt to get rid of the frozen fluid. All he managed to do, however, was get about half the snowball down his pants as well, which brought more laughter from Michael and Kapre.

Kapre laughed, "If you boys are done horsing around we can eat." He walked over to the table and lifted perfect 'over easy' eggs onto each plate. He then placed bacon, hash brown potatoes, and fluffy biscuits on each plate. He had already set the table complete with butter and homemade strawberry jam and fresh honey, Michael's favorite.

Phillip poured more coffee into each cup and the three men ate, laughed, and had a grand morning in preparation for their hunt. They talked about the elk that had gotten away, and there were many such stories, but today they would bag the biggest rack in history; this was a claim that they always made, but it wasn't an obsession with them.

With breakfast eaten, cleaned up and lunch packed, they saddled their horses and headed deeper into the mountains. The smell of pine was in the air and the snowfall had covered everything just enough to make pure heaven of an already holy place. Just ahead a deer jumped and ran for cover, white tail bobbing into a thicket. A distant wolf howled his triumph at killing the day's meal for his family. It was into this rugged wilderness that these fun loving men were about to travel; a place where the law of nature, survival of the fittest, rules.

Michael spoke, his breath visible in the cold air, "We better split up here. We'll ride to our usual spots and check back here just before dark. Remember, if you run into any trouble its three quick shots in the air as an S.O.S."

"Yes daddy!" Kapre and Phillip answered simultaneously as they rode off in opposite directions while Michael rode straight ahead.

* * *

Phillip was barely out of site of the others when he saw a blur to his right. Suddenly, a large grizzly bear stood before him growling. Without warning the bear's claws ripped through his horse's neck causing a spout of blood to splash the bear's fur. Phillip's horse dropped in its tracks, taking Phillip down as well. The bear's attention was focused on devouring the horse allowing Phillip to get up and back away slowly. He kept glancing back at a distant tree line, his only cover. What he didn't notice because of the disorienting snow cover and his own blinding fear was the ravine between him and the tree line.

When his foot stepped into thin air Phillip turned and lost his footing and half fell, half slid down the wall. He knew he would die in this fall but before this could fully register on his shocked mind, the collar of his coat caught on a bare branch that literally grabbed the material and hung him there, about seven feet down from the rim of the ravine. Despite the freezing cold he broke out in a sweat and started giving thanks to his maker for this reprieve. It was then that the life-saving branch gave a sickening crack and Phillip dropped a few inches more toward certain death.

Kapre reached his hunting grounds fairly quickly and started looking for tracks immediately. He had just dismounted from his horse to investigate the possibility of a fresh trail when he heard the shots. He couldn't be sure but they sounded as if they came from Phillip's .22 cal. pistol. Michael carried a .38 cal., which would have been louder and more urgent sounding. Kapre got back on his horse and headed off in Phillip's direction hoping this wasn't Phillip goofing off again.

Phillip's heart was beating at an alarming rate. He had managed to reach his .22 cal. Pistol and had fired the three alarm shots. At the same time the limb cracked again causing Phillip to scream hysterically and lose his grip on the pistol, which fell for and awfully long time before Phillip heard it hit rock. Phillip had tried to keep his eyes on the gun as it made its decent but dizziness overcame him then fear made him clamp his eyes tightly shut. Phillip whispered, "Oh, Lord help me now or meet me at the bottom."

Kapre galloped across the mountain range as quickly as possible. Within five minutes he spotted what was left of Phillip's horse. He saw the Bear dragging part of the horse off to his den. Fear gripped his heart. Where was Phillip? Was he crushed under the horse; before he could stop himself Kapre yelled, "Phillip! Phillip where are you!"

He heard a faint cry for help just as he saw the footprints in the snow heading off backward toward that distant tree line. Kapre walked his horse slowly in that direction and soon came to the ravine. He dismounted and laid flat on his stomach and looked over the edge. He saw Phillip some eleven feet below dangling over the ravine, with nothing between him and death but the collar of his coat and a very unstable branch.

"Phillip, hold still I'll get you out somehow. Try to reach up toward me."

Kapre reached as far as he could but lacked a good five feet of reaching Phillip's up-stretched hand. *'What a time not to have any rope'*, he thought. Kapre heard the crack just a split second before Phillip's ear piercing scream.

* * *

Michael and Tutor watched from a distant hill. Tutor said, "He's never going to figure it out in time." Michael just said, "Shush! Give him time and watch."

*   *   *

Kapre quickly surveyed the area for something to use as rope but to no avail; then in a split second; wait his clothing! Despite the cold Kapre stripped off his coat. Then his shirt, his pants and even tied his scarf into the makeshift rope. It wasn't pretty but it might just give him the distance he needed.

Kapre lowered that makeshift rope to Phillip and told him to grab hold and he would pull him up, but even with Kapre lying in the cold snow and reaching as far as he could Phillip could barely touch the leading edge of the cloth, it wasn't enough.

Quickly Kapre scanned the area and saw a possible solution. Daring but this situation called for extreme measures. There was a fairly strong bare bush at the edge of the ravine and Kapre tied one end of the cloth rope to the bush and the other to his right ankle. Then he crawled up to the edge and headfirst slid over the ravine's edge easing his way down the makeshift rope. A sharp rock tore at his cold flesh but in short order he was face to face with Phillip.

Phillip yelled, in surprise and shock, "What are you doing you fool?"

Kapre yelled back, "Do this quick or I'll get too cold to help you." He grabbed Phillips coat just as the branch it was hung on finally snapped completely. Phillip fell and screamed. He stopped screaming when he noticed he hadn't fallen. Kapre was straining to hold on. The knots he had tied pulled tight and one started to pull through.

Kapre yelled, "Phillip! Turn around and start climbing the rope."

Phillip turned and with Kapre giving his foot a boost, he was able to grab the material at Kapre's ankle and then get a handhold on the makeshift rope itself. He started climbing.

Kapre yelled up to him, "When you get up there, pull me up."

Phillip nodded his head but didn't have the breath left to speak. He climbed over the last of the ledge and collapsed exhausted and almost passed out. He was still lying there when he heard Kapre yell to pull. Phillip got to his knees and pulled on the clothing rope and started to move Kapre's dead weight as the slipping knot silently pulled through. Phillip was thrown onto his back, still holding the empty rope. Kapre for his part fell toward the earth and rock floor of the canyon at an alarming rate. As he was falling, head first to a certain death, Kapre found his thoughts, his mind, his whole being focused on one scripture. . . "The Lord is my shepherd. . ." Just before he hit bottom a flash of light brought him back to reality and he was at the feet of Michael, Tutor and Logos.

Kapre looked up and panted, "Was that The TEST?" They nodded, but none gave a clue as to the result.

Kapre said, "I failed didn't I?"

Michael asked, "Why do you think that?"

Kapre answered, "Because I got killed in The TEST. What good is an angel that saves his charge but gets killed in the process?"

Michael smiled and helped Kapre to his feet, "You did well my friend. You didn't panic, you used the materials at hand for the rescue, and most importantly you put the life of your friend before your own. Those are the qualities that you will need in great abundance in order to guard your charge on earth. This will be a very hard assignment, make no mistake of that. There are many who argue that we should give this charge to a more experienced guardian angel. I want you for the job. Will you accept your assignment without question or reservation?"

Kapre immediately said, "Yes, of course and thank you."

Logos spoke for the first time, "Don't thank us just yet Kapre. I'll take you to your charge and get you started on what is to be a very long and challenging assignment.

Kapre noticed that his sword once again rested against his leg and when he pulled it out of its sheath the shiny side wasn't empty any more but showed a man hanging from a cliff and Kapre in his shorts flying head first over the edge with terror etched onto his face.

Michael smiled and said, "Just a reminder that our dignity must sometimes suffer so we can serve others effectively, while keeping our sense of humor."

With Michael, Tutor and Logos all laughing, a stunned Kapre had taken his first step as a Guardian Angel.

CHAPTER TWO

TAKING CHARGE

Logos had his arm resting on Kapre's shoulder as they stood in front of the Mercy Clinic on Main Street; the name misrepresenting the evil that occurred within. Each day seventy-five babies lose their lives to greed, inconvenience and hard hearts. Kapre had butted heads with the abortion issue in his search and rescue duties but now faced it from another perspective; that of a Guardian Angel whose new charge's life was being threatened by a terrified, drug-ridden, fifteen year old girl, named Serenity.

Angels, like humans, do not know what the future holds and must rely on their faith in God for their plans to work. Logos was here to save the baby's life and get Kapre started on his journey.

Serenity stood in the rain just outside the clinic. She stood 5 feet one inch tall, blonde hair, a beautiful face, which was now smeared with make-up as her tears mixed with the rain that washed down her face. It was approaching evening and she knew that she would have to go in soon or chicken out again. Even in her drug clouded stupor she knew it was wrong to kill her baby, but she was also terrified to see what the drugs may have done to her child. Serenity was fifteen going on thirty. Despite her maturity through experience, she was still a terrified child. The father of the child had deserted her, as had her family. She was alone in a cruel and lonely world. She had thought this through and she knew that this was best for everyone concerned. She had earned the money for the abortion herself waiting tables and prostituting until she got too big. No one wanted to pay for an eight and one half month pregnant prostitute.

Serenity would have done it sooner but she hadn't the money or the nerve earlier. She had made several attempts but had always run away in fear. This time, however, her mind was made up. Chilled to the bone, cold and wet, she rubbed her tummy affectionately one last time then walked into the clinic and stood dripping on the lobby floor. The receptionist looked up from her work and with a sympathetic expression on her face walked over to Serenity, put her arm around her and moved her toward the hall which led to one of the exam rooms.

"I assume you're Serenity Clark, we thought you may have changed your mind, again. Come now, we must hurry, the doctor has to leave on time today."

She hustled her down a stark white hall to a small changing room, which was just as white and antiseptic as the rest of the clinic. The receptionist handed her a towel and said, "Here honey, dry off, strip off those wet clothes and put this gown on." With that, she turned her massive frame and left Serenity to her privacy.

Stunned that the time had actually come, Serenity looked around the small room. The walls were bare except for one poster which read in big, bold letters, located under the smiling face of a young girl, '**GOOD NEWS, ABORTIONS NOW AVAILABLE UP TO NINE MONTHS** (in smaller letters) **OF PREGNANCY', BUT DON'T PUT IT OFF TOO LONG.**

Without any further conscious thought Serenity methodically dried her hair, stripped off her clothes and then dried her body. She put the gown on and was tying it in the back when Machele Blakely walked in. She was a thin energetic woman of about thirty years. Her long black hair flowed onto the shoulders of her white nurse's uniform and reflected the light as she turned her head. Serenity just stared at her blankly.

"Good you're ready." She produced a syringe and said, "Lie down on the table honey and I'll give you something to help you relax."

Serenity, whose every instinct told her to bolt, did as she was told and laid down. Her fear hardened her heart to the inevitable. She felt the stick of needle and then nothing, she was out. Machele opened the door and pushed the gurney into the surgery.

As she entered, Dr. Nichols looked up and said, "Machele; is this the last one for today?"

"Yes Doctor this will be it. You'll get to your party on time." As Machele said this she untied and removed the gown exposing Serenity's naked body and painted antiseptic on the girl's belly.

Not wasting any time the doctor grabbed his scalpel, made a quick practiced incision that immediately exposed the uterus. He made a second incision effortlessly and without any conscious thought, gaining him access to the living, squirming baby held not so safely in his mother's womb. It was an important point of law that the baby be suffocated inside the womb. If the baby were to be removed first and then suffocated it would be considered murder, but if inside the womb it was just tissue. With a practiced hand that came from repetition, the doctor, without conscience, regret, or remorse, slipped the plastic bag over the baby's head and tied it tight.

The baby began to cry and struggle for life to the irritation of everyone present except the doctor. After just three or four minutes it had succumbed to the lack of oxygen and turned a Cimmerian shade of blue. The bag was removed and the corpse made a slight squishy thud as it was unceremoniously thrown into a metal bucket that sat on the floor for that purpose.

Dr. Nichols ripped off his gloves and told Machele to close for him and then quickly left the room. Machele had closed plenty of times for him, even though it was illegal. She got to work immediately. She sewed the uterus up and then started on the belly next. Something was trying to register on her mind, and then it hit her like a ton of bricks. The baby in the bucket was whimpering softly.

Machele froze. She forced herself to look and sure enough the baby was sucking on a bloody toe. Before that could sink in too far, Serenity started gasping for breath and then quit breathing all together.

Machele was there alone; she didn't know what to do. She ran out into the lobby, hands still covered in the young girl's blood. She looked through the front window and saw Dr. Nichols walking toward his car. She knew she couldn't catch him in time so she ran to the phone and called his cell phone. When he answered Machele yelled, "Doctor, the girl quit breathing get back in here." She slammed the phone down, saw the doctor turn and run back toward the building and then she ran back into the operating room.

The girl was already turning blue and the baby was still happily sucking on his toe. Machele stood by while Dr. Nichols did his best to bring the girl back, but even with all his experience he failed. The Coroner would later find that the anesthetic had reacted badly with the cocaine the girl had taken before coming into the facility. It would be deemed accidental overdose.

As for the baby, well they couldn't very well kill it now, so it was handed over to County Child Welfare System, put down as yet another failed abortion. It happened from time to time, but was not discussed; ever!

The baby boy was given a physical at the hospital and found to be addicted to cocaine but nothing else seemed wrong with him at the time. When he was older they would test his mental and motor skills, but for now they would dry him out and place him in an orphanage that specialized in infants.

*   *   *

When Logos came out of the Abortion clinic smiling, Kapre breathed a sigh of relief. "How did you do? Did you save him?" Logos nodded. "How did you do it?" Kapre asked excitedly.

Logos gave Kapre a piercing look and said, "It's a trade secret I'm afraid. Let's just say that I've done my job now it's your turn to watch over him." With that Logos was gone and Kapre was left alone with his new charge.

Kapre was excited, especially at first. He watched expectantly as the authorities named the boy child Justin Schaefer; Schaefer being his birth mother's maiden name. Over the next five years Kapre became rather complacent. No one had threatened his charge; no mishaps interrupted his fairly happy life. Nothing appeared wrong until his fifth birthday when they began testing him for placement in preschool. Everyone predicted that he would be of at least average intelligence because he walked early; toilet trained easily, and liked to play, although he mostly played alone. His caretakers even noticed that Justin spent a lot of time looking at the pictures in an assortment of magazines, especially magazines about computers. They were surprised therefore when Justin placed below normal on his first test. It showed him to have a below average IQ, his attention span on the test was almost non-existent. They labeled him as a learning disabled child, and no wonder with him being born addicted to crack cocaine. So when September of his first year of school came around, the orphanage put Justin in a special learning class. Justin just didn't seem to have any interest in school at all. He wouldn't turn in his homework, didn't answer questions in class and seemed utterly bored or overwhelmed, the teacher wasn't sure which. The only thing he seemed really interested in was leafing through books and pretending to read them, instead of actually studying his alphabet and numbers. The teacher tried to get Justin interested in his studies but when the staff psychologist diagnosed Justin with obsessive-compulsive disorder (OCD), she gave up and just let him look through books from the library during class. He was quite content and that allowed her to concentrate on other students who had more of a chance to succeed. She watched from time to time as Justin just sat and quickly flipped one page after another in these books. Justin was a small, thin child. He had pale skin, his head was covered with short, thick light brown hair and his deep green eyes were full of trust and peace despite his mental handicaps. Justin's behavior was very good for a child his age except for his lack of cooperation. Mrs. Harper had noticed that Justin had hastened his flipping of pages as one month flowed into another burning up his kindergarten year.

Justin's teacher, Mrs. Harper, picked up his books one day while he was at recess and read the titles. One book was a study of College level Physics I, another was on advanced Sociology through the ages, and a third was autobiography on the life of Albert Einstein. She shook her head and smiled, wishing Justin would try to learn as well as he flipped pages. Justin picked his own books each day, usually three large volumes which he would have flipped through by the end of the day. By the end of the year she estimated that he had flipped through about half of their extensive library.

Mrs. Harper sat in the teacher's lounge on the last day before summer break, which at the orphanage was only one month long. Mrs. Vicors, the first grade teacher came over and sat down with Mrs. Harper and several of the other teachers and they traded information about their students; each teacher sharing with the teacher in the class above their own. This would guarantee that any misconceptions about the children would be passed on from year to year. This is why it wasn't surprising that each teacher accepted Justin's diagnosis and his limited behavior from one year to the next without question; each assigning him a desk away from the other children, allowing him to sit alone with his books and just flip through them hour by hour, day by day, until he reached his sixth year in school and his twelfth year of life. It was on the first day of this sixth year in school that he was introduced to the most well liked teacher at the orphanage, Mrs. Links; who was known for her wit, her charm, and her undying belief that all children are special. She had been at the orphanage school for twenty-nine years. She was fifty years old, quite beautiful, single and determined to teach each child no matter their limitations. Nothing had prepared Justin for the intensity of her love, caring and wisdom.

It wasn't the fact that she had aged well and was still a beautiful woman, although Justin was beginning to notice girls and had an instant crush on her. No it was her eyes. The first time he looked into her deep, smiling blue eyes, which reflected hope, acceptance, and a caring soul, he was her prisoner. He wanted nothing more than to please her. He hadn't shown this kind of interest in anyone and frankly he didn't understand his feelings now but he did obey them. Gone was the desire to flip through books, a list books he had long since exhausted from the school's extensive library. Now when Mrs. Links asked him to do his schoolwork he readily responded and to her surprise did quite well. Every teacher there was very surprised to hear that Justin could actually read and write and do math on a sixth grade level. Miraculously Mrs. Links brought out an A student in Justin, but she had a feeling that there was more to Justin than met the eye. Justin for his part was getting the same feeling about Mrs. Links.

*   *   *

The Headquarters of the Johnson Empire covers three square miles of down town Chicago, but don't bother looking for it, because it is nestled a half mile below the foundations of the massive buildings which make Chicago famous. The Johnson Empire is the result of five generations of Johnson's who started with the dream of having the greatest "Think Tank" in the world and ended up with the richest most powerful secret organization in the world. Kings and Presidents have come to drink at the pool of knowledge created by the Johnson's and gladly paid the price. Since its inception it has grown into many fields including advances in medicine, military weapons, including government research and development of biological weaponry, space travel technologies, psychology, philosophy, business and many other varied areas of study that have proven helpful over the years. The current CEO of Johnson Enterprises and the oldest living Johnson, had over the years enlisted the help of the most gifted people alive and used the secret research of many deceased brains of the past. These adults and child prodigies are discovered and recruited by an army of teachers, business people, government employees which include police officers, senators, congresspersons, the FBI, CIA, and many Judges. These people are posted around the globe and it costs him a small annual fortune to maintain these "observers" but it has proven valuable time and again over the years. From time to time an observer will spot a potential child prodigy and will call his office so he can send out a team of experts to test the child.

Theodore "Teddy" Johnson sat back in his

meretriciously padded leather bound chair and rubbed his eyes. He had just finished reading a lengthy report from one his off-shore oil accounts and he was very pleased with the profit they reported. He got up and walked over to the bar that covered the entire east wall. Johnson was a short, powerfully built man who looked to be in great shape for his age of 65 years. He still had a head full of salt and pepper hair neatly cut. His hands were Herculean and nails impeccably manicured. He wore a $3000.00 blue suit whose shimmering material reflected the office light as he took the coffee pot from its heater and poured himself a cup of coffee, one sugar no cream, and walked back to his desk and sat down again, causing the complacent leather to gasp with pleasure. He took a sip of his coffee and was reaching for another report when the intercom chimed. It was his secretary, Mrs. Parsons. Her tone of voice spoke of her years of training and experience as a personal aide to one of the most powerful men in the world as she said, "Mr. Johnson, Don Black is here to see you on a subject of importance." Mrs. Parsons had been Johnson's personal aide for many years and had proven herself to be very helpful in weeding out people and subjects that would waste his time. So it was with confidence that he said, "Send him in Mrs. Parsons and thank you."

The door lock hummed then clicked as it admitted Don Black to Johnson's office. Black was a lanky gaunt man. He had long black hair pulled back and held in a ponytail by a gold elastic band. Johnson didn't look up as he told Black to help himself to a drink or a cup of coffee, his choice. Black smiled at Johnson's entirely business-like attitude. Black was only thirty-five but had risen quickly in Johnson's organization. Having been a child prodigy himself in figures and later in his perception of people. He had been promoted steadily over the years. He was now in charge of recruitment and resources and traveled the world testing potential associates for the organization. He wore black slacks and a white pullover golf shirt. He very seldom wore a suit but his clothes were stylish and expensive, paid for by the company through his inexhaustible expense account. Black poured himself a straight whiskey then walked over to a chair and sat down, letting it mold itself to his body comfortably. He had been in Johnson's office often but never tired of looking at the pictures on the wall, the trophies that spoke of Johnson's tennis years and even a few chess trophies, one of which was new and won just last month. There was a gallery of pictures of Johnson shaking hands with Presidents, Kings, Movie Stars, and some of the more distinguished business people.

Black was one of the few men in the world who wasn't afraid of Johnson and who felt quite relaxed and at ease sitting in his proximity. Johnson secretly enjoyed Black's courage and ease, but was gruff with him at times just to see if he could shake him up; he seldom could, however.

Johnson barked as he closed the report he had been studying, 'Well what do you want?"

Black took a sip of his drink and then spoke in his soft confident tone, "We may have found another child prodigy." Black took another sip, purposely making Johnson ask for an explanation.

Johnson smiled as he sat back and loosed his tie, "Well are you going to tell me about it or do I have to read it in one of these reports?"

Black smiled back and said, "I just got off the phone with Mrs. Alberta Links from The Orphanage for Unprotected Children." Johnson looked at his three page list of holdings which he owned and said, "Holding 27?"

Black nodded his affirmation as he continued, "It appears that she has a twelve year old male student named Justin Schaefer. His mother was a "coke-head" and died during a botched abortion attempt, but Justin mysteriously survived and ended up at our orphanage. His first year of school he was diagnosed with OCD, Obsessive-Compulsive Disorder. . ."

"I know what OCD is Black", Johnson said irritably, and then with an impatient wave of his hand signaled for Black to continue.

"It appears that all young Schaefer could do was browse through page after page of every book in their extensive library. It is full of books for all ages including many research books for the teachers. None of the teachers actually tried to teach Schaefer anything until he reached Mrs. Links in sixth grade. He's now suddenly holding an "A" average, seemingly with ease. The exceptional part is that Mrs. Links suspects that Schaefer was actually reading all of those books that he's been flipping through all these years. She first suspected it when she was explaining the computer to her class and she mentioned that a computer is like an artificial intelligence that is under our control. Schaefer raised his hand and bewildered Mrs. Links when he told her that he didn't want to contradict her but that her computer would not pass the Turing Test for artificial intelligence. He went on to explain that Alan M. Turing had written a paper in 1950; Computing Machinery and Intelligence, in which he devised the Turing Test for artificial intelligence and a simple PC does not pass that test. Mrs. Links had stared open mouthed at him and he realized his mistake at speaking and wouldn't answer any more of her questions. She called us to test him to be sure but her instincts have always proved valuable in the past."

Johnson was holding his breath and, when he realized it, he let it out with a sigh. No sixth grader talks like that unless he knows much more than he lets on. He spoke to Black in almost a whisper, "Do you think this could be the one? After all he already has the wisdom to hide his knowledge."

Black smiled at the twinkle in Johnson's eye, at his child-like enthusiasm. They had been waiting for the child that had been spoken of in the old prophesies which are found in the Black Book of Life; the veritable bible of Johnson's secret religious organization; a religion which has predicted, 'A child will be born who will have wisdom beyond his years and will bring the power to cure or kill the world. Beware not to expose this child to the light.'

Black nodded saying, "Yes, Teddy, I believe he may be the one and furthermore, as far as I can determine he is still pliable, he has not been exposed to the light."

Johnson whispered, "I want him Black. I want him now."

Black gulped the rest of his whiskey, stood up to leave and whispered back, "Arrangements are already being carried out as we speak.

The two men stared happily at one another for a moment, and then Black turned and left Johnson's office.

CHAPTER THREE

THE TAKE OVER

The first attack came like a swarm of angry bees. Kapre had become complacent over his first twelve uneventful years as a guardian angel. Not so much as a little nymph had bothered the boy, Justin Schaefer. Truthfully Kapre had been a bit disappointed in his charge. He didn't seem to be anything special, all he did was study, he had no spiritual sense what-so-ever. He didn't go to church, didn't pray, as far as Kapre could tell he had heard of God by reading the Bible once but only gained head knowledge from the experience. He never did anything dangerous for Kapre to protect him from and, for that matter, never even left the orphanage. Kapre was bored, and not a little ticked off at the obviously undeserved build-up this assignment had been given. Dangerous indeed! Important! Oh Yeah!

Then the first swarm of demons hit. First thing Kapre heard was an annoying buzzing in his ears. Then ten little mischievous demons appeared with teeth and daggers bared. They attacked Kapre without warning and without conscience. Kapre was sitting on the headboard of Justin's bed feeling sorry for himself as he watched his charge sleep. All ten daggers found their mark before Kapre could even think to draw his sword. The daggers were too small to do any permanent damage but they sure hurt. Kapre did a forward somersault and had his sword in his hand when he came back to his feet. Blood trickled down his chest, neck and arms. As the ten demons disappeared, five larger ones took their place. These demons were more experienced and more powerful in the art of war. Each was six feet tall, muscular and wielding large red swords. The farthest to Kapre's left attacked first taking a well-aimed swipe at Kapre's head. He ducked, parried and sent the demon flying through the air, smashing him against the far wall. The next two attacked at once and though Kapre expertly blocked them both the fourth and fifth attacked him from behind. He felt the painful blows as red blades passed through his back and out his front. There was a bright flash and Kapre was gone.

The five demons laughed and danced a triumphant victory dance. Suddenly they felt his presence and snapped to attention. Capt. Detestation flew in and landed amongst his soldiers. He was large for a demon, about seven feet tall, with a large muscular frame. He wore a black robe with a blood-red sash, which lay across his left shoulder and came together under his right arm. His feet, like his Master's, were like horses hooves. His face was shaped like an upside down triangle and was lined with many wrinkles that always kept his face in the shadows. Detestation's tongue absentmindedly flicked in and out much like a serpents and was split at the end, each side ending with a stinger. He bent over the sleeping boy and smelt him with his tongue. Detestation smiled, baring his teeth as he whispered, "We found him Master and we will take over his care." He stood, turned to his five soldiers saying in his command voice, "I charge you with his care and protection. Make sure he gets all this world can offer and above all be sure you keep all "bad" influences from this boy. We will not lose this soul to them!" As he said this he nodded his head toward heaven.

There was a red flash and he was gone. The five demons smiled at one another. They had just been given a field promotion to Sergeant. Then the responsibility hit them and they became nervous and very serious. Yes, they would make sure that no "bad" influences spoiled this boy's soul.

*   *   *

Kapre landed at the feet of Jesus with a thud. He lay there humiliated and defeated. When Jesus touched his shoulder he was instantly healed but his spirits showed little improvement. Jesus lifted him to his feet, hugged him and said, "The war is not lost my friend. I died yet live on and so do you. It was expected that the boy would fall into enemy hands. It must be so if our Father's plan is to work." Before Kapre could ask his forming questions, Jesus said, "Go now to Logos and he will prepare you for the next phase of your assignment. You will do well, I'm confident in your abilities and your loyalty. They hugged and Kapre puffed out to reappear next to Logos.

Logos slapped him on the shoulder and laughed, saying, "The first surprise attack is always the worst. Don't worry about it."

Kapre was a bit miffed when he said, "You could have warned me that this would happen!"

Logos shrugged his shoulders and said, "If I had warned you it wouldn't have been a surprise and you would have learned nothing. Tell me what you did learn from this."

Kapre thought for a moment and whispered, "That no matter how many years pass between attacks that I must always be ready, for there will always be attacks."

Logos smiled, "That's correct Kapre, now you're ready for phase two of your training."

Kapre stared at Logos for a minute and then asked, "Shouldn't we go back and protect Justin?"

Logos smiled and said, "Don't worry about him for now, we're working on it. Right now Tutor has a few more things to teach you. Learn them well."

Kapre's head was spinning as he was transported to Tutor's training grounds, "We're working on it, what does that mean?" Kapre yelled but Logos was already gone.

*   *   *

Reverend Robert "Bobby" Alexander Johnson was born to be the heir-apparent of Johnson Enterprises. He was everything that his father wasn't. He was twenty-two years old, tall (about six foot three) with a lean muscular body. He had handsome features, almost Roman looking with sharp cheek bones and chin and dark brown eyes. Unlike his father's, however, his were kind, compassionate eyes full of love and honesty. His ravine black hair was cut short and rustled gently as the fan oscillated back to him and he wiped the drool from one hundred year old Amanda Stevenson's chin. This was Tuesday and he volunteered at the Mercy Nursing Home on Tuesday. He loved talking and praying with the residents and helping in various capacities where needed. The residents had many life stories to tell and ached for someone to listen to them. Bobby did listen and prayed for them, with them, and read the Bible to those who could no longer do it for themselves.

You couldn't tell, by looking at him, that he was a millionaire in his own right. His slacks, casual shirt and loafers were all bought at a discount store. He drives a used car with high mileage and rents a modest apartment in the city. His father had set up a trust fund that he received on his twenty-first birthday last year. Bobby had made some wise investments and had turned his two million into many more and it kept growing daily. Bobby didn't like what his father did for a living, but he took the money anyway. He knew that with them being at odds and if he; Bobby, was to fight him, he would have to have funds, but Bobby never spent much on himself.

Bobby raised his voice, "Mrs. Stevenson just one more bite of applesauce left, open wide." He opened his mouth also as Mrs. Stevenson opened hers and squished the applesauce off the spoon onto her chin. Bobby figured that she only ate about a third of the food that she was fed. She smiled up at him, her round face glowing with happiness and peace as she patted his cheek, saying in a squeaky voice, "Thank you son." Her son Frank was eighty years old when he passed away over two years ago, but Bobby never corrected her. What harm does it do to let her believe her son is here taking care of her?

Bobby had just wheeled her back to her room, got her into her favorite armchair and folded the wheelchair putting it in the corner of the room. He said his good-byes and walked into the hallway and ran right into Justin Schaefer. Justin fell back and sat down hard.

Bobby looked into Justin's pale face and Bobby saw fear in the boy's green eyes. Justin was out of breath as if he had been running for a long time. Bobby helped the boy up and asked, "What's the matter Justin? Why have you come? How did you get here?"

Tears welled up in Justin's eyes and one dripped onto his cheek as he whispered, "They know Pastor Bob, they know."

Bobby sat down and lowered his head, praying for an answer. When he didn't get one he just hugged Justin to him and tried to soothe his shaking body. Justin whispered, "I tried to do what you told me. I didn't let them know how smart I was all this time, but the other day without thinking I corrected Mrs. Links about computer intelligence and I've been getting "A's" lately. I'm sorry Pastor Bob, but I really like Mrs. Links. Then today a tall man with a ponytail came and asked me a lot of questions. At first I tried to answer the questions wrong but that just seemed to excite him more. He kept after me until out of anger I just had to show him that I knew the answers and more than he thought. Now he wants to take me away to a special school. Mrs. Links said that it's a good thing but I didn't like that man. He's not kind like you or Mrs. Links and I would have to live in a place where he is one of the big wheels in authority. What should I do Pastor Bob?"

Justin had been spitting all this out in rapid-fire succession, hardly taking a breath. Bobby had been through this before with three other children from other places. He knew all about his father's think-tank and why he wanted Justin. His heart was sick. He had fought his father's adoption attempts on the other children and lost. His father controlled the Judges who always ruled in his favor.

Justin pulled on his sleeve to get his attention and then handed him the small New Testament that Bobby had loaned him. As he handed it to Bobby, Justin said, "They don't know that I memorized this book. I lied when the tall man asked me if I had ever read the Bible. You better keep it Pastor Bob, I have it hidden in my heart just as you taught me."

Bobby whispered, "Listen Justin. They won't hurt you. They will teach you many things and then they will want you to work for them. My father, Mr. Johnson will probably adopt you. I may not be able to get to you for years, but please remember this book, it is all true. I will be praying for you and the others, yes there are others, but one day I will find a way to get you out of there and you can use your talents for God. Will you remember me and God?"

Justin was still nodding his agreement when Don Black ran around the corner with two other men. He saw them hugging and his heart hardened with anger. He tried to keep his tone civil as he walked up to them and said, "Bobby thanks so much for finding our run-away for us."

Bobby, also with great effort to stay calm said, "Mr. Black, how nice to see you again."

Black smiled and asked, "How do you and Justin know each other?"

Bobby answered smiling back, "Oh, I volunteer at Justin's orphanage on Fridays. We've become great friends."

Hatred flashed in Black's eyes as he asked through

gritted teeth, "I hope you didn't spoil him with your archaic ideas about a God who can't possibly exist."

Bobby had learned long ago not to argue with this man, "No, your people would let me talk with the children but only about art, never about religion." Bobby was also an artist and had taught on Fridays at the orphanage for over a year.

Black bent over speaking into Justin's face as he gently grabbed his arm, "Well Justin it's time to meet your new father, Mr. Johnson, your adoption was just finalized. Mr. Johnson is Bobby's father too, though they don't always get along the best." Black looked up at Bobby and said, "Why don't you stop wasting your time and come work with us. You could have it all if you would just learn to trust your father a little."

Bobby patted Justin on the head, winked at him and said, "Remember Justin that I'll always be your friend and if you need anything just call." He handed a business card to Justin, who glanced at it, instantly memorizing it before Black grabbed it from him and said, "That won't be necessary." He threw the card on the floor and took Justin and walked away, the other two men trailing in their wake.

Bobby knelt down and prayed, "Father in Heaven please keep Justin safe from their kind. I know you have a plan for Justin's special abilities and I leave him in your hands for protection and guidance. I've done what I can until you guide me to do more." Logos put his hand on the young minister's shoulder and gave him peace. He smiled at Bobby and wished that all humans were as loving and pure as this man. Logos whispered to Bobby's heart, "It will all turn out well. God has everything under control."

Detestation laughed and spit, "Logos you bleeding heart. That man will never have the power to interfere with me or my Master's plans." With that he turned to follow his servants out of the Nursing Home. Just then the praying minister said, "In the name of Jesus Christ I bind Satan and all of his demons so they will have to flee and stay clear of Justin. Be gone Satan in the name of the Lord Jesus Christ!" Detestation and his minions screamed in rage as they were instantly transported back to their master by the power and force of binding prayer.

After the last of the foul smelling sulfuric smoke had dissipated Logos laughed loud and long, then whispered, "Detestation, just keep thinking that Bobby is weak, Please."

CHAPTER FOUR

THE SEDUCTION OF JUSTIN SCHAEFER

The worst had finally happened, but it wasn't as bad as Justin had pictured. He had been trying so hard for his entire life not to let on that he had knowledge beyond his years. He was afraid that people would think him a freak and lock him away somewhere. Then Rev. Johnson had warned Justin that his father, Mr. Johnson, would take him away to use Justin's knowledge for something evil. Justin had read the New Testament, he had not as yet been able to read the Old Testament, but he did believe in God. However, he wasn't very attached to God. Justin's mind worked best on information that he could see, feel, and touch. He had always known so many things and with his photographic memory he learned and remembered anything that he saw. He had never had any trouble recalling every bit of information that he needed. When he first started to recognize people as fellow companions Justin, at first, thought that all people could learn the way he did, but to his shock and eventual torture, this was not the case. It didn't take him long to learn that babies don't talk or read at age two, as he had. He instinctively kept his abilities to himself so that his caretakers would leave him alone to wander through the many books and magazines at the orphanage. As he was pretending to just flip page after page, seemingly without rhyme or reason, Justin was actually reading about many exciting things. There were so many things to read about that he never could have stood the starvation of knowledge that he would have endured attending classes as a regular child. Lately he had been experiencing withdrawal for he had long since exhausted all the reading material at the orphanage. Now, however, he stood in the largest library he had ever seen. The sight of all those volumes of knowledge quickly dissipated the fears and sadness he had been feeling just moments before.

Don Black watched and smiled with the realization that they had him hooked already. This had turned out much easier than he had expected. Like most people with abilities like Justin's, they just can't get enough knowledge. Their minds thirst for it like the body thirsts for water. Don had purposely started the tour of Johnson Enterprises with its enormous and well-stocked library and research center. He had watched Justin, on their path here, as they walked by laboratory after laboratory all of which had purposely left their doors open. Justin's eyes had grown larger and larger as he walked further into the complex and the importance of such a massive facility started to sink in. The auditoriums, Olympic-sized swimming pool, tennis courts, theaters, horse riding paths, nothing, however, would quite interest Justin like this massive room so full of knowledge.

Justin realized that people here were not going to hold him back. On the contrary they were going to encourage him to learn and study along with balancing things like eating, exercise, and playing at something of his choice. This was to be expected from adults and he would endure it well, but everyone would readily notice how Justin would fly through the latter things to get back to the first, his true love, knowledge.

Justin just stood and turned in a circle trying to take it all in. Don said as he gave Justin a gentle shove on the shoulder, "Go ahead and check out the books, it'll be all right." Don Black was happy with himself and with Justin. He knew with this kind of reaction that Justin would do anything to stay here and not try to leave before Black was finished with him. His plan was already forming in his own sharp mind as he watched Justin climb the stairs to a second floor containing thousands of books. Besides the row upon row of books there were tables with dividers on top and computers in each cubicle. Of course, all the books on the shelves as well as many more volumes were available in electronic form. One wall of the room opened to reveal drawer after environmentally controlled drawer containing optically encoded computer media with all the book material and room for multitudes more as needed. The books on the shelves were there because Mr. Johnson enjoyed the idea of printed books and they really looked impressive, anyway he could afford this type of excess. They purposely didn't allow their students access to the net because they wanted to control the type and content of knowledge that went into their children, their students, and their eventual mental slaves.

To men like Don Black and Theodore Johnson these children were a crop. They planted knowledge and ideas into fertile minds and in time harvested the best that they could produce. Once they were milked of all the research and inventions they could provide, or they got sick or unproductive, they had to leave the institute.

They were given a small pension for life, but none seemed to live long. They never saw any of the millions of dollars that the institute had made from the marketing of their inventions. Some were never told that their ideas had ever been put to practical use, whether in the space program or the many war efforts around the world or possibly in the pharmaceutical field. Medicine was big business and he who could invent and distribute the newest medicines became the wealthiest. Johnson Enterprises was a world leader in these and many other fields.

Don Black found that Justin wasn't afraid of him anymore and seemed to be adjusting very quickly to an overwhelming situation. This made Black just a little nervous but he couldn't explain why. No matter, as long as the investment in Justin paid off eventually. He led Justin out of the library to the cafeteria to eat supper then he would guide him to meet his new father, Teddy Johnson.

Even though they were deep below the earth they couldn't tell it from the huge, well-lit plaza they passed through. Justin actually said, "Wow!" as they turned the corner and saw the glory of the entire plaza. It was six city blocks long, five city blocks wide and four stories high. In the middle, the tile floors came together from four separate directions ending at a park covered with real grass, on which stood a dozen live oak, maple, and walnut trees. Each tree was large and had a round bench about its trunk. On the left of the park from where they now stood, a two-story waterfall, eight feet wide emptied itself into a ten-foot wide and four-foot deep pool that was stocked with many colorful multi-species of fish.

Justin ran to the pool whose five foot high glass wall allowed him to watch more live fish than he had ever seen in his life. He heard a roaring sound even over that of the waterfall and looked up in time to see about ten boys and five girls careening down a winding, curving, ramp which had its origin somewhere on the fourth floor from all appearances. The ramp was six feet wide and had sturdy clear railings made out of a strong clear aluminum. The roaring came from the many wheels of their roller blades coupled with the joyful whooping and howling of youth at play. Where the ramp crossed large hallways, on the North and East walls, a hidden laser light triggered a railroad style crossing arm, stopping all traffic whether bicycle, roller blade or pedestrian. In seconds the group had descended from the heights of the plaza and went zipping off in the direction of the cafeteria. When they were safely past, the crossing arms went up and the warning beep, beep, beep stopped. Justin laughed out loud at the sights and sounds of this fairy-tale land.

The plaza area also housed many shops where the students and workers alike could buy clothes, snacks, supplies, and toys. Don Black had his right hand on Justin's shoulder as he led him through the heart of the plaza's stores. He said, "Justin, if ever you need something from one of these stores, just take this card and hand it to the store clerk." Black handed Justin a shiny red card, which boasted of Justin's picture and his ID number and name. Across the bottom of the card were printed neat, bold, capital letters spelling out **'LEVEL ONE CLEARANCE'**.

Justin looked from the card to Black's smiling face

and asked, "What does level one clearance mean?"

Black looked down into Justin's overwhelmed face and answered, "It means that there is no monetary limits to this card. You may buy as much as you want, need, and can use. If something breaks just take it back to the store and they will give you another one, anything at all."

He stopped talking and let that sink in for a moment. On a whim he said as they passed an ice-cream shop, "Justin; why don't you run into this shop and get me a chocolate ice cream cone, and get yourself anything you want."

"Really!" Justin ran into the shop and asked the clerk behind the counter for two chocolate ice cream cones. The clerk asked, "Will that be one or two scoops?"

Without hesitation Justin said, "Two scoops, please."

As he waited for his order to be filled he looked out at Don Black who was talking on a cell phone. He couldn't make out what he was saying but he was laughing and seemed very pleased about something.

"How will you be paying for this young man?" the clerk asked as she put the cones in holders on the counter. He smiled up at her and handed her his card saying, "With this?"

She took the card and did a double take, seeming to check his picture twice. Almost nervously she said, "Thank you sir." as she passed it through a scanner and handed it back saying, "I hope you enjoy the ice cream sir and please do come back again."

Justin took the cones and started licking his while he walked up to Don Black and handed his to him. Don had put his phone back in his pocket by then and said,

"Thank you, Justin."

They resumed their walk toward the cafeteria and Justin held his card up with his free hand and asked, "Why did that lady get so nervous about this card when I gave it to her?"

Don licked some chocolate that was trying to escape down the cone and answered, "Because there are only four such cards in existence; yours, mine, Mr. Johnson's, and Pastor Bobby A. Johnson's."

Justin stopped walking and stood looking wide-eyed at Black. Black asked, "Does it surprise you that Pastor Bob has one?" Justin nodded. Black smiled and said, "It shouldn't. Mr. Johnson is a very generous man." Especially when he knows he is getting it back tenfold, Black thought, but he said, "Just because Pastor Bob doesn't get along with his father, Mr. Johnson would never revoke his privileges here. One day if he comes to his senses Pastor Bob could own all of this." As he said this last he made a sweeping motion with his ice cream cone.

Justin had been standing there listening, trying to get it to register in his mighty brain when he felt the cold stickiness of chocolate running down his right arm. He quickly licked at it and got it under control, then asked, "Why did Mr. Johnson give me one of these cards and not his other adopted children?"

Black bent closer and whispered, "Because he has been watching you very closely and he has decided to accept you as his own dear child. You are to inherit this if Pastor Bob insists on being stubborn."

Justin looked at Black and asked, "Shouldn't that honor go to you sir. You seem to run things, the way people treat you with such respect and sometimes a little fear I think?"

Black laughed as he bit into his cone, "Nothing escapes your keen eye does it son. Well don't you worry, Mr. Johnson takes very good care of me. The person who takes over Johnson Enterprises was preordained to do so. We thought it was Pastor Bob, but after researching your birth and after my testing you back at the orphanage we now believe that person is you. Now don't you worry about such things just yet my young Johnson..." Black noticed the quizzical look that Justin gave him. "...Oh, that's right I forgot to tell you. Your name was legally changed when Mr. Johnson adopted you. That has never happened before either. I hope you don't mind."

Justin searched his heart and mind and to his surprise he didn't. He finally remembered the card and pulled it out of his pocket. He hadn't noticed when he had first looked at it but sure enough in bold letters it had his name as **'Justin Schaefer Johnson'**. He looked up at Black and laughed, "You know it actually makes me feel good Mr. Black that someone loves me enough to take me in, give me their name, a middle name and all of this in one day." Justin made the same sweeping motion with his right hand that Black had made earlier, "I think I can get used to such wealth very easily."

Black's smile broadened, "You don't know how happy that makes me, Justin, and you'll find that Mr. Johnson is a very loving and generous father." (Just don't cross the old buzzard), he thought as they walked into the cafeteria to eat.

As Justin ordered pizza, more ice cream, and a root beer, Black took his spoon and banged it on the counter and said, "Let me have your attention please." Suddenly the noise of forks, spoons and knives hitting plates, glasses being set down, and the hum of hundreds of conversations at once all stopped instantly. "I would like to introduce the new heir to the Johnson throne, Master Justin Schaefer Johnson."

The hush was broken by a single person clapping then another and soon the applause had grown to a thunderous crescendo. Justin suddenly didn't know what to do. Finally he decided the only polite reaction would be to bow, so he did, several times.

CHAPTER FIVE

RESPONSIBILITIES OF AN HEIR

Theodore Johnson was just a little nervous. They had found the one predicted by the ancients and he didn't want to lose him like he had his son. He had been disappointed for years that the predicted one wasn't his son. All signs had pointed to him at first, but there were small things that didn't add up. The first was that Bobby just wasn't smart enough. Oh he's brilliant, but he's no genius. The predicted one had to be a genius. Johnson opened the large black book he had sitting in front of him. It was entitled, **'BOOK OF WISDOM'**. He opened it to the very familiar passage and read out loud, "The Chosen One will come unknown to mankind. He will be rejected by his own and will live alone in his mind until discovered. The man who discovers him would be wise to take him in as his own to train, educate, and mold into the one whom serves our Lord Lucifer. This child will have the power within him to destroy or to heal the entire world. The man who controls him will be most fortunate. Thus ends the prediction of Nephanisis; (1716)". Johnson closed the book and smiled to himself, repeating, "The man who controls him will be most fortunate."

Just then his phone rang. He absently picked it up and barked, "Johnson!"

On the other end Don Black whispered, "Now

Teddy put your nice voice on, I'm bringing your new son up in just a moment. Now remember what we talked about sir. With Bobby you shut him out thinking that he wasn't old enough to know and make decisions. You also never gave him much of yourself in time or affection; this needs to change. It will be awkward for you at first but as we agreed; you need to try hard and make it as natural as possible. Justin is a sensitive, pliable, genius, twelve year old, but he's lonely. He has a boy's need for a father who will love him, show him affection, friendship and trust. Let him in on secrets beyond his years, well you get the picture..."

Johnson wouldn't let anyone else talk to him like this, but this is what Black was paid to do and he was a genius in his own right, "I get it Black! We've rehearsed this enough, I'm ready."

Black asked, "Did the new chess board arrive?"

"Yes it did. It's an exquisite piece of work that set me back one-hundred-thousand dollars, but it looks like it's worth every penny. Where's Justin now?"

Black looked over his shoulder and said, "He's being overwhelmed by our roller blade kids who are falling all over him trying to suck-up."

"Wonderful!" Johnson said and continued, "You were right to announce him as heir. That removes so many problems he might have had with the other children. I don't think he'll get picked on at all, do you?"

"Not more than once anyway. Oh, he's coming over, got to go."

The phone went dead as Johnson hung up, sat back and took a couple of deep breaths. He suddenly clapped his hands once and laughed gleefully. He hadn't had this much fun in years. He knew the mistakes that he had made with Bobby and he wasn't about to make them again with Justin. He had the means and the incentive to treat Justin the way a child would want to be treated if they lived in this fairy-tale land built by Johnson to overwhelm all his children but especially 'The Chosen One'. He knew that Justin had the potential to be the Chosen One, but would he live up to his role? Time would tell.

Johnson walked over to the fireplace where a gas fire scorched a realistic yet fake pile of logs. He sat down in his chair at one end of a small square table upon which sat the new chessboard with the pieces set into their opening positions. The board was hand crafted from pearl white and ebony shaded ivory as where the pieces. He had to admit it was a work of art. He picked up his black king and held the cool piece in his hand. It was smooth and buffed to brilliant sheen. He hoped that Justin liked to play chess it was the one thing that he knew they could do together.

There was a knock at the door. Johnson got up and walked over to his desk and hit the lock/release button hidden under the lip of the desk and the door lock buzzed and clicked. When the door opened a small pale child preceded Black into the office. The boy stopped and stared at all the pictures, trophies and animal heads which were proudly hung on Johnson's wall. He was pleased to see the awe on the boy's face.

When Justin entered he took in the room at a glance and thought he had just entered the throne room of a king. The large desk sat on a platform making it higher than the chairs that sat in front. In one corner stood a full sized luminous silver knight's suit of armor, standing a little less than six feet tall. There were pictures of Mr. Johnson with some famous people, some of whom Justin recognized as movie stars. The walls were lined with animal heads, all proudly killed by Johnson himself. Cabinets with glass doors held many trophies for tennis and chess that told Justin of Johnson's interests. Justin had read three books on how to play chess with the masters and always wanted to pit his knowledge against a worthy opponent, now maybe he would get his chance. The degrees on Johnson's wall showed that he had graduated with a Masters in Business from Harvard University. He also had degrees from Princeton and Yale. He was about to ask how one person could have so many degrees when his eyes finally fell upon the man standing by the desk. He was an older man, short, with salt and pepper hair. He looked powerful causing fear and shyness to suddenly overwhelm Justin. He couldn't speak but just stood impressed by the man's presence. This is the man who owned all that he had been shown. This was the man who had chosen him to adopt as his own son. This was his father, but would he like what he saw in Justin? All of his fears and questions vaporized when Johnson smiled and said, "Come in son and give your father a hug."

Justin had never been hugged much. Mrs. Links had hugged him from time to time but she was the only one. Justin didn't know until that moment just how starved he was for attention and the contact of another human being.

With sudden joy he ran into Johnson's waiting

arms and the man picked him up and they hugged. Tears ran down Justin's face as he felt the man's warmth. He smelled of pipe tobacco, alcohol and after-shave; the smell of a truly worldly man. Justin drank it all in and loved it. They stayed that way for quite a few moments. When Johnson put him down, Justin noticed that he too was crying.

Johnson hadn't been ready for the power of his own emotions as he wiped tears from eyes that seldom entertained any. He instantly and even truly loved this boy that could very well be the Chosen One.

Black cleared his throat and said, "If its all right sir I'll just go work in my office until you two are finished."

Johnson looked at him, cleared his throat to regain control and said, "Yes, and thank you Black, for everything."

Black closed the door and left father and son alone to get aquatinted.

While Johnson and Black were talking Justin had wondered over to the chessboard examining it with admiration. Johnson walked over to the bar and asked, "Would you like a soft drink Justin?"

"Yes please. A root beer if you have it."

Just to be safe Johnson had ordered some of every kind of soft drink so he did indeed have it. "Go ahead and touch it if you like."

Justin had been itching to touch the chess set but it looked so expensive and he didn't know what was proper in this place. He picked up the white king and it felt cool as he twirled it between his hands. It was smooth, shiny and beautiful.

"Would you like to play?" asked Johnson as he came back with their drinks.

"Well, I've read all about chess but I've never really played the game."

Johnson smiled and said, "Well there's always the first time; white or black?"

Justin thought for a moment and wanting to pay Johnson back in some small way said, "I'll take black giving you the first move."

Johnson was surprised at Justin's manners and said, "That will be capital my boy. Justin I want you to be at ease around here. What I have is yours, remember that. You are free to explore our domain. There are some security areas that you will need an escort for safety purposes but I'll not keep any secrets from you. Do you understand?"

Justin, who couldn't possibly, at this early date, understand the magnitude of that statement, pulled his chair up on the black side of the board and smiled, "I don't know how to thank you Mr. Johnson..."

Johnson broke in, "I wish.....I mean I hope, if you feel comfortable with it of course, that you would call me Dad."

"All right Dad", Justin answered with eager innocence. I just don't know how to repay you for all that you've done for me already. It seems that suddenly I'm like Cinderella; like I've gone from rags to riches overnight."

"That you have son, but you'll get used to it soon enough; now let's play."

The game lasted for about an hour and was nip and tuck the whole way. Johnson finally put Justin in checkmate but just barely. Justin sat back and smiled at Johnson, "I thought I had you for a minute there."

"So did I Justin. That was an outstanding game for anyone, but you say that this is your first game?"

Justin just nodded.

"Well with the experience and exercise of actually playing the game you'll soon be able to put the theory that is already in your mind, into action on the board. When that happens few people, least of all me, will be able to beat you."

Justin liked the sound of that.

Johnson pulled out a cigar, "Do you mind?" Justin shook his head, amazed that this powerful man would even ask. "I'd offer you one son but you're just not old enough yet to be smoking."

Justin nodded his agreement.

Johnson held the flame of a solid gold lighter to the end of the very expensive imported cigar until it was properly lit and then took a few puffs. Sitting back in his plush chair and crossing his legs, he began his prepared speech, "Justin do you understand what it means to be heir to something?"

Justin answered quickly, "Yes sir..."

"Dad, please."

"Yes, Dad, it means that you are next in line to take over."

"Very good son; well you are now heir to Johnson Enterprises. I will be training you to take over when I can no longer do this job. It will take a lot of work even for someone with your type of mental capacity. You'll need to study the academic disciplines and train in the skills of music, fencing, business, and some sports activities, do you understand?"

"Yes Dad, I need a rounded education that includes many things so that I can fit into any type of society function and learn to manage people."

Johnson was a little surprised that Justin caught the total implication so quickly. There was a depth to Justin's reasoning that made even Johnson just a little nervous.

(I'm glad he's going to be on our side), Johnson thought as he laid his cigar aside in the crystal ashtray.

He thought for a moment and then said, "Justin, you will be given everything you want, need, and can use, but with that comes the responsibility of living up to your end of the bargain. As we take you through your training you will be included in many secret operations of this company. You will, therefore, have to be initiated into a secret society that is very discriminating. Not even my influence will help you with the Committee. You must pass their tests and satisfy them as to your loyalty, do you understand?"

Justin thought it sounded both exhilarating and scary at the same time, but nodded his head in the affirmative.

"You must assure me now that you won't get squeamish and turn back on me once you start. Can you promise me that you will be loyal and obedient to this society's rules?"

Justin not knowing exactly what he was promising said confidently, "Dad, I'll do whatever it takes to be a loyal son to you."

Johnson walked over to his desk and picked up the phone saying, "Black, bring it in."

Just moments later Black entered with a packet of papers.

Johnson stated factually, "Justin this is my new will. In it I'm leaving everything to you as my sole beneficiary, do you understand the enormity of that?"

Justin became dizzy at the offer of such generosity and simply nodded.

Black came over and handed Justin some papers and explained, "Now Justin these are contracts that we will ask you to sign, please look them over."

Justin glanced at them and saw as he flipped through the pages that he would be promising to keep secrets a secret, he would obey his father's commands even if he personally disagreed with the action; that he would promise to take over the business if anything should happen to his father. It also spoke of a secret society that he would agree to join when he was ready and that by penalty of death he would keep their business secrets to himself.

He looked up at the expectant men and smiled. What boy his age didn't want to belong to a secret society? It was all so invigorating. He took the pen they handed him and he signed the many papers that were then signed by Johnson as his legal guardian and Black as a witness. Then Johnson signed his new will legally making Justin his heir-apparent, which Black then witnessed and sealed making them all legal and binding documents.

Justin left Johnson's office, his head spinning, with a mixture of pure joy and a bit of weight from the new role he had taken on as heir to the kingdom of Johnson Enterprises burning in his gut.

THE ANTIDOTE

The suspense and surprises were not over yet! As Black led Justin down the hall from Johnson's office he found that his living quarters were not far from his father's office. They had turned left when they left his office and Black took him into the next room, which was Black's office. It was the same size as his father's except Black's carpet was powder blue while his father's was deep red. Except for a couple of modern art statues there was very little in Mr. Black's office. Black seemed to read Justin's mind and said, "I'm hardly in my office except to sleep, so I haven't gotten around to decorating much."

Justin asked, "You mean you sleep here too?"

"Oh, that's right! We didn't show you this in your father's office did we? His is the same." Black picked up a remote, "This operates the TV and stereo system. Watch." Black pressed a button and the wall to the right of the bar slid upward exposing an extensive library of books neatly arranged on shelves ten high with a space of two feet between each one. Yes, that's right each ceiling was twenty feet high and decorated with paintings of all types, each hand painted by the original artist. Each ceiling had two huge chandeliers hanging down and radiating its splendor. Black's desk was as large as Johnson's and it too was on a raised platform with chairs sitting down on the main floor below. There was no mistaking which person was important when you came in here.

Black nudged Justin's shoulder to get his attention, "Now watch this", he pushed another button and Justin watched in awe as the bar swiveled on its axis and stopped half-way around creating a large doorway.

They walked through and found a room, no two rooms. One was as large as the office space, the other about a fourth the size, which made a very large bathroom. The carpeting, walls and even the ceilings in here were covered with the best and most expensive of materials. Justin was overwhelmed (not for the first time today) and couldn't even make sense of all the pictures, patterns and designs he was now looking at. It reminded him of a movie he had seen once of medieval times. There were knights, dragons, angels and demons on Black's walls and ceiling. It was both grotesque and thrilling at the same time.

Black laughed at Justin's wide eyes and open mouth, "That's enough for one day young man." He took Justin by the arm with almost loving tenderness that he hadn't shown till now, and led Justin out of the spellbinding, hypnotic room.

When Justin first came back to himself they were already in the hallway. Again they turned left and stopped in front of the next door down. Black explained that he was to put his entire hand flat on the screen on the wall. He had seen Black do this at his room so he mimicked him. A light came on and scanned his palm and the computer said, "Name please." It was a seductively soft female voice, Justin liked it, "Justin Schae..I mean Johnson." "Please say your name again slower", the computer complained. "Justin Johnson." "Thank you and welcome home, Justin". With that the door lock buzzed and clicked and Justin entered the living quarters which were his and his alone.

Black explained, "Justin that lock works on your hand print and voice ID and yours alone. We believe in giving a person of your stature his privacy; for there will be times that you need to get away from your duties and studies and this will be your sanctuary."

As they entered, the full impact of Black's statement escaped Justin; for what he saw before him was beyond his wildest expectation. He sighed from awe and disbelief. What he saw before him was so unbelievably extraordinary and just what a twelve-year-old, no matter how ingenious, would dream of having.

Just like the other office rooms they had entered the office of Justin Johnson had a smaller version of the desk that Black and Justin's father had. It was on the same platform raised above the rest of the room. To his left was a bar just like in the others, except he would later find that his was filled with ice-cold juice, bottled water and soft drinks of almost every conceivable flavor. He would also find a very large freezer containing fruit; assorted flavors of ice cream, even already prepared chocolate and strawberry malts. Justin just stood there taking in the sights. Where the door swung in he found that they were standing at a railroad Crossing. The track ran around the walls of the office and in spots up the walls like a roller coaster. No it was a roller coaster Justin realized to his delight. He would find that it was operated from its only car that held up to four people. The track passed in front of the bar and then turned left, rising steeply upward, almost to the top of the twenty foot ceiling, then dipped suddenly almost straight down and around the rest of the room with two smaller hills, to add to the thrill of the ride, before coming down to the floor again and stopping just before the bar. The crossing gate at which they now stood would prevent anyone from being hit if it was in use when Justin buzzed them in, which he could do from the roller coaster's car even while he was riding. Justin noticed that the carpeting, black and white swirl was very thick and soft. He almost bounced across the floor as he ran to his new desk. The entire desk was black, but of what material he could not say. It was hard like stone, cool to the touch and very glossy. He could see his reflection in the desktop. As he sat in his chair that was a black leather swivel rocker very plush and padded like everything else, Justin noticed a panel of controls to his right. He tried to push one of the buttons but his finger hit glass and he jumped when a voice, no the same female voice said, "Please place your palm on the glass for identification." He did so and the computer seemed to sigh with irritation, "Please state your name, you should know the drill by now." Justin laughed as he said, "Justin Johnson." A section of the black glass on top of the desk slid so fast he didn't notice where it went but it was gone. He noticed now that the panel had been fake and was hiding a large remote control unit that he removed from its holder.

Black said, "For security purposes, I'd suggest you remember to lock that up when you are finished each time."

Justin just nodded and started pushing buttons. Under the track where it rises up high just past the bar, the wall slid up exposing Justin's own library. He would find that besides books on chemistry, biology and genetics it contained the top three-hundred classics of all time. The next button he pushed turned his bar like the others and he knew where that led. There were buttons marked for music, TV, in house movies (any he wanted and some yet to be released, from X-rated on down, he wouldn't be held back here), video games, computer games, and one button marked with a skull and crossbones.

"What's this one for?" he asked Black.

Black leaned over to see which one he was pointing to and said, "That one will open the secret chamber where we hold our meetings but it will not work until your father activates it. When he calls a meeting the "X" will light up and when you push it a small portion of your office floor will sink downward. Just slide down onto a stairwell that will lead you to the chamber. But for now young man, let's finish this partial tour; it is past time for you to be in bed."

The last thing Justin wanted to do was sleep! His head was swimming and he hadn't even scratched the surface of what his office contained for fun, entertainment and information assimilation. As they walked into his bedroom, Justin wasn't even thinking. He was in that neutral state that an overwhelmed mind will use to gather reality around itself so it can continue to function. Again, Justin stopped dead in his tracks, looked around slowly, and found he was having trouble breathing. He forced himself to take a long slow breath and then let his brain register what he had been seeing. The ceiling was covered with the old west. Cowboys rode galloping horses, twirling ropes over their heads in an attempt to capture and brand the new steers. Others were shooting rifles at Indians and Indians were returning fire with bow and arrows as well as rifles. One portion of the ceiling had more buffalo painted on it than existed in reality. It was a beautiful work of art. The walls had a 3-D wall covering, which was an exact replication of Dodge City, complete with boardwalk and swinging doors into the walk-in closet and the bathroom. Above the swinging door into the closet were the words "Barber Shop" complete with a red and white striped pole hung on the wall outside the closet. Over the swinging door into the bathroom were the words, "Longbranch Saloon". In one corner of the room stood a full size replica of a horse, saddled and ready to go. This Justin would later use to throw his dirty clothes on and find his clean pajamas. The floor was covered in a dusty brown carpet as thick as his office carpet but it completed the look of the "Town" in which Justin would live.

Justin entered the bathroom and immediately to his right was a shower stall for a quick wash. The rest of the right wall contained a bathtub about half the size of a large swimming pool that held four feet of constantly warm water completely recycled every six hours. The end closest to him was molded into steps, which he could use to walk down into the pool or he could just jump in. The top of the sunken tub was level with the tiled floor. From where Justin now stood he could see an entire ocean of fish life. The effect was created by the one-inch square tile arranged into a large mosaic of an ocean teaming with life. To add to the effect the entire wall above the small pool/tub was made of thick glass that formed an aquarium and seemed to magnify the size of the many live fish it contained. Justin couldn't tell how deep the aquarium went into the wall but he knew it was magnificent. To make it even more childproof, Justin would find later that other people were hired to feed and care for the fish. On the wall at the end of the tub/pool were switches labeled, temperature, whirlpool, with several settings for each. Next to the panel was a seat with arm rests and a headrest fastened to the tub at just the right height to sit down. Then depressing a button on the right arm the occupant could raise or lower himself into the warm pool of water to whatever depth he desired. There was also a sea green-blue urinal, toilet, and sink on the far wall. The sink was shaped as a large clamshell on a pedestal. Coming full circle on Justin's left was a dressing table with a tri-fold mirror standing six feet above the table. There was also an electronically movable bench in front of the table. On the table were brush, comb, aftershave, even though he didn't need to shave yet.

"Are you ready for bed Master Justin?"

Justin jumped at the new voice and Black laughed as he introduced, "This is Mr. Summons. This is an appropriate name because if you need anything you just summon him and he'll come, although he'll never be far away. He is your bodyguard, butler and nanny."

Both Justin and Mr. Summons made a face of disgust at the nanny crack, but it just made Black laugh all the more. Justin now noticed that the only blank space on the wall to their left held an, until now, hidden door, through which Mr. Summons had entered the bathroom. Black noticed Justin's line-of-sight and explained, "That door leads from your bathroom into Mr. Summons's rooms. He is the only one who can access his room and your room. While you are in your rooms he may go to his, otherwise he will be following you around. He won't interfere with you in anyway and you need to forget he's there. There is some danger with you being

the heir and all so if any trouble occurs Mr. Summons
will take care of it and you do whatever he tells you to do.
We hired him to help you, and he came highly
recommended so everything should work out fine. Do
you understand Justin?"

Justin nodded as he stared up at Mr. Summons
who was standing at attention. He stood about six foot,
six inches tall, was very thin but had a robust body. He
had an angular jaw, sunken cheeks and very pale skin.
He was wearing a luminous black suit, a long sleeve
white shirt with cuff-linked cuffs showing under his black
suit coat. Justin knew that if he had gotten closer he
could have seen himself in Mr. Summons's shiny black
shoes. To finish the picture Mr. Summons wore a long,
thin (about an inch across), black tie. Justin hoped he
could get used to this man. He was ominous looking,
standing there so silently.

Justin jumped again but this time it was Black
speaking, "Well I'll leave you two alone to get acquainted
Justin." He gave Mr. Summons a quick nod and got one
back in return. With that Black left.

Justin was a little nervous now. He was alone in
these very large rooms with this very eerie looking man
who looked down at him, opened his mouth and spoke in
a deep soft voice, "Master Justin, would you like to bathe
and get ready for bed?"

Justin only thought for a moment and thought he
would try his new wings, stretch his boundaries, "I will,
but first I'd like to ride my roller coaster."

"As you wish Master Justin; just press this buzzer
when you are ready and I will assist you."

Justin ran out into his bedroom, ran through it

with hardly a look and ran directly to the car on the tracks. He jumped in and read the control panel, which was simple enough. On the panel were three buttons that were labeled, start, stop, and door. Justin strapped himself in and with some excitement and perhaps some apprehension pushed the start button. Like most roller coasters it climbed that first tall hill slowly but as soon as it had cleared the crest it dropped quickly causing Justin to scream with delight. It rose up and down the other two hills around the flat (the crossing arm was down as Justin sped by) then it sped up the large hill faster this time and then repeated its circuit again. Justin lost count of how many times he rode around and around, but soon he was getting just a little motion sick so he pressed the stop button and after finishing its cycle the coaster came to a smooth stop just past the front door and before the bar where Justin had found it earlier. He got out, swayed and stumbled into his bedroom and through it to the bathroom where he ran smack dab into Mr. Summons, who seemingly hadn't moved from the spot where Justin had left him. Justin was about to fall backward but Summons caught him and held him up. Justin was going to thank him but instead he vomited all over Mr. Summons' black suit and shoes.

Summons picked him up and held him over the stool until he was finished and then sat him on his not quite stable feet. Mr. Summons said, "Master Justin, why don't you take off your clothes and climb in the tub and get cleaned up." With that he turned and walked into his own room and shut the door. In an impossibly short time, maybe thirty seconds, a minute at the most, and definitely before Justin had completed his own undressing, Mr. Summons returned looking as spotless as ever. He went out into the bedroom as Justin climbed self-consciously into the tub. The water was perfect. It was warm and relaxing. Justin sat in the seat strapped himself in, laid his head back and the chair sunk into the churning water up to his neck and he was asleep almost instantly.

Mr. Summons washed Justin's body, took him out of the tub and wrapped him in a large towel. After drying him he dressed him in fresh pajamas and laid him in his very large bed. Justin rolled over on his side without waking and Mr. Summons pulled the covers up to his chin. He stood there for a moment to make sure his breathing was normal and then he departed for his own rooms. As he left he clapped his hands once and the lights went out as several low-intensity night-lights came on.

Detestation stood over the sleeping boy and laughed. The five demons he had left in charge were explaining, "He didn't know what hit him sir. He was an overwhelmed child. It won't be a problem to bring him over to our side, sir; he's there now I'm sure."

Detestation stopped laughing. The hackles stood up on the back of his neck and he felt his strength leaving him again. He whispered, "It would be easy if it wasn't for that ignorant man of God who won't stop praying. We will have to take care of him before he messes up all of our plans."

The five demons hadn't seen their master look this irritated for a while now. They said in unison, "He can't stop us Master, he's only one Christian..."

Detestation cut them off angrily, "Yes, he's only

one but he's a praying Christian and they're the most dangerous kind. You better pray to our master that he doesn't interfere with us or you know where you'll end up!"

They knew and started shaking at the thought. It was then that the binding wave of Pastor Bob's prayer hit all six demons from hell causing them to writhe in pain. Together they opened their collective mouths and let out one desperate frustrated scream and again with desperate red eyes flashing and rotten black teeth gnashing, they were sent back to their master for punishment.

CHAPTER SIX

STANDING IN THE GAP

Pastor Bob had not always been a prayer warrior. Like most Christians he had to grow from an infant Christian to an adult prayer-warrior Christian with the power to fight Satan. Unbeknownst to Mr. Johnson his wife had been a secretly practicing Christian and she had seen Bobby saved before she died. Bobby had been seventeen when he knelt down and accepted the Lord Jesus Christ as his Savior while kneeling at his mother's deathbed. She died with a smile on her face, and her last words were, "I stood in the gap for you son, now you do the same for others. Save the children from your father's darkness. The Lord will help you son." Mr. Johnson had come in just in time to hear that last. He pushed Bobby aside and slapped the dead woman in the face several times. She was already far beyond any further harm from him. Bobby stood with his mouth open and couldn't speak. He hated this man so much he couldn't even express it. Mr. Johnson had tried to force Bobby into rituals that he just didn't feel comfortable with. Bobby looked at his father and smiled in such a way that sent chills dripping down his father's spine. Bobby said in an immature whisper, "With every breath I take I will curse what you are doing here. I believe in Jesus Christ and I will see the end of this work if it's the last thing I do!"

Mr. Johnson's partners were demanding that he kill his son. They said, "Your son will become a menace to us if you don't do what's necessary." With sadness and disappointment Mr. Johnson had taken out a contract on his son's life and it was carried out two days later.

Bobby had left the Johnson complex where he had lived all of his life. He had no idea where to go or what to do. He wandered the streets for two days until he entered the Mission of Christ on one of Chicago's many side streets. He sat down and ate a bowl of chicken noodle soup. While he was eating, Rev. Mack, as the patrons called him, sat down and asked, "Well son what's your story?"

Bobby looked up at him with red and swollen tear filled eyes, but couldn't speak. Rev. Mack seeing his distress prayed out loud, "Lord Jesus Your Name is Holy among us. You have all the power and glory that exists. I can see that this boy is sorely distressed." Rev. Mack laid his hands on Bobby's head as he prayed, "I stand in the gap for this boy Lord and ask that You touch him with Your peace and heal his heart. Heal the hatred, the broken heart, and protect him Lord with Your army of angels. Yes, Lord protect him for I feel much danger around this lad. You know all things Lord and You alone know Your plan for our lives. I put this boy into Your hands Lord and entrust him to your care." Then Rev. Mack did something that shocked Bobby; something only his mother had done up to this day; he hugged him. No man, not even his own father had shown him the compassion, love, and kindness that he felt in the hug he received. This bear of a man grabbed Bobby and held on tight. Bobby began to sob uncontrollably. He had been holding in all the fear, anger and pain. Now he let it all out, all seventeen years of it. His father had neglected him, beaten him, yelled at him, and disowned him. Rev.

Mack gave Bobby something now that he needed, a male role model of how to show compassion, love, kindness, concern, and best of all, how to turn to the Lord in times of distress.

After a long silence Rev. Mack wrote an address on one of the mission's business cards and told Bobby to report there for a bath and a safe, peaceful sleep. "You get a good night's rest and we'll talk again in the morning."

At this point Bobby would have done anything that Rev. Mack told him. He stepped out of the mission a different man from the one who had entered. He had a little spring to his walk and even started to whistle, until a woman walked up to him. She was beautiful and she smiled pleasantly as she approached.

"Are you Bobby Johnson?"

"Yes, but I..."

As soon as he had said yes she pulled a gun and shot him three times in the chest as she said, "Your father says he's sorry but you have to go."

Before Bobby hit the street the woman was gone, merging quickly into the gathering crowd and disappeared. Bobby had heard her comment and the hatred of his father returned. He was laying in the street getting colder by the moment when through blurred vision Rev. Mack knelt down by him and laid hands on his chest and cried out in a loud voice, "Yahweh Rophe - The Lord who heals - hear me now. Save this boy's life. In the name of Jesus I heal you Bobby, not through my power but by that of Jesus Himself." Rev. Mack continued to pray until the ambulance arrived and the paramedics took over. Bobby was long since unconscious, but he somehow heard all the prayers. He had seen the paramedics start their work on him and had then watched as they loaded him in the ambulance and sped off toward the hospital.

When Bobby came back he heard a nurse talking to Rev. Mack who had just arrived in the intensive care ward, "It's a miracle the boy lived this long. The next twenty-four hours are vital. The doctor says if he lives through the night he just might make it. The bullets seemed to have missed all his vital organs; we couldn't find any serious damage. If you hadn't held your hands so tightly on his chest and slowed the bleeding he never would have arrived here alive for surgery. Rev. Mack you saved his life."

"No nurse, Jesus Christ saved this boy's life. He has a great work for him yet, I can just feel it." With that Rev. Mack knelt down by his bed and prayed the rest of the night.

It took Bobby about sixty days to get his strength back. During those days, however, Rev. Mack taught him about intercessory prayer and how to stand in the gap for others who can't for themselves, just as Jesus has done for us. He made Bobby believe in the power of prayer and how we are called to pray day and night for others. He lived and happily agreed to work with Rev. Mack. He went on rounds to various charities and learned of the important things of life, a life of love and giving.

They were coming out of a nursing home almost two years to the day of the attempt on Bobby's life. Bobby saw her coming, and whispered, "It's her Rev. Mack."

As she approached the woman, not as beautiful as Bobby remembered, pulled a gun and as she passed she fired. In a flash Rev. Mack jumped in front of Bobby and struck the woman unexpectedly, square in the face with five hard knuckles. The woman went down, out cold and hit the ground before Rev. Mack did.

Now it was Bobby's turn to kneel and pray. He laid hands on Rev. Mack's chest and prayed, "I heal you in the name of Jesus Christ our Lord and Savior. Oh Lord who heals all, touch Rev. Mack and heal him now, please."

Rev. Mack opened his eyes as blood trickled from the corners of his mouth and he said, "Watch out; behind you!"

The woman stirred and Bobby yelled and quickly struck her in the face several times, his rage getting the best of him. He finally heard a weak Rev. Mack, "Stop it Bobby before you kill her." He stopped, horror filling his heart at what he had done. He yelled, "Oh no! I'm just like my father!"

Rev. Mack laughed weakly and whispered, "Don't worry Bobby, you're nothing like Mr. Johnson, but you are like your Father in Heaven."

Bobby ran into the mission; called 911 and then returned with an extension cord and used it to tie the woman up. An ambulance came for Rev. Mack while the police came for the assassin. They called in her ID and found a federal warrant had been issued for her in connection with eleven possible murders.

As they took her away she looked at Bobby and said through swollen lips, "Nothing personal kid."

She turned to go and Bobby shocked himself and

said, "I forgive you lady, for myself and for Rev. Mack. I pray now that in the name of Jesus Christ, Satan is bound and his demons must flee from you. I put you in the Lord's hands and may He deliver you from your sins." The woman laughed as she staggered between the two officers. Her eyes, however, held fear for the first time in her life. A seed was planted at that moment that would grow.

Bobby visited her all through the trial, until she was found guilty and shipped away to a federal prison for women. It had taken him a year but she had finally given her life to Jesus Christ and left for prison a different person. She would spend the rest of her days in prison but just how many souls she would save before the Lord called her home, only God knew? There were no more attempts on Bobby Johnson's life after that.

Now, almost five years after the attack, Rev. Mack and the now Pastor Bob knelt in their prayer closet that was a small office at the mission. Pastor Bob had taken over all of Rev. Mack's charities and had since added a few of his own. He had seen the Lord work many miracles through Rev. Mack's prayers and had learned much from the man who had become a second father to him; no, the only real father he had known. They had spent every waking moment; not engaged in mission/volunteer work; in prayer. He had learned the valuable lessons of how short one's life really is and didn't want to waste one moment of prayer. He was a very mature Christian and the Lord was pleased with him.

Rev. Mack rested his right hand on Pastor Bob's right shoulder as they prayed together. Pastor Bob prayed, "Oh, Lord Jesus I pray for Jonesey tonight. His gout is acting up again. Touch him with Your healing power Lord and make him comfortable..." His prayer was taken to heaven by Bobby's guardian angel, Aegis.

Rev. Mack interrupted Pastor Bob's prayer saying, "Bobby I must leave. I'm being called back to God for other duties. You will be fine now son. Just don't forget what I have taught you."

Pastor Bob was on the verge of panic and was going to argue with him but Captain Logos, who had taken the form of Rev. Mack, disappeared before his eyes. As he faded out of existence Rev. Mack smiled pleasantly and said, "Bobby, I have enjoyed working and praying with you; I'll see you again one day." And as he said this; he faded from Bobby's existence leaving Pastor Bob filled with the peace that comes from the realization that you have been entertaining an angel and that he had been taught by one who has seen God personally.

Aegis; who had by this time made it to heaven; laid Bobby's prayer before the Lord who nodded and said, "So let it be done." The angel suddenly stood at the feet of old Jonesey who was asleep at the mission. He touched his feet and they were healed instantly. In the morning Jonesey would awake to healed feet whether he noticed or not. Pastor Bob would notice and would remain silent about his own part in the process. He would also hide in his joyful heart the real identity of Rev. Mack and cover for his sudden disappearance.

There comes a certain power with knowledge and Pastor Bob became an even more powerful prayer-warrior from that day forward. "Lord Jesus I stand in the gap for Justin Schaefer Johnson tonight. I know he's the one my father wants to use for evil. Lord, all things are possible with You. I put Justin in Your hands and pray that You bring him to You, just as soon as it fits into Your plans and Your Father's Will. I just don't want to see the boy hurt as I was. Oh, yes and in the name of Jesus Christ I bind Satan and all of his demons who are no doubt celebrating the capture of Justin. Be gone, Satan, and all your demons with you in the name of Jesus!"

Captain Logos took this prayer himself and as soon as it reached the Lord's ears, Detestation and his horde had to depart suddenly and painfully. Justin slept a very peaceful sleep his first night in his new home.

CHAPTER SEVEN

PRAYER WARRIORS / SATAN'S CURSE

Kapre had just finished a debriefing of his current assignment and obtaining more information about what was to happen to Justin and it seemed hopeful. Unlike God, angels cannot see the future and are seldom given all the information; therefore, they have to rely on faith in their God just as humans do.

Tutor appeared in Kapre's room, "Hurry Kapre, Logos awaits!"

After Tutor disappeared, as suddenly as he had appeared, Kapre knelt down in God's presence and prayed, "Thank You God for Your constant help and for watching over me and my charge, Justin. I return to my assignment with great joy and thankfulness at Your trust in my service. I will follow the Holy Spirit into this battle gladly. Amen."

Kapre was transported to Logos who was standing in the midst of the Holy Spirit. As soon as Kapre appeared, he fell on his face in adoration of God in the form of the Holy Spirit for They are One. The non-consuming fire burned with brilliance not experienced anywhere else but Heaven. Kapre joined Logos in giving honor and glory to their God and singing his praises. Thus strengthened they suddenly were transported by the Holy Spirit to their destination; the prayer closet of Pastor Bob.

Pastor Bob was kneeling on the carpeted floor of

his small office at the mission. This consisted of a small wooden desk, office swivel/rocker chair which showed much wear and one book shelf which was full of books on prayer, Bible commentary and stories of other saints and their walks with God. Pastor Bob had found much comfort and knowledge in these books and had now grown to just reading the Scriptures. He was expecting a crowd of Christians who would arrive shortly at the mission to pray for Kathy Saunders; an eleven year old girl who has been diagnosed with pancreatic cancer. Prior to this meeting, however, Pastor Bob was praying for Justin as was his habit.

Aegis, Pastor Bob's guardian angel was kneeling with him offering up his own prayers to our Father in heaven for his charge and to strengthen his faith for the upcoming prayer meeting to heal Kathy Saunders. Aegis, if he had been standing would be six feet three inches tall and, as most angels were, very strong and muscular. At the moment he glowed in the presence of the Holy Spirit who permeated the entire office with His mighty presence. Aegis had his right hand upon the shoulder of Pastor Bob, a gesture of support from one bringing peace to his charge. The Holy Spirit radiated from Pastor Bob's face as he prayed, "Holy Father in heaven and my Lord Jesus Christ, Savior and Lord, please send my helper and Wisdom itself, the Holy Spirit. I need his boldness and faith to continue to fight in this prayer closet. My poor Justin is in the middle of the enemies' territory. He will be lied to, seduced with the evil of wealth and he is so young. I know Jesus that You can save him. Send the Holy Spirit to fill his heart with a desire to seek You out Lord. I place him in your hands but I will continue to intercede for him as long as it takes to bring delivery from that evil. . ."

As Pastor Bob was praying the first wave of the attack came in like a flood. First several demons rushed in from the roof and were immediately vaporized by the presence of the Holy Spirit. The same tongues of fire that make mighty disciples, prophets, and prayer-warriors for the Lord Jesus Christ, also makes crispy critters out of the enemy. As these large and fierce demons appeared, at first boldly and with confidence, then with faces reflecting shock and terror mixed with hatred as they were consumed, then vaporized by Holy Spirit fire. Aegis never looked up but kept hold of his charge who had tensed feeling the hatred that entered the room. Pastor Bob was an experienced prayer-warrior now and knew when he was under attack from the enemy but no longer feared it.

The second wave was just a little more careful and fearful as they entered the presence of the mighty Spirit of God, but fared no better than the first group of demons. The screams were horrible, the pain, the defeat, the torture they knew they would receive from their evil and vindictive master, Satan.

The Holy Spirit called his angels to action; not because He needed their help so much as He wanted them to fulfill their purpose; so Logos drew his sword and Kapre did likewise and suddenly the room filled with angels who had arrived from all corners of the world and heaven at the Holy Spirit's summons. The numbers were beyond count as they surrounded the simple mission on a dark back street of Chicago. As Kapre joined them outside his sword at the ready, he gasped at the contrast before him.

The mission and surrounding neighborhood were

awash in the glory of God's army. Just outside their range of influence were hordes of dark, sinister demons all swirling in a broad circle around the mission's neighborhood. They would attempt a strike at a point along the angel's wall of protection, in the hope that they could in some way hinder the Christians' prayers, but would in fact be destroyed instantly by the Holy Spirit filled warriors who would strike them down with their mighty swords that glowed with the fire of God; for who or what could stand against such might; no one; no one at all.

As the other Christians arrived at the mission for the prayer meeting; Pastor Bob got up and moved into the mission's chapel to greet his fellow Christians.

He watched as Kathy's family arrived; minus her parents who still prayed at her bed side in the intensive-care unit of the hospital. His eyes filled with sympathetic tears as he prayed, "Holy God we bring before You Kathy Saunders. As You know she is eleven years old and has just been diagnosed with pancreatic cancer. She is about to go through many painful treatments and I ask that You touch her sick body and heal her. Please God don't let this sweet girl suffer from this dreaded disease." Tears now streamed down Pastor Bob's face as he earnestly prayed for this little girl. Instantly six angels broke away and flew toward heaven with swords drawn. As they flew through the lines of the enemy and brought their light into the darkness surrounding and permeating the city up to the mission, several demons broke off to fight them. The six flew back to back striking death blows to any demon foolish enough to get too close. The demons fought hard but the angels persisted and passed through the veil separating this world from God's Heaven. When they entered the Lord Jesus Christ's presence they told him of the faith of Pastor Bob and the others and their request for the little girl. Jesus knew of her plight of course but was just waiting for a prayer-warrior to send the request.

Tears streamed down the face of Jesus, but they were tears of joy that he still had Christians on earth who had the faith to pray for healing, "Father out of the millions of Christians that we have saved from their sins, we have only a small percentage of prayer-warriors who have dedicated their lives to prayer, but still; look at what they do for our cause."

Jesus heard His Father speak in His heart and He smiled, "Thank You Father for hearing the request and answering it." Jesus turned to the six angels and nodded. They smiled and left His presence.

Pastor Bob continued to pray for Kathy Saunders with no evident result. What neither he nor most humans could see was the battle that raged between those six answering angels and the multitude of demons surrounding the hospital in which the little girl was preparing to start those treatments tomorrow. Pastor Bob for his part had prayed both at her bedside and in his prayer closet, and now in the chapel alongside other Christians. In that unseen space between heaven and earth the number of angels grew to three thousand and yet they still had trouble getting through with the answer. Finally, Pastor Bob turned to his group of men along with many of the women volunteers and they dedicated themselves to stay in this chapel and pray until they starve to death or the answer arrives. They had fasted for five days with nothing to eat and only water to drink and now they knelt in the most heart-felt and dedicated payer of their lives.

The number of angels grew to five thousand and the demons numbered in the millions because Satan could ill afford yet another miracle that would weaken his hold on humans in the area. He had spent years tricking even the Christians of the area to stay asleep filling their time with TV, buying and selling, and working for themselves while totally ignoring the spiritual world. As long as they didn't pray he would be all right. Now not only Pastor Bob but also eleven of his men and twenty of his woman had braved a fast and prayed for this one little girl. Satan marveled at the resources these humans and God would spend to save just one insignificant human being. God set up the rules and won't break them. Therefore, in order for Him to use His unlimited power on earth these humans must ask. Once Rev. Mack had left, Satan thought he was free and clear in this area, but Pastor Bob had learned to pray and had influenced others to pray. There had then been many battles such as this one; even more than when Rev. Mack was here.

Satan was getting very tired. He could only be in one place at a time and he had already spent far too much time on this little soul trying to drive her and her parents away from God. He knew it wasn't working and he wasn't going to waste his resources on this little girl any longer, not when there was so much easier prey about.

Logos, Kapre, and several other angels were cutting through the black ranks of demons that screamed, threatened then died trying to defend their evil master's plans. Suddenly the battle was over. Recalled by their Master the demons vanished and all opposition was terminated both at the hospital and the little mission chapel. Thousands of angels shouted, "Honor and Glory to Our God for wearing down the enemy."

The six original angels were already gone on their mission of mercy. They entered the intensive care room of the hospital and surrounded the little girl. They each touched her and instantly the foul disease left her. The Holy Spirit filled the room, the parents and the child. As the doctor walked in the Spirit of God also filled him. He took one look and he knew. He ran some tests and after a few hours he told the anxious parents that the disease was totally gone.

The parents shouted, "Praise God and His Holy Name."

Pastor Bob got off of his knees, which were very sore by now and answered the phone.

"Pastor Bob?"

"Yes."

"This is Saunders, she's healed! The doctor says that there is not one sign of the cancer. Kathy is healed." Then they sobbed together in joy.

Pastor Bob shouted to the others, "Kathy is healed, there is no more cancer." Shouts rose up throughout the chapel. Pastor Bob shouted into the phone, "Join us at the mission's chapel and let's give thanks to our God."

Kathy's parents, the doctor, the eleven men with Pastor Bob and the twenty women present and yes, even Kathy herself, all became dedicated prayer-warriors that night and Satan's fatigue grew more cumbersome as the weight on his shoulders was increased from the added heart-felt prayers that were to follow.

Kapre celebrated with the other angels and then

his thoughts fell back to Justin. What was he going to do now? How would he be saved from the evil in which Justin now lived? He didn't know how, but Jesus had promised that Justin would be delivered from the evil that ensnared him.

God the Father, God the Son, and God the Holy Spirit smiled as One. The sweet fragrance of powerful praise reached them in Heaven and Their Name was glorified, praised and honored once again. They were pleased.

Jesus whispered, "Thus revival in America begins!"

* * *

Kapre returned to his assignment. He entered the empty rooms of Mr. Summons. Justin was still sleeping peacefully in the next room. Kapre had long ago mastered the art of changing into human form. Seconds after he had entered the rooms in the heart of enemy territory, Kapre had retaken his disguise as the helpful, protective, Mr. Summons. He still didn't know how God managed to hide his true identity from the enemy but he trusted that God was all-powerful.

Mr. Summons quietly slipped into Justin's room and watched the child sleep his tranquil sleep. Mr. Summons (Kapre) knew that the years ahead would be hard but it was his job to protect this boy's life, his soul would belong to the Lord and it would be He through the service of the Nostrum who would move through human events to bring Justin safely home when the time arrived.

Mr. Summons sat in a recliner next to Justin's bed to wait patiently for morning.

CHAPTER EIGHT

GROWING IN KNOWLEDGE

Justin's earlier apprehension had dimmed. For two years now he had been the king of the kids at the facility. He hadn't been accustomed to all the attention at first and the fear of allowing others into his range of intelligence lingered. He quickly found, however, that very bright and intelligent peers surrounded him. Whether they were older or younger mattered very little to them or to Justin. On a daily basis he had at least thirty children up to his rooms in the evening for at least two hours. Each day he would invite new children and continue to rotate until they all got a chance to come up and be with him and his toys, then he started the rotation over again. It constituted a rather long list of children. On this occasion of his fourteenth birthday he had invited them all to the ballroom downstairs to celebrate with him. They were dancing to Rock 'N' Roll, eating pizza and drinking every kind of soft drink you could imagine. Theodore Johnson made sure there were never drugs or alcohol at the institute, for he didn't want to damage his investment, not that he opposed drug or alcohol use. The party was tame, though loud, and Justin was a natural host. He moved among his fellow students easily and Black and Johnson could tell that his peers really liked him. None of them thought to fear him for his position and rank because he never held that over them but rather shared what he had freely.

Justin was facing his first test arranged by Black. Black and Johnson awaited the result anxiously. They

95

had allowed him to be good and friendly so he would build powerful friendships and a charisma that would be useful in handling people, but now they had to test just how ruthless they could make him as well. They knew from experience that they couldn't just one day say, 'Justin we want you to kill this person or that person, no they had to start small and make him grow more ruthless with time. They were going for a perfect personality with a mixture of charisma and ruthlessness that Justin would need to hold this company and secret society together.

Black had made Mr. Summons take a solid gold statue of a horse out of Justin's room. Justin had bought it as a decoration for his bedroom and had reported it stolen to his dad, Mr. Johnson. His dad had been sympathetic and promised to look into it.

Now, one of Black's men carried the horse in to the Ballroom and started to hand it to a very surprised Justin Johnson. "Where did you find that?", Black called from across the room." Everyone fell silent and fear gripped the hearts of all in the room except for Justin. Instead his heart was broken with the thought that someone would steal from him. Johnson noticed the disappointment and knew that Justin was still too naive and needed this to thicken his skin.

The man with the horse still in his hands turned and yelled back, "It was in Scotty Lopez's locker." Scotty who knew nothing of this, turned white as a sheet and almost collapsed where he stood. Two of the many bodyguards who lined the far walls ran over and roughly grabbed each arm of Scotty Lopez. He was shorter than Justin and about three years his junior and his blue eyes filled with tears. His red hair was even more brilliant against his pale skin and his freckles stood out bolder as he was carried/dragged to the front of the room.

Black who had made his way over to Justin whispered into his ear, "As ruler of this empire you will be called on to do hard things which will include punishing transgressors. You can't allow anyone to get away with anything they do against you. The only options open to you are to choose in each case a fair punishment to fit the crime."

As Black stepped away sadness weighed Justin down. He had never had to judge anyone before and he didn't like it. Anger, however, began to fill his heart and he just couldn't tolerate the pain that this brought to his heart.

Mr. Summons who stood on the other side of Justin whispered in his other ear, "The evidence is circumstantial Master Justin; anyone could have taken the horse and put it in Scotty's locker." Inside, he was urged to yell, 'Don't do it Justin!' but he controlled his urges by making just the one comment.

Justin hesitated for a moment but in the end he glared at Scotty and yelled, "How could you do this to me? I befriended you and let you in my rooms. I've never judged you but have treated you all equally. Scotty I can't let you walk away free after such treachery. I must make an example of you, so the others will know better than to steal from me. I will not tolerate any crimes against me. None, do you hear? Scotty if I thought it would be best for the Institute I'd have you driven out of here but we need your knowledge and you can be trained to be honest. For now I'm taking you off my entertainment list. You are no longer welcome to come to my rooms to play. No one will befriend you and you will spend your time after school cleaning all the bathrooms in each store in the Plaza. If you fail to do this you will be kicked out to the worst orphanage that we own to continue your penance. Do you understand?"

Scotty was sobbing now and could only nod his head. He thought, 'I didn't do it Justin, please learn the truth, I didn't do it.' He couldn't bring it to words, however, and by that time Justin yelled, "It is so ordered and I will limit this sentence to six months this time, but don't ever repeat your crime." To the crowd he yelled, "The party's over! Go back to your rooms!" He grabbed the horse from the man who still held it and ran for the sanctuary of his rooms, bodyguards and Mr. Summons in tow.

Black and Johnson looked at each other; both smiled and whispered in unison, "Much better than I expected." Silence was all that covered the hushed crowd until Mr. Black yelled, "Well, you heard him, everyone back to your rooms. All activities are suspended and will not resume until tomorrow at 6:00 a.m."

As the room emptied the two men watched the faces of the boys and girls that left that evening and they all finally reflected the fear mixed with awe that they had hoped for. Justin had learned to strike out against pain and betrayal, even if staged, and his knowledge of pride and power were now growing in the proper direction. All that was left them was to increase Justin's own coldness of heart, greed and selfishness.

Detestation's smile grew into a full belly laugh. He watched his puppets damn this young soul and yelled, "Things couldn't be going any better! Make a plan, then work the plan, I always say!" Detestation shook his fist at heaven and yelled, "We have this one Logos and you can't have him back!" He looked around at his men and they all laughed with him as they celebrated the fall of one of God's chosen. They knew Justin was chosen by God for a purpose, but had no idea what that purpose was. They also knew that Satan had designs on the boy as well. This was a common theme with humans but the stakes seemed higher with this particular human.

Back in his rooms, bodyguards left outside, Justin cried for the first time in years. He flopped face down on his bed and sobbed for reasons not clear to him. Mr. Summons gently patted his back and rubbed his head, but did not speak.

Finally Justin rolled over and through his lessening sobs whispered, "What have I done Summons? Scotty was a friend of mine. This. . ." He held up the golden horse that he still held tightly in his right hand, ". . .It's not worth destroying friendship or another human being over, is it?"

Summons thought for a moment, and then judiciously answered, "Master Justin, you're fourteen, yet you're being asked to make decisions of a man. . ."

Justin sat up and yelled angrily, "I am a man!"

Summons nodded but continued, "Use your wisdom to think this through sir. You are fourteen with the brain of a scholar and scientist, but the emotions of a child." Summons held up a hand to stop Justin's next denial and continued, "I am not insulting you sir, but simply pointing out facts. You are being asked to make decisions of a mature adult who has had the years of experience needed to develop an emotionally mature adult. You are still learning to get your bearings. Give yourself time is all I'm suggesting. One sure thing about a leader, however, is that once you make a decision you need to stick to it. In this case whether or not Scott deserved your wrath, your sentence will help build character in the boy. Once it is carried out you can reinstate him in your good graces, thus showing the others that you are strong but that you don't hold grudges. This will build their respect and loyalty in your leadership.

"It's not my place to tell you how to decide in any given situation but I only suggest alternative ways to think and decide, the choice remains with your own freewill."

Justin had ceased his weeping by now and had gotten up to pace back and forth on the "street" of the western town that was his bedroom. He placed the horse on its shelf, wiped his eyes and said, "As usual Summons you make sense. Be a good fellow and very discreetly let Scotty know that I'm no longer angry with him, will you? See to it that he gets some goodies from me and swear him to secrecy. That should soften the brunt of his sentence and when the six months are up I'll reinstate him to full fellowship again."

Summons smiled, "Master Justin, it will be my pleasure. I may have underestimated your emotional maturity sir. You are showing more maturity than I gave you credit for sir. Keep this up and you will be a very good leader indeed."

"Thanks Summons. Now leave me. I'm going to soak in the tub for a while and then turn in for the night. Tomorrow I start my scientific duties for my father."

Summons went into the bathroom, laid out towels and a clean pair of pajamas and then entered his own vast rooms. Once there he knelt in prayer to ask his own Master for guidance and wisdom.

CHAPTER NINE

MONEY IS ALL THE GOD YOU NEED

Black and Johnson had retired to Johnson's Office after the abrupt dismissal of Justin's party. As Black poured the brandy and Johnson fell into his favorite armchair, both men still couldn't believe their good fortune. Justin had fallen right into their plan as naturally as a man falling into sin. He was obeying the laws of greed, anger, and emotional distance; a beginning of his journey as Satan's pawn.

Johnson spoke first, "Black, I made a mistake with my son, Bobby. I didn't let him in on our meetings at the Temple soon enough. Bobby really believed in the evil but it scared him. Then he reasoned if Satan existed then God must also exist and when his mother suggested that God did exist and that He loved Bobby, well it was a short jump to believe and betray all that we had worked for. By the time I exposed him to our society he had already formed the faith that I had forbidden. I won't make that same mistake with Justin. No, it's best for him to know the truth early."

Black brought the drinks over and handed one to Johnson, "And which truth would that be sir?"

Johnson took as sip of his drink then continued, "The truth that the only god in this world is money. With possession of money a man has power, position, things, and rules over his fellow man. That's all he needs. We can break him in slowly over the next few years on the ceremonies, being careful to explain that we don't believe this mumbo-jumbo but it's necessary to rule others. Make him believe he shares in some secret society and serves some mystical leader like Satan and he will be more controllable."

Black jumped in, "Yes, but Satan does exist and he wants Justin to believe in him."

Johnson snapped angrily, "I know he exists but the last thing he wants is for Justin to believe in him. The best way to get any child to believe in what you want them to believe in is to tell them it does not exist. We will expose Justin to The Society and let him form his own beliefs, which will hopefully be opposed to the ones we present to him. We will tell him it's just mumbo-jumbo and he will eventually seek it out for himself. We will just be careful to protect him from God's spirituality. We will teach him to believe in money and power, belief in our master will form with his constant exposure to demonic power which will eventually seduce him as it has us.

Black frowned, "I wouldn't let the leaders of the Temple hear you talking like that."

Johnson laughed, "It's the leaders of the Temple who suggested it! I can see by your expression Black that you are shocked, well don't be. Satan has for years headed a campaign of misinformation allowing the humans of the earth to believe in themselves instead of any spiritual beings. It's genius Black! If they don't believe in Satan they are less likely to believe God. Their coldness of heart, greed, and failure to accept the gift of God's Son are enough to bring them to our Father in the end."

Black was anxious now, "But Justin has to be much more active than that eventually, doesn't he?"

"We have time for that later Black. For now let us just bide our time and be sure we help Justin fall in love with and use the money to his best advantage. We can permanently damn his soul later, when he's older and deeper into the religion of money. We can then threaten to take the money away if he doesn't comply with the contract he signed. Belief will form when he himself seeks the power of the Master."

Black smiled down at Johnson saying, "You're playing a dangerous game here, Johnson."

Johnson looked thoughtfully at his drink as he whispered, "Yes, but it's my game to play and I'll play it the way I see fit. Justin is a genius but emotionally he is still a child. Now is the time to mold those emotions the way we want them to grow. We will concentrate on greed, power, wealth, sex, and many other vices that Justin will find impossible to free himself from. We will most certainly win Black. We have all the weapons in our favor. Our enemies have nothing."

The two men laughed heartily, smug in their own confidence. If they only knew who they were really matching wits with, they may have been less confident.

CHAPTER TEN

PLAYING DOCTOR AT FOURTEEN

Justin had taken a battery of tests when he arrived at Illumin two years ago. It was found that he already had the education of a very advanced student, far beyond college skills. He tested high in the medical field and was encouraged to study medicine and then research where he excelled. In just two years he had earned three Doctoral degrees; one in medicine, earning his medical degree, majoring in surgery. He earned a second degree in biology, specialty in genetics and his third degree in bacteriology. It was as a bacteriologist that he was finally hired by Illumin, Inc. to do research in their vast labs. Justin was not paid a salary for it was not needed since all of his needs and wants were instantly gratified, no matter the cost.

His research assignment was in bacteriolysis; the destruction or dissolution of bacterial cells. A further specialty would be bacteriophage; learning to destroy the various bacteriolytic viruses normally present in sewage and in body by-products.

Justin had learned to skateboard and traveled from his rooms the next morning to the labs using the skateboard tracks he had admired so much upon his arrival. He stopped in front of the door to his lab, expertly flipped the skateboard up and held it while he admired the plague to the right of the doorway. It read:

"LAB OF DOCTOR JUSTIN SCHAEFER JOHNSON"

He had supervised the stocking of the lab with proper equipment, supplies and personnel. At fourteen he was to be the supervisor of three men and one woman, all of whom were older and more experienced than he, but as had been proven by testing, not quite as smart as he. They had all agreed to do research under his command partly because he was a Johnson and Mr. Black had threatened horrible repercussions if they crossed Justin, but mostly out of curiosity that a fourteen year old could know so much about their field.

Justin took a deep breath and walked into the lab doing his best to command a supervisor-like presence. His staff was awaiting his arrival. He looked at the clock and saw that he was just on time; 8:00 a.m. He had eaten a quick breakfast in his room, fixed by Summons who had wished him well as he left.

Justin knew, by reputation, all the scientists who stood before him. He had studied their employee records and they, like himself, were all specialists in Bacteriology, each very young and very talented in his or her own way. Standing closest to him was Doctor Tracy Warner, age twenty, five foot five inches, one hundred ten pounds of well-endowed, perfectly proportioned femininity. She had been given special instructions by Black and was very ready and able to carry them out. Justin had no clue that he was about to get introduced to manhood so young. Her long blonde hair was pulled back in a ponytail and her black-rimmed glasses accented deep green eyes. Justin locked eyes with her, noticed her naturally full red voluptuous lips and instantly became self-conscious of his acne and what he thought of as his own very large ears. He blushed and looked to his next employee.

Tracy thought, *'Oh boy kid, you don't stand a chance!'*

Doctor Jeremy Bolder noticed Justin's blush and smiled knowingly. He was age twenty-five, the oldest member of the team, whose brown hair was prematurely balding. He stood six foot, four inches tall in stocking feet and wore as they all did; a white lab coat over jeans and pullover shirt with white thick-soled tennis shoes. His tall thin frame gave him a scare-crow look which caused Justin to smile back and reminded him very much of Mr. Summons, but not as spooky.

Next was Doctor Curtis Mayfield age nineteen, who at five foot, eight inches carried about two hundred and fifty pounds of corpulent flesh on his small frame. He sported long black hair and a full beard. He smiled at Justin then looked down as if awaiting orders.

Next to him stood Doctor Jerard Stromeyer, whose ebony skin fascinated Justin who hadn't seen many black people in his short lifetime. He stood six feet and carried one hundred ninety-eight pounds of pure muscle on his large frame.

It was Doctor Stromeyer who spoke first, "Doctor Johnson, welcome to the lab." He made a sweeping motion taking in the entire lab at once. It was a large room in which each scientist had his or her own work station complete with all the equipment necessary to carry out the research they had been assigned, including the most advanced computers available. Justin's station, which was the largest and the most opulently equipped, was located just outside the door to his right and, as he had earlier discovered, led to his large plush office. As supervisor he would be responsible for the reports and research papers that this research group would write. He would also be the one to present research findings to the entire medical board of which he was a member as department head.

Doctor Mayfield asked, "Doctor Johnson . . ."

Justin interrupted, "Justin please; why don't we just start off on a little less formal basis? We all know that we're doctors so why not just use first names for humanity's sake?"

Curtis Mayfield blushed and tried again, "Well then, Justin, I have checked all the supplies in but I didn't know what to do with these or what they were for." He pointed to three open crates that held bags of dirt, plastic bottles of cloudy water, and glass bottles of what looked to be body parts?

Justin laughed and explained, "That's for my research into bacterium. As you know bacterium is any class of microscopic organisms having round, rod-shaped, spiral, or filamentous single-celled or non-cellular bodies often aggregated into colonies or where motile by means of flagella. These live in soil, water, organic matter, or the bodies of plants and animals. Being autotrophic, saprophytic, or parasitic in nutrition and important to man because of their chemical effects on pathogens; I think it will round out our research and that is where I want to start. Have you all received the supplies and materials that you requested?" They all nodded so Justin continued, "Good. Now while I unpack these and get ready to begin, why don't each of you get started on your own research."

Tracy stayed behind as the others started off toward their stations. She suddenly stepped forward and wrapped her arms around Justin's neck and hugged him. Her perfume seemed to activate hormones that he hadn't discovered yet and he found himself hugging Tracy back enthusiastically. She whispered, "It is a pleasure to finally meet you Justin." She brushed her lips across his cheek as she stepped back and then skipped off toward her workstation.

Justin watched her hips as she skipped away; he then turned suddenly and walked into the private bathroom in his office. He suddenly felt the need to splash cold water on his face. He looked at himself in the mirror and noticed a very flushed face and felt a nervous knot in his abdomen, which twisted his stomach in a way that he couldn't explain. He thought to himself, *'Could she really find me attractive? No, she's just a friendly person. It was just a welcome as she said.'* But he couldn't help holding on to the hope that maybe . . . just maybe? Unconvinced he dried his face and went to his workstation and started unpacking boxes. Work is what he needed now he decided.

Noon arrived before Justin knew it and his co-workers invited him to eat with them but he told them to go on, he would follow shortly. "I'm setting up an experiment and it's in a sensitive stage that can't wait."

This happens often with scientists so no one thought anything of it. He had not looked away from his work so he jumped a little when a voice spoke close behind him.

It was Jeremy Bolder who said good-naturedly, "Don't take this wrong Justin, but I would be careful with Tracy if I were you."

Justin stopped what he was doing and turned to look at Jeremy, a surprising feeling of anger rising to the surface, "What do you mean?"

Jeremy held up both hands in mock defense and spoke hurriedly, "Whoa there big guy! I offer only a word of caution." He looked over his shoulder to make sure the room was empty and lowered his voice, "It's just that Tracy has, well, a reputation as a flirt, perhaps even a vixen."

Justin blushed involuntarily, "I don't know what you mean?"

Jeremy explained, "Vixen, as in tease, lose woman . . ."

Justin interrupted angrily, "I know what a vixen is Jeremy, I'm not stupid! What I mean is; what does that have to do with me?"

Jeremy smiled, "She's after you son. She didn't even try to hide her intent, she wants you."

Justin sat down on his stool and smiled. Could it be true? He had hoped he hadn't misread the signs.

Jeremy saw the reaction, "Now don't get me wrong son, I don't blame you for being infatuated with her. She is after all beautiful and which one of us wouldn't want a woman chasing after them, but you must be careful to be sure you let the right woman catch you. Besides, you're only fourteen and that may be just a bit young for what Tracy could offer you."

Justin cleared his throat and the earlier anger came back, "I may only be fourteen in years but I'm much older in experience. I think it would be best Jeremy if you keep your observations to yourself. In case you haven't noticed, I can do just about anything I want to around here. As a matter of fact I will do whatever I want to, with Tracy or anyone else!"

Jeremy had backed up at the outburst and again held up his hands, "Hold on to your hormones, Justin, it was just friendly advice. I know better than anyone that you have the freewill to do whatever you want to, but there are consequences to each decision. I just don't want to see you get hurt."

Justin, his experiment forgotten, stormed from the lab and skateboarded quickly, trying to catch up to the others and Tracy. Jeremy stood shaking his head sadly and watched him leave. He looked toward the heavens, then hands in pockets walked slowly toward the lunchroom.

The rest of the afternoon was tense for Justin. Jeremy didn't speak to him anymore about it but he caught him looking at him periodically during the afternoon. Tracy for her part hadn't paid him any attention whatever. She was centered on her work and her concentration was complete.

This all changed, however, at six when quitting time came. Jeremy left quickly without a word, but Tracy washed her hands and walked over to Justin. She put her arm around his waist and watched Justin finish his work. Beads of sweat broke out on his forehead as he felt the warmth of her hips leaning against his. His throat went dry and his breath seemed to come in difficult gasps.

Tracy looked around until her face was right in

front of his and asked, "Are you well Justin?"

Justin nodded nervously, unable to speak. The intensity of his reaction was shocking him. He was embarrassed, intrigued, and totally lost as to what to do about it. Should he ask her out? Should he run away as fast as possible?

Tracy smiled at him, "Would it be too forward of me if I asked you to eat supper with me tonight?"

Justin's knees went weak and he had to sit down suddenly. He took a deep breath and whispered, "That would be very pleasant."

Tracy said, "Wonderful; your place or mine?"

Justin looked confused.

Tracy kissed him gently on the lips, "I was thinking of a quiet and very private supper."

Now Justin knew he was dreaming and would have to wake up soon. He finally spoke even though it took much effort not to stutter, "Why don't you come up to my room in about an hour and I'll have Mr. Summons set up something for us."

Tracy thought for a moment and said, "Make it eight. A woman needs time to get ready Justin. I'll see you then." As she said this last she traced her index finger along the bottom of his chin and then ran off with youthful energy flowing through every cell of her seductive body. She had completed phase one of her mission.

Justin watched her leave then fell forehead first onto the table. He took deep slow breaths trying his best not to hyperventilate.

Mr. Summons was not pleased, "But Master Justin you're only fourteen years old sir! That's just too young in my book to be entertaining a woman alone in your rooms."

Justin replied stubbornly, "Who says? I'm my own master and I'll do what I like! You just do what you're paid to do!"

Summons mumbled something about impropriety but set up a table for two none-the-less.

In Mr. Johnson's office, he and Mr. Black watched the argument as if it were entertainment on TV. Black had arranged for hidden cameras to be strategically placed throughout Justin's office and living quarters. Justin had no clue of their existence.

Johnson was laughing as he said, "The boy looks very nervous, and perhaps Summons is right Black."

Black was watching quietly and just shook his head negatively, "Just watch sir. The only way to make sure Justin goes our way is to rid him of this naive innocence that he has. We must harden him some."

"I know that Black but first loves can be devastating. What if this plan of yours drives him to suicide?"

Black looked shocked, "Suicide! We have too many cameras and guards to let that happen; besides it will give us the opportunity to make sure he never marries unless we find it useful and we pick the bride. For the duties he is about to take over he can't allow soft lovey-dovey notions to stand in his way. The best way to remove them is to have him fall in love with the most beautiful cooperative woman we have and that is definitely Tracy. Let her seduce his innocence away from him; let him believe she is all his; then rip the elusion away with the cold hard truth that no one is faithful. I've seen it time and again sir; it will bring him around to thinking properly of women and sex. He'll learn to use them, be entertained by them, but never again will he trust one or confide in one. Then we will be able to trust him with the responsibility of the Society."

Johnson lit a cigar and let the smoke billow from his mouth as he nodded and said, "You're right Black; these are hard lessons; but you're right." They heard a knock on Justin's door. Tracy had arrived. Their collective attention was clued back on the monitor screen instantly.

Mr. Summons opened the door and towered over Tracy as he announced, "Miss Tracy sir."

He stepped aside and Tracy had to bend her neck back to look up at the tower of a man, "Thank you Mr. Summons." she said a bit nervously. She could sense Mr. Summons' disapproval of her and her intentions, but she chose to ignore him and his opinions; for she had a job to do and she would enjoy it, she realized.

Justin would have laughed at the two contrasting humans; one so tall while the other looked so short in comparison, if it hadn't been for the impression Tracy made on him. Her long blonde hair was still pulled back in a ponytail; her black-rimmed glasses accented those deep green eyes, which were now accented also with eye shadow and extra-long eyelashes. Her smiling lips were coated with a fresh supply of red lipstick and her complexion was perfect. Instead of a white lab coat she wore a long shiny evening gown with a low neckline and a diamond necklace that sparkled in the harsh lights of Justin's room.

She had never been here before and was surprised

how young Justin now looked in his own environment. She saw the roller coaster and other toys in this main room. She saw through the open bedroom door that it was made up like a western town. It was all she could do not to laugh at the youth and innocence of her target.

She smiled at Justin who still hadn't spoken but just stood there with his mouth open, "Justin would you mind if I freshen up before we eat?"

He suddenly came to life and said, "Of course Tracy. Right this way."

He led her into the bathroom and then realizing he had entered with her, he blushed and left quickly closing the door behind him. Tracy looked at the bubbling tub, the fish motif and decided that this would be the room for the final seduction. She would have a hard time in the other rooms, his age just screamed out at her there. At least here it was rather adult looking.

Johnson and Black were watching Tracy expectantly when she turned unexpectedly toward the camera and said, "You are going to owe me big time Black."

She smiled into the hidden camera, checked her hair in the mirror then left the bathroom. She reappeared in his bedroom and then again in his main living room.

Johnson whispered as if they'd hear if he spoke louder, "How'd she know about the camera?"

Black who still watched the screen spoke in normal tones, "I told you she's the best. Her specialty is stealth assignments. We have used her in the past with Senators, Congressmen, once even with President Collins."

Johnson looked at Black and exclaimed, "That was her that helped us get our law passed?" He said impressed, "Justin, my boy, you don't stand a chance."

Justin gently pulled her chair out for her and Tracy sat down. Her illuminating smile warmed his heart and he just about missed his own chair when he sat down, but he recovered well.

There was another knock on the door and Mr. Summons walked toward it as Justin explained, "I have ordered something from the kitchen for us. I hope you like porterhouse steaks?"

Tracy clapped her hands together and giggled, "Yippee! I love steak."

Mr. Summons rolled the cart up to the table, which was already set with the best china, silver, and two candlesticks each of which held a lit candle. There was a single rose lying on Tracy's plate and Justin smiled as she picked it up and put it to her nose.

Justin cleared his throat and said, "Tracy, if only I could be that rose."

Tracy looked at him seriously and said, "You will be Justin, much sooner than you think."

Mr. Summons cleared his throat and pulled the lids off of each china plate and sat the plates down in front of each young participants of this evening of seduction. Justin had ordered each a complete feast and some non-alcoholic Champagne for the occasion. However, when Mr. Summons opened the bottle he said, "There's a note here for you sir."

He handed it to Justin who opened it and read, 'Tonight I decided to make an exception for you. Enjoy some real champagne on your first date; Black.'

Justin whooped playfully as he handed the note to Tracy and said, "Does everyone now about our date?"

Tracy thought, 'Thank you Black!', but said, "You know there are no secrets from Black, Justin."

Mr. Summons questioned, "Are you sure you want to drink real alcohol Master Justin?"

"Yes Summons, I'm sure. Now if you don't mind we won't need you any longer tonight. You understand that I mean all night Summons. You can clean this up in the morning."

Justin looked nervously at Tracy and she nodded her agreement, a radiant, knowing smile allowing her pearly white teeth to sparkle in the bright lights of the room. With more confidence Justin said, "That's all then. Good night Summons, and dim the lights a bit as you leave please."

Summons hesitated only a moment longer, gave Tracy a look she couldn't read, but instinctively knew the meaning of, he then turned and walked into Justin's bedroom, heading toward his own rooms, when Justin yelled after him, "Oh and Summons. I want you to sleep out tonight."

Summons assured him that his room was sound proof and that not a sound gets through, "Also, sir you can lock me out from your side."

Justin looked at Tracy who shrugged her shoulders, and Justin waved his hand at Summons, "Very well then. Goodnight Summons."

After Summons had gone, the diners turned their attention to their steaks, complete with baked potato, salad, corn on the cob, chocolate mousse and of course the now, real wine.

Black watched them eat and said to Johnson, "We should have ordered something in ourselves."

Johnson agreed, "Why don't you call down for a pizza and some beer?"

Black did and then sat back down to watch the evening progress.

While they ate, Justin and Tracy talked of their work, their earlier lives since they were both orphans and then when they had finished the entire bottle of Champaign, Justin asked with a slight slur to his speech, "Would you like to ride in my roller coaster?"

Tracy looked at him, stood up and came over to him saying, "I was thinking of a totally different entertainment myself. Would you like me to show you?"

Justin's head was spinning between the effects of the drink and the hormones, which had long ago run away with any sense he might have had, and he simply nodded, allowing her to pull him toward the bathroom. After they entered and Tracy closed the door and made sure that Summons' door was locked securely she turned to Justin slipped out of her dress and let her hair fall over her now bare shoulders. She took off her glasses and using her index finger bent it toward her; calling Justin over to her.

His feet moved of their own accord all freewill gone with the call of his raging male hormones.

Johnson flipped the monitor off and Black moaned in disappointment. He thought, *'No matter I'll watch the tape later.'*

Johnson shook his head, "This is just too perverted even for me Black."

"That's what you pay me for sir. Just leave the

details to me and don't worry. I'll make sure that Justin remains safe. He's in good hands the lucky dog."

The two men laughed and finished their beer.

Tracy lay in Justin's bed listening to his now calmer heart beat as he slept peacefully. She almost felt bad for him but she knew her duty. She liked the boy and had not often found; not these days anyway; such naive innocence. Well she had taken care of that once and for all. He'll never be quite so innocent from this day forward and his education had just begun.

She got up quietly, got dressed, and laid the single rose on her pillow next to Justin's head. She crept out and headed toward her own apartment. She walked slowly thinking of Justin's trusting eyes. She opened her door, entered her apartment, closed the door, but before she could turn on the light someone grabbed her from behind and shoved her to the floor. She felt the weight of a body on her back. She clapped her hands and the lights came on and she turned in the man's arms and looked into the smiling face of Mr. Black.

Black whispered, "How is Justin?"

Tracy smiled back and said, "A bit older and more experienced I would say."

Black laughed, "Speaking of experience; how would you like a real man?"

Tracy giggled, "Anytime and anywhere sir."

Black whispered, "I'm free now."

Tracy pulled his face down and kissed him hard. She clapped her hands and the lights extinguished themselves as a fire of another kind was rekindled.

CHAPTER ELEVEN

PASTOR BOB'S PLAN

It had been two years since Rev. Mack had exposed himself as an angel and then disappeared from Pastor Bob's life. Bob still gave thanks to God for the experience as he prayed unceasingly for other's needs but he missed Rev. Mack's (a.k.a Captian Logos) guidance and the peace he instilled in Bob's heart. Bob had matured ever deeper in the spiritual life that God had set before him. He tried to always know and follow God's will but was having trouble with exactly what to do about Justin. He knew that Justin was now fourteen and he couldn't even imagine what his father and company was exposing the boy to; he knew it wouldn't be healthy, mentally or spiritually. Bob had tried to visit Justin on several occasions but had been turned away at the door each time. Finally, a homeless person had shown up dead outside the mission with a typed note, which read: 'One homeless for one visit.'

Bob had told the police that he thought his father had the man killed but they only looked at him like he had lost his marbles and nothing was ever done. Bob had received the message, however, and never tried to visit again. *"Chalk one up to Mr. Black,"* he had thought as tears rolled down his cheeks.

Bob was in his office kneeling on the new carpet that Kathy Saunders' father had given to him last Christmas over Bob's objections at the extravagance. Secretly he appreciated the cushion to his knees that it afforded as he settled in for another long session of secret prayer.

"Yahweh Tsidkenu, Lord of Our Righteousness, I give you much praise and thanksgiving for being my God. How can you ever use the weak individual that I am? I feel that I have failed you more than I have succeeded. No Lord, on second thought it is not me that succeeds or fails but it is Your power that works through me. It is all in Your hands and through the Lord Jesus Christ I am made whole.

"Yahweh M'Kaddesh, The Lord who sanctifies, it is You that I trust to make me holy and pleasing before my God.

"Yahweh Shalom, The Lord of Peace, it is You to whom I cry for peace in my heart and soul about Justin Schaefer Johnson. He is smart Lord and has a good heart. He could be so great a person and accomplish much for your kingdom, if only he was given the chance. I don't understand Lord why You, Who have such power, would let him be taken by such evil people. You know the effort I have expended on his behalf, both before and after he was taken, but I have failed. Nothing I can do as a human seems to help, so I am placing Justin in Your capable hands Lord and asking that You direct his path. If there is anything that I can do further, please let me know."

He was silent for a moment as he allowed those requests to rise to heaven and he meditated on what the Lord would have him do. Aegis laid his right hand on Bob's shoulder and prayed with him. He had also liked Justin and feared for his soul. He didn't envy Kapre the task laid before him.

Inspiration from the Holy Spirit flowed into both angel and human. The Spirit of God spoke almost audibly to Bob, "Build a hidden science lab for Justin." It was such a strange idea that Bob remained silent for ten minutes after it occurred to him. He had found many times in the past that the truest and most powerful inspirations from God had been short bursts all in one sentence just like that. No explanation or directions as to how; that would be revealed as he obeyed the first order. When he finally spoke it was a whisper, "Are you sure Lord?" The peace in his spirit assured Bob that he had heard correctly. "I hear and obey Lord. I will get started immediately. I'll have to find land, hire a sagacious company that has no ties to my father, and that's a tall order in itself. I'll need. . ."

The phone rang interrupting his train of thought. He toyed with the idea of not answering it but then realized that it would probably be someone in need of his help. He grunted as he got off of his knees and walked to his desk, "Pastor Bob. May I help you?"

A strong male voice answered, "Yes sir! You may find this strange and if you don't have any idea what I'm talking about I'll understand." There was a pause.

Pastor Bob waited but his patience was thinner than usual, "I won't know what you're talking about sir until you tell me."

"Sorry, it's just that this type of thing has never happened to me before. You see I was just praying and I felt this strong prompting to turn to the yellow pages. When I opened the book it fell open to churches and Mission of Christ caught my eye. I swear the Lord told me almost audibly to call and offer my services. You see

I was just about to move because I can't get work in this area. I'm an Architect and I had a disagreement with a corporation that wanted me to shave this and that off of the last construction project I had. Well, they fired me and have blackballed me. That's what I was praying about actually. My wife is seven months along with our fourth child and I need to work as you can imagine."

Pastor Bob had been listening and the joy in his heart made him interrupt the man and the joy was apparent in his voice, "This is wonderful! I know exactly what the Lord wants you to build! Wait do you design large buildings . . ."

The man said, "Office buildings, Subways, Hospitals . . ."

Bob said loudly with a little chuckle, "Enough already! You'll be perfect for the job the Lord has in mind. Let me guess something. The company you had a problem with was Illumin, Inc. right?"

"Well it was a Comminsky Construction actually; the General Contractor, that I had trouble with but I believe they were hired by Illumin, Inc., just as my company was. A Mr. Black was the gentleman, and I use that word loosely, who threatened me and then fired me when I wouldn't comply. He kept his promise and totally ruined me here in Chicago. I just couldn't do it though. I knew the Lord would provide for us somehow but this is beyond belief."

Bob laughed, "You haven't heard anything yet sir! Could you come over and talk with me now?"

"Sure just tell me how to get there, I'm not familiar with your street."

Bobby told him and hung up. Instantly he was

back on his knees, "Lord, You never cease to amaze me. I know that was verification that You want this done. I trust this man even though I have never met him nor did I even think to ask his name, but I know You have sent him to me for the purpose of fulfilling Your order. You've made sure that I have the money and I'm sure he'll have the expertise needed to get the project finished. This also gives me peace about Justin. You are God and can pull off anything You want and I should learn not to have doubts even when things look bad and even dangerous." An hour later Pastor Bob opened the door to a man who wore a rather expensive looking blue suit and held a leather briefcase in his right hand. Pastor Bob was wearing sweat pants and a sweat shirt with, "Jesus Died for YOU!" written on the front."

The man looked around skeptically and couldn't hide his shock at the rundown mission, "This is Mission of Christ?" he asked with a tone that sounded as if he was hoping to be wrong.

Pastor Bob smiled warmly not blaming the poor man, "You know I'm sorry but I didn't ask your name on the phone and I don't remember if I said mine. I'm Pastor Bob and yes this is Mission of Christ. I know it doesn't look like much but I have found that the people that come here won't go to the fancier missions, so I have not remodeled this one. I owned a mission about five blocks from here, modern, state-of-the-art everything, it used to be a hotel as a matter of fact, but no one will come in. They just don't trust fancy. So I sold it and kept this one the same. This one is overly full all the time and no complaints." Bob offered his hand, "And your name sir?"

The man switched the brief case from his right hand to his left and offering his now free right hand he said, "Sorry, my name is Chester Melvin and yes, you stated your name when you answered my call." He had a good grip and seemed confident in himself, which was a must for what Pastor Bob had in mind.

Bob stepped aside to let the man in and asked, "Would you like a soda pop Chester?"

Chester smiled, "Yes that would be fine sir."

Bob left the office, went to the kitchen, and returned momentarily with two bottles of pop in his hands. He handed one to Chester and walked around behind his desk and watched Chester take a nervous drink.

Bob waved his own bottle toward a chair in front of his desk and said, "Do sit down Chester. You're among friends now." Chester looked confused at Bob's use of plural and Bob said in way of explanation, "The Lord and myself of course."

Chester nodded but didn't say anything, waiting for the moment he could escape politely.

"Chester I hope you don't mind me saying this but you look disappointed."

Chester looked down at the bottle he was holding in his lap, seemed to make a decision and said, "You got my hopes up sir but perhaps you misunderstood me. Missions like this are usually asking for money not giving out large jobs. I would like to build something for you for free but I need to feed my family; like I said maybe I wasn't clear on that point." Chester stood as if to leave.

Pastor Bob waved him back down and when he

had regained his seat Pastor Bob explained, "I understood exactly what you said. Now listen to me very closely Chester. I was praying also about this boy genius I know. The Lord told me to build this boy a research and development center. I was in the process of making mental notes about it when you called. Your call coming from the Lord's prompting as it did tells me that the Lord doesn't really want me to build the center but only finance it. I take care of many charitable holdings in this city and here is where I belong. I don't know why but the Lord has given me a peace about you, so I'm going to take you into my confidence. I will hold nothing back and at the end of my explanation if you want out I would just ask that you keep what you know to yourself; fair enough?"

Chester nodded, "I'm sorry Pastor Bob, really I am, but I'm just a bit nervous. I've been out of work now for four months and my savings is just about gone, we no longer have insurance so the birth won't be covered. I'm sorry I shouldn't bother you with my troubles."

Pastor Bob rested his elbows on the desk and said, "On the contrary, those are legitimate concerns, so let's just address them first. I'm going to ask you to trust me sight unseen. You may verify everything tomorrow that I'm about to tell you and it won't hurt my feelings, if that's all right?"

Chester sat back in his chair and Bob could see that he had decided to trust him enough to listen, "Now, Chester, I have two more questions for you. What Architect firm did you work for when you got fired and were you ever in the service?"

"I worked for Manheim, Foster, and Gable and yes,

I was in the Army, Green Beret, for three years. I was in the service four years. I got an honorable discharge I assure you. I. . ."

Bob laughed when he saw Chester was nervous again, "Relax, this isn't a test. Have you heard the term Prayer Warrior?"

Chester smiled, "Yes, I have. Reverend Chesterfield, he's our Pastor, taught my wife and I about it."

"He's a good man."

Chester blushed and then explained, "I'm sorry, Pastor Bob, but I called Reverend Chesterfield and asked him if he knew you and he also said that you're a good man."

Bob laughed again, really warming to this man, "Careful, precise, a good fighter, and a strong prayer warrior, and on top of all that an Architect. You will need all of those skills and all the courage you can muster for the project I have in mind." Chester seemed to relax completely now, he was ready to hear Bob's pitch, "Chester, the company you worked for, as you know, is secretly owned by Illumin, Inc. as are many others. If it helps you to know, you didn't stand a chance against them. The Lord has been good to me Chester, in so many ways. The first way which will help you the most is that I'm filthy rich." Chester started looking longingly at the door again.

Pastor Bob laughed as he continued, "Oh, I know I don't look it but I am and as I said you will have ample time to check me out. You might as well know up front that the company that had you fired, Illumin, Inc., well it's owned by my father Theodore Johnson. My full name is Robert Alexander Johnson and that is where the similarity ends. My father is lost. I am a child of God. My father hates me for walking out on him and disowned me but only after he did the only honorable thing I have ever known him to do. On my twenty-first birthday he didn't fight the trust that he had set up for me and I received two million dollars. I had learned to invest at an early age and have done well over the years. If I had to, I could get my hands on three point four billion dollars tonight. If you needed more I would have to liquidate a few holdings; so money is not a problem that needs concern us at the moment." Bobby stopped and asked, "Are you all right?" Chester had just taken a drink of his soda and choked when Bobby had quoted the amount of money he could get.

After some coughing and turning red Chester whispered, "Go on, I believe you Pastor Bob; I don't know why exactly but. . ."

Bobby smiled, "Very diplomatic of you Chester, but check it out anyway. I want your loyalty and your silence, so I want you to trust me as I will need to trust you." Bobby took a drink and then continued, "Several years ago, I befriended a boy named Justin Schaefer, at an orphanage where I volunteered my time. I teach art among other things and I would go there one day a week. I noticed something about Justin right away. I'm sure it was from the Lord. It turns out that Justin is a genius. He's fourteen and holds three Doctoral degrees in Biology of some kind and he is actually a medical doctor as well. He is doing research for my father who hurriedly adopted Justin, for his own selfish reasons I'm sure. They won't let me see him but I pray for him all the time. Today while I was praying, the Lord told me to build a research center for him. That's when you called Chester. Up with me so far?"

Chester nodded and drained his soda bottle.

Bobby asked, "Want another?"

"No, sir, I'm good. Go on with your story. I'm finding it very interesting."

It was a relief for Bobby to hear that, "You see when you called that was verification to me that all this had come from the Lord and please call me Bobby."

Chester sat forward, "Let me see if I understand so far, Bobby. The Lord has asked you to build a research center for a fourteen-year-old boy who was adopted by your reportedly evil father. You have no idea how, when, or if ever you'll be able to get to the boy or if when you do, that he will even want to do research in it?"

Bobby looked seriously doubtful now, "Sounds pretty ridiculous when you hear it out loud like that."

Chester smiled and said, "On the contrary, it sounds as if it has God written all over it. Our Pastor told us that if God asks you to do something it will be God sized and this definitely fits the bill."

"I told you he was a good man. Well, you know about as much as I know. Do you want to help or not?"

"I suppose we are talking standard contract. . ."

"No Chester! No contracts! A handshake; I want the first step of this project to be very clandestine. Can you live with that?"

To his credit, the hesitation he did show was very short, "Yes Bobby, I'm going to trust you."

Bobby said, "Good", as he turned to his bookshelf and took some books off the self. Behind them was a safe that he opened with practiced precision. He pulled out a credit card and handed it to Chester. He explained as he typed some orders into his computer, "That as you can see is a Visa Gold card. It belongs to a corporation I started for just this type of operation. It has a credit line of one hundred thousand dollars backed by the corporation's assets. The name of the Corporation is Alexander Development Corporation as it says on the card. I have just made you President of that corporation and that card is your expense account. Alexander is based in Las Vegas Nevada and this is the address." Bobby handed him printed document, which now listed Chester as the President.

Chester looked confused, so Bobby said, "I accessed my firm via the internet and promoted myself to CEO with you as my President. You are now authorized to draw on the corporation's accounts for whatever you need. There are two vice-presidents already working there. They have been coming to work and doing a lot of charity work for local churches out of those offices and I want them to continue. Chester I have to ask this. Are you happily married?"

Chester looked offended, "We don't have a perfect marriage but yes it is a happy one."

"The reason I ask is that I don't want this project to consume you entirely. Work eight to ten hours per day but no more. Take off Saturdays and Sundays, holidays, and any of your children's events that arise. When it comes time for your wife, what is her name anyway?"

Chester said, "I'm sorry, it's Debbie."

"When it comes time for Debbie to deliver, I want you to drop everything and stay home for a couple of weeks to a month and just be with her. You may consider that an order. I have a feeling that we will not need this facility for a few years yet, so take your time in building it and do it right, do it thoroughly and most importantly, do it secretly."

Bobby stared into Chester's eyes for a moment and finally continued, "I won't pretend that this won't be dangerous Chester. There could be a real danger to your life if my father finds out. I think it will be best if we only speak in person; never call me, don't E-mail me, or write to me. If you need to get a hold of me after tonight, you will either have to travel here or have Cynthia call me."

Chester was taking notes, "Who's Cynthia?"

Bobby held up a finger, got up and walked out of the room. A couple of minutes later he came back with two more cold soft drinks and said, "Cynthia Caldwell and Beth Foster are the two vice-presidents I was telling you about. They are listed as Vice-Presidents of Charitable Distribution for the corporation. They are housed in four of the sixteen offices that our building holds. They know what they are doing and I don't want you to be concerned about them at all. I keep them very busy. They are both single mothers, at least for now; Beth has a serious boyfriend going; so who knows. They are well paid and earn every dime the corporation pays them. They have limited access to the corporation funds; only those earmarked for charity. I have already e-mailed them with the code word; Twelve-Melvin. I told them that if I ever activate the other offices that I would tell them the number of offices and the last name of the person who would take them over. They will check their messages in the secure computer account in the morning and will know that you are now President. They will have the offices cleaned and prepped. In the morning I want you to get on the internet and order any kind of furniture you want and have it sent to your office, the girls will see to it that it is set up. You can rearrange it if you like after you get out there. I never got around to it so the President's office is still empty. It is the largest corner office there is in the building. It will be large enough for your needs I'm sure and I think you'll like it. It has an attached private bathroom for convenience and parking is right out front. That reminds me, do you have a car?"

Chester was finding it hard to breathe and was turning a bit pale when Bobby got up and asked again, "Are you all right Chester? You're turning pale?"

After a few careful breaths, Chester's eyes welled up with tears and they quickly began to run down his cheeks, "God's mercy truly does come crushed down and overflowing, doesn't it?", and he cried full wracking sobs. When his tears subsided he said, "When I lost my job and couldn't find work I was so worried and now you have heaped upon me more generosity than I have ever experienced. You are being far more generous than I deserve. . ."

Bob patted his shoulder and explained, "It is God who shows us more mercy and generosity than we deserve, Chester, not me. All I ask you in return is that you treat the people you hire just as generously. Hire only people you can trust with our secret project. I will trust your judgment on that as well as all other details of this project. I will come out and visit occasionally and perhaps you can come here and report in every once in a while?"

Chester dried his eyes and said, "You can count on it."

Bobby returned to his earlier question, "Do you have a car, Chester?"

He shook his head saying, "They took that away with the job."

Bobby laughed, "I thought as much. Look I want you to fly out to Las Vegas with your family using the card for all the expenses. Find a home to buy and then pay for it out of corporation funds. Don't worry it's in the by-laws that the President and Vice-Presidents get a home and car from the corporation. There's a half-million dollar ceiling on the President's house; so if you want something bigger you'll have to finance the difference yourself. As for your personal car, buy a large family vehicle, and you'll be making enough to buy Debbie a vehicle of her choice out of your own money. Once you find a home that you like, buy it; you'll find the corporate check book waiting for you when you arrive and there will be ample funds to cover all of this. Then hire a moving company to move your family's belongings also paid by the corporation. By the way, how much did you make per year as an architect?"

"I was currently making eighty thousand per year, but with your generosity you don't need to. . ."

Bobby held up his hand and asked, "Do you have your check book with you?"

Chester reached in his pocket and handed it to Bobby no questions asked, after all there was only eight hundred dollars left in it.

Bobby did some typing while looking at one of Chester's checks, "I just transferred one hundred thousand dollars into your account Chester. This will represent your retainer. I then want you to draw for yourself, let's see." Bobby did a quick calculation and said, "Six thousand dollars per week starting on Friday next."

Chester jumped up and said, "That's three hundred-twelve thousand dollars per year! I. . ."

Bobby held up his hand and said, "Now don't worry that's not counting your annual bonus which will depend on my profits for the year. I have decided to give you a ten percent bonus based on profit from six of my most profitable holdings. If I were to pay you now on that. . ." Bobby was calculating again, pushing buttons on his computer's keyboard with practiced ease, "Let's see, if everything keeps going as is that would come to two hundred thousand and some change, but I make no promises."

Chester sat down again.

Bobby had sympathy for the man and handed him a tissue to wipe off the beads of sweat that had accumulated on his forehead and then a brown paper sack, explaining, "Put your head down and breathe into this bag for a moment. It will help.

After a few moments of this activity, Chester's color returned and he finally asked, "You're not some nut job that just escaped and filling me with a bunch of bull are you? No better yet I'm having a dream at home and I'm going to wake up in a minute and wish that this could really be true. Or maybe. . ."

Bobby slid the phone over to him and said, "Why

don't you come over to my computer, here is a list of the access codes to several of the accounts that you will now have access to anyway. Verify their balances, and then I want you to call home and tell Debbie that you got the job and that you will be staying rather late tonight, but that you will explain everything when you get home. I'm going into the kitchen and use the second line and have a pizza delivered so we can get down to business.

When Bobby came back in he heard Chester say into the phone, "I have to go honey. I love you too. I'll see you as soon as I can, don't worry."

Bobby sat down in the chair that Chester just vacated after he hung up and said, "The pizza will be here in forty minutes." He typed some more and then printed something out, "I decided to put your mind at total ease tonight." His printer started the task set before it and Bobby soon gathered the stack of printed sheets, which listed all of his holdings and their net worth, and handed them to Chester as he said, "I remind you how important secrecy is and the value of this list."

Chester looked at it for what seemed a long time, the color again draining from his face, handed it back, "I'm just in shock. I don't believe I have ever met someone as rich as you are."

Bobby laughed, "I was embarrassed at first when God blessed my investments so generously, but then I realized that one day He would tell me how to spend it as well. I have used forty percent of the interest on my investments each month to fund the many projects I am involved in. The rest of the interest I have been putting into Alexander Development Corporation. When you get there and check it out you will find over six million dollars of liquid assets not counting long-term investments. I can funnel you more as you need it.

"Chester, don't get the wrong idea about me. I, or rather God, is asking you to tackle a much bigger task than you can possibly realize right now. You will earn your money, but I am paying you this generously so money will no longer be a problem, which will let you concentrate on the task at hand. Be wise about it; save some, invest some, and be generous in return to others. God will return it to you tenfold. The money I'm paying you, God will return to me in other ways. So don't get hung up on wealth. Enjoy your house, cars, position, but don't lose sight that your family is the most important thing. Your kids will grow up so fast you'll wonder where the time went. What you'll be left with when they move out to live their own lives, is memories. Make them good ones, Chester."

Chester had been nodding his agreement and now stuck out his hand. The two men shook hands and Bobby said, "Enough of you for now, let's put our minds to the project itself.

"What I want you to do first is find and buy about six hundred to one thousand acres or so of desert. Build an electric fence with state-of-the-art security devices around the entire perimeter. Then hire a Chief of Security and however many guards it takes to guard it. Then design a large underground structure. I want it to contain a large apartment; four bedrooms with baths and a master bathroom off of the master bedroom, living room, dining room, kitchen, laundry, and a large office.

In the same structure, build a large research lab complete with walk-in cooler and freezer. You may have to research some labs to see what equipment is standard in most genetic research labs. I'm sure it will need bacterial safe containment enclosures as well, put them in or if you leave room for them we can add to it once Justin moves in. Then build a few small efficiency apartments for fellow workers or guests. I want two secure exits from this structure up into the structure that will be built, a bit later on the surface..."

There was a knock on the door. Bobby got up and answered it. In moments the transaction was done, tip given and hot pizza was in each man's hand, mouth, then stomach. Life was good.

After the pizza was gone and another soft drink consumed, Bobby started his narrative again, "Once that structure is complete, start on the second structure, which will use the first as a foundation. This upper structure will be the one that we will actually start using as soon as it is finished. I can already think of a couple of Christian research hospitals that could use a facility like that. We will contact them only after the first is secretly built. Whoever uses the top building must never know about the secret basement facility. Chester, when you hire your General Contractor, make sure he is someone that will keep our secret and the people he sub-contracts to must also be in the dark about the purpose for this facility. On the second building, we can use the same General Contractor but be sure he uses all new sub-contractors. This may help security."

Chester simply nodded and continued to draw. He had his brief case open and had already sketched out a rough blueprint of the floor plan. He looked at Bobby and asked, "How big do you want the apartment, the lab etc.?"

Bobby scratched his head, "I really have no idea. When you research the labs, discreetly of course, find out what size a generous lab would be. As for the apartment, make it as large as you would want it if you had to live there. I figure that Justin may want to marry someday, but for security purposes he may have to live there. Also Chester the entire *"lower"* facility will need to be bomb proof, to exceed the current air-raid shelter."

Chester looked as though he was trying to decide if he should ask or not, then decided finally to ask, "Bobby, just what is it that Justin would be researching in this lab."

"I haven't the foggiest, except that as a bacterial, virus and genetic expert, I'm sure he'll need high-tech and safe labs for that type of work. Like I told you Chester, take your time, research well, and then when the plans are finished bring them to me for final approval before you begin construction."

The men shook hands and Bobby called a cab for Chester. When he was gone Bobby got down on his knees again and thanked God for starting this project. Neither he nor Chester understood just how important the completion of this project would be for the human race.

Only God knew the entire matter. He smiled, as He looked down on these warriors for His Son Jesus the Christ. His plan was progressing right on schedule.

CHAPTER TWELVE

A NEW BEGINNING

When the sun crept up over the Chicago skyline the next morning, many lives had changed in subtle and not so subtle ways. There were opposing forces lining up for a protracted fight over the soul of Justin Schaefer Johnson. This battle would last for another eighty-five years and would affect the lives of many people on both sides, many of whom had no idea the battle was even being waged.

Pastor Bob's office of charity at the mission had now become the operations center for the war that had been inevitable since Justin's birth. Chester Melvin had just been promoted to General in this spiritual battle, which would become all too real much sooner that he could imagine. The secret operation they had launched last night would invariably touch the lives of an army of saints and sinners; the former trying to build something good for mankind, the latter trying to stop them.

* * *

Hidden deep within Illumin, Inc., Justin awoke from a deep and peaceful sleep. Memories of the night before played in his young mind and he thought that it must have been a dream. He picked up his phone and called Tracy to be sure it really happened.

Tracy lay in the arms of Mr. Black both sleeping as only people without a conscience could. Her phone rang and she turned over picked it up and whispered hoarsely, "Yes, what is it?"

Justin hesitated just a moment then said, "I'm sorry to wake you Tracy but I couldn't wait to hear your voice again."

Tracy switched to the sexiest voice she had in her arsenal and whispered, "I'm glad to hear your voice as well lover. I can't wait to see you today Justin, and then maybe tonight we could have a repeat of last night? What do you say?"

Justin's heart skipped a beat and he was giddy when he said, "Of course we can see each other again tonight. I wish we could just skip right to it and. . ."

Tracy laughed and said, "Easy there Justin. We have to continue to do our work each day. Don't worry I'll make that interesting enough for you and then tonight I have a few new adventures in mind to lead you through. Now get off this phone and get ready for work."

She hung up and snuggled back into Black's arms. His warmth fought back the coldness of the room as he said, "You know Justin's going to be like a child in a candy store for a while."

Tracy was thoughtful and then whispered, "Are you sure it's necessary to break the boy's heart to get your point across?"

Black smiled as he answered, "You truly like him don't you?"

She slapped his arm and said, "Don't worry I'm a professional, I won't let feelings get in the way, but it just seems a shame to build him up and then pull the rug out. He's so trusting and innocent."

"That is exactly my point Tracy. He can't run this

Corporation and become our High Priest as long as he is naive and innocent. He must be educated in the hardships of life. Don't worry though Tracy, I'll have another assignment for you by then I'm sure."

Black's cell phone rang and he reached over to his pants lying on the chair next to the bed, "Black."

An accented voice on the other end said, "You remember Chester Melvin, that Architect that you had fired some time back?"

Black simply snapped, "Yes."

"Well he met with Pastor Bob last night and they are planning to build a secret research center in Las Vegas. . ."

Black interrupted, "Why should I care what he is building?"

"Because he is building it for Justin Schaefer Johnson; he said as much."

"Get the recording to me ASAP and take out this Chester Melvin. I'm tired of him already. Then send a message to Pastor Bob so he won't miss the significance of Chester's death." Black broke the connection, lit a cigarette, and leaned against the headboard.

Tracy rubbed his chest and asked, "Trouble?"

Black put his cigarette out and said, "Nothing I can't handle." He kissed her before she could ask her next question and soon, with very little prompting they both gave into their lustful pleasures. Work could wait for another hour.

* * *

Across town Chester and Debbie Melvin were

ecstatic. Their ship had come in! They were set for life now and they had stayed up the rest of the night talking. They got on the internet and arranged a flight out today for Vegas. Debbie's parents would watch the children and they were going to house hunt later today. They had it all planned. They would sleep on the plane and then meet with the realtor they had contacted this morning. Debbie still could not believe that anyone would pay so much and give so many benefits. She knew her husband deserved it and could pull it off, but she still felt like it was a dream that they would wake up from all too soon.

Chester and Debbie took time to give thanks to God for his blessings and then they concentrated on packing, feeding the kids breakfast and got ready to leave.

*   *   *

Chester's guardian angel, whose name was Veracity, looked over at Ardor who was assigned to protect Debbie. They had also talked about possible dangers to this new job that Chester had taken. He was about to speak when Logos suddenly appeared before them. They stood at attention and saluted by putting right fist to left shoulder. The gesture had been used by angels to show respect long before the Romans had made it a salute.

Logos had an order and it was short and to the point, "Stall them this morning. Their life is in danger." He disappeared before they could ask questions but they knew what they must do. Angels have always used delaying tactics to save the lives of their human charges.

A missed bus, a stalled car. . . They looked at each other and knew what their most important priority today would have to be. It always disappointed their charges when inconvenient things happened to them, but most lived to appreciate it later.

Pastor Bob was praying in the Chapel when Chester and Debbie arrived. He was surprised to see them and his expression must have been easy to read. Chester smiled and said, "I wanted you to meet Debbie; before we leave." Pastor Bob noticed that she was very pretty with long blonde hair that looked as though it were spun from gold. Her deep blue eyes were intense and intelligent. She was almost as tall as Chester and would look very slender if she hadn't been seven months pregnant.

Pastor Bob remembered his manners and held out his hand, "Very glad to meet you Debbie. Would you like to take a seat?"

She glowed mysteriously as all pregnant women do, shook his hand; a smile beaming on her face but declined the seat saying, "No we can't stay long I'm afraid."

Chester explained, "We are on the way to the airport to fly out to Las Vegas."

Bob looked surprised, "Already?"

Debbie laughed and said, "You'll learn that Chester never wastes time."

Chester handed Pastor Bob a piece of paper, "I wrote down the hotel and number where we will be staying as well as the flight number. We'll be taking flight 303 from Chicago to Las Vegas. We'll be back in three days and I'll let you know what I've found."

Debbie put her right hand on the side of Pastor Bob's left arm and said as her eyes filled with tears, "Pastor Bob we just don't know how to thank you for what you are doing for us. We were I'm afraid, just a little miffed with God about the turn of events, then you not only turned our circumstances around but did it to such a greater degree than we could have ever dreamed."

Pastor Bob placed his hand over hers and said, "That is how God works sometimes, Debbie; He gives us far more than we would have even thought to ask for."

She stood up on her tiptoes and kissed his cheek and said, "Well thanks to you and the God we serve. I know that Chester will do a very good job for you. He really is very good at what he does."

"Spoken like a faithful wife. Don't worry Debbie; I already have the utmost confidence in Chester."

Chester laughed nervously and whispered, "Perhaps you two would like to be alone. . ."

Debbie slapped his arm and said, "Oh, you."

Chester hugged Pastor Bob and whispered, "Thank you Bobby." After he stepped back he said a bit louder, "Well we must be off, but don't worry I'll keep in touch."

Pastor Bob watched them leave and immediately fell back to his knees and prayed, "Lord Jesus, please keep them safe. They have no idea what they have stepped into. . ."

*   *   *

The man stretched, picked up his foam cup and gulped the now cold coffee and made a face at its bitterness. Then, as he discarded the cup and its astringent contents, he said, "You have that right preacher." He was in a van that was parked just down the street from the Mission. He picked up the phone and simply said, "The package is on the way, all is green." He hung up and put a new CD into the recorder and sent his partner out for fresh coffee and cold sandwiches, this was going to be a long assignment he feared.

*　　*　　*

Justin worked the best he could but his mind wasn't on his research this morning. He kept sneaking a peek at Tracy who would wink and smile at him. He was intoxicated with this new experience. He felt love deep and total for this woman and was already picturing them together forever. *'This is the woman I'm going to marry. Well, as soon as I'm old enough anyway.'* he thought happily as he transferred a culture to his growing field.

Jeremy Bolder watched the two youngsters flirt back and forth and just shook his head. He mumbled under his breath, "Poor Justin.", drooping his head sadly and went back to the experiment at hand. The other scientists working in the lab tried their best to stay out of the affair and just concentrated on their own work while secretly admiring Justin and his good fortune.

*　　*　　*

Chester and Debbie hurried into the airport and heard, "Last call for flight 303 to Las Vegas".

Chester spotted a wheelchair by the door and told Debbie to get into it. They only had two carry-on bags, which he placed in her lap and then ran. Gate 34 wasn't that far away they still had time to make it. Their rental car had died on the way here and they had to call a cab. Then it seemed that the cab driver timed each light so it would be red when they came near one. They were late and Chester had to make up time. He was still quite athletic and they got to the gate just as the last passenger was going through the door. They had made it.

*   *   *

Pastor Bob allowed himself to relax as he watched the afternoon ball game on the Mission's TV set. There were several of his homeless friends eating lunch and watching excitedly as their team hit another homer. Cheers filled the recreation room and Pastor Bob was cheering right along with them. Then suddenly the screen changed from the game and read:

STAND BY FOR A SPECIAL NEWS REPORT

Complaints arose from the baseball fans but their jeers died down once the news anchor appeared on the screen. He was wearing a blue suit, white shirt complete with red tie. His frown foretold that the news he was about to impart would not be pleasant, "Early this afternoon flight 303 from Chicago to Las Vegas crashed." Behind him the wreckage burnt itself into Pastor Bob's memory. Bits of aircraft were strewn as far as the eye could see. The anchor continued, "We go now, live, to Ben Smithers who is reporting from the crash site, "Ben."

"Thank you Jack; Ben Smithers here, reporting live from the crash site of flight 303 from Chicago to Las Vegas. I have just been informed by Fire Chief Sam Nichols that it is believed now that there are no survivors. What started out for many as a pleasure trip to Las Vegas ended in tragedy about an hour ago when for some reason flight 303 was lost on radar for no apparent reason. Investigations are pending. Airport officials said it would be hours if not days before they would know the cause of the crash. . ."

Pastor Bob had already dropped to his knees out of habit and was praying for the souls who lost their lives on flight 303 to. . ." Suddenly a fear that had been touching the back of his mind with its icy fingers; burst through and he jerked the paper out of his pocket and unfolded it with shaking hands. Beads of sweat broke out on his forehead and the blood drained from his face as he looked at Chester's handwriting and saw; 'Flight 303 from Chicago to Las Vegas.'

Pastor Bob fell backward and sat down heavily on the floor. Others gathered around him asking what was wrong. The ball game was back on but no one found it important or enjoyable any longer. Pastor Bob finally answered the repeated inquiries into what was wrong. He whispered to them, "I had friends on that flight."

Everyone was sad for him and patted his back and gave him their condolences. Just when he thought he was stabilizing another fear forced its way into his conscious thought. He whispered, "They know. Oh no, Lord! They know! Black did this!"

Pastor Bob got back to his knees and asked, "Lord Jesus welcome Chester, Debbie, their baby, and all the other souls on flight 303 into Your arms. Comfort them and give them Your peace."

Maxwell, one of Pastor Bob's regulars came up to him and handed him a folded piece of paper. Out of habit he took it, nodded his thanks, and read: 'Bob cancel all your Vegas plans before more innocent people die.' It was unsigned. Bob turned to Maxwell and yelled, "Who gave this to you!", but Maxwell just shrugged and walked away to get a cup of coffee.

Bob just rocked back and forth and cried out to his God for mercy and courage. He was still in shock five hours later and wouldn't respond to anyone, then the phone rang. No one could ever remember him being this upset before. Buddy answered the phone, "Hello? No I don't think he feels like talking to anyone right now." Now here Buddy lowered his voice and told the man on the phone, "I think he lost some friends on that plane crash and he's messed up right now."

The man in the van yelled, "Hurrah!"

A bit louder and skeptically Buddy whispered, "Are you sure? Man if you're messing with me I'll. . . O.K. don't have a cow." He put his hand over the phones mouth piece and yelled across the room, "Pastor Bob, there's a man on the phone insists that he's a friend of yours and insists that you speak to him."

Rage welled up in Pastor Bob as he yelled, "Black!" He got up, ran across the room, rudely grabbed the phone away from Buddy and yelled, "Black you've gone too far this time. . ."

Pastor Bob couldn't believe his ears when he finally stopped long enough to listen. A distant scratchy voice pleaded with him, "Bob be quiet and listen! This is

Chester!"

Pastor Bob sat down and turned pale for the second time today. His emotions were on a roller coaster ride as Chester explained, "I'm sorry about breaking our code of silence but as you know by now it doesn't matter. It can't be a coincidence that our particular flight goes down the day after we met. They're probably listening to us right now. . ."

The man in the van looked around guiltily; as if they could actually see him, but he continued to listen.

Bob interrupted anxiously, "But, how? What happened?"

Chester continued, "We arrived on a different plane than 303 naturally, I won't say which one. We were delayed after we left you this morning. My rental car broke down and the taxi ride was slow and almost made us too late. I pushed Debbie in a wheelchair and we ran to the gate and made it just in time. We were so relieved and started through the boarding door when we were informed that our seats had been given to a stand-by couple because we hadn't checked in an hour before time like agreed on the ticket. They were sorry but there was nothing they could do. They did help us arrange a transfer to another flight, so we had lunch while we waited. Then the news reports came over the TV in the restaurant. I'm sorry I didn't call sooner but I wanted to get us here safely first."

"You mean you're in Las Vegas?"

"Yes I am, Bobby, and nothing's changed except that I'm going to be much more careful from now on. I'm going to make security arrangements first if it's OK with you? Then I'll take care of other details after."

"Do whatever you feel is best. You can still back out if you want to Chester. I won't think less of you or anything."

"Not on your life, or mine either apparently. I'm not a quitter, Bobby! Look, I better go in case they try to trace this. Don't worry Bobby I know more about these types of things than you do and I have good connections. I'll get back to you when I can."

The line went dead before Bob could ask his questions but the momentary disappointment felt better than the immense mourning he had been going through. He yelled, "Yippee!" Then to no one in particular he yelled, "God is good!" He fell to his knees and started praising God and asked for His forgiveness at his own lack of faith. His respect for Chester had just doubled and he knew that God had been in his choice for sure. "Never a dull moment Lord," he said this with a smile on his face which echoed in his voice.

*   *   *

The man in the van was frowning now and was reluctant to make the phone call, but feared not making it more.

Black was in his office when the call came through. He picked up the phone without thinking of the action and said, "Black."

"Ah sir? Pastor Bob just got a call from that Chester Melvin fellow. Anders missed him; they missed their flight."

Black slammed the phone down and picked it back up just as fast and hit a speed-dial number, which was answered immediately, "This is Black! You missed him!

They missed the flight! I'm also not happy with the mess you made out there. I didn't approve taking out the other four hundred passengers, what were you thinking?"

"We made it look like terrorists. We. . ."

Black stopped him, "Never mind! I'll pay your contract off, but abort any further efforts until I call you again. We may let them start their plan and let it progress until I know for sure what they are up to. The element of surprise is gone so I'll have to make more subtle arrangements. Do you understand?"

"Yes sir; came the non-apologetic answer. Can't blame me for this guy's dumb luck; he should go out and buy a lottery ticket with luck like that."

Black hung up on him, his mind racing through several possible scenarios. He decided to put Pastor Bob and his friends on hold for a while, and just let the intelligence build up until it revealed clearer plans than he had right now. He couldn't see Bobby trying to kidnap Justin, or would he? What kind of research center would he try to set up and why?

There were four levels of security at Illumin, Inc. Level four was the everyday security level. At the other end was level one which was tight, very tight security. He couldn't run things that tight for very long, the tension was too great. He made his decision and picked up the phone again, "Raise security to level two and put Justin himself under level three." He hung up knowing that his orders would be carried out without fail.

He whispered to himself, "What are you up to Bobby? Whatever it is you're in way over your head. Bobby; of that I am sure.

A power greater than Mr. Black agreed and smiled

knowingly as He said, "Yes, and so are you Mr. Black; so are you."

CHAPTER THIRTEEN

CODE BLUE

Jack Miller walked over to the water cooler, drew a glass and gulped it down. That satisfied his thirst but didn't help wake him up. He had been up late installing a complicated security system for a large corporation right here in Tupelo, Mississippi. His company, Miller Securities, handled most of the security business in Tupelo but he also traveled extensively throughout the country setting up systems for small and large businesses alike. He even had a special division for home security, although his manager Wallus Morgan took care of those exclusively.

Wallus was at his desk in his office the door of which was just to Jack's left. He heard Wallus yelling, "I don't care what you've heard Bill that system won't do the job for you! You need a model X-357 at least, unless you want to just invite your intruder to dinner with you."

Jack walked away smiling. Wallus was a good man. Jack entered the employee lounge, a small room with a counter top, which held the all-important coffee pot. To the right of it was a refrigerator containing the soda, cream, lunchmeats and cheese that were used throughout the day by all the employees. Jack poured a black cup of coffee and took a sip. It was incredibly strong just the way he liked it and he started back to his office to work on some new bids.

Jack was only five foot five inches tall but had a sturdy build of pure muscle and he was in marvelous shape for fifty-five years of age. He was legally a senior citizen now but no one cared to remind him of it. In all honesty, he didn't look it because his short crew cut hair was still naturally brown, accented by bushy eyebrows over hazel eyes. He was still proud to brag that he had all his own teeth as well. Jack still wore a wedding ring on his left hand even though he had been widowed at the age of twenty-five when his wife died at the end of a two-year battle with cancer. He never remarried. This had occurred while he was a special field agent in one of the FBI's Special Services Security teams. He had landed that job right out of the Army where he was a member of the elite Green Beret from age eighteen to age twenty-two. He served for thirty years in the FBI until three years ago when he retired and started this security firm and enjoyed instant success. A person makes a lot of connections while in the FBI and some of those people owed Jack a favor or two.

He walked into his rather large exquisitely decorated office and stopped to sip his coffee while he admired the large swordfish hanging proudly on the wall behind his desk. Deep-sea fishing was one of the few recreations that Jack allowed himself. He started to dream about the next fishing trip that was coming up in a month or so when the intercom sounded.

He pushed the button and his secretary, Sally Smith said, "Jack there is a John Doe on the phone for you?"

Jack instantly tensed as he said, "Put him through Sally."

"Hello Jack, long time no see. This is John Doe - Code Blue - Las Vegas, sector B." The line went dead.

The color in Jack's face apparently drained because Sally, who had come into his office to see what this nonsense was about, asked, "What's wrong Jack?" He looked up and smiled with some effort and said, "Oh nothing Sally. Ask Wallus to step in here please."

She looked doubtful but complied. Jack knew that this call would probably come one day but now that it had he felt an excitement that he thought was long dead.

Wallus ran in and almost yelled, "What's up Jack? Sally said that you look like you've seen a ghost. To me, you look like the cat that ate the canary and enjoyed it."

Jack stared at his manager for a moment and said, "I'll be away for a few days. I have some business to attend to in Las Vegas. When I know more, I'll get in touch with you. There may be some duties in this for you, but I'll have to check it out first."

"Can't you tell me more about it Jack?"

"Not at this time I'm afraid."

Wallus had learned better than to push Jack too far and he let it go, "Well I'll be in my office", as he turned and left.

Jack hadn't seen Walter Boulder for six years now. They had met on one of Jack Miller's FBI operations. Jack needed help on securing a building that Walter's company was building for a suspected criminal element. Jack and some other agents had literally picked Walter up off the street as they had to do to people from time to time so as to talk to them securely. They drove up in a van, jumped out and at gunpoint no less forced the man into the van and took off down the street. Walter had handled it in stride as they figured he would with his Green Beret background. The two men hit it off immediately (brothers in arms and all that) and Walter had readily agreed to help them. He had gotten Jack onto the construction crew undercover and helped him install many hidden cameras and microphones. One night they had entered the almost finished building to put some finishing touches on the security setup when they were surprised by two armed gunmen. Walter had seen them first since they were behind Jack, he had yelled, "No!", and jumped in front of Jack as the first shot rang out. The bullet had struck Walter in the chest and as he fell to the ground Jack had already drawn his weapon and fatally shot both men. It had taken Walter six months to recover and Jack had visited him often during those months, cementing their friendship. The news had carried the headlines for just one day, 'LOCAL ARCHITECT KILLED IN ROBBERY ATTEMPT - ASSAILANTS FATALLY SHOT BY POLICE.' It had been child's play to alter the story and then to make Walter Boulder disappear into the witness protection program. He had been given a new name; Chester Melvin and they helped him get a new position in his field in another state. Since it had been a secret operation, however, they couldn't give Walter/Chester a medal. Jack, however, had offered something better. He had told Walter; now Chester, that if he ever found himself in a situation in which his life was in danger, to give Jack a call. He felt responsible for getting Chester involved and it was the least he could do. Jack had told Chester, "Keep it short. Call yourself John Doe and just say Code Blue which will tell me you're in trouble." Then he handed him a zip code book in which he had written down a sector number and a specific location in which to meet next to each major city in America. "This way if you have ears listening to your side I'll know where to meet you but they won't."

Jack never really thought his architect friend would ever need it but he was wrong. To Jack's credit, there wasn't even a moment of hesitation in his decision to honor this old debt. He genuinely liked Chester (it took some time but he had started thinking of Walter by his new name, Chester), and would do anything he could for him.

Jack found himself wondering what it would be like to be ripped out of your old life and starting over in a new one. Walter's parents had already died and he had no brothers or sisters, which made things much smoother. It was always hardest to fake your death when you had family who would mourn for you and then know you can never contact them. Jack shuddered at the thought of many angry witnesses who found that out the hard way. Luckily for Walter, it was immediately after his transition into the life of Chester Melvin that he met a wonderful woman got married and the last he had checked she was pregnant.

Jack had given Chester a number by which to contact him and when he left the agency he asked that any calls from Chester be patched through to him at his agency or even at home if they couldn't reach him here. Jack smiled at the prospect of finally getting to talk to Chester after all these years. What adventure had he gotten himself into now? Only time would tell. Jack broke his reverie and left for home to pack a small carry-on bag and get out to Vegas to meet his old friend.

CHAPTER FOURTEEN

REUNION

Chester had hung up with Jack and he and Debbie had gone to the airport to pick up her parents and the children. Very early that morning, they had called her parents and had them leave immediately so as to get everyone together here in Vegas and hopefully to safety. When they were all together and safe Chester told them all about Jack and the incident that had led to his change in life. He hadn't even told Debbie about it, not even in their most intimate moments. She had been a bit angry about the deception but her sympathy and pride in his adventure helped her to forgive him in the long run. She had explained that she was very proud of him and that not many people would get involved in something that dangerous.

That had been yesterday and now Chester sat alone at the agreed location. They had agreed to meet exactly twenty-four hours from the time he called Jack and that time was only twenty minutes away. This place had been listed as a coffee shop within a mini-mall but now it was a grand casino. Chester was hoping that Jack would find it and had located himself in the small bar just inside the entrance. He sat watching the door hoping to recognize Jack after these past six years that separated them. They were not supposed to contact each other except in the most dire circumstances, which Chester figured this qualified. He knew for this project he would have to have a man in charge of security that he would have no doubts about. That man was Jack Miller. As he sat and waited for Jack, however, he wondered if Jack would be willing to undertake such a project. It would obviously be a long-term project and as had already been proven it would be a dangerous project. Jack may be tired of intrigue and danger. Chester had no idea whether Jack had finally married and settled down or perhaps was tied up with some business at home. This trip may already be an imposition on his old friend. By the time Jack walked through the door and spotted him at the bar, Chester was feeling remorse.

The two men met half way and hugged. Jack said, "You're looking good Chester. I was worried that you might have been messed up or something."

Chester was genuinely glad to see Jack and answered, "Not yet my friend. Man it's good to see you. You married yet?"

Jack smiled as they walked back toward the bar and said, "Not likely to happen I'm afraid. Too set in my ways you know?" As they sat down at the far end of the bar and ordered a soft drink, neither man drank alcohol, Jack asked, "Look Chester we can catch up on each other later, I want to hear about this danger you're in."

Chester took a drink and waited for the bartender to step away then answered, "Settle back and get comfortable Jack, this is a rather involved story."

He set about telling him the story of his last job, his meeting with Pastor Bob, and all about the new project. "So you see Jack I'm going to need a Chief of Security that I can trust and I thought of you right away."

"Well that makes sense Chester but I'm still not

clear of what danger you're in."

"Sorry Jack I left out that part didn't I. Well the day after we met Pastor Bob we went to the airport to catch a flight here. Did you hear about flight 303 out of Chicago in route to Las Vegas?"

Jack nodded, "That was a terrible tragedy Chester."

"Well Jack that was our original flight. We were delayed and just missed the flight and had to take a later flight."

"That could just be a coincidence Chester."

"Normally I'd agree with you but Pastor Bob told me about this message he got about dropping this project or more people would get hurt. That makes it a sure thing in my book."

"Do you think they know that you are still alive?"

"And in Vegas? Yes. If you want the security job, Jack, your first duty will be to hire some people you can trust to protect my family, myself, and Pastor Bob back in Chicago. Then you'll supervise the security on the project site itself. We are going to refer to it as 'Operation Antidote', because that is what the research center will be called, 'The Antidote Research Center, Inc.' I can't explain why Jack, but I feel this project is important, maybe even to all of mankind, but we may never know that, not in our lifetime anyway."

Jack's mind had begun to grasp at details of what would be needed, "You say that money is no object with Pastor Bob?"

Chester smiled knowing that Jack had just said yes, "He has convinced me that money will be the least of our worries. We are, however, up against a very strong enemy here. One who probably has connections in the government, and no telling how high up. They have also proven that they have no respect for life, not if they would blow up an entire plane to just make a point. Think about it before you get yourself involved in this."

Jack ignored the way out that Chester had just given him, "I have thought about it and it's going to be a large project. I think my company can handle it though."

"You realize that I'm asking you to be a full time employee right?"

"No problem. I've been meaning to promote my employee Wallus Morgan to partner anyway. I'm sure in my travels I'll be able to throw some work his way while taking care of my duties for our project."

Chester liked the sound of that. He had said, "Our project", and it told him that Jack was now committed, so he asked, "What do we do first Jack?"

Jack took a moment to organize the thoughts that had filled his brain all at once, "First off, we'll need a base of operations."

Chester held up his hand, "Pastor Bob foresaw that years ago apparently. He has an office building that except for a small charity operation has twelve offices for our use. You let me know how many you will need for security and you'll have them."

"I'll only need two, one for me and one for the assistant that I have in mind. The rest of security will be at the site or in the field protecting you, your family and Pastor Bob. For the site, I'll hire an already organized security firm; they are pretty reliable, especially if you can afford to hire the best. I'll check around town and see who the best is. I've got a few individuals in mind that was secret service that would make good bodyguards.

"Chester, why don't you just leave this security stuff to me? You find the property to buy and start drawing up your plans and I'll watch your back. I can't believe we're doing this for a fourteen year old boy genius who may not ever want to use it."

Chester shook hands with Jack and said, "I really appreciate this, Jack."

"Don't worry, Chester, it's going to cost you."

Both men laughed and Jack left abruptly and Chester followed shortly after.

*   *   *

Justin couldn't have been happier. It had been a glorious two weeks now since he had met and started dating Tracy. She was the most wonderful woman he had ever met and, of course, the only one he had ever dated. He understood now why people liked falling in love. He hadn't given it much thought before Tracy had taken his life by storm. The sensations she had exposed him to, way before their proper time, were now totally obsessing him and left him weak in the knees and his thoughts addled. His research had gone nowhere since day one, he just couldn't concentrate.

Black was in Johnson's office talking about the fact that Justin had fallen much harder and faster than he had expected, "We may need to pull the plug quicker than I had planned, sir."

Johnson looked up from a report he was reading and said, "How is that possible?"

"It appears that Justin grabs at things with an intensity that seems to block out all else. This could be risky. Once we break his heart, he could either throw himself into his work with abandon as we hope or he may sink into a fit of depression from which he may never recover."

Johnson thought for a moment and finally asked, "Couldn't you warn that man-servant, what's his name . . .?"

"Mr. Summons, sir."

"Yes, tell him to watch Justin closely to make sure he does no harm to himself.

"I've been watching them together and I feared at first that they were building too strong a bond but now it may work in our favor. Yes, I think Summons may be able to soften the blow just enough."

"Well good! Make the arrangements. Let's get this part of Justin's training over with shall we. It's time he moves on to the more important job of finding the antidote to that latest government creation, the X-2 virus. Nasty piece of work but I think Justin's team can pull it off, providing, of course, we can get him back to work and with a clear head as well."

Black pulled out his cell-phone and made the call.

Justin was speeding along on his skateboard heading back to the lab after lunch. He hadn't been able to find Tracy but he figured she had stayed behind at the lab, working on an experiment. He was carrying a bag with a sandwich and chips in it that he had bought for Tracy. No reason she should starve while she works so hard. He was dreaming of the events they had planned for this evening; a movie, dinner, and then a night of love as only they could accomplish.

He happily greeted Jeremy Bolder as he walked toward his office, "Back already? Have you seen Tracy, I have her lunch?"

Jeremy warned, "Don't go in there Justin."

Without even pausing he barged into his office and stopped in his tracks as if he ran full force into a wall of rage and jealousy. Tracy and Jerald Stromeyer were completely absorbed in what they were doing.

Justin watched the surreal scene before him, not able to move or talk. The color drained from his face as her betrayal burst his heart. His thoughts raged, *'She lied! It's all a lie!'*, His voice squeaked as he whispered, "Tracy how could you?"

She opened her eyes but in no way did they alter their actions as she said, with no undo concern in her voice, "Oh Justin! We'll be finished in just a second, wait outside please." Tracy closed her eyes again and Justin just turned and walked out of the office and then the lab, walking blindly, not knowing what to do or where to go.

"Wait up Justin!" It was Jeremy Bolder, "Justin wait!" Jeremy grabbed Justin by the arm and forced him into a coffee shop just as they reached the Boardwalk. They sat at a table for two but Justin just stared into space with that hateful scene replaying itself over and over again in his broken mind, which was now severed from his heart.

Jeremy let him smolder for a while and then tentatively asked, "Are you OK Justin?"

Justin looked at him disbelievingly, "Am I OK? Of course I'm not OK! I just saw the woman I love making it with someone else. How can I be OK?"

"Justin I won't pretend that it doesn't hurt you, but you need to remember that even though you have seen unfaithfulness in one woman doesn't mean that all women are like that. There are many fine women out there who are faithful and are looking for a faithful man to be partners with."

Justin giggled. Then he laughed, softly at first, then loudly. People started looking at him until they recognized him, then they turned away nervously. "Oh don't worry Jeremy I've learned my lesson well about women. I know what they are good for and that's all they are good for!"

Just then Tracy came running in and ran up to the table and pleaded, "Justin, I'm so sorry. Things just got out of hand; I promise I'll never do it again. Please forgive me."

Justin had stood up during Tracy's pleading and suddenly he struck out with a right cross and knocked her down. Blood trickled from the corner of her mouth as Justin yelled, "Tracy you get out of this cafe, this institute, and definitely my life." He had squeezed those words out between gritted teeth as he tried to control his rage. Now, however he yelled, "Get out now before I kill you!"

Tracy, scared now, got up and ran before Justin could change his mind. He started to chase her but Jeremy grabbed Justin by the shoulders and whispered, "Let her go Justin, she's not worth killing. As a matter of fact try to forgive her so this won't fester in your soul."

Justin roughly pulled himself free of Jeremy's grasp and yelled, "Forgive her? Are you nuts? Not only shall I not forgive her, Jeremy, I will hold all women in contempt after this, because of her. I'll use them as she has used me and that's a promise. Now leave me alone!" Justin ran away without looking to see if Jeremy was following him.

Justin just ran aimlessly for an hour and finally found himself in Don Black's office. He fell into the office and stood there panting, completely out of breath.

Don watched him for a minute and then asked innocently, "What's wrong Justin?"

That was when the tears came. Justin sobbed uncontrollably as he fell to his knees. Don came over, put his arm around Justin, guided him back to his feet and led him to the couch. They sat down and Justin sobbed on Don's shoulder, hugging him desperately. He had finally cried himself dry and was soon able to explain to Don what had happened. Don was instantly furious and made a call. He ordered that Tracy Warner and Jerard Stromeyer be picked up and be brought to the Temple.

He led the way through the secret passage and he and Justin walked into the elevator at the end of the hall. This took them down several levels, deep into the earth under the installation that Justin had come to call home. When they reached the bottom the elevator opened into a large entrance hall, from the ceiling of which hung three large crystal chandeliers. The well-lit entrance led to stairs that were as wide as the room and led up to the pillared entrance of what could only be the Temple.

As they walked up the stairs Justin asked, "Is this where religion is carried out?"

Black put his hand on Justin's shoulder and said, "Religion is for fools, Justin. This is where we learn about wealth, holdings, power and revenge. This is where you will learn to become your own god. We all have a god hiding in us just waiting to come out. Part of becoming a god is learning that you command the power that allows people to live or to die. You will also learn that a Johnson cannot allow anyone to cross him and let them live to brag about it."

Just then two men dragged in Tracy. Her hands were handcuffed behind her and she was yelling, "Let me go pig. Wait till my boss hears about this!"

Black yelled out, "Gag that woman."

Justin had heard her but had mistakenly thought she was referring to him as her boss. Why did she think he would want to protect her?

When they brought her close to where Justin was standing she struggled and through the gag tried to speak to Don Black. Her eyes were pleading for him to stop this.

Black shoved his thumb over his shoulder and said, "Take her into the Temple."

Again two men came in and they had an unconscious Jerard Stromeyer between them. Don led the way and Justin followed him and the three men followed him.

The Temple was lit by large torches in holders all along the walls. Three more chandeliers hung from the ceiling but these too were non-electric oils lamps that cast eerie shadows, which danced to unheard music. Demons infested this place and made it feel chilly to the humans who dared to enter.

The men guarding the prisoners gagged Stromeyer as he came to and made the two prisoners kneel before Black and Justin. Don turned to Justin, "The best way to deal with unfaithful people is to kill them."

Justin thought he was kidding until Black handed him a forty-five-caliber semi auto pistol. It was just like the one they had him train with. He had enjoyed his shooting sessions but targets were much scarier when they became real people. Justin's fear had been dulled, though, with the video game that used a pistol just like this one and in which the job was blowing people to pieces, blood and all. Playing this for hours had dulled the meaning of life and death and Justin was confused.

He took the gun as Don whispered in his ear, "Take them out Justin. They don't deserve to live."

While Justin hesitated Tracy had slid the gag down enough to speak and she was about to expose Black's part in this mess, but Black grabbed the gun from Justin and shot her twice in the forehead. Justin's eyes grew round and he watched stunned as Tracy fell to the ground and blood pooled around her head. The shots were still echoing around the Temple chamber when Black handed Justin the gun and said, "Take care of this trader Justin."

All the pain came to a head and Justin screamed in his pain and pulled the trigger once, twice, three times, and continued to pull it until he ran out of ammunition. Jerard Stromeyer had stayed upright for the first four shots and then crumpled to the floor and was already dead when Justin finished emptying the gun into him.

Johnson, who was watching on his office computer, applauded and yelled, "Well done son!" he now knew that Justin was the right choice for High Priest of their Temple of Wealth and Power.

THE ANTIDOTE

A cold peace settled over Justin as he watched the sinners bleed onto the floor of the Temple. He had never seen a real dead person up close and it fascinated him. A chilly smile came onto his face as he watched the handiwork of his wrath. He was a god! He had the power of life and death in his young hands. A new kind of intoxication took over as his heart healed by becoming even harder against love and all that is decent in the human heart.

He was officially a worshipper of humanity and its god-like powers. He had tasted blood and would never be innocent again. Innocence was for fools as was trust, faith, and love. He knew now that he belonged here. This was his new home, his new kingdom; a kingdom to be ruled with a fist of cold steel and an even colder heart.

Justin turned to Don Black who had been watching him closely, "Here's your gun Don. Please clean up this mess. I have research to do."

Justin walked calmly away while Black with a chill of realization thought doubtfully, *'I may have just unleashed a monster; one that may not be as easy to control as I thought.'*

The demon Detestation whispered gleefully, "You have no idea how true that is Don."

*   *   *

Cynthia Caldwell and Beth Foster had become good friends over the years that they had worked together at Alexander Development Corporation. They were equally in charge of all charitable activities done by the corporation, which were many and varied. They

172

distributed everything from Bibles to food. They were on the boards of many homeless shelters, soup kitchens, and food pantries, which were run independently but that counted on them for supplies and leadership. It had taken them awhile to trust the generosity of Pastor Bob whom they very seldom got to see. He managed them from a distance with them reporting to him in the form of monthly reports sent to his Chicago mission. They had become accustomed to this arrangement and they had a few concerns now that he had activated the rest of the office building.

It was with dread that they awaited the arrival of this Melvin character. What would he be like? Would he interfere with their operation? Would their routine be upset by the presence of others working here?

It was these concerns that unconsciously caused a chip to form on their collective shoulders. It was this chilly mind-set that Chester Melvin walked into when he arrived at the office for the first time.

He walked up to the building; it was a two story modern looking building made of small white bricks that sported large black one-way mirror glass windows. The double door entrance was made of the same glass and when he walked through them he noticed that the lobby floor was covered with thick, plush blue carpeting. It was a wide room, which was empty except for a couch and coffee table on the right against the wall. On the wall straight ahead there was a large cross with these words sprawled underneath it in gold capital letters; 'JESUS IS LOVE AND LOVE IS CHARITY'. To the left was a blank wall except for a secure door with a keypad lock to the right of the door.

Chester liked it immediately. Just beyond the couch on the right were two doors and beyond them a hallway. Chester would learn later that this hall led to a small employee lunchroom. It also led to a stairwell to the upstairs food pantry that occupied the largest room on the right side of the building. A woman came out of the first office and asked, "Yes, may I help you?"

She was about five feet four inches tall with a slim figure that was complimented by a black pants suit and white blouse. Her lips were full and red; her long black hair shone brightly as it flowed over her black suit coat, but what struck Chester immediately were her intelligent gray eyes. He was not sure he had ever seen gray eyes and stared a bit long at them.

"I said, may I help you?" she said this with a bit of a bite in her voice.

Chester smiled and answered, "Yes. I'm sorry, my name is Chester Melvin. Pastor Bob has sent me to open the other offices for a project we are about to begin here in town."

Was that a frown? "I'll need to see some identification sir."

Chester walked over and showed her his driver's license and while she nodded almost disappointed that she had nothing to argue about, Chester caught on from her body language what she might be thinking.

"Who do I have the privilege of addressing?"

Beth held out her hand reluctantly and said, "I'm Beth Foster. Glad to meet you Chester." It was a lie that she didn't try very hard to cover up.

"I'm glad to meet you too Beth." This he said with genuine friendliness. Then he added, "Pastor Bob assures me that you and a . . ." He looked at his notes before he continued, "Cynthia Caldwell are very capable individuals and he has warned me not to get in your way or interfere with you in any way. Other than perhaps showing me around, I won't need to bother you at all. I think what you two are doing here is just tremendous."

Beth's heart melted some as Cynthia came out of her office, the second door on the right. She had heard them talking and wondered if this was the stranger they had been waiting for. Cynthia was a bit shorter than Beth and much heavier. She had a rather average body with average features. She wore her red hair in a bun and wore a long blue one-piece dress that went to her ankles.

As she approached Beth said, "Cynthia this is Chester Melvin and Chester this is Cynthia Caldwell. Cynthia looked him over for a moment and then said, "Beth and I are the Vice Presidents in charge of charity work for Pastor Bob and we. . ."

Chester could see that the ladies had really been traumatized by his arrival and took care to put them at ease. Looking first at one and then the other, he said gently, "Cynthia, Beth, I assure you that even though Pastor Bob has given me the title of President that he has also told me not to try to supervise you or interfere with you in any way. I won't have time for more than one task and I wouldn't try to fix something that is working so obviously well in any case. I will be hiring my own security and secretarial staff and just ask that you don't try to ask them about our project. It is a highly sensitive and secure project and no one will be allowed to talk about it. Is this a fair enough arrangement?"

Both women nodded reluctant agreement, both feeling relief and curiosity.

He pointed at the secure door and asked, "Are my offices through that door?"

Both women nodded again but it was Beth who added, "I had them cleaned as agreed but I didn't do anything about furnishings or anything."

"Thanks Beth for the cleaning, I'll take care of all the furnishings."

"It was messier than I imagined," added Cynthia, not to be out done, "Spiders and bugs everywhere. We had it sprayed as well, before they cleaned it. You won't have to worry about them now."

Chester laughed and said, "That's a relief. I hate spiders. Maybe later you can give me the name of the company you used and I'll set up a six month schedule with them."

They just stood there awkwardly for a moment, and then Beth said, "Well we might as well get this tour over with so we can get back to work."

Even though the words seemed harsh Chester could actually feel some warmth leaking through. He knew that these ladies were going to be fun to work with once they loosen up a bit. They walked over to the secure door and Beth punched in the code and the door clicked. She said as she opened the now unlocked door, "You can change the combination any time you like; I'll give you the book this afternoon."

Chester chose this moment to tell them about Jack, "A Jack Miller will be arriving soon. He is in charge of security and he'll decide about what kind and how much security will be necessary at this entrance point."

He could tell that the women were getting more impressed and curious by the minute.

Beth led them through the first door on the left and they entered a very large room. It was twenty foot by twenty foot and Chester's first thought was conference room as Beth said, "This is marked as a conference room Chester, but you can use it for anything you want." She flipped on the four rows of surprisingly very bright LED lights. Chester was glad of that, he liked bright lights. She had continued to walk across the plush beige carpeting to the opposite wall which was covered with an eight foot high and twenty foot long blind. She pushed a button on the wall and the blinds opened exposing a wall of glass. Just outside the window was the parking lot and small front lawn with its few small trees. Chester noticed that the walls were an off-white stone, topped off by an off-white suspended block ceiling with noise absorbing blocks which would stop any echo problems.

Beth was speaking again, "Each office has blinds just like this all motorized.

She led them out into the hallway and turned left. There were several doors on each side and Beth was passing them all as she said, "The other offices, both down here and upstairs are all the same; nine foot by nine foot square rooms, except your office Chester." She stopped at the last door on the right and led them through the open door. Chester caught his breath as he walked into a surprisingly large room. This was larger than the conference room; at least twenty-five by thirty feet. The wall to the left and the wall straight across was all one-way mirror glass from floor to ceiling. The blinds were already open. The view to the left was of the busy main street he had just driven to get here. The view straight ahead, however, was breath taking. In the middle of the glass wall was a sliding patio door. Just outside was a patio complete with a round table, chairs, and umbrella. Several lounge chairs and a brick grill with stainless steel grate were located at the far end of the patio. Beyond the concrete of the patio was green grass that sloped gradually down to a lake. Several ducks and swans swam peacefully on the surface of the water. The sunlight danced across the water and as his eyes followed the flow of the lake they fell on a large flower garden to the right. Octagon shaped concrete blocks made a network of sidewalks leading from the patio to the lake and the flower garden from several directions.

Chester whispered, "Do we own that?"

Beth smiled, "Yes we do. Pretty nice isn't it?"

Chester just nodded.

Beth added, "Just so you know, we use this a couple of times a year for cook-outs and fishing tourneys for charity. The lake is stocked with bass, catfish, and good-sized bluegill. We make a lot of money from those, so I hope. . ."

Chester raised his hand, "Beth we've covered this ground all ready. OK."

Beth blushed and nodded, adding, "Now in here is your private bathroom."

He hadn't noticed but the wall to the right did have a door in the far corner. He walked into a bathroom which was at least a fifteen-foot square complete with urinal, stool, sunken tub (which was also a whirlpool), and a shower stall, not to mention the double sink and large mirror that covered the wall over the sink. The floor and walls were covered with real tile and the faucets, flushing handles, and all other hardware were all made of gold. It was all bright, clean, and the air was even scented by a timed aerosol dispenser.

As they reentered Chester's office he noticed that the floor and walls that were not made of glass were made of what he would guess was real oak planks. He was embarrassed by the extravagance of it all.

Beth must have been able to read his expression because she said, "Impressive isn't it?"

Chester nodded and said, "Embarrassingly so."

Cynthia added, "Well you deserve it or Pastor Bob wouldn't have given it to you."

Chester was humbled again by Pastor Bob's generosity and asked, "Can you ladies tell me anything about Pastor Bob? We just met and I've just never met anyone as generous as he seems to be."

Both Beth and Cynthia laughed and Beth said, "We were both skeptical at first as well. I mean he gave us both new car leases, which renew each year, bought us houses that we never would have dreamed of owning, and the Christmas bonuses, well they're insane. To our shame we both wondered when he would proposition us, you know sexually." Both ladies turned red at the confession, but Cynthia was quick to add, "But in the five years that we have worked for him he has never acted in any way but a gentlemanly fashion. We have come to trust him totally and apparently he trusts us as well. We hardly see or hear from him. We send him reports monthly and he comes to the cookouts twice a year and that's about it. He's a marvelous man that either of us would marry in a minute, but he has never acted interested in anything but a brother/sister type relationship."

Chester didn't hide his relief when he said, "You know I'm really glad to hear that. He truly seems like a man of God and I'd be disappointed to find that he has a dark side."

Beth said, "Well if he does, we've never seen it."

Beth then led them back out to the lobby and asked, "Would you like a cup of coffee, Chester?"

He agreed and they led him down the hall, which was located just past their offices and into the employee lunchroom. This was a pleasant room that also had a corner view of the back lawn and lake and was furnished with vending machines, refrigerator, and counter top complete with microwave and coffee pot.

Beth said, "Just have a seat at the table there and I'll pour. What do you take in yours Chester?"

"Two sugars please."

He sat down, head spinning with the possibilities and blessings that this project could bring. Forgotten was the danger that, at this point, was sure to accompany it.

*   *   *

In Chicago, a cold wind blew as Pastor Bob made his way to the entrance of Illumin, Inc. He went through the door nervously but no one stopped him or interfered with him in any way. He went up to his father's office and walked in. His father, who had of course been warned in advance of his coming, was waiting for him at the door.

"What can I do for you Bobby?"

Bobby looked around, memories flowing back; some good, most bad, "I would like to see Justin if I could Dad. I haven't been allowed to see him in two years now and I think it's time that I talk with him."

Mr. Johnson looked at his son and had no intention of letting him see Justin, until Don Black walked in and said, "I think we should let him talk to Justin, Mr. Johnson."

Johnson looked at him the surprise showing on his face. Pastor Bob didn't miss the expression and wondered why Don Black would be pushing the reunion. He had fully expected to be turned down, especially after the threats and attempts on the lives of Chester and his wife. Could he be wrong about Black? Probably not, but he'd take anything he could get.

"I'd like to see him alone."

Johnson looked at Black for advice and saw Black smiling as he said, "Well, of course you can see him alone."

They led him to a conference room and twenty minutes later a tall young man walked in. Pastor Bob was shocked by the changes he saw in Justin. In just two years, Justin had become a young man that looked older than his fourteen years somehow. What had they put him through in these past two years?

Justin looked at him rather coolly.

Pastor Bob noticed he was wearing a lab coat and had a nametag, which read 'Dr. Johnson'. That surprised him.

Justin followed his line of sight and smiled as he said, "It shouldn't surprise you that I'm a doctor already Pastor Bob. You of all people should know that I was very smart when I arrived here, but unlike you, they didn't hold me back. In fact, they have done everything they can to advance my knowledge and training."

Pastor Bob didn't know what to say to this seemingly mature boy. He sounded and acted like an adult but somewhere in there was a scared fourteen year old, "Justin, I have longed to see you over the past two years but until now they wouldn't let me see you. I . . ."

Justin interrupted, "Mr. Black didn't think it was a good idea while I was training so hard to be interrupted by the past. I agreed that it was best and now after seeing you I know it was the right thing to do."

Pastor Bob was stunned and hurt by this cold reception, "Justin, I want you to have a chance to turn your life and soul over to God and . . ."

Justin laughed, "Don't bring up your arcane religion now, Bob. I have everything I need right here and don't need your primitive and hindering superstitious beliefs. I've learned how to get what I need and want; I don't need your God or your religion."

Pastor Bob looked around and whispered, "Justin, I believe that God has a plan for you to help mankind in some big way through your research . . ."

Justin sneered, "Mankind! What have they ever done for me? I believe it's time for you to leave." Justin began to turn around to leave but stopped and turned back, "Pastor Bob, I believe it would be better if you never came back. I don't ever want to see you again. Understand?"

As he turned to go Pastor Bob desperately called out to his back, "Justin if you ever need me, I'll be there for you." The door slammed with a thud that broke Bob's heart. The reunion was over.

CHAPTER FIFTEEN

CONFLICTING EMOTIONS

Justin left the meeting with Pastor Bob and slammed the door behind him without looking back. He was caught in a vortex of emotions all vying for mastery of his heart. On the one hand he had been happy to see Pastor Bob. He represented a peaceful and hopeful faith that led to a God bigger than life. On the other hand Pastor Bob represented something that would only bring pain, guilt and ruin to Justin in this particular environment that had no room for sentimentality or fantasy. Justin felt the call to belong to something bigger than him but he wanted to believe it was the concrete fact of his genius and what he could do with it. He knew little of this Savior he had once read about and the promises He made. He had no experience to back up this prophet's claims. He trusted Pastor Bob and if Pastor Bob trusted this prophet then so shouldn't he? Justin, however, could not think of giving up the feelings of mastery and power that he was growing into here at the institute, the power to take life or spare it. Nor did he believe that there could be forgiveness for the life and death decisions he had already made, or the immoral sexual acts he had already committed, so he abandoned himself to promiscuity and immorality. The ability to do his research without interference, and the encouragement to act older than he was without moral limits, as opposed to strict moral limits he didn't yet understand, made this an easy decision on the surface.

However, deep in Justin's soul a war was raging.

Justin ran away from goodness and forgiveness and toward the reality with which he had become comfortable. He ran as hard and as fast as he could to get to his room. His only fear at the moment was that the tears would find their way out onto his cheeks before he reached the privacy of his rooms. Almost there! One more turn! Yes! He put his palm on the lock/scan and was in his room in a flash. He continued to run into his bedroom and then jumped onto his bed as if he were diving into a pool. As soon as his face hit the pillow the tears came. They gushed and the pillowcase began to soak up the fluid.

*   *   *

Pastor Bob's abject heart broke painfully as he watched Justin rush from the room. It must have been reflected in his expression for Don Black said, "Don't take it so hard Bobby. You win some and you lose some. Justin has more maturity at his young age than you've ever had. He's a realist and you're not. I know of your plans to build a research center for the boy and your hopes to rescue him from a fate worse than death, but you saw him. Does he look abused? Did he not make it perfectly clear to you that he has chosen, as you should have, to help us better the world in some real and concrete way? It's for the best that you didn't spoil him for us as your mother spoiled you. Now go and don't waste your time or your resources on something that has no chance of ever happening."

Pastor Bob was stunned. His breath came with

difficulty. He knew that he had lost the fight already. Don Black and Bobby's father Theodore Johnson had won Justin over to their base and selfish ways. Without saying a word Pastor Bob stood to his feet and with difficulty made first one foot and then the other move forward stiffly. He left the room without saying a word, but his expression told the whole story. Black and Johnson waited until the door closed behind Bobby then they jumped up and down with glee. They had won, once and for all. Bobby would no longer be a problem for them. He was a defeated man and what was even better; Bobby knew that he was defeated.

Bobby walked down the hall, his shoulders bowed forward slightly, the pain and embarrassment of defeat making his walk a slow and painful one. He knew that he would never come back here again, nor was there anything he could do. If only Justin had held out some hope of conversion but Bobby had looked into his eyes and what he saw was hopelessness and darkness, nothing more.

Pastor Bob wasn't looking where he was going and slammed directly into a man who was walking the other way. The man caught him before he could fall and said, "What's bothering you friend? You seem to be wondering aimlessly, and from your body language and expression you'd think you just lost your best friend."

Pastor Bob looked up into the face of the tall man; he was six foot four if he was an inch. Pastor Bob looked into the man's deep blue eyes and saw; what? Hope? Wisdom?

The man held out his hand and said cheerfully, "Doctor Jeremy Bolder." He looked to be about Bobby's age, a bit taller, with a prematurely balding head of brown hair. Pastor Bob shook the extended hand and whispered sadly, "Pastor Bob Johnson."

The doctor looked surprised and asked, "Not one of "The" Johnson's?"

"Unfortunately, yes."

"Well I've never seen you around here, what do you do for the institute?"

"Nothing, thank God." was Bobby's quick reply.

"As I just said, I couldn't help notice that you seem down, perhaps even depressed pastor; is there anything I can do?"

"No, I'm afraid there is nothing anyone can do."

The doctor persisted, "Don't be so sure until you try pastor, what is it?"

Pastor Bob took a deep breath and sighed, "Well, I've been trying to save a boy named Justin . . ."

"Not Justin Schaefer Johnson?"

"Why yes. Do you know him?"

"Know him! He's my boss in the research lab. What are you trying to save him from?"

"Well I know my father uses a young genius like Justin to his own evil and selfish ends; destroying him and many others in the process and now he has added Justin to his trophy cabinet."

"You're that sure are you?"

"Why yes. I've just finished talking to Justin and he seems quite determined to be led astray."

The doctor smiled, "Pastor Bob, isn't the God you represent much stronger and wiser than your father and even Don Black?"

Pastor Bob looked into the man's eyes again with

growing surprise and even wonder, "Yes you're right of course. I suppose I had forgotten for a moment."

The doctor laughed good-naturedly and whispered in Bobby's ear, "That's not a good thing to forget. Remember that He who is in you is greater than he who is in the world." The doctor laid a hand on Bobby's shoulder and said, "Don't ever give up on God but rather pray with courage and wait for God's time."

Just then Don Black came walking up and the Doctor said, "Well nice to meet you Pastor Bob. Good luck to you."

Black said testily, "Don't you have some research to do doctor?"

"Just getting to it Mr. Black." The Doctor smiled pleasantly as He walked away.

Black watched the doctor leave with a concern and nervousness he didn't understand.

His concern grew when Pastor Bob said, "I'll be seeing you around Don." He walked away with a renewed bounce in his step. Black watched him until he was out of sight and decided that he and Doctor Bolder would have to have a talk, *'and soon'* he thought.

Doctor Jeremy Bolder, who for several hundred years had played many parts in human affairs while in disguise, was still Logos, General of the Nostrum. He got his tray of food and sat down across from Mr. Summons. "Well Kapre, how's it going with you?"

"Not well I'm afraid, sir. Justin is giving himself over to sin and corruption and I'm afraid he may not be able to come back from the abyss in time."

Logos/Doctor Bolder smiled and whispered to Kapre/Summons. "What is impossible for men and angels is not impossible for God. God has a plan, which is why we are here remember, but like Pastor Bob, we will just have to wait and see how this plays out over the next few years. Now eat up and get back to your charge."

CHAPTER SIXTEEN

INITIATION

FOUR YEARS LATER:

"Well son you're eighteen now. How does it feel?" Johnson was a proud father today on this; Justin's initiation day. Today Johnson, who was now seventy-one, would officially turn over his entire empire to his son Justin. After all Johnson couldn't live forever and he had been feeling tired as of late so he made the decision to get out and retire to his villa on a small island in the tropics (the location of which not even Black knew). His new wife Ginger, age thirty-five would go with him making his life complete.

Justin who was struggling with his formal bow tie smiled, "I feel a bit nervous dad. I know I've known the board members for six years now but to suddenly be their boss, well, I have to wonder who may try to kill me out of jealousy."

"Don't give it another thought Justin. No one will want to kill you, son. They have known for years that I was grooming you to take over. They all have what they want; they don't want to be in charge. Most of them have sons that will soon take their places and they too know that you are in charge. Legally, there is not so much as a flaw in the corporation contracts. You will now own the majority of the stock, a controlling majority. Their wealth is directly tied to your success. No, son, they will do all they can to make sure that you are successful.

This exercise today is just to show them you have the determination and the steel to do what it takes to rule. When we get to the boardroom they will inform you of some problems that are currently interfering with business and they will ask for solutions. I have confidence that you will have those solutions and the nerve to order them carried out. This will of course calm their doubts and fears and then we will go to your reception and celebrate."

Justin stood in front of the full-length mirror in his bedroom that he had completely remodeled. Gone was the western town, replaced now with a forest of real trees and artificial background that made it appear that you were standing in the rain forest. His king sized bed was in a clearing while the mirror he was admiring himself in was located between two trees. His dressing table and closet were located behind a wall of hanging moss that hung from a large limb of an even larger tree and would separate at the touch of a button.

Justin looked into the mirror and took stock of the man he had become. He was six foot tall. His figure had filled out in bulk and muscles. His pale skin had been artificially tanned; his brown hair was a bit darker now, long and styled. His sparkling green eyes still attracted women's curiosity and retained their hypnotic effect on the opposite sex. He had long since abandoned his jeans and sweatshirts for dark suits, white shirts, and various colorful ties. Today was to be formals and bow ties that he had grown accustomed to over the last four years.

His faithful man Summons held his tuxedo jacket open for him, and as Justin slipped into it Summons said, "You look sharp as usual sir."

Justin smiled and said, "You're a flatterer as usual Summons.

Summons laid the shiny black formal shoes down in front of Justin, "I just finished polishing these for you sir. You'll be the envy of all that see you."

While Justin put his shoes on, Johnson asked, "Do you have the results of your latest tests with you Justin?"

"Dr. Mayfield is bringing it with him dad. Don't worry it went well. The cloning breakthrough of the last couple of years has aided us in developing the most horrible viral weapon around. The government should be very happy and more importantly, they will pay top dollar for a share of the weapon."

Mr. Johnson asked, "Do I know the test subject this time?"

"You do if you remember Scotty Lopez.", Justin smiled to himself.

"Little Scotty? How did you get him to volunteer for that?"

Justin turned to face his father, "Well we never did hit it off after that little theft incident so I, well, I tricked him into it. He entered the chamber to clean it, we locked him in and well, he volunteered from there."

"Well done son! I know you will do well today." Johnson looked at his watch, *'almost five'*, he thought as he said, "We better get going son. The meeting is at five and the dinner is at eight or whenever the test is finished.

They entered the secret passage that led to the Temple. Justin had not been allowed to return to the mysterious Temple, not since he had administered justice there some years ago, and he was anxious to finally get to see it as a candidate for membership. He had pictures in his mind of human sacrifices, magic, and smoke hovering in the air.

They walked up the stairs that led to the mysterious interior. The steps were lined with board members and their sons and they all nodded out of respect as Johnson and his son passed. Justin, not sure what to do simply nodded back as his father did. It was almost anticlimactic when they finally reached the top and entered the Temple. Despite the old extravagance of the outside of the Temple which had inspired an awe and mystery in young Johnson for so many years now, was in fact something quite different on the inside. The Temple proper contained one large room furnished with a large oval oak table lined with ten over-stuffed leather desk chairs. Ten additional padded folding chairs had been added to the room, five along each wall on either side of the table. These were set up for the sons of the other Board Members who now entered the Temple, for the first time. At the far end of the room there was a door on the right wall which Justin would later find led to his second office, a bathroom facility, and a club room complete with computers, 3-D video screens, pool tables, chess sets and many more distractions for the board member's entertainment.

In the Temple/Board Room proper, the far wall housed a large black screen complete with a 3-D virtual reality camera/projector, which hung from the ceiling in front of the screen, just awaiting use by the Board of Directors of Illumin, Inc.

Each Board member took his seat and Johnson stood at the end of the table but didn't use his chair.

Once the other board members were seated he nodded to Justin and the other sons to take their seats.

When everyone was seated Johnson took his seat and announced, "This meeting of the Board will now come to order. I will remind the sons and heirs of each board member that whatever happens in this Temple is sacred and is never to leave this room. Is that understood?"

He locked eyes with each son until each gave him the demanded, "Yes sir."

"Today as you know I'm stepping down as chairman of Illumin, Inc. and my son Justin will be taking my place. This, as you know, will take place with or without your approval since we hold the majority of the stock, but I'd prefer a unanimous decision of acceptance from the board. You and your sons who will soon follow once each of you decide to retire will have to swear loyalty and obedience to Justin as you have each done to me. Is that understood?" This time the fathers and sons all said, "Yes sir." in unison, "One last thing. I have waved the exclusion of the sons for this meeting so that your boys could witness Justin's initiation, and at Justin's request they will be allowed at all future meetings, understood?" Again they all answered affirmatively.

"Good. With the formalities out of the way, let the examination begin. Justin."

Johnson indicated the podium at which Justin was to stand during the examination.

Justin's nervousness was replaced with the resolve, concentration, and discipline he had finely tuned through his training and research over the past four years and he was all business now. The board members looked more nervous than Justin did which he found very interesting and it added to his confidence.

This was the first time that Justin had been allowed into a meeting of the board and though he knew a few of the board members he had never met their sons, it had been arranged, therefore, that each board member would introduce himself and his son so that Justin would end up knowing each of them. He would study each of their files later at his leisure. Each board member would be allowed to give Justin one situation to solve or question to answer but that was all. The sons would have no participation at this time. It had been decided that the board members would be called on by age; oldest to youngest. That meant the privilege of the first question fell to Wilton DuBois.

Wilton DuBois was a man of seventy years; he stood about five foot seven inches in height and weighed a sparse 120 pounds. He had a full head of gray hair and his brown eyes were still sharp with intelligence and cunning.

"It is a privilege to meet you Master Johnson. I would at this time like to present my son to you; Clinton DuBois. Justin nodded his assent and watched as Clinton; a man of thirty stood up on his left. He was about five foot seven inches tall, thin, and his blonde hair was prematurely receding from his forehead. His brown eyes seemed less intelligent and even less interested in the proceedings than that of his father's.

When his son had sat back down Mr. DuBois continued, "In our time honored way we gather here today to test your skills and resolve by having you solve some problems that will face you as the chairman of this venerable body of leaders. Even though you come highly recommended both by reputation and stock holdings we will feel better if we witness firsthand how you solve problems, how you 'think on your feet', so to speak. So if I may. . ." DuBois gestured toward the remote in front of him and Justin nodded.

With Justin standing on the left side of the screen and DuBois on the right, the 3-D image of a factory wavered into existence between them. It was shift change and people were walking into and out of the factory. DuBois spoke, "Master Johnson. . . .'

Justin interrupted to the surprised gasps of the others and said, "Look Mr. DuBois and you others as well, let's start using first names here shall we? Now continue."

"Very well, Justin, this is an automobile production factory, holding 49 on the list, located in Milwaukee. It has been producing vehicles for over fifty years now, usually at a profit."

Wilton DuBois walked over to Justin and handed him a folder. Justin took it and opened it quickly studying the contents, "As you can see from the quarterly reports, this year it is not going to show a profit. What would be your answer to this problem?"

Wilton walked back to his seat and sat down awaiting an answer from Justin who was currently in deep concentration.

In a relatively short time Justin closed the folder and said, "It appears the factory is too old and outdated to keep up with modern demands. Luckily it is heavily insured. I suggest a believable accident that would destroy enough of the factory to warrant a large upgrade in equipment and automation. Close the factory for a short time laying off the workers that have been there for too long and reopening it only after finding them new jobs. Then hire new employees at the lower beginning salary packages with the insurance of course picking up the bulk of the tab for the new renovations. We would of course force the early retirement of the older highly paid managers and replace them with younger less expensive executives at a total savings or profit of . . ." Justin figured quickly in his head, ". . .of thirty-five million dollars the first year back in service."

Justin could see the pleased surprise on the faces of all the Board members, including that of his father. Wilton DuBois stood, bowed and said, "Very quickly and surprisingly accurately solved sir. Out of all the scenarios suggested that one was never thought of and seems to be the best one offered to date; very well done."

Albert Jackson, an African American, age sixty-eight, now stood and walked to the podium across from Justin. He stood a proud six foot two inches and looked to be in excellent physical condition. His coal black hair and neatly trimmed beard were still natural and his brown eyes sparkled with life and even a bit of humor.

"Justin. I would like to present my son, Roger Jackson." A young man of twenty-two stood about six foot. He was clean-shaven, he also had brown eyes, but his skin was lighter and spoke of a mix of white, which Justin would find later, came from his white mother. The young man smiled at Justin and then sat down.

Albert posed his question, the factory now gone and replaced by the picture of a man, "This man is a

State's Attorney who is threatening a thirty-six million dollar per year drug operation on the East Coast. Our representatives are very nervous about this situation. What do you suggest we do?"

Before Albert could sit down Justin asked, "Has this man been approached and offered a financial settlement, or that failing a substantial threat to back off?"

Albert nodded, "Both have been offered and refused or ignored."

Justin thought for a moment while all in the room looked on with growing respect and interest. Everyone slid a bit closer to the edge of his seat as Justin prepared his next question, "Do we have a suitable candidate to run against him?"

"Tried. Our man lost by six hundred votes."

"Do we have the politicians and a judge in place who could appoint our man if something were to happen to this man? Say a timely accident?"

Albert nodded.

Justin took a deep breath, rubbed his chin and said, "Then I recommend the appropriate untraceable accident and replacement of this man as soon as possible."

Again there was murmuring and rustling throughout the room and finally Albert Johnson said, "That is exactly the solution that was selected. Congratulations Justin. Applause broke out around the table. Even the sons applauded, caught up now in the proceedings. All were impressed with Justin's speed and accuracy in the solving of these problems.

Albert sat down and Senator Rotell Wilkerson

walked to the podium. "Justin I present my boy Ronald Wilkerson. Ronald stood and Justin gave him a cursory nod but kept his eyes on the Senator. He was a short round balding man of sixty-seven years. His brown eyes bored into Justin and he got right to the point, "As you know my Senate committee is responsible for military weapons research. We have made promises that it is now time to fulfill. I would like to hear how your research is coming."

Justin pushed a button on the podium in front of him and the door opened in the back of the room. Dr. Curtis Mayfield wheeled in an airtight glass cage on wheels. To everyone's surprise the cage contained a panic stricken Scotty Lopez. Scotty was dressed in overalls and still had his cleaning supplies with him. His yelling was muffled but his features told their own story of betrayal and fear.

Justin reached into his jacket pocket and pulled out a round silver pellet, "This pellet gentleman represents several years of research. I could spend hours trying to explain what this agent does but I thought a demonstration might save time and energy."

Justin walked over to the cage and said as he put the pellet into the delivery tube, "This gentlemen, is what happens to people who cross me." Justin smiled at Scotty calmly and pushed a button causing the silver pellet to be crushed and the agent delivered to the inside of the glass cage.

Justin explained, "The agent, named RFU63, is odorless, invisible to the naked eye, and as you will soon see, very deadly." Seconds after delivery Scotty's eyes went wide with shock as his skin began to boil free from his bones. Within thirty seconds all that was left in the cage was a small bloody mass of unrecognizable flesh and the unaffected cleaning supplies.

Justin explained, "The agent, even in very small amounts can be delivered by missile, can be air dropped, or can be hand delivered (although not recommended) and will dissolve biological material within a one mile radius per drop of agent, further if the wind is just right. It destroys within thirty seconds and dissipates into a harmless gas within two minutes." Just then there was a puff of white haze in the cage and then that too disappeared, "That white puff you just saw was the agent breaking down into harmless chemicals. It is entirely gone now, making it safe to enter the cage."

Everyone jumped at the hiss made when Doctor Mayfield broke the seal on the cage and opened the door. Justin smiled and said, "At least I hope that's how it works."

He smiled as worry and even panic flashed across the expressions of the Board members and their sons. It took a few tense seconds for them to believe that they were not going to share in Lopez's fate. Doctor Mayfield stood in the cage with no discernible ill effects and everyone relaxed and wiped the sweat beads from their collective foreheads as Justin continued, "This agent is very inexpensive to make, about one hundred dollars per drop, if you discount the thirty six million it cost in research. We will sell it to our government at ten thousand dollars per drop, quickly making up the research cost and even more quickly turning a profit. The government will pay even more for the antidote that will cost less to make, bringing in more profit. The antidote will be needed for our soldiers who may have to hand deliver this to the enemy."

A pale Senator Wilkerson sat down grimly satisfied that his committee would be able to sell this to the armed services.

Roger Dowling Jr. was next on the list and he stood as the doctor wheeled the cage out of the room and he paused, staring at the cage as it disappeared behind the closing door. He was sixty-six, thin and stood about six feet tall. Justin would learn later, to his surprise that Dowling Jr. was dying of liver cancer. Surprising since his hazel eyes spoke of confidence and strength. Dowling Jr. ran his right hand through his thinning white hair and said, "I would like to present my son Roger III. . . ."

Just then a disturbance was heard outside the door, then it was suddenly flung open, "I don't care what the rules say I have a right to be here!" A thud was heard and the hurried entrance of a five foot seven inch, muscular, and very determined red head followed the female voice. Her green eyes were ablaze with indignation as she yelled, "I'm the first born of the family not Roger the third."

Her father stood at the podium across from Justin and said, "Well maybe I should first present my daughter Amanda Dowling."

There was chaos throughout the room as board members and their sons alike objected to the presence of a woman at these sacred proceedings. Justin smiled, happy with the distraction. Two guards held the girl and tried to drag her out but she broke free by kicking the guard on her right he crumpled to the floor, unable to move. She then hit the second guard with the skill that years of martial arts training can give you, and now both guards found themselves on the floor writhing in pain.

Roger Dowling Jr. who had been calling for order finally got most of the room's attention and hurriedly stated, "This is your next test Justin. This has been an argument, no a thorn, in the side of our family for years. My daughter insists that she as first-born should take over my seat on the board. I present the problem to you and ask for a ruling on this issue."

It was obvious to Justin that Roger was using him to deflect the anger of his daughter from himself onto Justin. The question intrigued Justin who with his type of memory could recall the entire charter of this organization in seconds. This was obviously intended to be a man's group, but Justin said, "Gentlemen if I could direct your attention to article sixteen, section five, subparagraph forty seven B, you will find that the replacement of a board member will be by his first born only. Now it's obvious that they meant first-born son, but they did not in fact say that and I say that in all fairness we should stick by the letter of our own laws. This would of course mean that Amanda here is the rightful heir of the Dowling seat and shares. This is my determination." He pulled a second silver pellet out of his jacket pocket and flipped it into the air and caught it, "Any discussion?"

He looked at each terrified board member and finally said, "There being no further discussion needed, I welcome you to the board as a legal heir, Amanda."

Amanda who had calmed down while watching these proceedings looked at Justin with respect and perhaps a bit of attraction to his calm assurance.

Justin ordered, "Remove Roger Dowling III". The guards, who had by now painfully regained their feet, grabbed and unceremoniously dragged Amanda's very angry brother from the room.

When he was gone and Amanda had taken his place the next man on the list stood up and said, his face pale and his voice cracking, "I'm Gerald Jinkens and I concede that Justin is well qualified to take over as chairman and I see no further need of questioning."

He looked at each board member and received a nod from the remaining members who still had a right to ask their questions. Then he said, "With all agreeing I hereby welcome you Justin Johnson as the new Chairman of the Board of Illumin, Inc.

Applause exploded around the room and Justin bathed in the warmth of his success. It was close to eight by now and the entire group left for the formal dinner awaiting them. Many were in need of the drinks they were sure to find.

CHAPTER SEVENTEEN

HOPE

Amanda Dowling had faced and beaten fellow black belts in martial arts with less trepidation than she felt at this moment. She had won trophies in her first love; weight lifting, in which she rivaled even her brother. Yet, she had not felt the "butterfly" flutters that disturbed her stomach now as she sat in the waiting area to Justin Schaefer Johnson's office. She had been immediately attracted to him when she had barged into the meeting room last night. Every man there had looked at her with those shocked and contemptible expressions on their collective faces; all that is except Justin. With a sparkle in those deep green eyes, he had smiled approvingly. She had become lost momentarily in those eyes before she had snapped back into the reason for her sudden appearance.

Now, however, doubt crept its way into her mind and heart as she waited to see this young man who now controlled over fifty percent of the corporate stocks. His father would, of course, retain ownership of those stocks until his death but Justin Schaefer was now the power that would drive the corporation forward. He could help her or hold her back and her hopes were that he would help. Judging from his actions and attitude of last night, he seemed intrigued with the idea of having a woman on the board, or perhaps he was just hoping to make points with her for sex. Yeah, that was probably it. From her young experience all men were alike when it came to that

205

area. It would seem that they all have only one thing on their minds; conquer every woman you come in contact with, and then move on to the next. Her sexual drives were normal but power drove Amanda even more passionately and lasted longer than the momentary satisfaction that sex provided.

Her reflections were interrupted suddenly when the secretary finally said, "You may go in now Miss Dowling." The secretary watched as Amanda stood up and walked straight backed in perfect poise into Justin's office. Was that envy or jealousy she saw sneaking across the secretary's cold expression? Amanda didn't know nor did she care as long as she was in the driver's seat.

If she had been expecting a prim and proper young man dressed in perhaps a blue suit, white shirt, tie and matching jacket she was surprised to find Justin sitting back in his chair, feet on the desk, his young powerful body covered with jeans and a Notre Dame sweatshirt. His feet had no socks but where stuffed into large tennis shoes, the souls of which looked well used. He smiled and waved her into a chair in front of his desk and indicated with a single finger that he would be off the phone soon.

She sat there quietly listening as he finished talking on the phone, "I don't care Mr. President! No! That's your job, sir!" Amanda watched as he gave her a wink as if he were listening to a child with no real important information to give. She was amazed when she realized that he was speaking to the President of the United States with such ease, familiarity, and even contempt. It was at that moment that it sunk in; Justin

Schaefer Johnson was the most powerful man in the world and he was only eighteen and not elected by the people.

"Look Bob! You and I both know the importance of getting that bill passed. Now, I don't care how you do it but I better not have to have this conversation with you again. That's all I wanted to hear Bob. Tell Sally hello for me and I'll see you next month at the State of the Union Ball."

Justin hung up, smiled at Amanda, and dismissed the fact that he had just called the President of the United States, Bob."

"What can I do for you Amanda?"

The question threw her off for a moment, "I don't know Justin; it was *you* who asked *me* to come in remember?"

Justin laughed as he bounced to his feet and walked toward the bar, "Oh, that's right! Sorry! Want a soda, beer, whatever?"

"A diet cola would be good Justin. Is it all right if I call you Justin?"

"By all means Amanda; I want us to become friends. I have some plans in mind for you."

'I bet you do you male . . .'

The thought must have completed itself on her face because Justin stopped, the smile dropping from his face as he said, "I'm sorry, Amanda, I didn't mean anything . . .well, sexual. I don't know about you but I find power much more stimulating. I thought I might have read you for the same type of temperament. Was I wrong?"

She smiled, relieved to hear Justin say that, "No,

you hit it just right. I'm also into power. I like to chase my own man, in my own time, and in my own way, but I never let this entertainment interfere with powerful goals."

Justin handed her the diet cola as he asked, "Does your brother, Roger, have a black eye today?"

"Why yes he does, and he knows now not to question me further on this issue. He'll be no further problem. How about the rest of the board? Foresee any problems?"

Justin laughed as he returned to his own chair, "None that they'd dare say to my face."

There was an awkward silence. Amanda raised an eyebrow as if to say, 'you asked me here remember'.

Justin leaned forward, took a sip of his beer, then asked seriously, "Amanda, this won't be a very sensitive question but it is important. How soon can you get your father to step down?"

She knew what he was getting at. Her father was dying of cancer and wasn't very strong anymore but she hadn't wanted to push the issue. Justin just sipped his beer and watched her closely, looking as though he were ready to sit there till doomsday if necessary. She finally let out a breath that she had been unconsciously holding and answered in a whisper, "I hadn't really considered pushing him to step down, Justin. Why?"

"Remember this has nothing to do with you being male or female but has everything to do with your personality."

She was beginning to regret that she had put up such a strong front against any romantic involvement, but she nodded and waited for Justin's explanation.

"I have some plans coming up very soon and I need a second in command that I can trust. I think that person is you. Interested?"

"Who wouldn't be Justin, but I thought Don Black held that position."

"Don't you worry about Don Black, Amanda, worry about taking your father's place. How soon?"

"Well he has been feeling worse lately, I'll see if I can influence him to step down immediately. Can I have a day or two to feel him out on the subject and then get back to you?"

"That would be great Amanda. Hey did you catch that new episode of The Quest? I liked it when. . ."

Justin had the ability to give his visitors whiplash due to the speed with which he changed subjects. They had talked about many things for the next five minutes then suddenly she found herself standing outside his office, dismissed, and most likely forgotten. Amanda had never met anyone like Justin before and she knew now beyond a shadow of a doubt that she had grossly underestimated the man. He was many times more charming, powerful, and intelligent than she had even thought, and she thought she had been very generous. Hope began to well up in her heart that she may have finally found a man that she could call an equal, a partner, maybe even husband. Yes, with this meeting came a new hope, a new plan, and a totally new direction to her life. Amanda Dowling felt the joy of a new challenge and she knew that she was up to it.

THE ANTIDOTE

*   *   *

As Pastor Bob stepped out of the gate at the Las Vegas airport he spotted Chester almost immediately. He overheard Chester explain to his small son that he couldn't fly with him this time because they were going to a restricted project. He gave up and asked Debbie, "Honey, please rescue me here!"

Debbie ignored him and ran up to Pastor Bob and hugged him. It had been over two years since his last visit and she was still very grateful to him for all he had done for them. Her four children also ran up to Pastor Bob and each hugged him in turn and then the two men hugged.

Chester smiled, "It's been too long Bobby."

Pastor Bob nodded agreement and said, "That it has Chester. That it has. I didn't expect to be greeted by the entire Melvin clan."

"Well Debbie and the kids are going to go out to eat and see a movie but they wanted to see you first. We'll be at the site for a few days, so it's a hello and farewell greeting combined."

Bobby looked down at their youngest and said, "Little Chester Jr. is sure growing like a weed, and the rest of you, well you're getting just too pretty for daddy's comfort I'm sure."

Chester smiled and joked, "Amy, our oldest, has a boyfriend already."

Amy blushed and yelled, "Daddy, he's not my boyfriend!"

After Bobby had greeted each of the children and had walked with them to the heliport, Chester and Bobby said their good-byes to the rest of the family and made their way out to the waiting chopper. The waiting area had been deceptively quiet as they opened the outside door and stepped into the churning wind and the whooshing sound made by the powerful blades of the helicopter as it warmed up in preparation for their departure. Some airport official took their bags and stowed them in an outside compartment as they climbed into the chopper. They had barely buckled in when the chopper lifted off and turned sharply north and climbed swiftly into the air while gaining forward speed at the same time. The nose dipped slightly forward and the two men experienced the child-like excitement that always accompanies flight. The noise of the engine and passing wind was muffled as they put on their headphones. They could now talk through a microphone directly to each other.

The pilot could hear them talk but he was an employee of Antidote, Inc. and had the appropriate security clearance, so it was with confidence that Bobby asked, "Chester how is the site coming?"

Chester had waited for a long time to be able to say, "We are for all intents and purposes finished, Bobby."

Bobby smiled for he knew that he was about to see his dream realized, or at least part of it. They still had to get Justin out to the site and that didn't seem to have much of a chance at this point.

Chester seemed to read Bobby's mind, "Jack will give you an update on Justin's progress when we get to the site."

Both because of the difficulty in speaking over the

noise and the beauty of the desert rushing past, just a hundred feet beneath them, both men watched silently, as off to their left, the sun began to drop below the horizon. Neither of them ever tired of the majesty of God's creation and enjoyed it every chance they got.

In the four years since they began this project, Bobby had not once been out to visit the site. He had come to the office in town and even went to Chester's house for a visit once, but usually left the same day to get back to Chicago. This time he had been warned to clear a few days off his schedule and be ready to be impressed.

"The Antidote", as Bobby had dubbed the site from the beginning, giving no other reason than it had come to him while he had been praying one night, was one hundred-fifty miles from anywhere. Nothing but flat, barren, desert surrounded the site. Chester pointed at a gray outline of a block building just below them, its beacon light was blinking on and off in lonely vigil, "That's the fifty mile perimeter defense system. Your perimeter is fifty miles on each side giving you two hundred-fifty square miles of desert to hide in. There is one system on each of the four sides of the site property and it lets us know if anything is flying, walking or crawling toward our post. This is made possible because the perimeter is dotted with ground sensors that warn us the minute anything enters our defense perimeter. We should be approaching . . . Yes, there it is."

Chester pointed just as Bobby saw a large square of lights. Chester explained, "That is the five mile square outer perimeter electronic fence that surrounds the site. The lights show that it is live and they also illuminate the warning signs leaving no doubt that this is private property and to stay clear. The smaller square of bright lights is the one-mile square inner perimeter defense; an electronic fence which surrounds the compound itself. The large single story building that you see in the spotlights there is a legitimate pharmaceutical research facility in its own right, called, as per your instructions, "The Antidote Research Facility. The "real" Antidote Facility is located below that. The other buildings there," he pointed off to one side, "Those are the temporary living quarters for scientists and support staff who will be moving in soon. Jack has an army of security personnel already in place, some of which have been working from the start of the project."

Chester stopped talking and looked at Bobby and noticed the conflicting emotions dancing across his face. Tears ran down his cheeks co-mingling with the smile on his lips as Bobby whispered, "Hopes Chester. I still have high hopes."

CHAPTER EIGHTEEN

CHECK

Don Black had been listening to Justin on secret wiretaps ever since he had arrived at the corporation about six years ago. He had studied his every conversation, business meeting, and written word. He had played chess with Justin many times and from that had developed a profile on just how Justin thinks and maneuvers. It was quite a surprise for him when he overheard Justin inform Amanda that he would gladly give Don's position to her. At first he thought Justin was just playing her for a sucker, but as he thought about it he began to feel the first signs of anger. *Maybe this upstart was going to make a move on me,* Don thought; *it wouldn't be the first time that someone has come after me, but all who tried have ended up dead.*

Don figured that Justin had to know by now that not so secret bugs were planted everywhere in the office, his living quarters, the lab, everywhere. If he knew, however, why would he warn Don ahead of time that he was planning on taking him out? If he didn't know then Don had given him way too much credit. Either way Don decided that Justin was just too much of a threat to keep around. All the board members had learned the hard way that Don was the real power behind the corporation and what he said would go. In short, they feared him. Don had sensed lately that they were beginning to fear Justin more and his plan had been forming for weeks now. It would appear that he couldn't afford to wait any

215

longer.

He had called for two of his "soldiers" who were just now walking through his door. He focused immediately on the three machine-guns that they carried. He hadn't told them to bring him one but they had and he was beginning to feel in charge again. He didn't say a word but grabbed his machine-gun and lead them into the hall walking to the door just down from his own. The secretary gasped when she saw the guns but just sat still, hoping that by this lack of activity she might remain alive herself. It worked, the three men pushed past her desk and Don Black keyed in the over-ride code to Justin's office. The door clicked and Don pushed it open and walked swiftly into the room, gun raised, and a big smile on his happy face.

Justin looked up from his desk and thought Don looked very strange. The smile, that's it. Justin had not seen Don smile much in the years that he had known him.

Don felt nervousness for the first time since his plan's inception. Justin had three machine-guns pointed at him and yet he just sat there smiling like he had the upper hand. It was then that Don noticed the plastic. The entire floor was covered with plastic drop cloths. Don looked back and noticed that the door had closed on its own and he knew without a doubt that it would be locked.

Don turned back to Justin, "I see that you anticipated this move Justin."

Justin smiled, "Anticipated it? I engineered it. I knew you would be listening to me, I knew you would feel threatened, and I knew you would react quickly and efficiently." Justin smiled proudly.

Don smiled back, "You have learned well, Justin. I don't know what your little plan is but whatever it is you can't get out of this alive. This will end in a stalemate at least."

As he said stalemate, Don pulled the trigger on his machine-gun and his two soldiers did the same. Don even yelled at the top of his lungs in anticipation for the shots that should be ripping through his own body about now, but nothing happened. To his dismay, when he and the others ran out of bullets and the dull clicks of firing pins falling on empty chambers subsided, Justin was still sitting at his desk fully healthy and still smiling.

"Don, do you know how much it will cost me to repair all that damage? Oh well, I can afford it can't I. You have made sure of that and for that I thank you. Right about now you're asking yourself, how is this possible? Am I right?"

Don just nodded while his mouth still hung open and drool dripped onto the plastic. "Well Don, I knew that you would use your usual straight forward and violent approach of gunning me down, so I rigged a holo-projector to project my image from the next room. I took the extra precaution of sealing this room off from the office that you're in because well I don't want the gas to get to me. If you'll notice sitting in front of me on the desk is a little clear plastic box that is now riddled with holes. I'm surprised that you didn't destroy it with all those bullets but if you had we wouldn't be able to have this conversation at all. In the box you will notice the small silver ball resting in its holder just waiting for the electronically operated metal plate above it to be activated by me which will in turn smash the ball. You were there Don. You know what the gas contained in that ball did to Scotty Lopez, don't you. If you look up Don you will see three more of those boxes attached to the ceiling as well, one can't take any chances with a man like you, Don. You taught me that. Well, it looks like checkmate Don." Justin pushed the button and all four silver balls were smashed at once. The two soldiers ran for the door but as Don had suspected it was locked.

Don looked at the projection of Justin knowing he had but seconds left to live and said, "No, Justin not checkmate but merely check. Checkmate is when your opponent has no moves left but even in my death I can still out maneuver you. I must say though that you have become a worthy opponent,"

Years of discipline had allowed Don to stay calm as his skin melted from his body but he had been hoping for a little more panic on the face of Justin when he informed him that there were more things that he could do. Doubt suddenly hit his heart at about the same moment that blackness hit his mind. Within seconds there was nothing left of the three men but a bubbling puddle of goop.

Justin told the men waiting with him to wait an hour and then go in and clean up the mess. They just nodded and left; fear forever etched in their hearts and minds.

Amanda turned to Justin and watched as he smiled back at her. Justin whispered, "If you want out now is the time to tell me, not later when I need you to be strong."

Her head was spinning, her stomach threatened to

empty lunch onto Justin's desk, but to her credit she just shook her head and smiled back at Justin.

Justin seemed to make a decision and whispered, "All right then. You wanted power, now you have it. You can move into Don's office immediately. Go through his things and throw out whatever you don't want or keep it all, I don't care. You will start learning the ropes and taking over his duties as soon as possible. I will have some additional things for you later."

Justin stood up and was about to leave but stopped and turned around, "Tell me, Amanda, did your father really just die, very conveniently I might add, the same day that we talked, or did he have some help from you? Don't lie to me", he warned.

Amanda thought about it for only a second and answered, "He wouldn't step down Justin, I had to help him decide that his time had come and gone."

Justin smiled, nodded, and then left the room.

CHAPTER NINETEEN

KATHY SAUNDERS

Kathy Saunders had been a volunteer for Pastor Bob since she was eleven, following her miraculous delivery from cancer. At seventeen, she had just finished high school and was helping Pastor Bob unpack the latest shipment of food for the food pantry and soup kitchen. They were accustomed to working together and she felt totally at ease with Pastor Bob. He was always a gentleman and almost like a second father to her. He often acted like a worried father and it made her smile when he shifted into that mode.

Pastor Bob stopped suddenly, holding a box of cereal that he was about to put with the afternoon giveaway items and asked, "Now that you're out of high school, Kathy, what are your plans? "

Kathy continued putting cans of soup, beans, and tuna into her bag as she answered, "My parents and I are looking into scholarships that will allow me to train for a career in medical research. I want to help others to get over diseases not only through prayer but also through research into diseases. Does that sound unrealistic to you, Pastor Bob?"

"Absolutely not Kathy! As a matter of fact, I'm glad you have chosen that route. I would like to offer you an opportunity to work in a new research project that I'm starting just outside Las Vegas. I have just finished building a state of the art research facility and am starting to man it with personnel who will be dedicated to the cure of many diseases that presently plaque the human race. I would like to have you on board someday. Interested?"

He saw the shock on her face, then the joy, then the expression of disbelief, "Pastor Bob, we, my parents and I, have been praying that the Lord would make the arrangements and show us a sign as to which way I should go. This is nothing short of an answer to our prayers."

Pastor Bob felt good as usual that the Lord had blessed him with the finances to help people and he said; "Now, here is how it will work Kathy. I'll hire you right now and pay you a monthly salary of say two thousand dollars. You'll have full medical coverage; and, of course, as an employee you'll have all of your schooling paid for, including books, room and board and a company car. For this, you will have to sign a contract promising to commit to two years at our facility in Vegas. At the end of the two years, you will have the opportunity to stay or go to a company of your choice. If you stay, you will, of course, be eligible for a raise and an upgraded employment package."

As he had described the job and its benefits, Kathy had turned pale and had sat down in the folding chair to her right. Her breathing came with difficulty as she began to hyperventilate. Pastor Bob handed her a small paper sack and said, "Breath into this."

After a few minutes she emerged from the bag, her color returning to her face and tears streaming down her cheeks, "Pastor Bob, how can I thank you? I'll talk it over with mom and dad but I know what they will say. They'll say it's too generous and it is."

Pastor Bob smiled and whispered as he kissed her

forehead, "It's my standard package for students, Kathy. If they have any questions they can call me and I'll prove it to them. I recognize and reward talent, and you have more than talent, Kathy, you also have real faith. That's very rare today and I need you. Think it over, talk it over, but I hope you will say yes. Now let's finish our work and then you can go home and talk with your parents."

Pastor Bob knew what the eventual answer would be and he smiled as they finished the task at hand.

CHAPTER TWENTY

DON BLACK'S FINAL MOVE

After eight years of patrol, twelve years as a detective, one very rocky marriage, the ups and downs of rearing a teenage daughter, and finally the all too familiar divorce, Detective Rachel Longstrum never tired of the adrenaline rush she got from the high-speed chase. Her car fishtailed around the corner and she was still on the perp's tail. Many of her career advancements had been due to the luck of timing and the skill of carry-through, just like this chase. How many officers can be going by the exact bank at the exact time that the bank robbers try to flee from their crime? One minute Rachel and her partner Detective Bob Smith had been calling in lunch break, the next they were being shot at and were the only unit in the city within range to give chase.

"Kick the windshield out Bob, I can't see!", Rachel laughed as Bob who had been on the force a bit too long and who had eaten a few too many burgers tried to get his foot above the dash to kick the window out. He finally gave up, taking the shotgun out of its lock-holder between the seats and used it to bash the windshield out onto the hood. He then fired off some rounds at the car just ahead of them. The back window of the suspect's car disintegrated and the passenger fell forward, red liquid spraying the side of the driver's mask; one down one to go.

"Bob! I'll try to pass and pull up next to him and you take him out, OK?"

They had been partners for four years now so no answer was really expected, Rachel gunned the car and weaved around the sedan in front and prayed that the oncoming car would veer off which it did just as the explosions in her ear from Bob's .38 caliber snub nose told her that three shots had been fired into the robber's vehicle. The car they were chasing veered to the right suddenly and smashed through a fortunately deserted storefront window.

Rachel slammed on the brakes, turned the wheel so their car swung around and was going back toward the store. As she hopped the curb she slammed on the brakes and jumped out of the car, her own 9 MM drawn and pointed at the driver's side of the getaway vehicle.

She yelled, "Police, come out with your hands up." There was no response and her heart was racing as she quickly and carefully slid herself toward the car, her arms outstretched, a double-handed tense grip on her weapon. As she peered into the car she saw the driver was slumped over to his right side. Bob was bringing up the other side.

Rachel stood her ground watching both driver and passenger who had slumped to the floor on Bob's side; due to the impact with the store-front. She was watching for movement as Bob opened the passenger door. Suddenly the passenger raised a weapon toward Bob and Rachel opened fire putting two slugs into the back of the robber's head. Bob jumped back as if he were the one shot and exclaimed, "Thanks Rach, that was a close one!"

With her weapon still extended in her right hand

Rachel reached through the open window with her left hand and felt for a pulse on the driver's left carotid artery.

Feeling none she holstered her weapon and walked back to their car and called in, "Operations this is Detective Longstrum, chase terminated, black and whites on the scene. Need Supervisor and coroner on the scene, two perps down." She threw the Mike onto the seat and walked to the front of her car and sat on the hood. That's when the adrenaline hit her and her hands began to shake. She always hated this part of the adrenaline rush. When the action was over there was nothing to do with all the extra adrenaline already coursing through your blood stream so you just sat there and shook like you had palsy or something. Officers from the black and white ran up and secured the scene.

Rachel had her head resting in her hands in an attempt to stop them from shaking so much, tears of anger and frustration threatened to drip from her eyes so she angrily wiped them away with the heel of her palms and barked at the officers, "Make sure those weapons are right where the perps left them when IA gets here."

"Yes Ma'am!" The officers gave her and Bob some distance to recover.

'Internal Affairs, now there's a group for you. They police the police!', the thought came with such force and venom that Rachel just shook her head at what was to come; the eternally long hearings, the third degree, IA trying to prove that you must surely have done something wrong.

'No I won't think of that now!' Rachel thought as she stood up and paced back and forth in front of the car.

She suddenly stopped, "Bob, let's go across the street and get a cup of coffee while we wait."

Bob nodded, understanding the real message, as Rachel nodded toward a bar across the street. From the moment they shot the suspects, they were on administrative leave until the investigation could be conducted. They each took out their weapons and handed them to the officers who were securing the scene.

"We'll be over there when supervision gets here." Rachel said.

The officer's nodded, totally understanding the need, as Bob and Rachel headed for an eighty proof cup of coffee. They walked through the crowd, which had steadily grown since the incident. The crowd parted for Rachel and Bob; as the Red Sea had parted for Moses and the Israelites. They took the first two stools they came to and Bob ordered, "Whiskey with beer chaser for both of us. The bartender set two shot glasses on the bar and slopped them full. As they downed them, he set two full mugs of beer down in front of them and as they gulped those down he poured them two mugs of one part coffee and nine parts whiskey. The bartender had served many officers in this type of situation, and was an expert in what he called his "special coffee".

Rachel allowed the whiskey to roll its burning way down her throat and took satisfaction in the instant calming effect it had on her nerves. She grabbed the beer and downed the cool liquid in three gulps and with a hoarse voice whispered, "Wonderful!"

Both she and Bob picked up their mugs and would nurse their "coffee" slowly as they waited for the inevitable storm to come. Hollywood made shootings look so easy on the movie screen. Moviegoers were never shown the mountain of paperwork, the interrogations, the three-day suspension with pay while you see the department's shrink. All this had to happen before you were given your weapon back and told to get back to work; just to repeat the entire process again far too soon; when the next perp decides to take a shot at you.

Bob finally looked up from his drink and said, "I'm getting too old for this Rach."

Rachel smiled and patted his hand, "I know Bob. You've only got another year and you can retire. Just hang in there."

"Too many more days like this one and I'll quit early and take the cut in benefits."

Rachel laughed, "What; and miss out on all this fun?"

Bob wiped his forehead and smiled, "When I was in my twenties, it was fun. Now at fifty-four, it's insane. Next year I'll have my thirty in and I'm out-a-here." this last he said as he gestured with his thumb like an umpire at a Sunday afternoon baseball game.

Rachel smiled at Bob and stood up. She kissed the top of his sweaty bald head causing him to flush bright red as she said, "You'll get to open your cop bar just in time to have all sorts of war stories to tell. Now come on; let's get out there and give our preliminary report and get our tired butts home, shall we?"

*   *   *

The chase had begun at three thirty that afternoon and it was now after one in the morning. Rachel lived in a nice apartment, not fancy but a comfortable two bedroom. The second bedroom was for her eighteen year old daughter, Becky, who just started college at Loyola University here in Chicago; studying to be of all things, a lawyer. It was her dream to be a prosecuting attorney someday.

'At least she won't be defending those perps', thought Rachel as she shed her empty shoulder holster and unclipped her badge from her belt and threw it on the entrance table. She put her foot up on the chair and ripped the Velcro harness open from around her ankle where she kept her off duty/back-up .38 caliber snub nose and locked it in the drawer of the lamp stand.

She looked at herself in the mirror that hung waiting on the entranceway wall and whispered, "Whoa Rachel, you look like you've been through the mill." Her hair, though short, was nonetheless windblown, her lipstick was smeared, and her eyes, with all of her effort were still puffy and red from the unwanted yet persistent tears. Her white blouse was stained under the armpits and her black slacks were still dirty from sitting on the car's hood.

Rachel made her way into the living room to the answering machine which sat on an end table next to the couch. The light was flashing, warning her of messages waiting patiently for her return. She almost passed it by but long standing habit forced her to stop and push the mailbox one button.

A deep male voice said, "You have three new messages and fourteen old messages", beep, "High mom! Just called to let you know that I'll be staying at Kenny's tonight; we can argue about it later." beep, "Rachel it's your mother; just checking to see if you're still alive. I haven't heard from you this week. Well bye, call soon." beep, "Detective Longstrum, this is Icicle. I have something for you, the drops been made. Pick up at your convenience." beep, "End of messages."

Despite her fatigue, the sound of Icicle's voice brought the thrill of mystery to Rachel's heart. Icicle had left many items of interest over the last five years, which had led to some very important arrests. Rachel had no idea how he had come to pick her for these anonymous gifts but they always proved true and important so it was no surprise to her that she found herself backtracking, putting everything back on and heading out the door. She'd never sleep till she found out just what it was that Icicle had left this time.

*   *   *

Don Black had not trusted many people and he had his own network of agents who only knew what they had to know to get their assignments done. He had also gotten smug in his later days, thinking that everyone would do exactly as they were told without question or variance. Therefore he had no doubt that the day he was double-crossed and failed to check in with Icicle that the package would be delivered to Detective Longstrum just as he had ordered. He had underestimated the resentment that had built up with the only person he had really trusted; one meaningless female slave whom he had loved too much and had sent on too many little errands. Recently he had sent her on an errand to deliver a package to Icicle. The enclosed instructions had stated that in case of Black's demise and upon his failure to check-in with Icicle daily that he was to deliver that package to the detective. What he hadn't counted on; was the female messenger opening the package and looking at the contents before delivering it to Icicle. He also had never dreamed that she would spy on the drop and watch Icicle pick up the package; thus discovering his identity. This lowly female operative was the only human alive today who knew both; who Icicle really was and what damning evidence was in his possession. Now the only question left was what she would do with this information. It was no easy decision for her but she finally came to what she considered the most prudent course of action.

The female operative was Tracy Warner; the woman whom Don Black, with the help of some Hollywood special effects, had pretended to kill in the Temple with two blank shots to the head. The Temple was just dark enough that the switch from the live Tracy to the holographic Tracy went undetected by everyone except Tracy and Black. So, when Tracy and Jerard knelt in front of Black and Justin only one was a live person, for a short time. Black had assigned Tracy the task of making Justin fall in love with her only to crush his young spirit by having Justin catch her making love to Jerard Stromeyer. The plan had worked perfectly; Justin became in one act both cynical and a murderer (since only the first two bullets in Black's gun were blanks making it possible for Justin to kill Jerard) thus making it easier for Black to control him from that day forward.

Tracy, however, had resented what she had been

forced to do to Justin and had therefore informed Justin of the entire plot and Don Black's part in it. She had the distinction of being the only woman to have fooled Don Black and live to enjoy it.

She now picked up the phone to call her employer, Justin Schaefer Johnson. Justin had, in his own way, forgiven her, and trusted her as much as he could trust anyone, but like everyone else in his life; he used her over the years to accomplish his own goals; she owed it to him after all, didn't she? He had thus out maneuvered Don Black having learned his lessons in manipulation quit well for one so young.

*   *   *

Rachel had picked up about five mysterious packages from Icicle over the last five years and the information they contained had always led to the arrest and conviction of very important people. What she hadn't realized was that the information was only part of the reason for her success. The most important part was the strings that got pulled by Icicle, behind the scenes. It was Icicle who had kept the many powerful people off of her back in the past allowing her to chase after and "bag" the important people that Don Black had incidentally wanted out of the way. She was a good cop but she never really saw the bigger picture and why should she. She saw a good bust and took it and her career soared. She never would have believed the powerful moves of deception that went on behind the scenes nor would she have liked knowing that she was an unwitting pawn in a much larger game being played by Don Black.

Rachel walked through the bus station and after making sure that she didn't have a tail, she walked to the locker and put her key into the lock. She opened the locker and pulled out the black cloth satchel it housed. She closed the locker and walked away without looking back or checking the satchel's contents.

*   *   *

Roger Dowling III had resented Justin for forcing his father's hand to accept his daughter Amanda as his heir. He further resented the pressure Amanda had received in being forced to kill her father when he wouldn't retire. He had agreed to become Icicle about five years ago when he realized that Justin was winning his sister over and would in reality take over eventually. Don Black had put plans into effect that he had promised would place Roger in a position to take over as director of Illumin, Inc.; when and if anything were to happen to Black. Roger was willing to stay in his place and Don had convinced him that his plan would work and that they would give young Justin enough rope to hang himself and then he would suddenly be out of the picture and the Dowlings (with Roger not Amanda as director) would finally have the position that should have been his in the first place. Now Don Black was dead and the emergency plan had to be activated. It was with great relief and satisfaction that Roger had called and left his message once again as Icicle.

He lay back in his bed smug in the knowledge that he was about to exact his revenge on the young upstart, Justin Schaefer Johnson. When he turned out the light he didn't even notice the small cracking sound of the small silver ball opening to release the RFU 63 under his bed. Within seconds Icicle was dead and Don Black's final move was terribly crippled. Now only Detective Rachel Longstrum stood in the way of Justin's complete take-over; but, as with all excellent chess players, Justin still had some options open to him.

CHAPTER TWENTY-ONE

CHECKMATE

This was big! No this was huge! Stretched out before Rachel on her living room floor were several items. Two or three DVD discs, reports on something called RFU 63, and enough documentation to convict everyone from this Justin Johnson the creator of RFU 63 all the way up to the President of the United States. The discs were full of human experimentation of RFU 63 and many other biological weapons sanctioned by the United States Government and tested on its own citizens. The terrorist attack on a New York subway with some unknown biological weapon was not terrorists but a carefully planned experiment by our own government. Rachel was still horrified by what she had seen on these DVDs. The subway incident had been recorded and carefully documented as an experiment. Individual people were trapped in glass booths and exposed to these agents and died horrible deaths.

Rachel paced back and forth in her living room talking to herself, "Who do you go to when your own government is the criminal? What can I do with this?" She felt sick to her stomach. She had always been proud of America and her profession, but now . . . ?

"How can I ever look at our government with respect again? Someone has to pay for this, this, outrage!"

Rachel walked over to the table by her front door and began to strap her off-duty .38 to her ankle. Just then her front door exploded inward and just as she drew her weapon she saw the entry-team force their way through. The pain caused by several rifle bullets entering her chest and severing her aorta never had a chance to register on her brain before the blackness overtook her and Rachel slumped to the floor dead.

The men who assaulted her were dressed from head to toe in black material. They worked fast picking up all the evidence from the living room floor and removing the disc that was still in the player. Using gloved hands, they filled the cloth satchel Rachel had carried home with cash and cocaine leaving only Rachel's fingerprints. They secured the crime scene and waited for the black and white units. The story that would air in a few minutes would tell of another cop gone bad; the government's crime and Justin's secret would remain just that; secret.

*　　*　　*

Logos, in the guise of Dr. Jeremy Bolder still worked with Justin on a daily basis, as did Kapre in the guise of Mr. Summons. They met very few times but when they did they met for lunch usually in the company cafeteria as they were doing now.

"Logos I just don't know what I'm supposed to be doing. I can protect Justin's life but we seem to have lost his soul entirely. He's given himself over totally to the enemy it seems to me. He has orchestrated several murders to date, made decisions that have put thousands out of work, and doesn't seem to have a conscience at all. He has become very hard of heart and there appears to be no innocence left. He listens to my advice but never takes it. Am I doing something wrong?"

Logos finished his sweet tea then whispered, "If you remember Kapre, I have been guardian to several men throughout history who it seemed had gone over to the enemy for a time, but who in time came to their senses and became great forces of good for our Lord. Saul is a good example. I guarded him during the time he was killing Christians and jailing them all in the name of God. As you know he finally came around and became the great evangelist who opened the Lord's saving grace to the Gentiles."

"Yes, but at least he was acting for God and not Satan. Justin doesn't seem to believe in God or Satan. He just believes in what is good for him."

"Kapre, we told you that this assignment would be difficult didn't we?"

Kapre/Summons nodded, and Logos continued, "Well, this is the hard part; guarding a human who is exercising his freewill even when it is destructive to him and others. You must remember, however, that our Lord has a plan that includes Justin Schaefer Johnson, and we must trust His judgment. Evidently, somewhere down the line he will be made aware of his soul and its sins and when he does you must be there to save him from himself. He will be crushed by the weight of his sins and he'll need the freeing power of our Lord's love and forgiveness, which will come in the form of Grace. He won't have to deserve it but simply accept the gift that Jesus has already offered.

"So, in short Kapre, you aren't doing anything wrong, you simply need to stay focused and have faith that all will turn out for the best. If not, the deciding factor will be Justin's freewill."

Kapre had been nodding his agreement but he added, "I understand, Logos, but it doesn't make it any easier to watch."

Logos laughed, "When it gets easy to watch, you let me know and we'll reassign you immediately."

The two men/angels parted company to carry out their respective duties.

*   *   *

Her cell phone rang several times before it could penetrate her dreams. Amanda stirred and tried to get out of Justin's bed but his arm was heavy on her shoulders. She finally slid out from under it and stood up on the soft carpet. She retrieved her coat and took the annoying phone out and flipped it open, "Hello, Amanda here, this better be. . ."

Justin sat up in bed just in time to watch the color drain from Amanda's face making her tousled hair look even redder. She fell to the floor, sitting down unceremoniously, "What? How?" She listened a little more and her pale face began to turn red, starting from the neck and moving up to her ears and then her face in total.

Amanda slammed the phone shut cutting the connection and with unbelievable speed she jumped up and ran to Justin's side of the bed and punched him in the jaw. Blood trickled from the corner of his mouth and she pummeled him over and over with her fists, yelling the entire time, "You killed him! It could only be you with this new agent RFU 63 of yours!"

Justin tried to defend himself the best he could but Amanda was strong and fast and she would have killed him right then and there if not for the intervention of Mr. Summons. With strong arms he clamped her in an unbreakable vice-grip and held her in place.

Justin yelled over her protestations, "Amanda calm down! What are you talking about? Killed who?"

Amanda continued to struggle but was no match for Mr. Summons and she began to tire as her hoarse cry continued, "I was just informed that my brother, at least what's left of him, has just been found in his bed dead! Melted! Melted Justin, just like that Lopez kid."

Exhausted Amanda went limp in Summons' arms and wept quietly.

Justin showed his first signs of conscious with tears escaping from his eyes. He wiped them away angrily then lied, "How can you suspect that I would hurt your family, Amanda? I sell that formula to the government you know that. Obviously, your brother had made enemies in high places and was eliminated. I had no reason to hurt him, now calm down and think."

Mr. Summons carried her to the bed and laid her down and she curled up in a fetal position. Justin's right eye was swollen shut from her attack but he sat next to her and gently rubbed her hair. Mr. Summons seeing that the danger had passed left the room, having difficulty watching his charge lie through his teeth. Justin held Amanda's head in his lap and rocked gently back and forth and came to a decision suddenly.

Without stopping to think about it he said, "Amanda I think I trust you about at much as I have ever trusted anyone lately. If you are going to be my second in command, I must be able to trust you with my life. So here goes..."

As he hesitated, Amanda sat up and dried her eyes with the handkerchief Justin offered her. Justin looked into her face and said, "I had to take your brother out just as you had to take your father out, Amanda. Your brother was a spy for Black under the code name Icicle. He has betrayed us all to the police so he had to be eliminated. Amanda think about it. Your brother was bitter about you usurping what he considered his rightful place in the scheme of things. He, therefore, struck back in the only way he could; in a way provided for him by Black. Now that Black is dead, your brother passed on incriminating evidence to the police that will bring us and our government down and it's not the first information that he has passed along like this."

Amanda tried to get angry but she knew where her loyalties lie. She said, "Yes, Justin I understand quite well that it had to be done under the circumstances. I only ask that in the future, if you are truly making me your number one person that you consult me about any further eliminations. We must work in unison in the future. OK?"

Justin stared at her for a while and then said, "I'll agree on one condition Amanda."

"What is it Justin?"

"Will you marry me? Let's be true partners in everything. Will you?"

Amanda didn't need to think long. She smiled and kissed Justin hard on the lips as all anger and fear drained from the couple, as they joined forces against the world.

*   *   *

Senator Rotell Wilkerson was the only person on the Illumin, Inc. board who knew the truth. His operatives who carried out the black ops at Detective Longstrum's apartment and at the Dowling residence were sworn to secrecy and he had no reason to betray Justin Johnson, not yet anyway. He had quickly obtained the needed government contract for the purchase of RFU 63 and the further needed research, which would bring millions of dollars into the corporation. His own share plus the "under the table contributions" of this one deal alone had added millions to his own considerable personal wealth. He was a happy man. He had learned early that in politics all rules must be put behind you. You did whatever it took to get the job done. He had been Justin's secret advisor for several months now. He knew that Don Black, smart as he was, just wasn't in Justin's league. He liked the boy and what's more he recognized talent and Justin had it all; brains, courage, and most important; a total lack of conscience. He saw Justin's potential not only for research but also for politics. He had youth, good looks, money, and a natural cunning that made Rotell proud.

Rotell began with dreams of becoming President of the United States, which Senator doesn't, but his opportunities had passed him by. Now he was too old and his son was, well, an imbecile. Ronald could perhaps become a Congressman, maybe a Senator, but more likely an Ambassador or cabinet member. He was simple and would do whatever he was told to do.

Justin on the other hand had a photographic

memory, was a walking library of facts, and had the determination to do what is needed to get the job done, as this little test had proven. With Justin's agreement they had just beaten several powerful men at their own game. Don Black had made his move on Justin. Black's plan had been to topple Justin with Detective Longstrum's help and then replace him with Roger Dowling III. Don had underestimated Justin and his connections with Wilkerson. Don didn't miss much but he had totally been blind to the Senator's coaching of Justin and it had proved to be his undoing.

Now for part two of their plan. If Justin could pull this off, there would be no doubt of his ability to maneuver, conspire, and to rise to a position of power from which no heights would be out of his reach. The Senator smiled to himself as he entered the White House to talk to President Bob Spalding who would be at the end of his second term in just two years. They would work together to bring Justin into the political arena. The Vice-President would then be elected for eight years and then one more President would reign before Justin would be ready for the Oval Office. First would come several years as Senator, then when old enough perhaps Vice-President first, and then the top office of the country. Senator Wilkerson knew he would probably not live to see it, but he could take comfort in the fact that he knew exactly where to start in launching the boy's career.

CHAPTER TWENTY-TWO

ANTIDOTE
RESEARCH FACILITY

FOUR YEARS LATER:

The small two-passenger jet was black in color and had no markings of any kind. The skin of the craft was made of top-secret stealth material that absorbed all radar, radio, and light frequencies. It was also equipped with the new whisper anti-gravity engine, which had advanced with each generation of re-invention. This one was so efficient that the pilot could hover just ten feet over your head and you would be unaware of its existence. The pilot now hovered at five thousand feet above the ground, and opened the cockpit's clear bulletproof canopy. He watched the paratrooper, who was covered from head to toe in black material with only an oval hole for the eyes. He climbed out onto the wing, centered himself, and then simply fell backward; arching his back as he did so.

The air roared past the man's ears as he turned over onto his belly and held his arms and legs out wide; to catch as much air as possible. Even then he was dropping toward the earth and possible death at the rate of one hundred seventy-six feet per second. As he fell he tapped a button on a black box attached to his chest strap causing it to vibrate slightly which told him that the motion detectors below him were now suddenly jammed.

245

The jumper could see the lights of the five-mile outer perimeter fence below him, the square of lights of the one-mile inner perimeter fence, and the lights from the facility buildings themselves. It reminded him of a bull's-eye on a target. He put his hands to his sides trying his best to track toward the bull's-eye but he was fighting head winds and would have no canopy time in the air to direct him. Below a thousand feet his audible altimeter was screaming at him as he pulled his pilot chute. He only had one chance at this low altitude deployment, for if something went wrong he had no time to deploy his emergency chute, and in fact hadn't worn one.

As he raced toward the ground the pilot chute deployed, caught air and began the process of releasing the main chute. For one terrifying, adrenaline filled moment the holding pin hesitated to pull away from the parachute container but finally gave way to the pull of the pilot chute. He heard a slight rustling sound as the ball of fabric rose above him, unraveled and fought the onrushing air for mastery of the situation. At this moment if the lines were to tangle and the chute failed to open, he would Roman candle to his death in seconds. Finally the deployed canopy supported his full weight. As his descent was halted, a break line snagged whipping him one hundred and eighty degrees away from his target. He grabbed the brake line and his straightened course happened to be directly toward the quickly approaching fence. He only had seconds to react. He flared, leveled his descent, raised his feet, and barely cleared the top of the fence which was topped with deadly razor wire. Normally he would land into the wind but the snagged break line caused him to land with the wind at his back. This forced him to hit the ground harder than he intended. He rolled with the jarring impact, pulled the RSL allowing the chute to leave his shoulders and float gently to the ground. From the time he fell from the jet until now, only thirty seconds had passed.

He ran to the outside of the one-mile perimeter fence of the Antidote Research Facility, laid the black box gently on the ground in front of the fence and quickly took a twenty foot wire out of the pocket of his jump suit. He hurriedly clipped this to the fence with specially attached clips, each placed one foot apart for this purpose, allowing him to make an area on the fence measuring six foot from the ground up, then six foot over, then six foot down to the ground again. He plugged one end of the wire into the black box and flipped a second switch diverting the electricity along the newly attached wire and effectively giving the man a six-foot door, which he now cut out of the fencing on three sides using a small laser cutter. He pushed the fencing forward careful not to touch the still hot edge and walked through the opening and closed it after himself. He saw the buildings in the distance; two new two-story apartment complexes for the scientists and the single-story research building. It was to this building that the man was interested in going. He ran quickly across the open area, jumped forward and rolled head over heels coming to rest behind a large bush just as a spot light swept over his location with its revealing bright 10 kw of light that turned night to day wherever it landed.

That had been close! The man pushed a button on his watch and a dim green light illuminated the dial; Midnight was only one minute away, he was cutting this mighty close. He had chosen midnight because that was when the guards changed shifts and the most confusion could be generated. It was, however, when the most guards were there as well. He unzipped his black coverall outfit and pulled the dark hood off of his head and buried them in the bush. From a bag he had worn slung over his shoulder until a moment ago, he removed a guard hat and gun belt. The uniform he had worn under his coveralls. He now donned the hat and gun belt and ran toward the building's back door. As he ran he pulled a remote out of his pocket and pushed a button. The green light on the black box that still sat by the fence about a mile away now turned to red and instantly sirens wailed as the motion detectors, intruder alerts and video cameras suddenly were allowed to read the intrusion. The back door opened and two armed guards ran out toward the fence not even noticing the guard standing behind the door. The fake guard eased himself into the opening and stood inside as the door closed gently behind him. As guards swarmed the fence line for the intruder he walked down the hall to a door marked: "Employees with red passes only." Oddly enough, no employees of this facility even had a red pass but no one knew that. The intruder took out an instrument that looked like a small thin screwdriver. He placed this in the lock, pushed a button, and after a short burst of power, a whirring sound and a click, he was able to turn the lock and open the door. This door opened onto a secret elevator. He closed the door behind him, the light stayed on and he inserted his power key into the panel unlocked the access door and hooked a small instrument to the console's keypad and pushed a button. The first section on his display lit up and numbers began to rotate until it stopped on six. It repeated this until all six numbers appeared allowing him to key in the access code and the elevator dropped toward its destination. This particular elevator only went to one place; the secret research facility located about a half mile below the known facility. Before the door opened the man took out yet another box and attached it via magnet to the back of the elevator and switched it on. When the elevator door opened he pushed the hold button and the door remained open. The box that he had placed in the back of the elevator caused all the surveillance cameras to blank out so the guards above, had they even been looking at them would have suddenly seen nothing on their screens.

As the man approached the large vault which held millions of dollars of untold secrets he was suddenly startled by the command, "Halt and be recognized!" He froze in his tracks, his hand half way to his revolver.

The guard holding the assault rifle warned, "I wouldn't do that if I were you." The man didn't. A second guard came up behind the man and removed his revolver and handcuffed his hands behind his back.

*   *   *

It was an hour later before Jack Miller, head of security, walked into the vault area. He wasn't a happy man. It was the middle of the night, an intruder had penetrated millions of dollars worth of security precautions and no one had made coffee yet. The latter was soon corrected and he took the offered cup and sat down in front of the man and ordered the guard, "Take the cuffs off of him." The guard only hesitated for a moment and then complied. "Now leave the coffee, but I want you guards to leave us alone down here.

The shift supervisor looked frantic as he protested, "But sir!"

Jack wasn't having any arguments as his expression clearly warned the man. "Yes sir." was all he could say as he complied. Before he entered the elevator Jack yelled, "And turn off all the security cameras to this area while I'm down here." They had found the black box and had deactivated it, but hadn't removed it. The guard simply switched it back on. The man looked back, frowned, and said again, "Yes, sir."

When the guards had left Jack stood up and shook the man's hand saying, "I sure didn't expect you to get this far Stan." Stan Peterson formerly an operative for the "non-existent" Black Ops; now a hired agent for the CDC (Centers for Disease Control and Prevention); indisputably the best of the best when pitted against any security system in existence.

"Sorry Jack but this will cost you about ten guards and at least one upgrade in systems that I could see. I wasn't expecting you to have this area manned, that was your saving grace as I see it."

Jack smiled at Stan and said, "If you had made it into the vault you would have been stunned with a mighty jolt of electricity that unless deactivated automatically nails the first person through the door."

Stan smiled back and pointed to his bag that still sat on the table, "May I?"

Jack nodded.

Stan took a small piece of equipment to the vault,

attached it to the door and pushed a button. A slight whirring sound, a click and Stan opened the door to the vault and walked in. He did not get shocked which in turn shocked Jack who jumped up, knocking his chair over, and said, "What did you do?"

"That's obvious Jack. I deactivated it."

Jack picked up his chair, sat back down and poured them each another cup of coffee. He pulled a cigar out of his suit coat pocket, "Want one Stan?" Stan nodded and the two men just sat quietly and sipped coffee and puffed without speaking for about ten minutes.

Finally Jack broke the silence, "Well Stan, what does this do about our potential contract with the government?"

"Don't worry Jack; since you gave me the heads-up; I was able to get my company assigned to your facility and a good thing too. I researched your blueprints, floor plans, schematics and as good a job as your security team has done; I still found one flaw. On one of the blueprints there was an unexplained "empty" space which turned out to be your elevator to this secret part of your facility; the part you don't want anyone to know about. I have purged it from the system. I'm also ninety-nine percent sure that the agents or spies that the government has secretly placed into your employment know nothing about this lower level facility."

He reached into his bag and pulled out a report and handed it to Jack saying, "This will give you all the information you need about the guards, their wives, the system's upgrades and the spies so you can make sure that this part of the facility remains a secret. Read it; then destroy it.

"As far as the government will know after I give my recommendations is that they are entering into business with a legitimate research facility; all of which is above the desert floor. Most facilities we investigate are broken into at least twice before I can approve them, but that won't be necessary here. You've done a good job, Jack. You have state of the art instruments and all but ten of your guards are loyal and efficient. However, it only took me a month of visiting local taverns and bowling alleys to get to those ten from whom I gathered most of your access codes and they didn't even know they gave them to me. They were sloppy and they talked to their wives way too much. All I had to do was send a female operative into the beauty shops to ask a few questions and listen, and then bingo, here I am. If you replace those guards and the systems that I have recommended; all of which are in that report, this facility will be in use within two months and be as safe and secure as it can be.

Jack stood up and again shook Stan's hand, "Thank you for all of your help here, Stan. By the way, how did you get into the grounds without being spotted?"

"Now Jack you know I don't reveal trade secrets."

The men laughed, poured some more coffee and talked about old times as long time friends tend to do.

CHAPTER TWENTY-THREE

DOUBT

Doubt is a dangerous thing for an angel. It is not quite a sin but it gets close when the doubt starts eroding his faith. Kapre/Summons watched as the fat slimy demons had a field day around Justin. Justin, like most humans, had no idea that he was becoming ever more relaxed with the heavy burden of sin. He could no longer feel its weight directly nor did he give it much thought, but with each sinful act the next gets easier. Justin was entangling his life in forces, which were fast growing larger than Justin could control. He had been taught that his power over his circumstances depended on his mastery of the universal force; a non-personal power which traversed the entire universe and was immersed in all things. Once one learns to master it or tap into it, then one has complete control over one's life and destiny. Justin was further instructed that he could influence other people's decisions if he wanted it badly enough and meditated on it deep enough. What he wasn't taught, was that demons actually carried out the deeds asked for and that there was a price to pay for their services. The more Justin called on the demons the more control they had over him.

Demons, of course, mastered the take-over of the human race long ago and met with very little resistance these days. Few humans even believed in Satan or his demons anymore and even fewer believed in God. Like Justin, about as close as they would concede was that there is a universal force that permeates everything and is itself usable and pliable to the wishes of a human master.

Justin was a murderer, an adulterer, a liar, a cheat, and a shallow man, all of which he did in the name of business. These facts are what weighed Kapre down at this moment. He was charged with keeping this young man alive and was supposed to believe that somehow he would be converted and saved to the Lord's purpose someday. Right now, at this particular moment, that seemed very unlikely. Kapre couldn't remember what he had expected some twenty-two years ago (counting the time from Justin's entry into the world and unexpected survival) when he was assigned to this case but he didn't expect to be guarding another "Attila the Hun". He had pictured himself guarding some great man of God that was in constant danger because he was carrying out God's Will, not a man that was so obviously working for Satan and his minions. It made Kapre feel dirty and cheap, like he himself was working for the enemy.

Justin Schaefer was one of the ten wealthiest men in the world. He was chairman of the Illuminate, (Il-lu-mi-nate; with the "a" being pronounced short and the "e" being pronounced long). It was now, however, known as simply Illumin, Inc.

Justin's illustriousness, virulence, and total lack of sensitivity to others made him the best chairman this organization has seen in decades. He had far exceeded anyone's expectations of him and many had underestimated him to the privation of their lives.

Now in a surprise move the proposal and courtship of Amanda Dowling was to culminate today in their marriage. The joining of these two great families would bring eighty-six percent of the corporation under their control and this would make them even more inexorable as a team.

*   *   *

Amanda was controlled by a high-ranking demon named Sway; but her angel Radiance who had watched over her since her conception sadly watched as she spiraled into a life of sin and darkness. He nodded at Kapre and then flew out of the room. The Holy Spirit had asked Kapre/Summons to protect her as well as Justin for he needed Radiance for another task. The Spirit had said, "Shortly Aegis; Pastor Bob's angel will come and help you with them."

*   *   *

Ever since Justin had started hanging out with her, Kapre had stayed in the human form of Mr. Summons but he still wasn't sure how the Lord had prevented these demons from knowing his true identity. They had not tried to influence him as a human, probably due to his low stature in life or perhaps some further miracle of the Lord. Even so he sensed that Sway was beginning to suspect that Mr. Summons was more than he pretended to be. It was just a feeling. One handicap that Kapre had as an angel in the humble service of Justin, was that he could actually see the demons but had to pretend that he could not. This was difficult, especially when the foul smelling Sway got right in his face, testing to see if he was indeed aware of him. It took all of Kapre's concentration to act like he didn't notice; just as he now had to ignore Radiance as he left.

As Justin and Amanda stood at the altar in the Temple to exchange vows, Mr. Summons watched from the back of the audience as the demon Sway flew around and around the couple laughing. He was overjoyed to see this union for a couple of reasons. One was the prominence that it gave his human charge, which in turn earned him a promotion to Lieutenant. He had also found out just today that even though Captain Detestation had taken a special interest in Justin Schaefer all along and had up to today been personally assigned to him, he was now turning that duty over to Sway. Two prizes in one place, what an honor. Captain Detestation was here in person to make the promotion and transfer and to give Sway some last minute instructions. Then he was off on some other important assignment that would apparently be taking up a large portion of his time. This turn of events was fine with Sway but made Kapre/Summons very nervous.

Mr. Summons looked over the crowd and found Dr. Jeremy Bolder who was Logos in disguise and his heart slowed some. He couldn't have made it these past years without Logos being right with him in this building, but after today he also would be alone. Whatever it was that Captain Detestation was leaving to do, Captain Logos was also assigned to by the Lord. No explanation just, "You'll be fine Kapre, keep up the good work."

The nervousness returned to Kapre when he realized that he would be totally alone in this den of vipers. Or would he? No one who follows the Lord is ever really alone but was he up to the challenge?

These and many other doubts raced through his being as he watched the end of the ceremony and everyone left for the reception, an event to which he was invited to serve. Service! Well that was his specialty, after all, both in human form and as a guardian angel. *'Come on Kapre! You can do this!'*, were his thoughts as he began the long walk to the reception area.

CHAPTER TWENTY-FOUR

A PLAN ONCE MADE

The past six months of their honeymoon had been the happiest days of their lives. Justin and Amanda had made a whirlwind tour of the world. At least, they visited the richest and most fun parts of the world; France, Germany, England, Ireland, Canada, Africa, Japan, China, Holland, Switzerland, and Italy. Upon arriving back in the States, they were driven from New York to Chicago with many stops along the way for site-seeing.

They were exhausted, but in that good way, from having stuffed all the fun you can into the shortest amount of time. Amanda found to her surprise that Justin spoke fluently, the language of each country that they visited and this helped them immensely. He had also surprised her with his ability to enjoy himself to the fullest and still run their organization from wherever they found themselves. This, of course, was made easier with the vast communications network throughout the world. The network consisting of communications towers, satellites, communication laser beacons plus some newly updated ultra-broadband wireless networks made audio, text and video communication available anywhere on earth and beyond. They had toyed with the idea of totally cutting themselves off from being bothered but they had both agreed, wisely, that too much could happen in six months and that they had better stay on top of things.

The honeymoon now over, however, it was time for them to decide on a course of action, a plan if you will, for the rest of their lives. They were both twenty-two years of age and both powerful members of the richest and most influential of organizations in the world; for most people that would be enough, but not for them. Justin for his part had tired of research and had turned this over to others. He had in just four short years, however, created three of the deadliest weapons in the government's secret arsenal; the latest and deadliest of course being RFU 63. The other two were deadly enough viruses but worked slower and were longer lasting making them hard to use or control. The government mostly used these in third world countries were the ill effects least concerned the US interests, but still did their part to control the population of these countries.

Amanda had taken over Don Black's duties as Justin's hatchet man or woman in this case. She was twice as devious and cunning as Black had ever been and had already proven her worth. Justin still did not know how she did it but she had in some way convinced all of the old men to retire from the board and put in their places their younger sons. Both Justin and Amanda had agreed that it would be much easier dealing with men closer to their own age.

Senator Rotell Wilkerson agreed to coach Justin in politics even though he was now seventy-one. He could still play the game and had promised to get Justin into the inner circle of all the right people. His son, Ronald Wilkerson, had been (in a not so direct manner) appointed the Ambassadorship to London, England, and was very content. He would be at board meetings via holo-satellite feed, just as many members were from time to time.

Amanda had, at first, no clue to how high Justin's ambitions ran, but when she learned of it she agreed that they should not stop until he was President of the United Sates. Justin had explained that he had only eight years till his thirtieth birthday when he would be eligible to be a Senator. He would run and win a seat in the Senate and hold it for four to eight years and then run for President or Vice-president depending on how things were in the country during that period. In the meantime, he would spread a generous amount of money around to the right members of Congress; Representatives and Senators. He would also fund many government projects, building a history which would come in handy when he ran for office.

They also agreed that with Justin's amazing ability to consume books at a superhuman pace that he should read every biography, autobiography and history book available. He would start with but not limit himself to United States history and personalities. Then he would move on to other countries so that he could deal with other leaders with a more than average intelligence that they would hopefully come to respect and perhaps fear.

The largest concern Justin held in his upcoming education, however, was the study of Christianity and the Holy Bible. Even though he didn't believe in it, he did fear it for some unidentifiable reason. Morals could only be a distraction and not an asset in his opinion and he feared what exposure to these ideals might have on him. Amanda promised to help him keep perspective on real life during this time and that seemed to ease his concerns for the time being. Either way, they knew that they had to be professing Christians to get elected in the United States; so one does what one has to do.

Mr. Summons, who had accompanied them on their honeymoon had overheard many of these plans and had set a few goals of his own. He knew that the knowledge that Justin sought could only strengthen his own chances of bringing Justin over to the Lord's side, so he therefore secretly prayed anew for the saving of Justin's soul. His own faith had gained a boost from this knowledge and he knew that the Lord would arrange circumstances as they needed to be for Justin's eventual salvation experience.

The plans once made were forgotten by the couple as they settled into living their very active, productive and fulfilling lives.

$$*\qquad *\qquad *$$

Chester Melvin; President of Alexander Development Corporation had finished the final preparations of the Antidote Research Facility, also known secretly as The Antidote. Even after eight years of working on the project he didn't have a clue as to how Pastor Bob was going to get Justin Schaefer into it or if he ever would. One thing he was sure of, however, was that it was the best stocked, equipped, and most secure facility available in the United States today, bar none. The government (through the CDC) had contracted the facility to research cures for disease as well as the study of genetically altering and producing food which could eventually be used to feed the world. The United States was already years ahead in this research and production of this type of agriculture but more research would keep it that way.

Pastor Bob had asked Chester to stay on as director of the facility but Chester pointed out that his expertise was in designing and building, not in management. He had arranged over the past year to start his own firm with the nest-egg he had saved from this "generous" project and would be leaving soon to devote all of his time to that endeavor.

As his second choice, Pastor Bob picked up the phone and called the security division at Antidote, "Hello. Security, Officer Windsor.", an uninterested male voice answered.

"This is Pastor Bob Johnson. May I speak to Major Jack Miller please?"

"Yes sir! Right away sir!"

His renewed excitement surprised Bob, who had to smile at his own simplicity and habitual humility. (Bob often forgot that he owned all this and to the employees he was that mysterious owner from Chicago).

"Hi Bob how you doing?"

"I'm great Jack. How are things there?"

"Running as smooth as silk of course; to what do I owe this honor, Bob?"

"Well Jack, the place is up and running and I'm in need of a Director and I'd like you to consider taking the job."

There was a long silence, then, "Well, I had hoped to tell you this in person at your next visit Bob, but well, I'm going to retire. I'm now sixty-three years old and

Beth Foster and I have been dating for the past four years now. Well, Bob, we're getting married, and we're going to travel around the country and enjoy what's left of our lives."

Bob was stunned but he recovered quickly, "Congratulations Jack. I'm really happy for you both. I'll be sorry to lose you both but I wouldn't hold you back even if I could. I would ask one favor of you though."

"Anything Bob" Jack said.

"I would like you to pick the best head of security you can find and offer him or her, the same package you have now."

"That will be very generous of you, but why doesn't that surprise me? At any rate I do have a man in mind, if I can get him."

"Who would that be?"

"You remember a few months ago when we had the government surprise inspection by the Black Opps paratrooper by the name of Stan Peterson?"

"Yes. And I understand that he gave us a lot of help both in personnel and equipment suggestions?"

"That's right. He's young (but has a vast array of experience for his thirty-five years), bright, energetic and guess who's wanting to get out of the business management role soon?"

"You're kidding?"

"Nope and I took the liberty of contacting him to see if he would be interested in my job, but I haven't heard back from him yet."

"Do you think he would take it?"

"Bob, I really don't know what his plans are, but it would be a good deal for him and he would most definitely be qualified."

"Is he a Christian? You know that we are trying to conduct a Christian operation there."

"From speaking to Stan the night he was here, he indicated that he does believe in Jesus as his Savior but that he hasn't attended a church in years."

"Well that's a start. We can fill him in a bit more when he gets there. If the Lord wants him he'll be there, if not, keep looking. Well, Jack, I have to run, but I'll come down there for the wedding. I am invited, right?"

"You bet and thanks."

"No, Jack, thank you for all of your good work. I couldn't have set this up without you. Call me with the wedding plans and I'll be there."

*   *   *

Kathy Saunders couldn't believe that graduation day had finally arrived. She had just turned twenty-one and had been totally free of cancer for ten years now. A day hadn't gone by that she hadn't thanked God for what He had done for her and for sending a friend like Pastor Bob Schaefer, without whom she would never have had the opportunity to attend and graduate college. She was graduating fifth in her class which wasn't easy with the classes she had taken. She had a Major in Genetics with a minor (at Pastor Bob's suggestion) in research administration. She had many friends; many of whom envied her making a job out of going to school, and getting paid for it, then also having a job waiting for her when she got out. Not many of them would be that fortunate and she knew it.

Kathy had plenty of intelligence, personality, beauty, and on top of all that retained her humility and gratitude for all she had been given. It had never occurred to her, even for a moment, to stiff Pastor Bob, even though she had been offered many lucrative positions (anyone of which would rival being a researcher at the Antidote). A promise, however, was a promise and Kathy kept hers. It was no surprise to her then, when at her graduation party, Pastor Bob came up to her and said, "Kathy, I would like to speak to you for a moment."

"Certainly Pastor Bob and I bet I know what about."

"I bet you have no clue." smiled Pastor Bob.

Kathy gave him a quizzical glance as she followed him out of the room.

As they walked outside on a beautiful spring day Pastor Bob began, "Kathy, I was really hoping to ease you into this offer slowly. Let you get some research experience at the facility, then manage an office or two and perhaps in a few years offer you the directorship. The problem is that time and circumstance won't allow it. I need someone that I can trust implicitly. Your moral character and honesty are more valuable to me than twenty years of experience."

He stopped, grabbed her shoulders and gently turned her to face him. Then spoke slowly and clearly, "You're under no obligation to accept this offer for I know it will mean a lot of responsibility at a crucial time in your career and development, but I would like to have you as my Director of the entire Antidote Research Facility."

Bob paused and let that sink in which from her

suddenly pale face he knew it had, "You would have the final word on which research would or would not be conducted. You would be over all other department heads and would be responsible for dealing directly with the government and other corporations for contracts and funding. You see now why I asked you to minor in administration."

When Kathy found her voice it was weak with fear, "Pastor Bob, I don't deserve this honor, nor do I know if I can pull it off. Let's face it. I have no experience for such a huge and important job."

Pastor Bob raised his hand in protest, "From past experience of observing you over the years I know that you have real courage, fortitude, a kindness and gentleness that are needed when dealing with my staff, and most of all I know you have a genuine love for God and faith in His power.

"Kathy, when God asks you to do something it is usually larger than yourself, and something that can't be done without His help, that's how you know that it's God doing the asking. And you know that what God asks you to do He will give you the wherewithal to do it."

Pastor Bob was still holding Kathy by both shoulders like he was going to shake her, but rather he patiently waited for her to give a response. She closed her eyes and he knew that she was praying for guidance and must have received it for she opened her tear filled hazel eyes and said in a humble whisper of a voice, "I accept."

Bob smiled at her, hugged her, then took her by the arm and they continued walking as he added, "Now I know your parents will have a million questions so here are some answers. The Director starts out at a salary of one hundred thousand dollars per year, not counting percentage bonuses, medical, dental, eye care, a retirement package that I'll explain later and the other usual amenities; a new company car each year, a clothing allowance, and a rent-free apartment at the complex. The director's apartment at the facility is the largest and most comfortable, and of course you'll have a large corner office with windows. . ."

Pastor Bob had been talking and just now realized that Kathy had pulled away and had taken a seat on the bench that they had just passed. She sat with her head between her knees; she was hyperventilating. Then he noticed in addition that she was sobbing softly and that confused him, "What's wrong, Kathy?"

She came up for air and in rapid-fire speech she said, "Oh Pastor Bob! We didn't want to worry you but dad got laid off at work this week and now I'll be able to help them. Thank you so much!" She jumped up and hugged his neck, then ran off to tell her parents the good news."

It was Pastor Bob's turn to sit on the bench. It never ceased to amaze him how God's Holy Spirit worked everything together to help the most people he could. He made a mental note to talk to her father about a position in one of his charities, for Pastor Bob was still habitually kind and helpful.

CHAPTER TWENTY-FIVE

TEN YEARS LATER

On television and computer screens around the world the stunningly beautiful face of WNN Anchorwoman Patricia Perkins appeared and her soft, sensual voice pulled the attention of any who weren't already glued to the screen. WNN's rating had gone up an amazing ten points after hiring Ms. Perkins. Her lithe, well-proportioned body was covered in an expensive no nonsense blue business suit and white blouse which accented her oriental features, consisting of olive skin, full red lips, and tawny slanted eyes that drew you in and held you there. Her raven black hair, cut in a short but stylish fashion, completed the persona which brought envy to most women and fantasy to most men.

After her introductions, her face was reduced to a small square and placed at the top left of the viewer's screen while the rest of the screen showed disturbing unrest in the Middle-East, as Patricia said, "Word has reached us that just thirty minutes ago Senator Justin Johnson, who was on a peace keeping mission to Israel, has been shot."

Patricia was removed from the screen so the entire screen could show what had happened via satellite feed right from Israel. A black sedan pulled up to the terminal and armed Israeli Soldiers surrounded the Senator's car. The now familiar smile of the young Senator from Illinois appeared as he stepped from the vehicle and waved to the crowd. He stood six foot one inches tall as he straightened up, had a muscular build, his longish hair, the color of harvest wheat, styled in a wave behind his ears, fluttered gently in the hot breeze. He was wearing a dark blue suit with a white shirt and red tie. The silver cuff-links holding his shirt cuff together on his raised right wrist glistened in the sunlight as he walked and waved in slow motion. He was the picture of health and a poster-child for what the typical American male should look like. Suddenly from the crowd there appeared, also in slow motion, and with a circle of red drawn around him so the audience couldn't miss the implication, the world watched as the man in the tunic drew a small hand gun, and rapidly fired two shots toward the Senator. The Senator's face suddenly lost its smile as he took on a pained expression and the Senator fell, in slow motion, behind the police, who for their part opened fire on the assailant killing him at the scene. After a momentary time lapse froze the screen, the audience then watched in real time, as an unconscious Senator was hurriedly loaded into a waiting ambulance, placed there for just this possible contingency, and rushed to an undisclosed hospital.

Patricia's small square picture reappeared at the top left corner of the screen as the entire shooting scene replayed itself silently behind her. (She paused here for effect, then continued in a serious, sincerely sympathetic voice as she dramatically dabbed a stray tear away with a Kleenex. The staff who watched her had no doubts that they watched an artist at work.)

"As you know, the freshman Senator from Illinois made a large splash as he entered the political arena just two years ago when he appeared, as if out of nowhere, and took the Illinois Senate seat in a landslide decision. Little was known about the Senator except that he is a self-made billionaire in his own right. Some say he's a genius in business, scientific research and now in politics, but most of all he is known for his charitable work. The fame of his humanitarian efforts preceded his entrance into political life and didn't stop upon his arrival. Since taking a seat in the Senate, Senator Johnson has spent, to date, thirty-eight million dollars of his own money to alleviate suffering in third world countries. He has ties to research facilities which have led the war on AIDS and many other illnesses that plague the world's population. Senator Johnson even hints to a miracle cure, or rather, a miracle antidote to all disease may be possible one day."

"Now in his latest humanitarian move as peace-keeper in Israel, someone has struck him down in his youth and may have ended what promised to be a brilliant career in politics. Most people had heard of Justin Johnson even before he ran for the Senate and we have found over the years that most women loved him and most men admired him." (She was adding the past tense to pull out all the suspense and sympathy she could from her audience.) Behind Patricia, the scenes of the shooting had replayed about three times and were now replaced with scenes of Justin, smiling and laughing as he helped out at numerous charitable functions around the world. Scenes from his campaign and even scenes of other politicians talking about the rumors that Justin Johnson may have had the Presidency in his sites.

After exactly three minutes of these carefully presented scenes, which flashed on and off the screen in rapid succession, Patricia said, "We must stop for a short break but do stay with us as we bring you the latest on the shooting of Senator Justin Johnson."

Patricia took a drink of her bottled water as make-up experts ran up and touched up the spots on her face that were melting in the heat of the spotlights and the tears that she had expertly allowed to dribble down her cheeks. Patricia whispered softly, to no one in particular, as she stared off into space, "If Justin lives through this incident, he'll be hailed as a hero if not a saint. He owes me big time." No one else spoke, which was surprising because breaks were usually full of everyone trying to speak over everyone else. Now, however, everyone just nodded their silent agreement.

Just as the cameraman was counting down, three, two, one - - they handed Patricia three sheets of paper. She was looking them over as the red camera light came back on, indicating that they were again on the air.

Patricia looked up slowly from the papers and smiled, "Welcome back to WNN's extensive coverage of the shooting of Senator Justin Johnson. Word just in (She held up the sheets of paper) Senator Johnson is expected to recover from the wounds he received just about forty-five minutes ago." (The shooting scenes repeated behind her silently as she spoke) "He was shot twice by a would-be assassin as he approached the airport to meet the plane which was to bring him back to the States. The assassin himself, as yet unidentified, was pronounced dead at the scene."

Patricia turned her swivel chair to the right and looked into a second camera. "In other news. . ."

*   *   *

Amanda had finely arrived in Israel and was hurried into the hospital room in which Justin was recovering. The armed guard closed the door behind her and they were left alone. He smiled up at her as she rushed to his bedside and hugged him without thinking.

"Ouch! That hurts honey!"

"Oh, I'm so sorry Justin."

"Getting shot hurts much worse than I expected Amanda."

"It's worth it though, honey. You're being hailed as a hero just as we had hoped."

"I know. I've been watching my life pass before my eyes on the TV screen and I'm even convinced that I'm a saint. That idiot collapsed my right lung, I could have died."

"Honey, the poor sap I hired did die, and it had to appear real didn't it?"

"It was real Amanda and for a moment I was afraid that he really wanted to kill me."

"All the better my dear. Now stop whining and bask in the glory of our victory. The Presidency is as good as yours. After this, the President himself may step down and invite you to take his place."

They looked at each other for a moment, then laughed and said simultaneously, "Nah! That's leaning just a bit toward fantasy."

Amanda smiled and continued alone, "In your campaign that news footage of your being shot will be priceless, as will the many appearances you'll make between now and then, telling the nation just how close to death you came that day."

Justin looked up at Amanda and asked, "Did you cover your tracks well?"

She frowned in mock pain at the question, "Of course I did buster; totally non-traceable to us."

Justin was staring off into space as he whispered, "Just how do you get a person to do this and for free no less."

Amanda smiled, "He was told that we need coverage for our cause; you're election, and that his cause, going to heaven, would be assured if he became a martyr. He jumped at the opportunity. His people will take responsibility and credit for the assassination attempt on the United States representative of peace with Israel. Both of you look good with only one act of violence."

"Well, Amanda, I have to admit that you're brilliant. When you first approached me with this scheme I really was tempted to believe that you wanted me out of the way for some reason." Amanda made a fist and made as if to hit his sore shoulder. He was quick to add, "But honey, I decided that you were just exercising your brilliance and I was yet again correct."

She hugged him, instead of hitting him, and they kissed, long and deep.

*   *   *

Kapre (who had stepped out of the role of Mr. Summons and now invisible to the humans) stood and watched, shaking his head. He thought, *'How can humans so flippantly use the gift of life to gain popularity with their fellow humans?'*

To an oblivious Justin he said, "Don't you know son, that the assassin had every intention of killing you quite dead. If I hadn't deflected the fatal bullet which instead of landing in your heart, landed in your lung, you would be dead right now and living in eternal damnation. One day you're going to realize just how close you came to eternal death."

Kapre knelt down by the bed and prayed earnestly for the quick salvation of Justin Schaefer Johnson. This had been just a little close for Kapre's tastes. He was counting the hours, days, years, whatever it took, but he wanted his charge safely, once and for all, in the freeing and saving Grace of Jesus Christ.

CHAPTER TWENTY-SIX

PASTOR BOB'S LAMENT

When Pastor Bob first heard Patricia Perkins' report his heart faltered momentarily. He thought that Justin was dead and thus all of his plans and dreams futile. What's more he thought of Justin spending eternity in Hell and he began to cry out for his soul. Bob had brought many souls to the Lord and understandably he was disappointed that the very soul he had worked so hard to save was cut down before he could bring him over to the Lord. He had first cried out angrily to the Lord and then with a broken heart he had slipped into a quiet depression, all within moments of hearing the first report.

Praying softly Bob said, "Lord forgive me my insolence. You do the saving not me. You guide others to You not through me but rather through the Holy Spirit. I didn't mean to try to take credit or blame, for it just isn't..."

He stopped praying when Patricia came back on and told the world that Senator Johnson was alive and would most likely recover from his wounds. Hope returned as did an intense resolve to bring this project to a head. Pastor Bob started to pray with even more intensity. He asked the Lord to please pull out all stops and to bring Justin to his knees so that he would begin to see his need for salvation. His fellow Christians thought he had lost his mind long ago with this project. "The millions you have already spent on Justin could have been put to better use on the poor", they would lament. "Stop dreaming and move on to another soul, or perhaps many souls and leave the Senator to his fate", they would advise him. Everyone else around Pastor Bob, it seems, could see what Senator Johnson was truly made of morally. They were not fooled by his act, as the rest of the world was and as apparently Pastor Bob. Pastor Bob had by necessity brought the project to the attention of a few of his closest Christian business advisors. Men and women who had faith in him and his ministries but who, to a person, had advised against this project from the beginning, but who in the end had also finally relented and offered their full support. They trusted Pastor Bob's close relationship to the Lord even though their faith and understanding in the project itself was limited.

Pastor Bob, however, would cling to his hope until the end; trusting the Holy Spirit's prompting against all the well-meaning advise of his advisors. He would fight for the soul of Justin Johnson until there was no hope at all. Bob had prayed long and hard and felt strongly that the Lord did not want him to give up on Justin and that was that. His advisors had finally ceased to argue with him on this issue and just let it drop. It was his time and money after all and if he wanted to waist it, well he still did plenty for everyone else; let him have his dream project. Pastor Bob understood their reluctance and lack of faith in the project because his own faith was strained to the limit at this point; yet his resolve to see it through was as solid as a rebar reinforced foundation.

*   *   *

Two weeks after the shooting incident, Pastor Bob was praying for Justin and all of his other projects when the phone rang and he heard a woman's voice "Is this Pastor Bob Johnson?"

"Yes, may I help you?"

"I'm an aid for Senator Johnson your step-brother. He asked me to call you and tell you that your father has passed away."

Pastor Bob sat down and asked in a hoarse voice, "What happened?"

"I'm sorry Pastor but I really have very few details but the Senator is getting back from Israel tomorrow morning and asked if you would meet him at Dorfine's Funeral Home in the morning at 10."

"Yes, tell him I'll be there." He hung up the phone and buried his head in his arms and wept bitterly over the loss of his father and his lost soul. He really hadn't hated his father but their lack of relationship was now hard to bare. He would never get the chance to apologize, or make up, or rebuild their relationship, and more importantly he would never be able to lead him to the Lord.

*   *   *

Theodore "Teddy" Johnson, one of the "top ten" wealthiest men of the world lay naked on the cold porcelain embalming table. All his life, he had received the best of everything and today was no different, for very few people were embalmed by the director himself.

Billy Williams was busy enough doing the directing and managing tasks for the corporate owned Dorfine Funeral Home. Mr. Dorfine had been fifty years dead but they kept his name because it was still respected in the area. Very few people even realized that the funeral home had changed hands twice in the last fifty years. When he heard that Mr. Johnson had died he had insisted on personally taking the case. Johnson Enterprises sent him more business than any other corporation and he would give Teddy the best his profession had to offer.

He had just finished embalming Mr. Johnson and was washing the corpse with his main embalmer, Al Jones, when the phone rang. Al dried his hands, activated the earpiece and said, "Dorfine Funeral Home, Al speaking. Yes, hold please." He tapped the earpiece and said, "It's Senator Johnson's office for you, Billy."

Billy dried his hands and tapped his earpiece receiver saying, "Mr. Williams here. How may I help you? Yes that would be fine. I'll expect them at ten. That's fine, thanks."

As he double tapped the receiver to hang up and grabbed a towel to dry off Johnson's corpse, he told Al, "The Senator's office got hold of Pastor Johnson and both brothers will be here at ten in the morning. Now, that will be interesting. I hear they haven't spoken in ten years or more."

Al didn't answer; he just stared at the Johnson corpse with a strange look on his face. Finally Billy asked, "What's with you Al, is he breathing or something?"

Al jumped slightly, then laughed, "No, of course not. I was just comparing Mr. Johnson to poor Mrs.

Wimpleton over there." He pointed to the corpse two tables over; there were five tables in all. "She has been a poor widow on a sparse $1400.00 per month pension for twenty years and then there's Mr. Johnson who's worth billions, yet they both ended up here on our tables, just two pieces of cold meat."

Billy smiled, "Yeah, it makes you think doesn't it."

Al nodded, "If it wasn't for the fact that I believe in an afterlife, it would be depressing. Mrs. Wimpleton had nothing here, financially anyway, but everyone has been praising her for how she has touched their lives. Her visitation may end up being larger than Mr. Johnson's; at least the visitors will be more sincere in their grief. I also believe her soul is already enjoying more joy than we can imagine. I wouldn't even want to imagine what Mr. Johnson is experiencing right now. I . . ."

Billy spat in the sink and growled, "Don't start your preaching again, Al. I don't believe all that Christian stuff. When you die, your dead and that's the end of it."

Al grumbled under his breath, "You're going to miss out on all the fun one of these days, Billy."

"What was that?"

"Oh nothing, Billy, nothing at all."

*   *   *

Senator Justin Johnson's heart was breaking. This was unusual for him and he didn't like it. Theodore Johnson was the only father that Justin had ever known and he had been good to Justin. He had taken him in when no one else would. He had given him everything he had ever wanted and had paved the way for his current political career. He had made him heir to a fortune and had helped him become the head of the most powerful organization ever to exist; the Illuminati, or as it is known today, Illumine Inc. Teddy Johnson had even, in recent years, introduced Justin to the world of Spiritual enlightenment. Justin had trained for the past few years in the art of Astro-projection (Out of the body experiences). As in everything else, Justin had learned quickly and was fully involved in projecting his will on others and getting them to do what he wanted, without them even knowing it. He had obtained his own spirit guide through the elusive world of the cosmic spirit or force. His faith in this self-serving, "I'm in control" religion was so strong that he had been able to strangle the seeds of Christianity planted by his brother Pastor Bob Johnson so many years before.

Now, however, in this time of emotional need he was finding that his "religion" was leaving him empty and alone. The impersonal cosmic force was no lover of the individual. It could care less about one person's need but instead operated for the better good of all mankind and if a few individuals or their needs were ignored along the way, so be it. Most of the time Justin agreed, but today he needed some love and understanding. Some comfort and some hope wouldn't be bad either, but he didn't find it in his session with his spirit guide this morning. His guide told him that his dad had been reabsorbed into the cosmic force and would find rest for a time until he was reincarnated into another life. He said he had grown much in this life and would be rewarded in his next incarnation for the deeds committed in this one.

Karma, the universal law of justice, would balance the good and evil acts committed by Teddy Johnson and he would rise to the next level of existence accordingly.

In his mind, Justin understood and for the most part agreed with all of these doctrines, but in his heart he wished for the comfort of a loving and personal God, who cares about the individual. He longed for the hope that Pastor Bob had introduced him to so many long years ago. With Justin's copious memory, it was virtually impossible for him to forget the stories his brother had taught him, nor could he forget any of the words he had read in the Bible in his studies. His analytical mind had recalled both sets of lessons and compared them before Justin could stop the process and to his surprise, his current belief in reincarnation and a universal force, fell way short of explaining death and the future compared to the faith in a personal God, held by his brother Pastor Bob. Even though he and Pastor Bob had not spoken for years and they were legally step-brothers rather than natural blood brothers; in this moment of grief, Justin realized that he loved Bob as a brother and could not think of him as anything less than a brother and with this thought his doubts about Christianity began to wane.

The Senator's thoughts were invaded by a new argument, *'No! Christianity would only bring destruction of everything I have built over the years. I have fame, wealth, power, and a future . . . but no real love, comfort, peace, or personal wealth.'*

Justin was startled at the intensity of that last thought. He became aware of an emptiness that he had managed to ignore most of the time, but now it was an inflamed and festering wound in the center of his soul. Tears began to stream down his cheek and his face turned red when he realized that Amanda was watching him closely.

She hugged his arm and whispered, "Hold yourself together Senator, now's not the time to lose your self-control, now is it?"

He took a handkerchief out of his pocket and wiped the tears away and just nodded. His wounded soul, however, filled him with an emptiness and doubt that threatened to rip through his hard exterior, as they approached the funeral home.

*   *   *

Pastor Bob Johnson sat in the waiting room of the Dorfine Funeral Home, Bible open on his lap, but with eyes closed he concentrated on a prayer for the salvation of Justin's soul. He whispered, "Father, I remain full of hope that You are reaching out for Justin's soul. Help him to see the need to turn back to You, Lord. You can reach him, Lord, I know you can. Please fill me with Your Holy Spirit and the hope and strength that He brings. . ." Just then the front door opened and Senator Justin Johnson walked into the Funeral Home.

Pastor Bob inhaled sharply for the man before him was a shell of the man he had just seen on television. There were dark circles around his eyes and he appeared to have been crying. The woman next to him brushed the long red hair out of her face and locked those hard, cold, green eyes on Pastor Bob. Bob shivered slightly as he stood to greet his brother.

Justin stopped to look at his brother. Pastor Bob radiated a peace and a love that Justin had not found in another human being and he instantly loved this man again. It didn't make sense at all but he couldn't stop himself.

Pastor Bob didn't know what to expect when Justin almost ran to him and gripped him in a desperate hug. Bobby gladly hugged him back and tears of joy ran down his cheeks. Then to his surprise Justin whispered in his ear, "Oh Bobby, I need your help! I know now that you've been right about everything but I don't know how to escape my life. I've made promises that I can't break. I've chosen a path that pulls you along whether you want to go or not and no one turns from the faith without paying a great price. I'm not ready to pay that price yet but I want what you have. I want to feel loved Bobby, just loved."

Bobby hugged Justin tighter and whispered, "I love you Justin; I always have and always will. More importantly God loves you, just because you're His child. You don't have to impress him just love him back and accept what His son Jesus has done for you."

Bobby held Justin at arm's length and said, "I'm always here for you Justin, any time, any place, just call and I'll be there." They hugged again until Amanda walked up and grabbed Justin by the shoulder and actually pulled him away from Bobby, saying as she did so, "Come on Justin let's get this over with. Remember we have that dinner meeting at six."

Justin began at that moment to see Amanda through new eyes and it scared him and at the same time angered him. Where was the compassion, the tenderness

. . . 'No! Stop it! I have to stop thinking like this. I'm just feeling hurt from the loss of my dad. That's all it is.'

With that Justin stood up straight and in a flash he was the tough Senator again, the new age disciple that he had been trained to be. His belief had been shaken, however, and he would never be the same from this day forward; even though he didn't fully realize it yet.

*   *   *

After the arrangements were made and Pastor Bob was driving back to his office, joy filled his heart. He had finally seen, and for the first time, a slight crack in Justin's wall of denial. It was no less than a miraculous answer to his prayers. It came right at a time when Pastor Bob was about to give up hope.

Bobby's heart was also heavy with his only lament.

He prayed, "Lord Jesus I'm so sorry for the doubt that was creeping into my heart. I was beginning to think that I had lost Justin forever. I should have known that Your Holy Spirit was working on the man every time I prayed and more. I put Justin in Your hands Lord and I know that You can and will win him over eventually. After our encounter today, I have hope that one day Justin will use the research center that you have had me build. I don't know when or how You will accomplish it, but I will never doubt you again Lord. Thank you so much for my renewed hope and faith. You have filled my soul with renewed vigor, happiness, and hope . . ."

In his joy and happiness Pastor Bob didn't see the van full of teenagers who in turn didn't see the red light ahead of them. The driver was bending over to pick up a CD he had dropped when his passengers screamed, "Watch out!" His van shot into the intersection and collided with Pastor Bob's car right at the driver's door. The next words out of Pastor's Bob's mouth would be said directly to the face of Jesus Himself. Bob's duties on earth were finished and his rewards would be beyond even his active imagination.

The angel, Aegis, had watched over Pastor Bob these many years and was very proud to escort him to the waiting arms of Jesus. As Jesus hugged Bobby and Bobby enthusiastically hugged Him back, tears of joy intermingled on their cheeks. Aegis left Father and child to their reunion and left for the next stage of the operation they all knew as Operation Antidote.

CHAPTER TWENTY-SEVEN

SATAN'S ATTACK

Satan knew that he was slowly losing his hold on Justin Johnson and he was angry at the knowledge and was swift to discipline his disciples when the need arose. The first thing he did was to strike down his biggest contender for Justin's soul; or so he thought. He orchestrated the demise of Pastor Bob and to his surprise, if truth be told, he succeeded. The car crash finally snuffed out one of his most active adversaries. He reasoned that with Pastor Bob out of the way, Justin would fall in line with his plan as first anticipated. It wasn't the first time that Satan had miscalculated his efforts nor would it be the last.

*   *   *

Amanda saw the change in Justin after this morning's meeting at the funeral home and she feared it. He sat beside her in the limo and was distant and cold toward her. Yet she saw in him a growing warmth that she could not explain and feared to search it's meaning too deeply. She knew that he was hurting from his loss but there seemed to be something deeper working in him; something that seemed dangerous yet unidentified.

Even as she sat thinking desperately of how to broach the subject, an aide's phone rang and was answered with, "Senator Johnson's office". He listened for a moment and then turned to the Senator and handed him the phone saying, "It's the State Police for you, Senator."

Justin took the phone and said, "Senator Johnson."

He listened for a moment his face turning even more pale if that were possible and with trembling hand he handed the phone back to the aide.

Amanda whispered, "What is it Justin? What's happened?"

She held her breath as she anticipated that some new catastrophe had befallen their campaign. Justin looked at her and whispered, "That was the police. My brother has just been killed in an accident. Oh God, Amanda, he's dead." He shook with new sobs as a smile crept across Amanda's face.

'Thank the Universal Force!' She thought as she hugged Justin happily. As she pretended to give her husband comfort her thoughts raced, *'With him out of the way, I can get Justin back on track and stop all this nonsense talk of Christianity, love, and Salvation'*.

She hadn't recovered fast enough and had unknowingly allowed Justin to see the smile that passed quickly across her features and he sensed her elation and her thoughts but he hid his own reaction from her as a plan began forming in his newly washed soul. He knew now what he must do. He must become President! He must become what he had pretended to be and more; even if his life would be cut short for his efforts. He had no illusions about the men he dealt with. He knew their power and what they would do once they discovered his betrayal; but they would not discover it soon enough to stop him, of that he was sure. As they drove back to their residence Justin prayed silently, deep in his thoughts, and for the first real time in his life, *'Dear Father in Heaven, I come before You humbly for the first time in my life. My brother, Bob, has tried so hard to reach me and I believe he did so on this last day of his life. Through him, I saw Your love and kindness shining through his eyes. I felt your compassion through his own and I desired it greatly and resented its absence in my own life. You, however, are kind and merciful and have not withheld from me Your Grace and Mercy. I know You have saved me from the Abyss that my sins have created and for that I am eternally grateful. Give me the courage to stay the course now that Your Holy Spirit is instructing me as to my new duties. It is, You, Lord, who places people in power and You who direct them even if they do not know it themselves. I know it now.*

I would have liked to have more time to talk with Bob of these things but I know now that you will guide me through Your own Holy Spirit. My soul has now learned what my brain has always known. The words of your Scripture that were hidden in my heart even as I studied them so as to deceive my public, are even now flowing into my heart and soul and I finally understand what it was that Bob would have me know; the Spirit behind the words. I first ask You, Father, to forgive me all of my sins; and they are many, through the gift that Your Son Jesus gave to me on the cross. I now know and accept Jesus Christ as my Lord and Savior and I ask that You fill me with your Holy Spirit. I am no longer afraid of Him or You and desire Your presence and guidance in my most complicated life. I will do what I can to bring love, joy, and peace to the earth but all through Your Will, Lord, and Your Power.

I will also show love to Amanda and hope that I can win her over to our side before it is too late for her. Thank you Lord for Your goodness and kindness to Your most humble servant.'

At that moment a peace filled Justin's soul. Mr. Summons (Kapre) who sat across from him in the limo smiled and nodded to Justin and it was at that moment that Justin recognized him for what and who he really was and to his further surprise it did not seem strange that the Lord would send an angel to watch over him and perhaps even protect him from evil and harm. So it was that courage was added to his new found peace and the line was now drawn.

*   *   *

Satan stormed, fumed, yelled, stomped, and punished, but he knew that all was lost. He would destroy Justin Johnson if it was the last thing he ever did. He would crush him to pulp and feed him to the vultures. How could this have happened? How could he not have seen it coming? Justin had gone over to the enemy - Just like that! Once done, he was forever out of Satan's spiritual reach but not out his mortal reach. Justin was surrounded by Satan's hoards and he would suffer and die for his treason!

After hours of uncontrolled rage, Satan settled down to aim all of his cunning, evil, and hatred toward one man; Justin Johnson; traitor and enemy. All of his lofty plans lay in ruin and the enemy now held the high ground. Satan had once again played right into the hand dealt to him by God. Would he ever best him in just one plan? *'Yes! Of course I will! What am I thinking? Of course I will!'* But he never would.

* * *

Justin was at the same time repulsed and drawn to Amanda. She was still what he once was and he knew that he would have to treat her as a fragile flower. She could yet bloom as God had always intended for her to bloom but she could also just as easily wilt if she rejected God's invitation. How to reach her was now the largest question on his mind.

Their limo wove its way through the streets of Chicago as they held one another, Justin with love and tenderness and Amanda with bitterness and fear. *'What has happened to Justin? He is a stranger to me now and I don't know what to do with him. Is it just the strain of losing his father and then his brother so closely together? No, there is more to it and I'm afraid that his brother has infected his soul with this Christianity non-sense somehow. But how damaged is he? Can I win him back? Can I keep him on track?'* These and many other questions raced through Amanda's desperate mind as they pulled into the residence and office complex of Illumine, Inc.

Their footsteps echoed in the parking garage as the couple and their servant Mr. Summons walked toward the elevator. Amanda was smiling (not easy at the moment) and was holding lovingly onto Justin's arm as she asked, "Justin, are you still going to run for President?"

Justin smiled down at her and answered, "Of

course I am honey. Nothing has changed our plans. How we carry them out, however, may change some. I would like to sit down some time after the funerals and discuss our future and some ideas that have just come to me. I think you may find them intriguing to say the least."

The elevator door opened and the three entered as Amanda asked hesitantly, "What kind of ideas honey?"

"Not yet, honey." was all that Justin would say for now.

As the elevator door opened onto their floor Justin asked "Mr. Summons, could I see you in my office for a moment please?"

Mr. Summons, who had already started off toward his own chores, stopped and said, "Well, of course sir."

Justin turned to Amanda and said, "I'll be along soon. I want to talk to you before you get involved in anything this afternoon."

Amanda gave him a quizzical look but nodded and went into their apartment. Justin, with Mr. Summons following walked down to his office and went in. Justin asked Mr. Summons to shut the door and then he went over to one of his large leather armchairs, which sat with its twin in front of the now cold fireplace and sat down, directing Mr. Summons to take the other.

Justin stared at Mr. Summons as if seeing him for the first time and then hesitantly said, "Sir, this is new to me. The Holy Spirit has been communicating to me almost nonstop since I prayed the Salvation prayer on the way home. I understand that you are an a. . ."

Mr. Summons held up his hand palm out (a sign for silence) and got up. He walked to the desk and took a pad of paper and a pencil and came back and retook his chair. He wrote for a moment and then handed the pad to Justin. On it he had written;

> "Your office is bugged sir and I think I know
> what you are about to say. Yes, I'm an
> angel and I have been assigned to protect
> and guide you through the many trials of
> your life. I have many things to tell you but
> we must first get this office swept and we
> must do it ourselves."

Justin nodded and whispered, "Couldn't you just. . ." He waved his hand like a magician with a wand, but Mr. Summons just smiled, took the pad back, threw it into the air and it disappeared as he said, "I could yes, but things must be done conventionally when they can be."

Justin got up and pushed a button on his phone, "Yes, Mr. Johnson?" His secretary, Samantha Bearinger, answered. "Send in the SDDS right away please." (Justin had developed an above average state-of-the-art bug sweeping system, Surveillance Device Detection System, not long after taking control. He had used it once to discover the devices in the office, but hadn't felt the need to again after removing his rivals.) "Yes sir." Samantha frowned; at what she wasn't sure, then it hit her. Justin had never said please to her in the two years since his wife, Amanda, had hired her. One of her many duties, besides secretarial was to keep Amanda informed of things. Since Amanda was head of security for Justin, this was easy. Amanda was the person that she was to contact with any security question, so she picked up the phone and called, "Mrs. Johnson?"

"Yes", Amanda answered, "What is it, Samantha?"

"Mr. Johnson has requested the SDDS, I thought you should know."

"I'll take care of it."

Amanda hung up and thought, *'What are you up to Justin?'*

Justin and Mr. Summons had sat patiently and talked about the funeral arrangements and about Pastor Bob as brother and friend until Amanda showed up with the SDDS. "What's up?" She said as she entered and started sweeping the office.

Justin stood up and took the sensing unit from her and said, "I'll take care of it, honey." Amanda frowned and was about to protest but Justin just said, "Be patient, honey and I'll talk to you shortly. I just want a few private moments with Mr. Summons here and then I'll call for you. We have a lot of plans to make Amanda, so be ready."

Justin smiled at her and though she was apprehensive, she nonetheless obeyed and shut the door behind her as she left the room. It just took five minutes for Justin to find the two small "bugs" and reconfigure them as active to whoever was listening, but in reality they were now silent. It took another couple of minutes for the equipment to verify that they were now totally protected and Mr. Summons nodded his agreement of Justin's assessment.

Justin sat down across from Mr. Summons still not sure as to how to approach this subject but as always Mr. Summons made it easy by saying, "Don't be afraid Justin. I have always been here for you and will still be if a bit more openly than I anticipated. If the Holy Spirit, however, has deemed to give you my identity then I shall cooperate with him fully."

Justin took a breath, for he had forgotten to breathe for several heart beats. He looked at his servant, now guardian, with new eyes. He was tall yes, muscular with the look of a warrior more than a servant, *'Funny I never noticed it before this'*, thought Justin as he leaned forward on the edge of his seat, "How do I address you, sir?"

Kapre sat back comfortably and said, "When we are quite alone you may address me as Kapre, for that is my Angelic name, but in public treat me no differently than you did before. In the world's eyes I must still be your faithful servant, Mr. Summons. Also, Amanda must not know my true identity unless she makes a profession of faith and would not believe you in any case until she did; agreed?"

Justin nodded, "Yes, certainly, but I may find it difficult to treat you the same now that I know that you are an angel from Heaven. Before we get into specifics of my future could you tell me what Heaven is like?"

"I'm sorry, but it would be like trying to describe blue to a person born blind. Worse it would be like describing what life in the world will be like to a baby still in the womb. I won't leave you totally unanswered, however, for I will tell you that living in Heaven is being immersed in the presence of God forever. That will have to suffice as an explanation for now, however."

Justin understood even if he was a bit disappointed. "Well, to the subject at hand then. As you know, I will begin my bid for the Presidency of the United States at the end of this year, or at least that was my plan before this morning. Now, it's still God's will for me as far as I can tell, but there are several problems, with my new life in Jesus being thrown into the mix. How can I be an effective politician with this new burden of being honest and upfront? I must be Christ-like and the powers-that-be will not like it one bit. They will fight me once my stance is clear and if they can't stop me they will try to kill me. I've seen it done and have even been a party to it. Then there is the problem of the fake attempt on my life that we set up. . ."

Kapre smiled, "As for that, it wasn't fake, Justin. The assassin had every intention of killing you until I deflected the bullet to a less lethal portion of your body."

Justin turned pale and sat back; his mighty brain working double-time to absorb this new information. After a moment Kapre continued, "Amanda knew it was real as well as some on your committee. You are already a target for those of the enemy who are jealous of you so you won't be in any more danger than you were before; less actually since you are now saved and the loss of your life won't now lead to the eternal loss of your soul as it most certainly would have until today. You have caused me to hold my own breath more than once.

The Lord has ordained that you will be the next President and in years to come you will be much more than that. He has given you the talent to bring much relief to the human race through research and the healing of the body. Up to now you have been using that talent to destroy and kill but you have been forgiven for those despicable acts and you should try to put that behind you now. Search your vast memory of the Scriptures, which you could not help but memorize at your first glance and you will find that there are many stories of men and women who started out poorly but by Grace and courage ended on top of their game with God's help. You can be one of those men with God's help and that is why I'm here. I will help with advice and protection as I'm directed by my Lord. I ask only that you listen and measure my counsel carefully before you act. Your freewill has not nor will it ever be impeded by me or your God but you would be wise to follow our directions carefully if you want the best results allowed to you.

My first advice to you will be to allow the bad things you have done in the past to carry you forward into your more informed future. God can turn things that you and others meant for ill into blessings right before your eyes. Accept this as a gift and run with it. As far as your future is concerned, trust the guidance of the Holy Spirit, as it is made known to you directly or indirectly through myself. Try to win Amanda over if you can but be faithful to her in all things for she is still your wife, saved or not.

Shortly you will be introduced to a woman by the name of Kathy Saunders. She is the director of one of Pastor Bob's 'pet' projects called 'The Antidote'. You will also find that she is listed as the sole heir to his vast fortune for he trusted her explicitly."

At the mention of Bob's name Justin became sad, at the mention of inheritance he become instantly angry but he didn't understand why. Kapre didn't miss the expression on Justin's face nor its implications, "Don't take it personally, Justin. Bob wasn't certain you would be saved and this project was very important to him; to all of us. He knew that if anything were to happen to him that Kathy would be the best person to assure that all would move forward as planned.

Anyway, I'm telling you this so that you can help her and The Antidote when you are President and to help them is helping yourself, but I cannot tell you how just yet. Now..."

Kapre stopped short because Justin was staring at him with a blank look, "What's the matter now?"

Justin blinked and then smiled shyly, "I'm sorry, this is just a lot to absorb all of a sudden, even for my abilities. Kapre, have I treated you badly over the years?"

Kapre was in turn surprised at the question but answered readily enough, "I really can't remember Justin for everything you did before today is forgiven and forgotten not only by God but the angels as well. You have a clean slate, my boy, so use it wisely."

Justin was silent for a moment then said, "Thank you, God, and thank you, Kapre. Now, since I know who you really are shouldn't I promote you or something?"

"Being your servant is enough for me, Justin, and it gives me better access to you than most positions would. Just insist on having your personal servant wherever you go and that will do. Remember, not a word to anyone about my real identity. Not everyone gets to see their guardian angel nor do many people even give us much thought, but we don't love them any less. You are being given opportunities that not many people on earth get, but much is being asked of you in return, for one short life. I think that's enough for today. Talk to Amanda and see if you can get through to her.

Remember to love her no matter how she reacts and also remember that you cannot make someone accept what you have accepted. You invite them and then leave them to their own freewill and to God."

Kapre had gotten up and walked to the door during his statement and when he was finished, he turned, opened the door and walked out of the office. Justin looked at the closed door for a long while not really thinking of anything in particular or perhaps everything at once, but eventually he stood up. He felt tired, no, exhausted would be more like it. Justin reached his desk and pushed the intercom button , "Samantha would you ask Amanda to step into my office please?"

"Certainly Mr. Johnson", came Samantha's cheery voice over the line.

Justin walked to his bar and poured himself a drink and fixed Amanda's favorite as well. He stopped in mid mix and thought, *'Now that I'm saved can I drink alcohol?'* He went over everything that he had read and learned over the years and decided that the "Word" says not to drink to excess and that it's not what goes into your mouth but what comes out that makes a man unclean. *'I'll work it all out in time!'* Justin thought as he carried the drinks back to the chairs and waited for Amanda to arrive.

Amanda stormed into the room her green eyes on fire with rage and indignation. Her face was as red as her long hair which was severely pulled back and tied into a ponytail. She paced back and forth in the room after slamming the door behind her. Mumbling something under her breath about what Justin could do with his secret meetings and rubbing elbows with the servants and all this talk about Jesus, she in time finally stopped and turned on the subject of her rage; Justin.

"Justin, what are you thinking? Just what are you planning to do now that you have religion; how am I going to protect you and run a campaign if you're going to throw it all away for that half-wit brother of yours?"

Amanda saw the look that Justin fired at her and she fired first, "Don't you look at me like that Justin Johnson! We have made commitments to some very powerful people. We have made promises that cannot be broken! You choose now? Right before the campaign starts; you pray for forgiveness? You asked God to accept you and you accepted the gift of His Son?"

It was Justin's turn to look surprised and Amanda saw the unasked question in his expression, "You prayed out loud in the car Justin, didn't you know that? You were so sincere, so distant, yet so rapturous that I couldn't bring myself to interrupt you. Oh Justin, tell me that you have come to your senses and that you're not going to get all religious on me now!"

"Amanda, please sit down and take a breath. I don't know exactly what I'm going to do just yet. I still believe that I am to run for President; it's just that instead of faking being the good guy, I really want to be the good guy. I have changed Amanda, instantly, in the twinkling of an eye, I'm no longer who I was. All that I have ever studied about Christianity has become crystal clear in my mind and soul. Jesus Christ really did die for our sins. He died so that we wouldn't have to. Amanda, please try to understand and join me. Ask Jesus into your own heart! He will come in and take away your old self and fill you with His Holy Spirit. Please join me so that we can make the rest of this journey together. Just confess your sins, ask for forgiveness, and accept Jesus Christ as your Savior and yes, it's really that simple!"

Amanda walked over to Justin and slapped his face. Hard! It staggered him. He stumbled back. He remembered something that he had read about turning the other cheek and Amanda slapped him again, just as hard as before, yelling, "Don't ever talk to me about this again, Justin. Do you understand me?"

He nodded and wiped the blood away from the corner of his mouth and then found that tears had overflowed the lids of his eyes and were running down his cheeks. He felt an old anger trying to rise within him - *'How dare she slap me like that! Who does she think she is? I'll never be able to do this if I can't control myself now. I must!'* he thought as he took deep shaky breaths and then a peace and calmness came over his features and Amanda gasped. Standing before her suddenly was a different man than she had known all of these years. There was a depth about him that actually caused her fear and yet she was drawn to him almost against her will. She was fascinated by something deep within him that she as yet couldn't recognize or experience. Thoughts came into her head uninvited, as she backed toward the door, *'Could all of this be true? Could there really be a God? Could there really be a Holy Spirit that would and could dwell deep within each of us to comfort us, to guide us?'* She wanted that too she suddenly realized. She wanted it, as all humans do, if they are honest with themselves; yet fear welled up in her and she suddenly and desperately wanted to run from the room away from this man, from whatever lurked deep within his eyes.

Her back was against the door now and she slid down and started crying like a baby. *'What's happening to me?'* her thoughts raced as she sat there confused. She sat there crying, tears of shame filling the hands that covered her face; not only shame, but her shame? *'Why am I feeling shame?'* She thought as Justin came over and sat on the floor next to her. She turned to him and buried her face in his shoulder and wept cleansing tears that racked her body for some minutes.

Justin just held her afraid to speak or even to breathe. *'What do I do now Lord?'* His thoughts raced as he watched God work right before his very eyes. As Amanda raised her eyes to look into his, it was his turn to gasp. He saw terror in her eyes. She was afraid and looked trapped. At first Amanda's lips moved but no sound came out. Then as Justin leaned closer he heard her croak out a whisper, "Help me, Justin! I don't know how. I want to have what I see in you, but I just don't know where to start." Justin held her to him, a ray of hope welling up in his heart. A growing joy that he couldn't identify was filling his soul. They faced each other, knees touching, still holding hands and Justin began to confess to Amanda everything that he had ever done, including, yet again, the murder of her brother, along with many other things that shocked Amanda, yet made her feel closer to Justin than she ever had. Then Amanda to her surprise confessed everything that she had ever done or thought to do to Justin and for him including the details of her father's murder. It was his turn to be shocked but not appalled. When they had unloaded every sin they could think of Amanda then said, "Justin I am truly sorry for deceiving you. I am sorry that I was a party to your assassination attempt, one that was real, not fake. You were supposed to die and I knew it."

Justin began, "Su..., Someone told me that you knew." She stared into his sympathetic green eyes, her shoulders slumped forward with the weight of her sins and she whispered, "Yes, Justin, I knew! I had thoughts of taking all for myself but was truly glad that we failed in our attempt, if that helps anything." She waited for what seemed an eternity, until Justin finally smiled and said, "I'll forgive you if you'll forgive me." Amanda held him tight and laughed, "Yes! Justin I forgive you. Do you really think that God will forgive me too?"

"Amanda I know He has forgiven us both, but let's ask him now anyway."

Amanda kept her face buried in Justin's shoulder and began hesitantly to pray, "God you have heard my many sins, will you please forgive me as your son, Jesus Christ, has promised me that You would? Jesus will you come into my heart and life and fill me with the same Holy Spirit that I have witnessed in Justin's eyes tonight?" (Let me pause for a moment in my story telling, dear reader, and ask you this life altering question; have you prayed that prayer in your life yet? Now is the time. Do not delay another moment, so when you see the Lord next, you can tell Him, 'Yes, I was invited and I responded in the affirmative before it was too late.' His Grace will accomplish all else that is needed. Welcome to the Kingdom of God which is as close as your soul. Now, allow me if you will, to continue with our story.)

They continued to hold each other on the floor in front of the office door as a peace fell upon them and a deep peaceful sleep enveloped them.

Kapre watched with satisfaction as Amanda's demon, Sway, flew from the room in terror, screaming that he would be flayed alive for this failure on his part. He thought as he fled, *'How is this done? We took every precaution! This can't be happening!'*

As he left Pastor Bob's angel Aegis was suddenly standing next to Kapre who said, "Well Aegis did you get Bob home?"

Ageis smiled and just nodded and then added, "I'm assigned here now. Strange isn't it Kapre?"

"What's that Aegis?"

"Just how clean and fresh a room feels after the Salvation of a soul is performed by the Spirit?"

"Fresh as a spring day." said Kapre as both angels enjoyed the peace of watching their newly born charges sleep like the babes they were.

*   *   *

The pleasure and joy of the angels had not diminished at all when the sun slowly peeked through the tinted windows of Justin's office. The only two humans in the room were still wrapped in the peace of sleep and in each other's arms. Their backs still leaned against the door of the office, so it was quite a surprise to them when they were awakened by Mr. Summons, who said, "Time to wake up sleepy heads.", as he laid a tray on the small table between the two leather armchairs. On the tray was a silver coffee pot, two cups, cream and sugar dispensers (also silver), and two plates of French Toast with pre-warmed maple syrup already steaming on top of the pats of butter which were just melting enough to spread out over the top of the toast.

The couple became aware of the smells of toast and coffee even before they were aware of Mr. Summons. Amanda was the first to jump up and ask suspiciously, "How did you get in here, Summons?"

Her security instincts had told her that they had been leaning against the only door into the office.

Mr. Summons smiled, winked at Justin and then calmly announced, "I'm an angel, Amanda. One of the perks is passing through solid objects undetected."

Amanda's mind could not wrap around that as she said, "I don't care. . .", then her mind caught up and with her mouth still open she just stared first at Mr. Summons then she turned her attention to Justin who simply shrugged his shoulders.

Amanda finally wiped her sore eyes and walked over to one of the leather chairs and sat down. Then she looked up and said, "Look, up until last night I didn't really even believe in God but I suddenly found myself asking Him for forgiveness and accepting His Son Jesus into my heart. I still don't know why but it did and does feel right. Now, however, you are asking me to believe that Justin's servant of several years is really his what; Guardian angel?"

Summons smiled and said, "Yes, that is exactly what I want you to believe; no, that's what you really need to believe."

"I may need help there." Amanda said as she poured coffee for herself and Justin who had taken the other armchair during their exchange.

"I was given permission to tell you about myself so that you would be able to believe faster and therefore be able to help Justin in the years ahead with his mission, which incidentally is also your mission now. I am also able to tell you that you have a guardian angel as well Amanda; his name is Aegis."

Justin perked up and asked, "That means guard doesn't it?"

Summons smiled as he answered, "It also means preservation and that is how it pertains to him."

Amanda was trying to remain calm, not wanting to lose her new-found peace, but she was having trouble believing any of this, "You don't seriously believe all this do you Justin?"

"Yes, as a matter of fact I do Amanda; in God, in angels, in Salvation."

"I want to Justin, I. . ." Amanda broke off to take a drink of coffee just as a brilliant light caused both she and Justin to cover their eyes.

Mr. Summons broke in, "My real name is Kapre, Amanda. It means young or innocent in our language. Our Master has allowed me to show myself to you in my true form but not completely. To see me fully as I am would kill you just as dead as if you saw God in His true form. You will one day but not in your present form."

Amanda had just taken a sip of hot coffee as Kapre was talking and she spat it all out, dropped the cup and fell to her face just as Kapre began to speak and his luminescent form seemed to fill the room. It was more than just the light that filled her heart and that of Justin with fear. There was a presence that penetrated their very being and caused, well, fear in their very souls. They buried their heads in their folded arms and shook from head to toe, then suddenly just Mr. Summons was standing there again saying, "Fear not my children for I am here to protect you, not to hurt you."

They still couldn't move. Their minds were trying to make sense of what they had seen. Summons/Kapre had begun to glow suddenly, then the flash of blinding light which immediately disoriented them both. Through the light they saw a beautiful being of light from which emitted a power that neither had ever felt before. It began to crush them and they thought that they would surely die just from looking at this being. They felt shame at being a mere human and they felt unworthy of life itself. It wasn't clear to them when exactly they had ended up on the floor, but after Kapre spoke softly to them, "not to fear" they tentatively looked up and then slowly got up.

Kapre asked Amanda, "Do you believe me now?"

It took two tries for Amanda to get the words out but she finally said, "Yes, Kapre, I most certainly do. I would ask though, why don't you show yourselves to everyone so that everyone will believe?"

"Faith is needed in most cases. Our Master in His infinite wisdom says that He wants people to believe because of faith and the testimony of others. Very few humans ever get to see an angel and of those that do, fewer ever get to tell about it. You two, for instance, are asked not to speak of us except to each other. You are asked not to speak even to other Christians about it. Very few people would believe you anyway and you will have enough burdens piled into your lives as it is without adding the complications of that one.

"I'd like to get back to your mission for a moment if I may?"

Both humans nodded and sat there waiting for whatever information Kapre was willing to give up, "Justin is to be President of the United States, Amanda." Amanda started to speak but Kapre stopped her when he raised his hand palm out, "I know the objections you will have but this is where your new-found faith must kick in and you allow our Father to do His work. Everything is possible through Him who sustains us, Amanda. He has declared this to be true and so it will be. You, Amanda, will be First Lady and you will have the opportunity to do much good during Justin's two terms in office. Justin you also have much good to do then and after. There will be many trials but God has allowed you this inside information so that you will both have the courage necessary to carry out His plan. I will also be around to help you through it all."

Amanda asked, "Will I get to meet my own guardian angel, Kapre?"

"Alas no, Amanda; He wanted to show himself as well but the Lord said no. You will, of course, meet him on the other side someday, but not yet."

"What is heaven like Kapre?"

"Nothing you could ever comprehend, Amanda, but anything that you could ever wish for.", Kapre wished he could describe it to them but there were just no words that could really do it justice, "Now, one final warning - You may call me Kapre when we are alone in a secure room, but all other times just treat me as the servant, Mr. Summons, O.K.?"

They both nodded and became aware that their stomachs were actually unknotting from the newly formed faith and knowledge that had entered their souls. The breakfast, untouched and now forgotten was cleared away by Mr. Summons, who was back in human form, as the couple left the office to get cleaned up and prepare for the painful, exciting and intriguing days ahead.

CHAPTER TWENTY-EIGHT

NEW FRIENDS

The board members were there with their sons and their wives if they had one or an "escort" if they did not or if their wife was out of town. It looked like a Gala of "Who's Who" instead of a man's wake. Everyone who was anyone had to be seen there or be in danger of being ostracized from their society. Mr. Johnson had been embalmed by the best as could be seen by his peaceful, almost life-like appearance. He was dressed in a tuxedo complete down to his patent-leather shoes which of course were hidden beneath the closed lower lid of the coffin. His upper half, however, looked as though he had just laid down for a nap right before or after a dinner party and that he might arise at any moment and participate in the festivities. And festivities they were; with everyone drinking Champaign, eating caviar, and doing business as usual; same game different players. When one player dies another takes his place; in this case Justin Schaefer Johnson had already been given "most" of the power in Illumin, Inc. but now with Mr. Johnson's death, "all" interest, properties, and under-the-table agreements pass directly to Justin, or to stay with the mood of the event Senator Johnson; for it was all very formal and cold? Yes, cold would catch the mood just fine and if anyone thought that the mood could not get much colder they had not yet seen Senator and Mrs. Johnson.

When the couple entered the room everyone stopped to smile their sympathy at the passing couple, but as they passed a strange thing happened. Every smile and bright pleading look changed as the couple passed; they changed into a dark, angry, even hatred-ridden sneer followed by an even deeper sense of fear. If anyone had been watching from a distance they would have thought it much like a sunny, flower blessed valley overtaken by a sudden and severe thunderstorm. Each person in their turn from the lowest to the highest felt the hatred and then fear for feeling the hatred. It was not safe to hate a man as powerful as the Senator. Each was afraid that he would read their feelings in their faces so consequently they turned away from the couple as they passed so that by the time the couple reached the casket everyone in the room had their backs to the couple except for Mr. Johnson of course who could neither feel nor move any longer.

By the time the couple had paid their respects and had turned around, however, the mood had passed and everyone was back in their "suck-up" mode. Hands were clasped loosely, firmly or luke-warmly (none of the importance of which was lost on the highly trained couple). Condolences were given and maneuvering for position had begun. As they dealt with the couple of the hour, everyone recognized that a change had come over them, but not the reason for it. They could not see their own personal demons cringing and leaning as far away from their charges as they could and still maintain control of them. They couldn't see {as the demons most certainly could}, that this couple was now filled to overflowing with the Holy Spirit, yet they knew that there was something quite different in their demeanor.

Justin leaned over to Amanda and whispered, "Don't look now but Brice Saunders Jr. at two o'clock approaching with his latest conquest no doubt."

Amanda looked up and to her right and saw Brice walking toward them with a woman on his arm. She looked to be in her early thirties, dressed in a blue evening gown that made her pale cream-colored skin look even paler. Yet, the same pale skin made her short-cut brown hair and her hazel eyes even more distinct. She was a beautiful woman when all her attributes were added up and Amanda took note of the men checking her out as she passed.

Brice Saunders Sr. had passed just last year and Brice Jr. had made a good replacement on the committee since that time. He was known for his dating habits and since he was short, chubby, and not all that attractive, it amazed the other men of the committee that he always seemed to attract the most beautiful of women.

Brice beamed his best smile as he approached the couple and said as he finally arrived in front of them, "Justin. Amanda. I would like to introduce to you my cousin, Kathy Saunders. Kathy this is Senator and Mrs. Johnson."

Kathy shook hands first with Amanda and then with Justin. Their grasp lingered as they stared into each other's eyes. The pause lasted just long enough for jealousy to rear its ugly head in Amanda's heart, then they let go of their hands and the moment passed in silence as Kathy spoke, "It is very nice to finally meet you both. Your brother, Pastor Bob, has told me so very much about you both. I am very sorry about your loss, Senator. I didn't know your father but I know how much it hurts to lose a father; mine passed two years ago next month. The loss of your brother is very dear to my own heart for he was a very good friend of the family."

Brice interrupted, "He was much more than that Kathy, surely, for him to leave you all of his fortune, estates, and holdings."

To everyone's surprise, Kathy slapped Brice on the face as she spoke in deadly earnest, "Brice Saunders Jr. you have a dirty mind to imply that there was anything but deep respect and brotherly love between Pastor Bob and myself. He was always a gentleman to me unlike certain other people I could name!"

Senator Johnson tried to save Brice from digging himself in any deeper by saying, "I knew my brother well enough to believe you, Miss Saunders, and I apologize for Brice's rudeness." He gave Brice a look that chilled the young man's heart and inflamed Amanda's own.

Brice, not being all that bright tried to recover by saying, "I just thought. . ."

Kathy cut him off by slapping him again and yelling, "I know exactly what you think and you can just keep that filth to yourself!"

Brice rubbed his cheek and slunk away before any more damage could be done.

Kathy turned to the couple and apologized, "I am very sorry for my behavior but I have wanted to do that since we were children when I caught Brice peeping into my bedroom window one night as I changed for bed. I haven't much cared for him since I'm afraid. When he insulted Pastor Bob I just couldn't hold back. Again, I'm sorry for my lack of control. . ."

It was Amanda's turn to interrupt, "Nonsense, my dear, Brice is a slug and has been getting slapped like that since I have known him. I, myself, may have slapped him a time or two except for the fear that I couldn't stop at a mere slap."

That brought a chuckle from both Justin and Kathy. Justin's brain had been spinning since the mention of Kathy's name until he finally remembered that it was Mr. Summons who had just mentioned her name to him, "Kathy, aren't you the director of The Antidote?"

Kathy smiled and her face held an expression of surprise as she said, "Yes, I am. As a matter of fact, I have directed The Antidote for about ten years now. Were you aware Senator, that Pastor Bob built the facility for you to personally have a place in which to do your research?"

"Yes, I have just recently become aware of that fact."

This caused Amanda to give Justin a quizzical look, "I wasn't aware of that Justin."

Kathy stated innocently enough, "I would like to invite you both to visit the facility as soon as you can fit it into your busy schedules."

Amanda became aware that Kathy was a potential friend to her husband and on a deep instinctual level knew that her husband's future safety may count on this woman. Her old self found it impossible to trust anyone but her new spirit seemed to find trust reluctantly but not impossibly. Yes, trust and gratitude grew quickly in Amanda's heart toward this woman and she instinctively reached out to her "Kathy, we would be more than happy to visit you at The Antidote. I'll have my secretary call yours and make the arrangements."

This pleasantly surprised Justin as he added, "Yes,

it is about time that I see the place that is doing our governmental research on the immune system isn't it?"

For a second time Kathy was surprised, "You know about our CDC contracts?"

"Yes, I was on the Appropriations Committee that approved and recommended the research to the Senate. I'm very glad to see that the research is in your hands. I believed then and more so now that if my brother trusted you, that you could certainly be trusted, but until his death I'm afraid I was never personally attentive to the details once my committee's part in it was played out."

Kathy smiled and said in parting, "Again, it was very nice meeting you both and I will see you again tomorrow night at Pastor Bob's visitation." then as an afterthought, "I will see you both there won't I?"

The Senator understood her doubt but assured her, "Yes Kathy, my brother and I made peace the very morning that he died. As a matter of fact. . ." Now he drew closer after looking around and whispered in her ear, "Amanda and I were both saved just last night. We will need to talk to you about what to do next, but let's wait until tomorrow night shall we?"

Kathy stepped back as if slapped. Her stunned expression brought sudden joy and laughter from the newly saved couple and it was Amanda who said, "Yes, Kathy, God does work in mysterious and miraculous ways as I understand you have experienced in your own life."

Kathy smiled, pleased with this new turn of events, and after giving both Justin and Amanda a big hug, followed by a big kiss on each cheek, she then said as she walked away, "Till tomorrow then; brother. Sister;

and by the way Pastor Bob never entertained any doubts about this outcome" She fairly beamed with happiness for Pastor Bob and the couple that he had somehow lead to the Lord just before his sudden death.

The rest of the evening was full more of politics than mourning but it was finally over and the young couple went home to continue the mourning process and to forge new plans.

*   *   *

As the young couple arrived the next evening for Pastor Bob's visitation they could tell from the start that things would be much different this evening from last evening. For one thing words of sympathy were conveyed in such a way that they carried sincerity and love. The couple, who had entered, was already drained and exhausted from Mr. Johnson's visitation the evening before and the funeral held that very afternoon. They had just had time to go home and change clothes before the limousine was there to pick them up and drop them at the Dorfine Funeral Home once again. From the start there was genuine joy in the fact that they had been "Born again" just two evenings before. No expectations were heaped upon them, instead the relish of pure joy and happiness that two more souls had found their way home into The Kingdom was the main theme of the evening.

Justin and Amanda were escorted around the room by Kathy who introduced them to many of the current and past employees of The Antidote. "Justin. Amanda. This is Jack and Beth Miller. Jack was the Security Director at The Antidote for many years and

Beth was Director at the Alexander Development Corporation, one of Bob's charitable organizations."

The Millers looked to be in their seventies but very well preserved. Jack extended a strong hand to Justin and said, "It is very nice to finally get to meet you Justin, and, of course, you as well Amanda." Beth shook their hands vigorously and expressed her own joy at their meeting and then Kathy moved the couple on to the Melvins' who they learned now had seven children and owned and operated their own Architectural Firm.

"This is my fiancé Stan Peterson" Kathy announced proudly and to Amanda's relief. Justin and Amanda both recognized the "military" way in which Stan carried himself. Stan Peterson they learned was the current "Director of Security" at The Antidote and would be working with them soon to get their clearances confirmed for the visit that was planned for the near future.

The entire evening was a whirlwind of introductions and light-hearted bantering among friends. No talk of business this evening; that could wait for another time which was another difference from last evenings visit. These people seemed more genuinely interested in each other as individual people and what they had been doing with their lives and catching up on ministries and family events rather than what could be gained by the "proper" contacts. They did not maneuver for position or compete for attention from the "bosses" but treated each other as true brothers and sisters in the large family of Jesus Christ. Even though they mourned respectfully for Pastor Bob there was no hopelessness and definitely no callousness among them. Life seemed to carry more meaning to them than mere business, politics, or "out scheming" the competition.

When Justin and Amanda finally had time to concentrate on Bob, they found that through the almost magic skill of the Embalmer, all the trauma of the accident was hidden from their sight and Bob looked as if he was in normal, peaceful sleep. They knew now, through the Holy Spirit most likely, that Bob was at peace with the Lord he had served so faithfully. Money, power, position; these things had never impressed Bob and he had not been corrupted by them in the least. He had been a good steward of the things that the Lord had given to him. This was made apparent by the many "visitors" who streamed by to pay their last respects. They included the young and old, rich and poor, and not a stranger in the bunch, at least to Bob.

Both Justin and Amanda felt a new love and respect for Bob and desired for their own lives to mean as much when it came their time to pass on. Together they promised to help each other to accomplish God's purpose for them if it was at all possible. Justin found that he was even happy that Bob had left his entire fortune, charities, and The Antidote facility to Kathy Saunders. He and Amanda agreed that even though they had only known her for a short time that they could see why Bob had trusted her so completely.

Kathy for her part had felt bad about it and had talked about working something out with Justin, but Justin stopped her and said, "I won't hear any of it, Kathy. Bob trusted you with it because he knew that you would carry on the work and ministries that you had already shared. I have ministries of my own and will not have time to help you for a long time yet. God is leading Amanda and myself in an entirely different direction from you, however, it does look as though we will be working together some. The government contracts with The Antidote to name one, and hopefully in later years I will be able to come there myself to complete the research that I began so many long years ago."

Kathy's radiant smile spoke of her joy at finally hearing those words, "Bob would be so proud and happy right now to hear those words, Justin. He prepared everything with you in mind and when you are ready all the room you need will be made ready for your sole use."

Justin bent over and kissed Kathy on the cheek and to Kathy's surprise so did Amanda. Amanda was able, by the end of the evening, to cast off all jealousy. She knew that she could totally trust Justin with any woman because the Holy Spirit had taught her about trust and that it really did exist.

When Justin and Amanda left the funeral home that evening they were richer by several friends; brothers and sisters. Their hearts were lighter as was the load they had handed off to Jesus as they entered their new ministry. They would now run for President with new agendas and purposes in mind. They no longer feared the Committee though they were no fools to think that their task would be easy or go unopposed.

In the weeks after the funeral they both got baptized and started going to churches wherever they found themselves on Sunday and they began to grow in their faith. At the same time, preparations were made for Justin's announcement of his candidacy for the office of President of the United States.

CHAPTER TWENTY-NINE

TO THE WHITE HOUSE

Two years had now passed since Pastor Bob's funeral and Senator Justin Johnson had still not visited The Antidote; Justin's time just was not his own anymore. Twenty-four months of eighteen hour work days and sometimes more with appearances, talk shows, radio spots, news media promotions, and on and on to infinity. Surprisingly the Committee liked the change in Justin, "Makes him more human, more sellable", they would say; as they added more events to his already inhuman schedule. In the end it worked, however; and on one cold, windy, and rainy evening in early November, he and Amanda got the great news that Senator Justin Johnson was now President-elect Johnson.

They were in their suite of rooms atop the Republican Convention Center in Chicago watching along with the rest of America when the final results were tallied and his opponent; incumbent President Bob Morris officially gave his concession speech becoming the first one-term President in two decades. He came across as a good-sport but all that knew him personally could tell that he was hurt and shocked by the large margin of votes Justin had received.

As Justin and Amanda watched President Morris laid his sword at Justin's feet, figuratively speaking of course, the door of their suite opened and there were suddenly twenty men in black suits pushing everyone out of the way and they surrounded the couple where they sat on the couch. They held their breath as the obvious leader of the group reached into his suit jacket and pulled out a. . . .an ID and badge as he said, "Mr. President, I am Special Agent Robert JoHansen and will lead the "A" team of your protection detail. This is Special Agent Beverly Pickerton and she will be in charge of the First Lady's team. Your code name is "Falcon" Mr. President and yours Mrs. Johnson is "Falconet". You have thirty minutes to freshen up and change, and then we will escort you to the stage area where the nation awaits your victory speech."

"Sir it is our responsibility to keep both of you alive and we would like you both to agree from the start that all and I mean all activities will be cleared through us before you go off to any function, meeting, trip, or even to the bathroom sir. Both you and your staff are being asked from today on to include security in the "loop" so we can plan and execute safety plans well in advance of your going anywhere."

Justin didn't like that and it apparently showed in his features but if he was going to object Agent JoHansen made a preemptive statement cutting him off effectively, "I know, Mr. President, that this is a lot to take in all at once but by law and tradition your protective detail must have your cooperation and take charge from this day forward. Rest assured, sir, that I know my place. I know that you are the boss but it is for that very reason that in matters of security that you try to humor me in this request. When there is more time you will have the opportunity to research each of our files and if you want to request replacements later, that will be well within your rights, but for tonight and the rest of this week, we are it. Do you agree to these terms for now, Mr. President?"

The agent stood at attention waiting patiently for Justin's answer which when it came was a submissive nod and the deal was made; at least for now. Immediately agents thoroughly checked the bathrooms for "bugs" or listening devices of any kind, bombs, or hidden dangers and finding none took up positions outside the bedroom doors, strategic locations throughout the suite and in the hall outside the suite.

Mr. Summons stepped forward and asked that the couple follow him into the large bed and bath complex which adjoined the plush sitting room that they now occupied and pointed out a fresh suit for Justin and dinner gown for Amanda and left them to their privacy, however short-lived it might be.

After a very un-relaxing shower and when they had changed into the awaiting clothes, the couple was literally hustled to the elevators, each surrounded by these strangers that were now apparently in charge of their every movement. Agent JoHansen spoke into his sleeve, "Falcon is on the move" and Agent Pickerton seemed to speak into her watch saying simply, "Falconet, is on the move - same location." The ride down in the elevator was tense and silent. As the car came to a halt the rear door opened into a bright if narrow hallway down which they were again hustled and then through a curtain which to their surprise lead them onto a large stage in the convention hall itself and they suddenly stood before their large uproarious constituency. The roar was deafening but Justin and Amanda held hands as they walked up to the waiting podium.

The agents broke off and took up positions that left them discretely positioned to the sides and rear of the couple. The Teleprompter read; "Wait for applause" and stated "smile and wave, sir.", as if Justin and Amanda hadn't just spent years doing just that.

Suddenly Justin's mind went blank even if his expression did not and smile and wave was all he could think to do in any case. After a long five minute outburst from their adoring fans and workers, during which time Justin's professional life flashed before his mind's eye, the hall slowly became as deafly quite as it had been loud and the time had arrived to speak. The prompter started to roll and years of training luckily kicked in and President-elect Johnson spoke his first words as the newly elected President of the United States.

The speech which was etched into his sharp mind came back as he read the first the words from the prompter but then, as was his habit, continued from memory, "I want to thank President Morris for his kind words and would also wish him all the best for what his life will bring to him in the future." He paused for the applause that followed then continued, "As in the past, many opportunities face us in the months and years ahead and we will face them and solve them together." More applause. "Our campaigns, though heated at times, have for the most part been positive, as will be my term or hopefully terms in office." Many happy shouts of "Eight years! Eight years!" resounded through the hall from the many fans and three minutes passed before Justin could continue. "I am gratified with the large vote of confidence that the American people have given me this evening and I want to assure the citizens of both

Parties that I am their President. I. . ." Standing ovation - longer than hoped for, yet bolstering Justin's confidence he continued, "I want to assure anyone who helped with my long campaign that your efforts will not go unappreciated or unrewarded by my administration which will strive to make America a stronger, healthier and safer place in which to live, work, and raise your families."

"My campaign promises are just that! I promise. . .!" Elation and uproarious applause. "To the press which has always treated me fairly, I promise access like you have never had to date, and as you read these words in print tomorrow you will know that they must be true." Delight from the press and a joy and hope which began to raise in their very souls, showed in their eyes, their nods of approval and their applause. "To our children, I promise that they will finally learn the best lessons, in the best facilities, from the best teachers that money can buy. I challenge educators to turn in my report card one year from my inauguration day." Thunderous applause and "We promise we will. You can count on it.", shouted a good-natured President of the National Teachers Association.

'This next topic is delicate but I ran on this platform, so here it goes,' he thought as he took a deep breath and let it out slowly. As he began to speak a hush of anticipation swept the crowd, "Another issue which has been ripping our country long enough is the fact that every law abiding citizen should have the right to carry a weapon concealed or unconcealed. . ." The roar that arose from the crowd made it impossible to speak so he took the opportunity to sip from the water glass that sat

at his right hand. The water was cold and soothing as it slid down his parched throat. He was surprised to see how steady his hand was. Justin was also surprised that the water was actually lemon-aide; sweet and tart and very refreshing. *'I'll have to find out who the thoughtful person was that gave me my favorite drink and thank them in person, that will brighten their day.'* He had time for another sip and took it as the crowd settled in for some more words that they had been waiting forever to hear from someone who could finally bring about everything they had been promised for so long, "The criminals will always have weapons because they don't care about the law or those who enforce it. Our citizens have voiced the request to help police themselves and I believe they should be given the chance to protect themselves and their families. Most certainly before and since 9/11/2001 numerous citizens have proven themselves quite capable of thwarting hijackings, carjacking, and assaults of many kinds. Let's give them the means to do the job right. Shall we? "

The hysterical crowd tried to break into his speech again, but this time Justin kept on speaking and they were forced to quiet down or miss a possibly historic words, "Some people argue that there may be more shootings if everyone is armed and I agree there might be, but perhaps it will be the criminal who is shot instead of an innocent by-stander like little Jennifer Jackson who was playing at a local McDonalds with her mother looking on. They were having a nice peaceful afternoon outing, when a crazed gunman came in and opened fire. Jenny's mom had to look on helplessly, as her little girl was gunned down in cold-blood. She told me herself that she was defenseless to stop the man and even got shot herself for trying. Ten people died that day and fifteen more were wounded and left behind to remember their loss and the helplessness that they all felt."

As he paused, Justin raised his hand toward the balcony and said as a beautiful young woman stood, arm in sling, "I would like to introduce to you Jenny's courageous mother, Mrs. Josena Jackson."

The crowd stood one and all; the pro and the con, for all respected a courageous spirit, and a grieving mother, and the applause lasted for five minutes. She sat down after a few moments, tears running down her grateful cheeks and once the deafening applause died down, Justin continued, "You know who finally shot and killed the maniac? Yes, the armed police. If anyone of those customers had carried a weapon, much fewer of our citizens would be dead today and wouldn't have had their lives ripped away from them that day. Yes, the maniac would have been shot much sooner and little Jenny could have been spared, for she was the last to die in that group."

Justin looked out over the crowd and noticed that not a dry eye was to be seen in even the most skeptical of his opponents. Taking courage from that fact he continued, "I will ask strongly that both the House and the Senate quickly pass bill number 13687B giving the citizen the right to bear arms as protected by the Constitution of the United States."

There was no holding the pandemonium that followed. Balloons fell from the ceiling, mixed with confetti, the flashes from cameras threatened to give Justin a sun burn and he feared he would see black and white spots before his eyes for the rest of his days. He smiled as he watched the joy of his constituents as they celebrated. He toyed with the idea of ending his speech on this note but he knew that his writers would flip if he left out this next part so he waited patiently for everyone to settle down. He sipped more lemonade as he waited and when he found a large enough gap in the celebration he stepped back up to the microphone and forged on, "Now there are two sides to every story and there are dangers to everyone carrying a weapon; so to address this there will be a one month waiting period to obtain a permit to carry a weapon. The person will have a thorough criminal history check while they take a twenty-four hour gun safety course. They will not be able to carry long guns, machine guns, or any explosive launcher-type weapon of any kind. We want them to protect themselves not blow up an entire block. Hunters, target enthusiasts, sportsmen and competitors can own equipment designated for these areas of interest, such as shotguns, rifles and specialized handguns, but these can only be carried as the law now provides. Handguns will now be allowed out in the general public either strapped to your side or concealed on your person. To those who worry about us going back in time to the Wild West and the quick-draw challenges of old; I say that the same laws that stop the police from just shooting people down will also stop the law-abiding citizen from just shooting first and asking questions later. We are a Nation in which its citizens are asked to have integrity, common sense, and responsibility, so let's give it to them."

Justin paused here for emphasis and the applause filled the silence as he thought it would. He was organizing his thoughts for his next topic, a topic even more controversial than the guns; foreign policy. It came upon him almost unnoticed. A little extra sweating at first, then he noticed that his heart was speeding up against his will and he was powerless to stop it. Nausea hit next, followed by dizziness and shortness of breath. He picked up the pitcher next to the glass and refilled his glass and took a healthy drink trying to settle his stomach and everything was suddenly normal again. When the glass was half drained again he was ready to start in, "The terrorists of the world are holding their breath tonight to see if getting elected will have changed my resolve to rid the world of their destructive philosophy - let me assure you that it has not!" He looked into the camera as if speaking directly to the world-wide terrorist, Omar Zinnarzer, himself, he pointed at the camera and said, "Omar, I'm coming after you sir, and I will hold you personally responsible for any further attacks on this country!" He shouted this last part and held his pose for emphasis, then continued, "Not since September 11, 2001, has anyone dared to attack our country so vilely and cowardly as you have done just last month when your handy work in Chicago, Illinois toppled the John Hancock Center destroying Water Tower Place and severely damaging surrounding structures. Also, your failed attempt at exploding a nuclear weapon on United States soil resulted in a dirty bomb that only temporally disrupted downtown Michigan Avenue and Lake Shore activities. For this you will pay sir and dearly!"

Justin knew that he would probably have won the election anyway but not by the large margin he had done if President Morris had reacted more forcibly to this vile act. Instead of taking quick and forceful action as President Bush had done years ago he hesitated and tried to negotiate a settlement with Omar which backfired in his face and lost him any chance of retaining his office.

He held himself up using the podium and tried to continue but the wave of nausea which overtook him also robbed Justin of consciousness and the newly elected President collapsed in front of an entirely shocked nation. Medical teams that are always on hand but very seldom used and never seen; rushed onto the stage and surrounded Justin and were in turn surrounded by the Secret Service; thus ended President-elect Justin Johnson's first speech to the nation.

*   *   *

Later at the hospital the answers that the doctors needed were obtained because of Agent JoHansen's quick thinking. When the new President-elect collapsed JoHansen kept his cool and his team collected the pitcher and glass from which Justin had been drinking. It was transported to the hospital along with Justin and at his insistence was tested to see what it might contain. The answers were as surprising as they were shocking.

The news aired on all of the networks, who however sympathetic and sad, had to carry news of this magnitude. As it always had, the news monopolized all networks and preempted all previously scheduled programs.

Patricia Perkins once again found herself covering

an assassination attempt on the person of Justin Johnson. She had her technicians dig up the old footage of then Senator Johnson being shot and then added the earlier scenes of his speech and his eventual collapse and with true emotion as well as respect, but with the theatrical expertise for which she was so famous, she reported everything that they would release from the hospital, which was far too diminutive for her appetite.

She sat at her desk in the studio and continued her report as new information arrived. Sitting next to her was a woman dressed in a white doctor's coat. Patricia spoke, "This just in from an undisclosed hospital here in Chicago. The doctors have now determined that the lemon-aide that President-elect Johnson had ingested during his monumental speech was laced with Propafenone, Lanoxin, and Metoprolol. Joining me here is Dr. Beatrice Moltice a prominent heart surgeon in her own right. Doctor what can you tell us about these drugs?"

She turned to the doctor who said, "Patricia, all three of those drugs have been used for many years on patients that have suffered heart failure or irregular heartbeats and they have allowed many to live longer more productive lives. Given to a healthy person, however, a strong dose of those combined drugs can very easily bring on the very heart attack or irregular heart beat that they were made to prevent."

Patricia asked, "Doctor Moltice what are the chances that these drugs might cause death?"

"Unfortunately, Patricia, a sudden introduction of these drugs into a healthy body can very easily cause death. The dosage is the key of course. Just how much did the President-elect drink?"

Patricia had the answer waiting, "We have looked at the video of the speech again and have determined that he had consumed almost two full glasses before he collapsed. Can he survive this dosage doctor?"

"Patricia I cannot say without also knowing the concentration levels and how fast the counter measures have been administered. . ."

"I hate to interrupt Doctor but we are getting network feed that we must air now." Patricia turned to the camera and said, "We now join a taped broadcast from terrorist Omar Zinnarzer".

On screen across America and the world for that matter; a short, rather fat man in a white robe sat on the floor behind a small table. His face was hidden by a large, rather wild beard; he wore a turban and had small spectacles on the tip of his nose as he read a prepared statement. He spoke in a dialect that most people could not follow but an interpreter was dubbed over his words so all could understand him and grew very quickly to fear him.

"I am Omar Zinnarzer, religious leader of the Muslim world. Where my predecessors have failed I have been successful. It was my agents that reached out and snuffed the life of this Infidel who would attack the Muslim peoples. Allah has reached out his hand and given the victory to me. I warn the American people to take a lesson from tonight's victory. If I can snuff out this powerful man, I can then snuff out the weak-minded infidels that follow him. I warn you now - don't drink your water if you want to live and may Allah be praised." thus ended the first worldwide speech of the new extremist, self-proclaimed leader of the Muslim world.

* * *

    Mr. Summons had gone unnoticed and thus it was easy for him to leave the earth momentarily and return to his Master. When he returned as Kapre, invisible to the doctors who were working frantically on President Johnson, he had no trouble standing at Justin's right shoulder. He placed his hand there while he prayed for his charge as he had done on many occasions before. The Lord had assured him that Justin would live through this ordeal and Kapre's faith held even when a doctor suddenly yelled in a panicked voice, "Flat-line! Charge the paddles!" Someone placed the charged paddles into his waiting hands and he yelled, "Clear!" No one had time to clear before he let-go the charge into Justin's body and Justin's body involuntarily raised itself from the cold stainless steel table on which he lie. Fortunately no one was touching him, however, and the doctor yelled, "Recharge to three hundred!" A nurse yelled, "Charged!" The doctor yelled, "Clear!", once again and let the power pass through Justin's body once more. Nothing happened. He took a long hypodermic needle full of adrenaline and punched it through Justin chest directly into his heart and then zapped him again, and again, and yet once more; nothing.

    The doctors having exhausted all that they could do stood with bowed heads and listened to the solid flat-line beep of the heart monitor. The frustrated doctor yelled, "Shut that thing off!" Then he ripped his gloves off angrily and threw them on the floor. As the nurse reached for the "off" switch on the machine the constant unbroken beep went silent for a second and then began to beat rapidly at first and then to slow into a normal sinus rhythm. The doctor who had already started walking away stopped and listened; not believing what he heard. He and his team rushed back to the table and he yelled, "Vitals!" After listening to them once and after they were repeated to him a second time he laughed. He turned to Agent JoHansen and said, "The President-elect, it would appear, is out of danger. I don't know how, but his vital signs are all back to normal. He's back!"

A sigh of relief passed through the room and the new First Lady was sent for and soon burst through the door. She was angry at having been kept outside through all of this but relieved to learn that her husband was alive. The doctor soon explained, "He will be weak and dizzy for a while longer but the danger has seemed to pass. He should be fine now. "

To their surprise she yelled, "He won't be fine until he can speak to the world and tell them that he is fine. Omar Zinnarzer must know that he has failed! The world must know that he has failed! How soon can he speak?"

The very power of this woman took them all by surprise and no one even thought to argue with her. Well maybe they thought about it but then dismissed it as too dangerous.

Surprisingly it was Justin who answered her question, "As soon as they can bring a clean suit in here for me to wear." JoHansen made it happen. And so it was just twenty minutes later, sitting in a wheel chair, behind a desk in one of the doctor's offices, that Justin again addressed the nation and the world, bringing joy to most but fear to many.

Justin smiled and when he spoke it was as if nothing had really happened, "I'm sorry for the interruption and I hope that this broadcast isn't interfering too much with your normally scheduled programs. Just let me say that Omar Zinnarzer's attempt on my life has failed because he doesn't really serve Allāh al-'Ab (as he calls God), but instead perverts God's very teaching and for this he will suffer at God's own hand. God's right hand, the Lord Jesus Christ will take care of our enemy I am sure. He has given us the skill to fight people like this and we will assuredly use that skill to the best of our ability, have no doubt about it. And Omar, I'm most definitely coming after you with all the skill and resources that a Commander-in-Chief has at his disposal. To this, I will add prayer. Prayer that the Lord Jesus Christ can lead you to Himself before I can get to you! You are, I'm afraid, a mad-dog and must be put down." Here Justin paused to wipe the sweat from his forehead and then continued, "As to the people of America. If you will allow me a few days rest I promise you that I will get back to work as soon as the doctors release me to do so. Thank you."

The camera was cut and Justin passed out once again, but it caused no panic this time for he was only asleep and far from danger. Amanda rushed to his side and hugged him and then followed helplessly as he was wheeled back to intensive care where his vitals would be monitored for a day or two until he could be transferred to his private room which had been prepared and secured immediately upon his arrival.

CHAPTER THIRTY

THE TROUBLE WITH COMMITTEES

All the fathers had either died or retired and the sons and one daughter had taken over but they all retained their family seat on the Illumin Committee, as had been the case for several hundred years. Never before, however, had one, let-alone two of the Committee risen to king or queen, and never had any gone to the White House, personally filling the two most powerful positions in the world.

Special Agents JoHansen and Pickerton had many secrets about Presidents and their wives tucked away in their hearts but even they had been shocked by this new set of secrets with which they had been entrusted. With only one week remaining in the transition period between election and inauguration President-elect and Mrs. Johnson had sworn the Special Agents to secrecy and then told them of the existence of the Committee and the broad power that the group wielded. They had to know if they were to protect the two most powerful people in the world. The agents knew they were powerful but had no idea just how powerful. They were about to find out that if you peeled an onion long enough you would descend through layer after layer of secrets until you finally reached the inevitable core; In this case that core was The Committee and then the leaders of the Committee; President and Mrs. Johnson.

The agents had just spent a week locked in the secret meeting hall of the Committee located far below Johnson Enterprises in Chicago. They now knew the entire sordid history of not only the Committee but of their President and his wife; the murders, the experiments, and all the other illegal activities. They also learned of the couple's transformation through the Saving Grace of Jesus and were convinced of the couple's sincere desire to do what was right by the United States and all humanity across the globe. These weren't the first questionable homicides they had covered up for Presidents nor would they be the last, but the vast scale of activities rivaled anything they had seen to-date. They had ridden a rollercoaster of emotions as they had read through the volumes of secrets that had titillated the world for eons. They learned who had really ordered the Lincoln assassination. They learned who shot President Kennedy and who ordered it and why.

Most importantly they learned that the First Couple controlled the power, the money, and the laws in this country and the world for that matter. At first fear had set in; for how could they be allowed to live with this knowledge? Then they wondered if they had been spoon fed lies that would discredit them if they ever tried to blow the whistle on the Committee. President-elect Johnson assured them that his only motivation was that he needed at least two people who knew everything there was to know and that he could still trust with his life and that of his wife.

The first couple sat across from the agent couple in this secret chamber far below the earth and Justin asked the much anticipated question, "Can we trust you both?

Will you still serve to protect us and help us in the cause set before us, even knowing our sordid and evil past?"

As both couples eyed each other, Justin had his hands resting on a stack of black file folders. Each folder contained the entire history of each of the Committee Members, none of whom were yet known to the agents. Justin had to have their sworn loyalty before he could divulge that last piece of the very complicated puzzle.

Robert JoHansen looked over at his wife Beverly Pickerton and nodded. After a couple more tense moments, she nodded back and Robert turned to Justin and said, "I serve at the pleasure of my President."

Beverly Pickerton looked at First Lady Amanda Dowling Johnson and said, "I serve at the pleasure of my President and the First Lady."

Justin and Amanda smiled first at each other and then at the Agents and Justin continued, "Even when we leave the White House this information must remain secret forever, do you understand and agree?"

More quickly this time the couple nodded and the tenseness of the past week was gone and a new mission was begun.

Justin stood up and paced back and forth for a moment and then stopped and looked at the couple which were now closer than family and said, "We are about to face some unique challenges. To date, the Committee has always had the pleasure of controlling the President of the United States by one method or another. They will try still, but with the added problem that the President and First Lady own most of the shares of the entire organization and hold the two top positions on the Committee. This will be the first time in American history that the President and First Lady may very well influence if not control the Committee, and they are not going to like it. They are going to threaten, back-bite, undercut, and stall any project that I come up with where they disagree. They may get frustrated enough to try to take my life and maybe even Amanda's life, but they mustn't get away with it and that is where you come in. You must not only watch for the usual dangers a President and his family face but you must also monitor the activities of these most powerful men. This you must undertake personally because we cannot afford to bring anyone else into the loop. The Committee must never suspect that you have learned all the things that we have already revealed to you nor what we are about to show you. I need you to know so you can understand my future actions and not suspect my motives. You must trust me no matter what appears to be happening. Amanda and I will be walking a tight-rope unparalleled in history and we will need trusted friends who we can literally trust with our lives. Do you understand?"

Special Agents JoHansen and Pickerton said in unison, "Not really, no, but we do trust you both and will do what you ask without hesitation. We are used to secrets and danger and you have just brought us to a much higher level of clearance than we ever expected to reach or even knew existed, for that matter; but we are on board, of that you can be sure."

Justin and Amanda smiled lovingly at the couple in front of them as Justin pushed the large pile of black folders across to them as he said, "Here is the last of the light reading you will need to commit to memory. Each folder contains all the information you will need to know about each Committee member and their family histories. It's a lot to learn and you only have a couple of more days in which to learn it. I want you to study these in your rooms upstairs while Amanda and I meet with the Committee. These are copies that I want you to burn in your fireplace as you read them. I have people watching the movements of each Committee member, and I'll fill you in later so you can take over their supervision personally. You will need to understand who they are and what they control so you will be able to figure out a strategy to protect us from them as needed.

"Our jobs at the White House are inseparable from our duties to the Committee and we will need to balance them no matter how precariously. Remember, that trust between us is crucial and there will not be time for explanations at the time orders are given. Obey first and any explanation that we can give we will as time and circumstances permit. We will be counting on you two for many things, not least important of which will be to cover for us to the press, the government agencies and especially your subordinate agents as needed. There will be times that we will need to appear to be in one place while we are in reality in another. Agreed?"

The agents just nodded, took the folders and they all left the room.

Mr. Johnson and Mr. Black would have been proud of Justin and Amanda, Christian stain and all, if they had lived long enough to witness their progress.

*   *   *

Everyone was at his or her assigned place at the

conference table when Justin and Amanda arrived. For several months now, Amanda had attended all of the Committee meetings and had even run them in Justin's absence; but for this one, Justin decided that he needed to be present. Justin was the official President of the Committee with Amanda being the Vice-President because together they owned a majority of the organization's stock. They had been on the Committee the longest, even though all the sons of former Committee members have been present from the first arrival of the couple, but had not been voting members themselves till recently. One by one, however, their fathers had either died or retired and all the sons had now become full voting members in their own right.

Fear of Justin and Amanda had not lessened much since "they had gotten themselves saved," because they were still shrewd business tycoons and some didn't know just what being "saved" meant and they weren't about to be the first to find out. In other words, they didn't want to cross Justin or Amanda and they avoided anything that smacked of betrayal. Justin and Amanda knew this and used it to their advantage whenever they could which was most of the time, currently.

Justin and Amanda represented many firsts on the Committee and that made them very valuable commodities as well as all the businesses that they represented. This was the first and only time that the Committee had "real" Christians amongst them, nor had they ever had a President of the United States as their President or a First Lady as their Vice-president. At first, both of these facts made them nervous until they saw an increase in business profits, with the added benefit of reduced violence throughout the organization. Intimidation was replaced with true concern and goodwill toward fellow workers and customers. What a concept! And it worked!

Amanda had "witnessed" only one time; giving them the facts about Jesus and what it meant to be saved and then left it up to them to seek out more information. None had as yet, and no pressure was put on them to do so and that helped them relax for the most part. As a group, they were beginning to see the benefits of a life filled with the Holy Spirit and it wouldn't take much more time before some of them would approach either Amanda or Justin to learn more. As a group, they had witnessed the transformation that being saved had brought upon Justin and Amanda and they were beginning to think that all the negative propaganda that had been forced on them as children, about Christians, might have been exaggerated if not outright lies.

On another front; for the first time the most powerful office in the United States was held by the same man who ran the rest of the world from behind the scenes and it seemed to simplify things considerably. Justin, Christian or not, they felt was the best man for the job. They truly wanted to back Justin and Amanda in the new trend that was creeping slowly into the way they operated.

It was into this new, less hostile and increasingly more trusting atmosphere that Justin and Amanda walked now into calling the meeting to order. They took their seats at the head of the table and the Committee stood as they were accustomed. Justin took a few moments to make eye contact with each member and then began, "As most of you know by now, Amanda and I have become Christians and as such we can no longer follow the customs of our fathers. We ask, therefore, that the Committee members bear with us as we implement a few procedural changes to our meetings. Usually at this time we open with a short meditation to invoke our spirit guides and then ask Lord Lucifer for his guidance. Amanda and I will, of course, use this time to pray to our Lord Jesus Christ and ask for His guidance. You may proceed as you normally do. I think in time you will see that Jesus has more power, love, and wisdom for us than Satan ever did, with rewards that are just as good for you as Satan's were evil. As Amanda has pointed out to each of you, we are available to help you make the transition from one "Master" to the other; all you need do is ask.

With those words, Justin and Amanda bowed their heads and a very uncomfortable minute went by; then two; then three and finally after five minutes, Justin looked up and could tell that in the confusion of the moment, the other members of the Committee had forgotten to meditate or invoke Satan for help. This brought hope to his heart and courage to go on.

Justin began, "I know that when Amanda and I turned our lives over to the Lord that this put fear into your hearts and perhaps some resentment. To your credit, however, I never once got wind of any assassination plots and for that I am grateful. Many of you have even seen the wisdom of the Holy Spirit coming through in our business dealings and have shown enough wisdom not to turn down the profit that it produced."

This broke the ice and everyone laughed and relaxed. They were his Board of Directors again and he felt that they were settling in for business much as they had in the past, before all the changes. Whether occult members or Christians they were all businessmen and he would feed that commonality first.

After addressing many business ventures with his usual skill and to their satisfaction, Justin now turned to his Presidency, "The next item on the agenda is my Presidency. I am aware that I am the first person to hold both the Presidency and the Chair of the Committee. Since our organization is a secret organization the By-laws Committee has ruled that I need not step down. Is this agreeable to everyone?"

He looked around the room and saw nods of assent. He was aware that there had been a long and unfriendly debate about this issue but in the end the vote had been unanimous in his favor. He knew that but still had to make them say so to his face.

"I call for a vote of obedience and loyalty. Amanda?"

Amanda, who as Vice-Chair kept the minutes, now read the names one by one, while Justin watched each of them closely, "Charles Blackard?"

Charles looked up and said, "Aye."

Amanda smiled, "Amanda Dowling Johnson?" She answered herself with a sincere, "Aye."

Then she called, "Roger Jackson?"

He took a little longer which neither Amanda nor Justin missed the significance of, "Aye."

"Brice Saunders Jr.?" To the surprise of all in attendance Brice stood up and said, "I have a few questions first." Angry mutters from around the room, but he pushed through them to continue, "Now be quite and let me speak. I know we had this all out but Justin wasn't here to answer these questions and I believe it to be very important." He stared them down until his eyes rested on Justin who simply nodded for him to continue.

"Justin, we debated for hours about this and what impact you being elected President would have. Then we had to come back and debate further about what impact you and Amanda becoming Christians would have. That as you very well know, flies in the face of tradition and may very well bring the Master's wrath down on us. As yet we haven't felt his sting but that doesn't mean that it isn't coming. I, for one, am very much afraid of him and don't want to find myself fighting him."

Justin smiled and nodded as he began, "First of all let me deal with the first question; that of my being President. I have given it much thought; and as a member of the Committee, you no doubt remember that I have talked at length with you all, but I'll nonetheless give you a short synopsis of that report. As President, I'll be in a very good position to help Illumin, Inc. You will also be in a very good position to help me as well. With me being the same man in both positions, I'll have the same goals in mind as both, therefore, doing away with the usual friction that arises between us and the Presidency. I already know, like every previous President came in time to see; we control all commerce in the world and nothing gets done without going through us. It has always behooved them to cooperate as it does me as well. I, on the other hand, have the inside benefit of making decisions from the perspective of both the President and the Chairman of the Board of Illumin, Inc. and that can only be advantageous to us all.

"Now as to your second question, Brice. How will our being Christian effect things? Well as you can see, it has improved business almost overnight. The God in Heaven has chosen to bless our efforts, if we will only change our tactics. He has asked that we stop our violence, be more charitable, try to really feel compassion for the weaker people of the world and let him help us fight the more evil elements in our world. You are confused into thinking that Christians are weak and that we cannot step up to the plate when opposed by evil; but you are mistaken as you will soon learn when we come to the next subject on the agenda."

Everyone, including Brice, looked down at the agenda and saw the name Omar Zinnarzer and knew that they hadn't reached the hardest subject on the agenda yet.

Justin continued, "Amanda and I have assured you that we would not preach to you about Jesus Christ and what He has done for us but we only ask that you watch how the Lord goes before us and how practical He is. If along the way you want to participate in that mutual love and respect, then we will work with you so that you can get a full share in the Grace that Jesus offers. Does that answer your question Brice?"

Brice was now very uncomfortable and whispered, "Not fully but it will do for now. My vote is, Aye."

There was a sigh of relief around the room and Amanda continued quickly, "Sam Jinkens?" "Aye", was his almost too quick reply; everyone just wanted to get this part over with.

"Alphanzo Ingraham?"

Alphanzo had flown in from Italy for this historic

meeting and would fly back later in the day. He stood and said, "With pleasure! Aye."

"Jason Mooreland?"

"Aye."

"Wilbur Sunbeam?"

"Aye."

"Clinton DuBois?" For this name Amanda turned to the bank of screens on the wall to her right. Clinton had chosen to stay in France and answered from his screen, "Aye."

"Denver Jones, Jr.?"

Denver smiled at Amanda and simply whispered, "Aye."

"Ambassador Ronald Wilkerson?"

Ronald had taken the Ambassadorship to London and had fallen right in with English Society and so was pleased as he said from his own screen on the wall, "Aye."

Amanda said to Justin, "Eleven Ayes! Vote will be unanimous if you vote in the affirmative Justin."

Justin smiled at the Committee and said, "Aye."

Amanda finished, "Vote unanimous! The Committee has just officially given its approval and power to Justin Johnson." Amanda put her pen down and waited for the next item.

Just then Mr. Summons walked into the room pushing a large cart on which were to be found, sandwiches, coffee, iced soft drinks, and cold fruit.

Justin waved a hand toward the cart and said, "A ten minute break to use the restroom, and then help yourselves to some refreshments. No alcohol, I'm afraid, just yet. I want you all thinking clearly for this next few hours.

*   *   *

Special Agents JoHansen and Pickerton lay in their bed and enjoyed their relaxed and blessedly faithful relationship. They had been married for many years now but the joy of the marriage bed was no less intriguing to them than when they first consummated their marriage.

On the way back to their room, they marveled at the size of Illumin, Inc. They also were impressed with the number of children that seemed to fill its enormous Board Walk. They had strolled through the stores and had even been tempted to take in a show, but they knew their duty. After picking up a few needed items, they had found their room and had begun a study of the Black files which had lasted almost non-stop for two days now. Last night, however, they had finished and had fallen into bed together and were instantly asleep. This morning Beverly had awakened first and had no trouble enticing her husband to more romantic pursuits. Later, they were about to call for room service, which they had found was available quite by accident, when the phone rang.

Beverly leaned over Robert and answered it, "Yes."

She sat up suddenly holding the sheet in front of her as if the person on the phone could see her, "Yes, Mr. President. Right away Mr. President."

She hung up and said, almost sadly, "Bob it's time to go. The President-elect will meet us in one hour. We'll just have time for a shower and a quick breakfast." Bob just looked at her till she pushed him out of bed playfully and yelled, "Well! Get moving, mister!"

CHAPTER THIRTY-ONE

OMAR ZINNARZER

Omar looked back at Camella; his sixth out of fifteen wives. Last night had been the second night in a row that he has spent with Camella. He found early that by favoring one wife he made the others jealous; and thus they tried all the harder to please him. Oh yes, they argued amongst themselves but that didn't concern him.

He would shower them with attention one minute and ignore them the next and for some odd reason this rudeness made them try all the harder to please him as well. He ruled his terrorist organization the same way. Omar made others argue amongst themselves and thus they didn't argue with him; not that they would dare, anyway.

Omar thought himself in a fairly good mood considering how his best operatives had bungled his attack against America's newest President. Perhaps his good mood was due to the fact that he had found a scapegoat on which to lay the blame for this failure. It mattered very little who shouldered the blame as long as it was not himself.

The men came to attention as Omar cleared the cave entrance. It still galled him that he had to live out in the desert when he had a perfectly comfortable palace back in the restored and reorganized section of Tehran. At least, he thought it still stood. He knew the bombing would have to come soon. That is always how the Americans react to their attacks. Sting an American and they sting back; it was the way of things.

It had been a hot day but the evening brought its welcome cool breezes which rustled Omar's white robes as he walked into the circle of soldiers that pulled the traitor to his feet. Omar had recalled Ishmar when he had found that the President-elect still lived.

Ishmar was about to plead for his life when Omar yelled, "Silence! Cut out the dog's tongue." One of the men standing by, drew his knife and using tongs, pulled a length of tongue out of the struggling man's mouth and sliced it off with a large curved knife.

They let Ishmar drop to his knees and bleed into the sand. Omar yelled, "See what happens to failures." He pulled his American made .357 Smith & Wesson revolver from his belt, pointed it right at Ishmar's head and pulled the trigger.

When he had replaced the revolver he yelled, "I'll meet with my chiefs in ten minutes." With that, he turned and walked back into the cave he used for his living quarters, which was adjacent to the one he used as his command center.

*   *   *

President Johnson sat at his desk in the newly occupied Oval Office smoking a cigar and enjoying a moment of free time with his Chief of Staff Patricia Meyerson. Patricia had learned in the first month since Justin's Inauguration, not to argue with the President about smoking in the Oval Office; and now that he had taken the oath of office there was no stopping him. The fact that it violated Federal law didn't seem to faze him in the least. As he lit up, she simply pulled a small battery operated fan from her pocket, turned it on and pointed it in the President's direction.

Justin noticed the move and smiled as he said, "You know, I once peeked through the crack in my private office door," he pointed at the one they both knew so well, "And to my surprise; just as soon as I left the office, a maintenance man ran in here and emptied my ashtray, and sprayed the best smelling citrus air freshener I had ever smelled. I have often wondered since if he sits just out of reach of my senses just to spring whenever I leave the office?"

Patricia smiled in turn and said, "He has a pager, Mr. President. Whenever you leave the room he gets paged and the screen reads, 'Citrus - Oval Office', or whichever room it is that you just left. Remind me to bomb our friends in Cuba, if ever you are incapacitated for a few moments."

The President looked up from a brief he was reading, "Why on earth would you want to do that?" he said knowingly.

"Why...for sending you that case of cigars that you thought it such a shame to waste Mr. President."

"This is just one of very few vices that I allow myself, Patricia. You wouldn't want to deprive your President of his vices now would you?"

"Only if I had a say in it Mr. President." She smiled.

They had a good working relationship from the start. Patricia was all business but luckily she did have a sense of humor and needed every bit of it to deal with the work environment around President Justin Johnson.

Patricia was in her sixties, very proper in her dress and in her manners. Tough as nails when need be. Her clear sky-blue eyes shone with intelligence and humor and her gray hair was neatly styled. She could bake cookies for her grandchildren and two hours later give orders like a drill sergeant. Justin was lucky to have her and he knew it.

The phone rang and Patricia answered it, "Yes, We'll be right there."

She hung up the phone and stared off into space for a moment before saying, "They think they've found him, sir. They're waiting for us in the war room."

Justin's cigar had gone out unnoticed some time ago and he absentmindedly placed it in the ashtray as he stood.

Patricia picked up the wooden box that still contained plenty of the subject cigars. Justin found earlier that he was looked upon as more of a man's man to the Joint Chiefs of Staff, gathered awaiting his arrival so they could brief him on the current situation, the first time he offered cigars all around at their first meeting; the ice was broken and he was accepted as one of them. That had been one month ago and now it was a tradition. Patricia bore it like the good-sport that she was and they all laughed good-naturedly at her little fan. They did stick to juices and fruit for snacks as a compromise to Mrs. Meyerson, who had readily proven her worth.

The Generals, Admirals and staff rose as the President entered the room, followed closely by Patricia. They sat seconds after the President took his seat at the head of the table. The leather chairs were large office chairs, stuffed to the max and they sat around a large oval table with a highly polished ebony onyx top. Patricia handed the box to the President and as he removed a cigar, she produced her fan. The box was passed around the table to the "brass" but the staff present had to provide their own smokes.

As Justin lit his cigar, he said between puffs, "The smoking lamp is lit, gentlemen." That was their cue, their permission, to light up in the presence of the President. When in the presence of the President one did nothing first; one waited for the pleasure of the President. Justin, being used to that type of treatment all of his life didn't have as much trouble getting used to it as past Presidents had.

Justin sat back and blew a large billow of smoke into the air and it was sucked up through the silent exhaust fans located in the ceiling. "OK gentlemen, what do you have for me?"

General Mead stood and pointed to the large screen which was located about twenty-two feet in front of the President and stretched from floor to ceiling. A picture became visible and with a pointer the General showed the layout, "Mr. President, what you see here and here", he pointed to the left of the screen, "Is our black-ops teams, who are awaiting your orders to attack." There were two sets of figures; six operatives per group.

Now he pointed to the center of the screen, "This is live infrared feed coming in from the Zagros Mountains of Iran, and this red figure here, according to our intelligence, is Omar Zinnarzer. The smaller figure is one of his wives, and these fifteen in the adjacent area are his personal guards.

"For the past two months since his attempt to kill

you, Mr. President, he and the rest of the world have been expecting you to bomb the h... I mean the heck out of Iran and its allies. Also our intelligence tells us that your total refusal to speak of the attempt and lack of action have him baffled.

"He has just begun to spread the rumor that you are a coward and that he can walk in any time and take America from you."

Justin sat forward and to the surprise of all he was smiling, "I know General what the rumors are and that my approval numbers have dropped from the 97% approval rating down to an my all-time low 54%. One thing my country and my enemies need to learn right from the beginning, however, is that I will not be intimidated into taking action willy-nilly. My reactions will be studied, calculated, and not preceded by a lot of meaningless talk.

"I have always understood, General Mead, that you military types like action, not talk, am I wrong?"

The General and other military leaders smiled to each other and got a chill down their collective spines, as they thought, *'Now here is a man!'*

Justin for his part was thinking, *'What they don't know is that by having The Committee behind you, one doesn't need strong approval numbers and the approval of other country leaders because The Committee controls them.'* What he said, however, was, "When we get done with Mr. Zinnarzer, General, the terrorist community and other less than friendly countries will be less likely to strike out against us. The action you are about to get approval for, coupled by my statement to be delivered with pictures in about one hour, will set all rumors to rest."

The Joint Chiefs, their staff and yes, even Mrs. Meyerson, looked at their Commander-in-Chief with a little more awe and even a bit of fear. They hadn't seen this side of him at all. Not through the campaign, not through the two months of preparation to take office, and definitely not at the Inauguration. They had secretly wondered if Justin could really handle the responsibility of being President. Their doubts had grown when he didn't even show anger at Omar Zinnarzer; but now they saw deep into a cold, calculating mind which had been honed over the years to deal with all aspects of life.

Justin stood and said, "At your convenience, General." He pointed toward the screen, "You may rid the world of one mad dog."

As Justin sat down the General ordered into the microphone, "Team leader Bravo; Operation Stamp out Omar is a green. I repeat, Operation Stamp out Omar is green."

The General sat down and they all watched the screen. The two groups of figures converged on the caves in question. They looked like miniature men and women with transparent skin with red internal organs showing. As they entered the first cave with Omar's personal guard, red projectiles shot out from one group and then the other but none from the personal guards.

Justin watched as the red figures of Omar's guard dropped one or two at a time until they were all prone; dead. Next the two teams converged on the second area in which Omar held the woman, presumably one of his wives, in front of him for protection. More projectiles and both figures dropped like stones; a moment of static and then, "This is team leader. Omar is stamped! I repeat, Omar is stamped; it is confirmed." The two groups left the compound in seconds and were gone when more red figures appeared from the opposite direction.

The screen went blank and all but Justin hooped and hollered and even hugged. They slapped each other's back and held up their cigars in victory. When they realized that Justin hadn't joined them they calmed down and looked nervously toward him.

Justin looked up and smiled coolly, "Don't stop on my account, please. You deserve your victory dance. That was expertly done and I want each member of those teams to receive the Presidential Medal of Valor. Forgive me, but I just don't take pleasure in killing people and I hope I never do, but don't worry, I will always order whatever needs to be done to protect the American People."

Justin stood and walked out, leaving in his wake, men and women who had just witnessed the finest balance of justice and remorse that they had ever seen.

CHAPTER THIRTY-TWO

COMMANDER - IN - CHIEF

Patricia Perkins had been surprised when the President-elect had called her at her WNN office and asked if she would come to Washington and take over duties as his Press Secretary. She was famous in her own right and she knew it would help his popularity (not that it needed any help of course) but none-the-less it wouldn't hurt. WNN was more than happy to give her a leave of absence for the duration of his term(s) of office. (They hoped of course for some exclusives which they would receive).

That's how Press Secretary Patricia Perkins found herself standing in front of the Press Corps waiting for the President of the United States to make his statement. Neither she nor the press got to see a copy of his speech because Justin very seldom had one written. With his memory and the ability he had to think on his feet, he did quite well most of the time. He had speech writers, of course, but even when written, his speeches were only passed out to the press after the speech.

This had brought rumbles from the Press Corps, rival politicians, and even Patricia herself, but to no avail. Justin had proven that he would do things his way and that was that.

It was a surprise then, when Justin had handed her a copy of the speech; no "his" copy of the speech, just thirty minutes ago. She had read it and turned pale. She had just pulled herself together enough to start the news Conference; which would be carried by all the networks. She stepped out onto the newsroom platform located in the White House, and said, "Good evening ladies and gentlemen. As usual copies of the President's speech will be available after the news conference. The President will be making his comments and then leaving with no questions at this time. Later this evening, however, there will be a call-in WNN special interview, 'An hour with the President, himself'. News people as well as the public will be able to call in and ask questions at that time."

Everyone stood as the President entered and walked up to the podium. Patricia proudly announced, "The President of the United States".

"Thank you, Ms. Perkins." Justin looked into the camera for a moment and said, "Please bow your head while I take a moment to thank my higher power, Jesus Christ. You may join me or pray to whomever you worship." He bowed his head and said, "Lord Jesus Christ I want to thank You for delivering us from our enemies this evening. I ask that You give me wisdom and that You always deliver the enemies of the United States into our hands."

He looked up and again just looked out over the crowd for a moment. Just when the silence was getting awkward he began his speech, "At 5:30 p.m. Standard Time, two Special Forces Teams penetrated the stronghold of Omar Zinnarzer and eradicated his personal guard with extreme prejudice. They then proceeded to personally shoot down the coward as he held one of his wives in front of him as a shield. The teams then safely removed themselves from the compound. "

He waited while whispering rose from the Press Corps in front of him. As expected, some were elated and some were appalled. He ignored both reactions as he continued,

"Twenty minutes after our teams successfully removed themselves, the several charges that had been set earlier by our teams successfully exploded, totally eradicating Omar's immediate family, friends, and his top leaders and their families."

"There has been much talk lately about my inactivity or lack of addressing this situation. As you can tell this evening, I am a man of few words when it comes to this type of thing. I have spent my time talking with the leaders of the free world, who like me, are fed up with Terrorists and gave their reluctant approval of the operation.

"Casualties are estimated at about one thousand persons; men, women, and children. The leaders of all Terrorist Organizations were warned that we would be taking action against them for the attempt on my life and the many terrorist attacks around the world which also killed many men, women, and children without any warning. It saddens me that they did not heed these warnings and that they seem to hold their wives and children in such little esteem. The blood of these innocents will fall directly on the heads of these godless and gutless leaders. "

"I stood at the hospital just over two months ago and promised Omar Zinnarzer that I was coming after him. This evening I kept that promise." Justin paused here to take a drink from a water bottle handed to him by Special Agent JoHansen himself. As he took a drink the

Press Corps stood as one body and applauded the President.

When the applause died down and they had regained their seats, the President continued as if nothing had happened, "This is just the beginning of a war that will hopefully end terrorism as an organized activity all over the world. Once we have accomplished this task; the other world leaders and I hope to start working on the other pressing matters that have plagued our world for far too long; hunger, poverty, ignorance, and illness."

Again the drink and the applause, "I have been in contact with the American Farmers; the most productive in the world I might add, and they have agreed to donate literally tons of corn, wheat, and dairy products to alleviate the suffering of our fellow brothers and sisters around the world and I invite other world leaders to follow our example. This will be done with negligible price increases to the world market but will save the lives of millions of our starving brothers and sisters around the world."

The room exploded in applause and cheers both here and in living rooms around the world.

Justin thought, *'This next part caused the Arab Nations to come unwillingly kicking and screaming into the spirit of charity but the Committee did its job well and they finally agreed.'*

To the audience Justin said, "I have been in private negotiations with our Arab brothers and they have agreed to help us offset the cost of giving this food away by selling their surplus oil supplies at just above cost. That will instantly bring the cost of all types of petroleum fuel down drastically."

The Press Corps exploded into applause again and no one could remember so much substance in just one speech. They weren't hearing about promises of what might get done, what might be tried, but rather what had already been accomplished.

"This experiment was tried to see if we could share our wealth and perhaps equalize the conditions and cost of living not only for our own citizenry but also for those more unfortunate than ourselves around the world."

Justin was a bit nervous now but pushed on, "I have been attacked by my fellow Christians who have mistakenly accused me of being the Anti-Christ because I'm working with the world leaders on these many problems." Here Justin leaned toward the camera and whispered, "Really it's because I have not hidden the fact that I drink a beer now and again, and yes I have been known to smoke a cigar or a pipe from time to time. I enjoy a good meal and I enjoy dancing with my wife, as all of you can attest. To the Christians listening tonight I must say, please read Luke 6:43-45."

"To my non-Christian friends, I will not apologize for my belief in Jesus Christ as the only Savior, who alone can bring us to His Father. Please read John 3:16-21 in our Holy Scriptures."

"I must unfortunately come back to the business of Terrorism. On the screen behind me, you will see a group of Terrorists who are creating the Anthrax Virus to release in our country. The estimates are that if they are allowed to complete their mission, no fewer than three hundred thousand of our men, women, and children will die. They will not be allowed to finish, however, due to the excellent combined cooperation of both our intelligence community and that of our allies. What you are about to see was accomplished with a very secret special forces team of just three persons; with the support of course of our armed services as back up. I put the terrorists on notice; that if just one three person team can do this type of damage just what do you think will happen to you when we get really serious? Now, as you watch live from a hidden camera; (he knew that everyone including the terrorists would wonder just how that camera got there; and he would just let them all wonder) as he continued, you will see what will happen to biological Terrorists that do not cease immediately. I would warn you to have your children leave the room at this time. What you are about to see is not pretty."

On the screen several men in white coats, heads covered with white caps, and white masks over their nose and mouth. All that could be seen of them were their eyes and that would be too much in one more minute. They were working in an expensive lab with all of the best equipment.

Justin continued, "The air-born agent we will use to stop these terrorists in their tracks is so top-secret that I can't name it or give details as to how it works, but I have decided to show you what it does."

Just then the terrorists grabbed their throats. Blood began to ooze from the corner of their eyes. Their white caps, masks, and lab coats were soon soaked in blood. Each of the men and women in the lab were dead almost instantly.

Justin looked into the camera as the scene faded, "This was the only warning that terrorists will get. Call it off! If you do not, I will authorize a wide-spread operation that will leave you all looking like these men and women. The choice is yours and the blood is on your heads if you don't stop all plans for violence immediately and may God have mercy on your souls."

With that Justin walked out on a room. It had fallen silent. The news reporters and the world stared at the back of an undisputed Commander- in-Chief. They understood now that he had just declared himself Commander-in-Chief of not one army but two; not one war, but two.

CHAPTER THIRTY-THREE

STATE OF THE UNION
(FIRST YEAR)

Amanda was enjoying being the First Lady. Her new faith in the Lord had given her a genuine love and empathy for people and she was a natural at helping charities. She approached this new task with the same determination that she had her duties at Illumin, Inc., tempered somewhat by the calm and peace that emanated from her these days. She had just flown in from Atlanta, Georgia, where she had dedicated a new children's wing to the fairly new Atlanta Memorial Children's Hospital.

Amanda was in a good mood as she and special agent Pickerton rounded the corner and saw special agent JoHansen standing at attention outside of the door to the Oval Office. She was amazed how this married couple could ignore each other while on duty. Without a word agent Pickerton took up her position opposite her husband as Amanda knocked once and entered the Oval Office.

Justin was leaning back in his chair and reading, as usual, some report or other, but when he saw Amanda enter he jumped up and they were hugging before the door had a chance to close completely behind Amanda.

"Welcome back, honey. How was Atlanta?"

"Oh, Justin it was so happy and so sad at the same time. Those poor kids! Most of them are dying of Cancer or some other wasting type of disease. It's bad enough for adults but those sweet kids. Justin you have to get the labs to continue your work on the eradication of disease as we know it. Please?"

Justin held Amanda at arm's length and smiled down at her and wiped a tear from the corner of her beautiful green eyes as he said, "Amanda, you have become the most loving person I have ever met. Who would have thought that we would actually and truly care about people? The 'old' us wouldn't have."

The couple kissed for a long moment and when they parted Justin said, "I'll see what I can do. Instead of Illumin though, why don't we finally visit The Antidote and see what they have there. I've been thinking a lot about it lately and I think that they may be set up for just that type of research. I can share my ideas with them and get them started in the right direction anyway."

"That will be great, honey, but when could we go. You've got the State of the Union coming up in two weeks and then the Middle East Peace Conference, and then. . ."

"Amanda, I'm the President of the United States, surely I can get a couple of days off for a little working vacation, right?"

They both laughed knowing that it wouldn't be all that easy, President or not, but they had made up their minds and they would see it through somehow.

*   *   *

"Mr. President", Patricia Meyerson; Chief of Staff, had to almost run to keep up with Justin as he took long strides towards the waiting helicopter. Amanda was on board waiting for him as he had been detained with a last minute phone call.

Patricia, forgetting herself in her desperation, actually grabbed the President's shoulder, turning him around and causing him to stumble. She soon found herself in the vice-grip hands of agent JoHansen, "I'm so sorry Mr. President but the Joint Chiefs are insisting that you stay here, just in case the situation in the Middle East flares up, as they expect it will. . ."

Justin's moment of surprise and anger, passed quickly, but must have registered on his features for Patricia had turned white when she stopped to realize what she had done. People had been fired for less. To help ease the moment, Justin smiled. Then he said gently, "Look, Patricia, there will always be one emergency or another to contend with but this trip is just as important. You're my Chief of Staff, so handle it and keep me informed with hourly reports if you have to, but please let me get going. I'll only be gone two days and I still have a week till the State of the Union, so don't worry."

"Yes, of course Mr. President," Patricia said to the President's back as he hurried for the chopper as agent JoHansen released Patricia. Thunder rolled in the distance and the sky was growing dark and a cool breeze brushed her hair with the coming storm. Patricia shivered as she watched the chopper take off and head toward the Antidote Facility. They would make a couple of refueling stops and then straight on to the Antidote.

Neither she nor the President knew of the real storm that was about to hit America.

*   *   *

The Antidote Research Facility, Inc. had been crawling with Secret Service agents and technicians. Administrator Kathy Saunders and her fiancée, Security Chief Stan Peterson, were surprised and impressed with the preparations that went into a visit by the President. Everyone at The Antidote had to submit to background checks and security was tightened even more than usual. Stan cooperated, of course, but chafed at the implication that he didn't have an airtight secure facility.

Kathy's schedule had been radically affected as well. She had spent too much of her time lately running errands for this advance Presidential Team, as they called themselves. They seem to have more authority than God Himself, or so they think as they give orders freely and expect them to be carried out. What shocked Kathy more than it did Stan was when the snipers and other armed guards arrived the day before the President's date of arrival. From armored car patrols at the fifty mile perimeter, the five mile perimeter and just outside the one mile perimeter, to the canine patrols inside the compound, to the snipers on the roof, they had heard they numbered about a thousand men and women all total. There were added to that about one hundred technicians of one kind or another that installed a bank of forty communication links, satellite up-links, and a room full of video monitors, which would give the President the capacity to keep in touch with the world.

Their red arm bands flapped in the early evening desert winds as they stood and waited at the heliport for the President's arrival. They had been told to keep the arm band on for the snipers had orders to shoot anyone on the grounds without one. (They felt as though they meant it too).

They had also been informed that the President and his staff would arrive wearing white arm bands on their arms and that when he arrives they could greet him briefly and then he would be hurried into the safety of the facility.

The air about them suddenly vibrated with the heavy blades of the President's personal helicopter. The thud, thud, thud, of the blades could actually be felt by the awaiting crowd even before the low range thump, thump, thump, was finally heard and the small strobe lights of the black speck could be seen approaching in the darkening sky as it moved quickly toward the facility.

*   *   *

John Black; an expert marksman; had been assigned to Presidential sniper details for three President's now. In all that time he had never had to fire his weapon and hoped he would never have to. The adrenaline flowed unabated each time the President drew close to the secure area, however, and John's alertness was sharp from years of training. The first thing he had been taught was to treat each arrival and departure as if it were his first. It had been good advice for this detail could get boring if you didn't stay sharp.

His position was on top of the single story administration and research facility while the other snipers were located on the two story residential buildings on either side. There were four snipers per building each facing a point on the compass. Since he was a senior sniper he drew the direction that overlooked the heliport. He looked through his scope which he had switched over to night vision. The people below him looked like green figures, each with a bright florescent red arm band. They were made of special material which made them shine for the snipers. To the naked eye they just looked red but anyone trying to match the red would be surprised to know that the snipers wouldn't be able to see a plain red ribbon; that would be a deadly mistake.

John heard a boot scuff behind him. He left his rifle on its tri-pod, drew his .45 auto pistol as he turned onto his back and pointed it at a surprised security guard who yelled, "Wait! I was ordered to bring you coffee."

John's pistol didn't waver as he drew special glasses out of a sleeve pocket and put them on. The man's red ribbon glowed showing its authenticity. John put the glasses back into their assigned pocket and said, "Thanks. Just set it down there", he pointed to a spot to his right. The man did so and withdrew quickly. John watched until the man had passed through the roof entrance door and it latched behind him.

John thought, *'I wish people would stop trying to be nice.'* The coffee was tempting but his standing orders were not to eat or drink anything from anyone just before the arrival of the President. If the other three snipers had followed that rule they might have been alive when the President arrived. The thunder of helicopter blades ruffled the air around John and he put his pistol away and continued to scan the crowd below through the night scope of his FN-A2 sniper rifle.

*　　*　　*

Justin and Amanda looked out the window of their helicopter and were impressed as they watched the fifty mile perimeter fence light up just as the sun slipped below the distant desert horizon. The smaller five mile perimeter fence came into view followed quickly by the facility itself. It was made up of one large single story building which they understood was the actual research facility, with a couple of two story buildings which housed the employees of the facility. Kathy's personal office and apartment was located in the facility itself.

Justin watched absentmindedly as he approached the facility. He had made many of these trips and except for the fact that this was built by Pastor Bob this was just another visit to another of many facilities that demanded the President's personal attention. As they approached, Justin put the reports into his brief case and handed it to his personal aide Peter Highston. He was only twenty years old but had proved very efficient and seemed to anticipate the President's every need even before the President knew he needed it.

Peter said, "Please put this on, Mr. President." He handed him a white ribbon and pointed to his own on his right arm. He then handed one to Amanda just as the helicopter touched down.

*　　*　　*

John Black watched the helicopter through his scope and as it touched down he checked in with command, "Position one check." He heard the others check in and then a nerve was struck when command said into his head phone, "Check in position two, three." But there was only static on the com line.

John watched as the President and his entourage stepped off the aircraft onto the heliport. The waiting crowd began to merge with the President when command yelled, "Condition red - Cover position two and three."

John knew something was wrong, but those positions where on the other two buildings and facing the heliport. One of the other three snipers on each building would have to cover those positions but they would be in place in time.

*   *   *

Justin and Amanda saw Kathy and Stan and smiled as they reached each other and hugged. Justin had forgotten just how beautiful Kathy was. Her Hazel eyes shone with joy, her short, no-nonsense, brown hair wasn't disturbed much by the breeze. She was short but well-proportioned and just full of life.

Amanda was hugging Stan who was still in extremely good physical condition and looked as though he still had his cat-like reflexes.

Kathy said, "Welcome President and Mrs. Johnson to The Antidote."

Just then Agent JoHansen yelled, "Gun", and knocked the President and Kathy down, just as his wife, Agent Pickerton knocked Amanda and Stan down.

*   *   *

John Black had been alert and watched the greeting through his scope. He saw the agents pull their guns and run toward the President and First Lady. He quickly scanned the crowd just in front of the President and saw that everyone had the proper arm bands, but one man, wearing the overalls of a maintenance man was pulling a machine-gun from the unzipped front of his garment.

Without thought he squeezed the trigger.

*   *   *

As Justin hit the pavement he heard a loud retort just as a man in a maintenance outfit yelled, "For the people of Allah!" as he pulled his weapon. Before he could bring his weapon to bear, however, his skull exploded from the impact of the high-velocity sniper's bullet. Justin was struck by the surprise on the man's face as his lifeless body tumbled to the ground. The gun clattered to the ground and all was deathly silent for a moment. Then the agents were manhandling the President and First Lady into the facility.

*   *   *

At that same moment, in St. Louis a timer was counting down; three two, one; the resulting explosions at each base of the St. Louis Arch shook the structure violently. Underground hundreds of tourists died instantly. On the outside the Arch seemed unaffected for a moment or two. Then slowly, unbelievably, the Gateway to the West slowly toppled onto many more tourists. The people in the observation area, who just moments ago had been enjoying the scenery, watched in a surprisingly detached way as they fell six hundred feet to their deaths.

*   *   *

At that same moment, in Washington D. C. the first successful nuclear device to be used against the United States released the fury of its split atoms and lethal neutrons directly over the White House. The structure was crushed instantly as well as vaporizing all organic life. As the plume of the mushroom cloud rose over Washington the destructive wave moved out in all directions destroying buildings and all life within a five mile radius of ground zero. This took just under ten minutes or so but the destructive forces would go on for months in the form of fall out. Fifteen minutes after the explosion, ash and debris fell from the sky mixed with unseen radioactive poisons. The device was a combined thermal nuclear and neutron bomb that had been constructed with ground and then powdered Loadstone as part of its core which enhanced the E(lectro) M(agnetic) P(ulse) characteristics of the device. The resulting EMP destroyed all electronic equipment on the East Coast as well as five states inland. All air, ground and shipping traffic instantly halted paralyzing any attempts at assistance efforts. Planes fell from the sky, trains went out of control (since there were no functioning brake systems), cars stopped functioning where ever they were and all water traffic just floated aimlessly. Everything came to a standstill for a 700 mile radius around Washington. People were stunned and had no idea of what happened given that all communications in the area were destroyed. There was no way to call out and no way to broadcast in.

*   *   *

Peter Highston was shaking. In his twenty years of life, he had never been through such a terrifying few seconds. His tall, lanky, frame was bent over, hands on knees, head down, trying to regain his composure. Sweat beaded up on his forehead, his short brown hair was messed despite its shortness, and his brown eyes were glazed over. Justin had hired him as his assistant because he was a genius with three Doctoral degrees; one being in political science. He had been one of the many orphans who had lived and been educated at Illumin, Inc. Even at twenty Justin could see Peter's potential and wanted to have access to his vast knowledge. Over the last year as President, Justin had found Peter's advice to be precise, accurate, and uncannily prophetic.

Peter had just recently warned him that the Middle East terrorists would try something soon. He had been all to correct. Kathy walked up to Peter and handed him a glass of cold water. Peter looked up, took the cup and said, "Thank you mum," as he took a drink.

They had hustled the President, his wife, and most of his staff into the President's temporary command center in the research facility. They hadn't been there five minutes when the phone rang. Peter answered and listened for a moment and Justin watched as Peter's face turned even paler than it had been.

Peter looked even worse by the time he whispered, "It's for you, Mr. President."

Justin took the phone and assuming it was Patricia Meyerson checking in, "Couldn't wait Patricia?"

"I'm sorry, Mr. President", a male voice said, "This is General Hamerstien at NORAD, Mr. President. I'm sorry to report to you that five minutes ago, terrorists set off explosives at the Arch in St. Louis and totally destroyed it, killing hundreds. At the same moment, an atomic weapon was detonated over the White House causing destruction for about five miles in all directions. The only good news I have to report is that the radioactive cloud is being swept out over the Atlantic Ocean instead of inland.

"We received a call right at the moment of detonation from a man that identified himself as a follower of Omar Zinnarzer and claimed these acts in his name. He told us Mr. President that you had been assassinated as the bombs went off and we were worried until I heard your voice."

Justin had fallen into a chair and found it hard to breathe, as he thought, '*all those people dead? What madness would allow people to do these things? Why was I spared but not them?*' These and many other questions raced through Justin's mind as he tried to process this new chapter of history. The people around Justin wondered what was affecting Justin so radically until he put the phone on speaker-phone and asked, "General what are the casualties?"

"It's too early to say sir, but the experts say that

from ground zero; the White House; that for five miles in all direction anything organic was vaporized. That would mean that everyone in the White House and surrounding buildings are gone. There will probably be survivors a little further out but they will die quickly from the radiation if not removed and treated quickly."

Tears ran down Justin's cheeks, "May God have mercy on their souls. General, are we sure that it was Omar's group?"

"We just have the phone call so far, Mr. President, but Intelligence is looking into it."

"Verify it quickly General and get the Joint Chiefs together. . ."

The General interrupted, "Sir, if you'll remember the Joint Chiefs were at the White House waiting for your return."

Justin felt numb, "Then get the next in line that are still breathing and gather them somewhere safe for a conference call.'

"Yes sir! I'll get back to you."

The line went dead.

No one spoke for a while. Then Justin briefly dished out the information that they hadn't heard and many in the room also sat down. Tears were running freely when Justin finally recovered and said, "All right people, we have to start thinking of what form our response to this monstrosity will take. Peter, as of now, you are my new Chief of Staff."

Peter jumped up and squeaked, "But Mr. President, I'm not old enough yet."

Justin waved his hand in the air and said, "I don't care about your age, but I need your brain so get yourself together mister and start thinking about our response."

"Kathy, may Amanda and I use your office for moment?"

Kathy looked up, drying her red-rimmed eyes and nodded.

Justin said, "I want a secure line routed to her office now." He and Amanda stood and walked out. Kathy led them to her office and then left them alone.

As soon as they were alone, the couple fell into an embrace and wept, praying to God for guidance.

CHAPTER THIRTY-FOUR

OPERATION SANDMAN

One year ago when Omar Zinnarzer made his attempt on Justin's life; then, President-elect Johnson, had studied the problem hard before he made his response. He had decided to make a surgical strike against the man responsible and had as a result taken out Omar and most of his local followers. This had been a warning to the terrorist community not to mess with the United States or this particular President. That warning had not only been ignored but their retaliatory response had been worse than expected by most experts. Peter Highston had been alone in the opinion that they would strike again and that it would be extreme, possibly even nuclear. Though unpopular he would not deny his gut feelings on this and as it turned out he was absolutely right. That was one of the many reasons why the President had promoted him to his Chief of Staff. Another reason was that Operation Sandman had been his idea as well and just as unpopular.

Justin had put the plan into effect and then put it on stand-by when nothing else happened. It had remained in a ready status for almost a year now and that is why only four hours after the attack on America by Iran, President Johnson was ready to make a public announcement.

Patricia Perkins as Press Secretary had accompanied the President along with a small press corps. They had used their connections to get national and even some world coverage of the President's response.

Justin had exercised for an hour to burn off stress as he talked on a headset to his new Joint Chiefs and to some of the Congressmen and women who survived due to being out on the campaign trail instead of in Washington. The same happened with the Senators who survived. They all knew about Operation Sandman and even the ones who had opposed it no longer did. With a green light from the United Nations, given reluctantly, Justin had left the gym and had showered, shaved and dressed in his best business suit.

Kathy's office had been transformed over the last four hours with the Presidential Seal Plaque now hanging on the wall with three American flags on either side. Her desk had been cleared off and small American flags set up on each corner. Justin took a seat at the desk and had three stacks of papers sitting in front of him.

For the past three hours, shocked Americans were joined by equally shocked people from around the world, as they all watched video of the St. Louis and Washington tragedy was described to them in detail. Video had appeared from satellite feeds about an hour before the President went on the air. It showed unprecedented destruction around the District of Columbia (Washington DC). It also showed the monstrous cloud that was finally dissipating over the Atlantic Ocean.

After four hours of coverage and not one statement from the President, the people began to fear that he had indeed been hurt in the reported attack on his life. It also made them ready to listen when he did finally appear on their screens.

A squadron of fighter jets had been assigned to fly the skies around The Antidote and Special Forces were air-dropped to shore up patrols around both perimeters. Any aircraft flying over The Antidote without permission would be shot down without question; for they would have been warned before the fifty mile perimeter.

On screens around the world appeared the beautiful, if serious face of Patricia Perkins; who as the President's Press Secretary had accompanied the President to The Antidote along with the Press Corp; announced, "Ladies and gentleman, the President of the United States."

The picture faded, showed a waving American flag for fifteen seconds and then faded onto the President as he sat at his new desk; in what would become, at least temporarily the New White House.

"To my fellow citizens and to our friends around the world, it is with a heavy heart that I verify all the reports of the cowardly attack on American soil by the Republic of Iran. Hundreds died as a result of an unprovoked attack on the St. Louis Arch; the Gateway to the West. At the same moment, a nuclear detonation leveled Washington DC killing more than half of our Congress men and women and a third of our Senators. With them, hundreds of thousands of American citizens; including service men and women, entire hospitals, schools, office buildings and on and on until it numbs the mind and saddens the heart. I would ask that we have a minute of silence to ask our God to bless them on their journey home." Justin watched the second hand on his watch as he bent his own head to ask for God's help.

Exactly one minute later, he continued, "An attempt was also made on my own life and my entourage by an assassin at an undisclosed location. I am happy to report that at least that attempt failed due to the skill of the Secret Service agents assigned to my security detail. Details of that will be forthcoming."

"As I speak, a state of war exists between the Republic of Iran and the United States of America. Let us also bow our heads and ask that God have mercy on their souls."

* * *

Up to this moment the citizens of Iran were celebrating in the streets of Isfahan. American flags were burnt and then Iranian citizens danced on the ashes. This scene was repeated in Tehran, Mashhad, Esfahān, Tabriz and Karaj, just to name a few major cities. The American oppressor had been put in his place the people screamed. Allah had delivered them into their hands; or so they thought.

At the height of celebration simultaneous detonations wiped out the Nation of Iran.

* * *

Justin again watched the second hand on his watch and at the end of sixty seconds he looked up and said, "At precisely this moment of silence, ladies and gentlemen, Operation Sandman was executed. At staggered times, six of our new Stealth 450 bombers left our base just south of Sakakah in Saudi Arabia, each escorted by over seventy stealth fighter jets, and they each reached their assigned targets just at this moment. Each jet, simultaneously, dropped a medium yield nuclear bomb on the following Iranian cities; Tehran, Kermanshah, Mashhad, Shiraz, Tabriz, Esfahan and finally Ahvaz which have been wiped from the face of the earth. I will not endanger even one American soldier on Iranian soil. If this retaliatory effort is not enough, we will bomb them again. "

"Syria has been implicated in the monstrous act toward our country and if we find out that they were involved, the cities of Aleppo, Damascus and Homs have already been targeted and will also be wiped clean with a nuclear strike."

Justin looked into the camera and pictured himself staring at his enemy. After a full minute of silence, he said, "Let it be known that we will tolerate no more American casualties in these cowardly attacks. When attacked, we will strike quickly and completely; wiping out any country involved in the attack. The time of playing games with the American Giant are over. You've stirred our anger to the point that we have no tolerance left. If you have eyes, then see. If you have ears, then hear."

At just that moment satellite feed was seen on screens around the world as one nuclear plume after another spoke of the death of Iran. The world was stunned. The picture zoomed in from a satellite passing over Iran at this moment and destruction swept across the face of the earth as never seen before. Millions of humans were snuffed out in a heartbeat.

Justin's determined features reappeared, "Make no mistake. America has never tried to rule the world. We have always tried to help where we could. We have rebuilt nations; we have fed millions with the sweat of our brow. We have sent medical aide to uncounted nations and the only thanks we have received in return is hatred, hostility, and violence. Even though it is tempting to just leave you to yourselves, we will still help where we can. However, we want to be clear here, we will not tolerate any further violence toward us. If we are in your country helping your citizens and we get attacked for it; we will withdraw immediately and completely and you will receive no further help from us. If you attack our soil; well you have seen what will happen to your country. So if you want to meet Allah, make sure that your entire country wants to meet him for it will. That is all!"

With that the feed was cut and as agreed the news media started showing nothing but humanitarian efforts carried out in the recent past by the United States.

Justin slumped forward on his desk and wept for the death of his own citizens and for those of Iran. His decision weighed heavily on him but he didn't see any other way to protect America but to set the cost so high that no one would ever want to pay it again.

Amanda and his Special agents closed in on him and he whispered, "Please get me out of here. Please."

CHAPTER THIRTY-FIVE

THE ANTIDOTE

It had been so academic to Peter when he drew up Operation Sandman. Now that it had been carried out he couldn't handle its enormity. He had planned the destruction of millions of human beings; snuffed out like so much chaff among wheat. He hadn't slept in the week that had followed; he was afraid of what awaited him in the dark world of dreams. He was damned and he saw no reprieve.

Justin wasn't far behind him but he knew something that Peter didn't.

Justin entered the room and spoke softly, as if Peter would bolt if he spoke too loudly, "Peter, this is Mr. Summons my, well servant. He is very wise and I thought it might be good if we both talked with him about our decision. First of all Peter I want you to realize that the responsibility for Operation Sandman is mine, not yours. I asked you to come up with different ways to deal with this threat. I didn't accept it at first and look what happened. I then chose to activate the plan. You did not make that decision. Now, let Mr. Summons talk to us and perhaps he'll have some answers for us."

Peter looked up and wiped tears from his eyes, "I'm damned and I can't see a way out."

Mr. Summons sat down and spoke gently as he laid a hand on Peter's shoulder, "If you feel damned then you must believe in God, right?"

Peter nodded and whimpered softly.

"Then you must know that God has an unlimited capacity for forgiveness. He placed you and Justin here at just this moment in history to make these decisions and I don't think he will damn you for them. Even if He didn't have you carry out such a plan, and I don't know that, He will forgive you for it if you will humble yourself and ask."

Peter looked up hopefully, "I couldn't be more humble, Mr. Summons. I feel crushed by the weight of my choices."

Mr. Summons smiled, "Jesus asked that you bring your heavy burdens to him and he will exchange it for a light burden."

Peace passed through Mr. Summons into Peter Highston and he lay down on a couch and was instantly asleep.

Mr. Summons looked up at Justin and said; "Now sir, it is your turn to sleep. You will do no one any good if you collapse from exhaustion, now will you?"

Justin smiled and said, "Thank you Kapre for helping. I know God has forgiven me but what if they don't listen. I have to act tougher than I feel all the time so they will take me seriously. People have been saying that I'm a monster for what I have done. Some think I'm Hitler reincarnated, some think I'm the Anti-Christ. How do I know I'm not? Some want me impeached and then arrested for war crimes."

"Like I told Peter, Justin, God put you here to make the decisions and not those people. Everyone has an opinion, Justin, and you listened to them all, you prayed, and then you made your decision, so stick by it. Keep seeking God's guidance in the future and remember that only He knows the real answers to questions like these."

As he spoke, Mr. Summons had placed his hand on Justin's shoulder and he too drifted into the peace of God and into a deep, peaceful, sleep.

*   *   *

After the traitor who had sent the poisoned coffee to the snipers had been found and arrested Justin and Kathy had convinced each other that their staffs could be trusted with whatever secrets she and Justin wanted to share. It was then that Kathy shocked Justin with the existence of the secret Antidote lab and apartment far below the public research center. It turned out to be perfect for his needs as President. Under the circumstances, his advisors had told him to set up his headquarters right here. Security was tight; the Apartment was adequate to the First Couple's needs. The communication center had been set up prior to his arrival but they moved it to one of the labs on this lower level. All the labs, which had been dormant, just waiting for Justin to use them, would be temporarily turned into offices for his staff; all the labs that is but one, which Justin would use for his own research. The Antidote would in effect become the new White House; in function at least.

After much debate, it was decided over Justin's objections that he shouldn't go out into the world for a while. Tensions were high both in this country and abroad. Justin sat in front of a bank of monitors and watched the opinions of the world unfold.

"This is WNN's Special Report; Operation Sandman - Plus one week. Our President is still hold up in the research center called The Antidote, and has not appeared in public since his history making decision to obliterate Iran. We have gathered opinions from around the world on this decision. . ."

What appeared next began to knot Justin's stomach. One person after another appeared and had their say. A young American woman, "I think President Johnson should be arrested as a war criminal, convicted, and summarily executed!" An older gentleman, "You have to admit he has brass ones. I say this should have been done long ago." An elderly lady, "All I want to ask is how you can put such a cheap value on human life young man?" A teen girl, "They did destroy Washington and the Arch what else could he do?"

The English Prime Minister, "Good show old chap. Stomp the buggers before they can stomp us, I say." An older lady on the street, "I've lived too long I'm afraid. The world is beyond me now."

A UN spokesman, "President Johnson did everything according to the rules and got prior approval for Operation Sandman, so if you blame anyone, you must blame us all. We just hope that this drastic step will put an end to any further violence."

A Christian spokesman, "The end of the world is at hand and President Johnson is the Anti-Christ. Watch for him to demand that we get branded on the forehead and worship him next."

Justin switched off the screens. He threw a remote across the room and paced wildly back and forth in his new operation center. Amanda watched him closely but didn't say anything yet. Finally Justin wound down and turned to her and yelled, "For a week now, the same thing over and over. Even the people that applaud me turn my stomach at how trivial they treat this; the others? They think I'm a monster!"

Amanda sat forward, "Not all of them said anything like that. A few did, but a few more applaud your actions."

"Applaud my actions? I just said that I'm not looking for applause, Amanda. . ."

Amanda stood up and yelled back, "No Justin, you're looking for absolution! Well, you won't get either from me."

Justin stared at her his heart at the breaking point. In a softer voice, "What you will get from me, Justin, is support. No one should be faced with this type of decision, but you were and you decided correctly in my opinion."

Amanda approached Justin slowly and wrapped her arms around him and held him tight. The pressure in his chest had built to the point that he thought for sure that he would have a heart attack. In fact, he would have welcomed one; a fatal one. He collapsed to the floor, the comfort he had received from Mr. Summons last week, was used up, gone like a puff of smoke. Amanda followed him to the floor, still holding on to him tightly. He wept as she rocked him back and forth.

*   *   *

The angels Aegis and Kapre watched the couple unseen but not unnoticed. Aegis had his hand resting on

Amanda's shoulder and Kapre had his own on Justin's. They were praying for the couple's peace. As the weeping subsided, Justin held Amanda back and they just lay there on the carpeted floor and slipped into a peaceful sleep. Each angel knelt by his charge giving them strength and peace; praying that the Holy Spirit would fill the couple anew and bring them wisdom. Neither of them knew then just how powerful the answer would be, when the dawn came.

CHAPTER THIRTY-SIX

HOLY GHOST POWER

The couple still lay on the floor holding on, one to another when the breeze awakened them. Their minds were fuzzy with sleep so it took them a moment to realize that something was different. Unseen by the couple were the two angels lying prostrate before their God; the Holy Spirit.

Justin stood first and helped Amanda to her feet and then it hit them. In the middle of the room was a swirling fire. It consumed nothing but their hearts. They fell to their knees, shaking with the fear that comes from respect for the power of their God. His very presence brought awe to their souls and they too lay face down before their God. There was no heat but the fire soon consumed all of their fear, their dread, even their doubts and soon all that was left was God's presence.

There was no loud booming voice from the fire but instead a calm, loving voice, sang a song whose beauty finds no description in the written word. The couple knew instantly that their God was completely overcoming them and soon nothing was left of them but what God intended for there to be. It was a miracle without signs. They lay there crying from the sheer joy of the experience. God was talking directly to their souls and they could in no way understand with their minds, the language He used, but their hearts retained it all. They had no way of knowing how long the experience lasted but when suddenly they were alone in the room again they cried for the loss. Then to their surprise, Kapre and Aegis were standing over them in all their angelic glory and they announced as one, "Why do you lay there wasting time? You know what you must do. Do not fear your assignments but instead trust in the God that lives in you. You now know Him almost as well as He knows you. Many have wished to experience what you have just witnessed, now rise and go."

The couple blinked and the angels were gone but not so the Spirit that would never depart from them again.

*   *   *

When the Justin and Amanda emerged from their apartment everyone knew on one level or another that the couple had changed. They carried themselves with confidence and had an atmosphere of peace and tranquility that just had never been there before. They were friendlier, kinder, and more patient with everyone and every situation. Gone was the fear and indecision that had plagued Justin this past week or so.

Oh, they never spoke to anyone of their experience. How could they? What could they say that would even come close to explaining what they had experienced? No the experience was meant for them and them alone. So they went on together in quiet contentment that they had met their Creator, and also friend. What an awesome knowledge to know God as He really is and to still be alive to contemplate it.

Justin called for a news conference and he reluctantly received it from his press secretary, Patricia

Perkins, who tried her best to explain that it just wasn't a good idea just yet. Justin just smiled and she finally said, "Yes, sir."

The world waited with baited breath.

Justin wore (for the first time ever mind you) a white suit, white shirt, white tie, and even white shoes. He was so white that he had the illusion of glowing, or was it an illusion? Who knew for sure, but it did have the expected result; purity. He looked clean; white as new fallen snow.

Coupled with his soft voice, even his most adamant enemy was impressed with the power that seemed to emanate from this man.

After a few moments of silence, Justin spoke softly, giving his words even more power somehow, "My brothers and sisters of the world. We live in hard times and there are wolves among us. Ever since 9/11, 2001 we have tried to fight terror. We have prayed for peace but peace was not forthcoming. The wolves among us only grew bolder and showed even more contempt for God's people. You cannot plead with wolves. If you want to save the flock you must at times eradicate the wolves. Iran was such a wolf. They have called for the eradication of America for years and now have tasted their own curse.

"This is not a good time to be a wolf . . . and if you are going to attack my flock. . ." Here Justin leaned forward and spoke in a whisper which brought a chill to the spines of his enemies, "Be ready to feel my staff!"

"To my allies I say, let's get on with life and build peaceful societies, prosperous societies, and finally thankful societies. I, for one, want to thank God my father who has so blessed my life that I must give thanks daily. I personally am also thankful for His Son, Jesus Christ, for saving us all from our sins and making it possible to go to heaven someday. . ."

It was, at this point, that people from around the world began to realize that they could understand Justin in their own language and without an interpreter, "I know this will probably cost me the election even more than blowing Iran off the face of the earth, but here goes; Jesus Christ has a message for each and every person in the world. Most of you are listening to this broadcast and so you know that this message is from Jesus, true Son of God, you are now hearing me in your own languages. This is a sign that the message I deliver now came from God and not from man.

"God wants you to know that he loves each and every one of you. He has watched the suffering of the flock for years and has decided to lessen our suffering and pain. He has told me today in a vision that I will, before my death, discover a way to cure all disease. This will alleviate much of the suffering that is being endured in every nation of the world."

"This may be hard to believe from a man who has forced peace on earth through violence, but it is none the less true. On the one hand I will, as long as I'm President, promise you that the wolves of this world will pay the heaviest of prices if they attack us or any of our allies. On the other hand, I offer you salvation through Jesus Christ and His additional gift of a cure for all illness. I do not know at this time what form this cure will take, but I believe that God will give me the wisdom to find it."

"To that end I will run the government from The Antidote, since the White House lay in permanent ruin and the area won't be safe for many years to come. There will be a special election in two months, on the second Tuesday of March, for those states that lost their Senators and Congressmen or women."

"There has been much talk about me resigning . . . That will not happen. I do not apologize for killing a rabid wolf. I will, from here, lead our country to a more prosperous time, a safer time, and a more blessed time. I call all Americans back to a time when we were one nation under God. Repent your ignorance of God and His ways and turn back now. He will respond in kind and pour out blessings upon our country and any other country that will join us in the worship of His son, Jesus Christ."

"Despite what some people are saying, I am not the Anti-Christ, which by the way is why I feel it appropriate to speak of God, Jesus, and their plan of Salvation. I am a servant of Jesus Christ and my life belongs totally to Him. A house divided cannot stand; so if I'm for Jesus, then it stands to reason that I cannot be the Anti-Christ. I am not a monster; the monsters were those who attacked us in a cowardly sneak attack and want to cry foul when we strike back."

"In the past, Presidents have been criticized for not doing enough in response and now I'm criticized for doing too much. Well, I stand by my decision and say publicly to the world that I will do it again and again until Terror stops attacking us or they are totally eradicated like the wolves they are."

"What little bit of free time I do get will be spent in

a lab trying to find that cure that God did not promise to hand to me. He said I would have to look hard but that I would find it, so be patient and look forward with hope."

"This speech has been no trick. The power of the Holy Spirit has filled me and I speak in tongues; languages that I can speak fluently without learning them. This is the power that the Holy Spirit had shown in the early days of the church so that diverse peoples could join together united under the banner of Jesus Christ. Let's do it again shall we. Join with me to gather around the only hope left for our world; the Son of God; Jesus Christ."

"I have arranged for numbers to appear on your screens no matter where you are in the world. You may phone in and ask more about this saving Grace of Jesus Christ. Can I pray of you?"

Screens all over the world faded to black and then the numbers appeared and stayed on the bottom of the screens for the next two hours of programming. The phone banks were swamped from that day forward.

Over the next three years, Justin kept his promises. He ran the country with skill, compassion, and a firm grip. He spent two hours a day on the phone talking to people about Jesus Christ and he spent four to five hours per night in his lab looking for the promised cure.

Unseen but not unfelt by the world, the Holy Spirit of God washed over the world in a tidal wave of unheard of proportions. Converts flocked to Christianity by the millions from all countries, from all walks of life and from every faith. People were slowly turning back to God and to hope.

CHAPTER THIRTY-SEVEN

TRANSITIONS

President Justin Johnson ran unopposed in the next election. His first term decisions had proven to be correct it seemed. Peace spread throughout the world. Even Israel and the Arab Nations seemed to get in the spirit of peace. Ireland, which had been split for centuries, brought Catholic and Protestant differences to a point of understanding and the violence ended when the prejudice ended.

Against his advisor's wishes Justin and Amanda traveled the world speaking on peace and "The Brotherhood of Man". They also answered the many questions thrown at them about their own conversion to Christianity and many were converted by their witness. The Committee had totally converted to Christianity and it just was not the same organization. Instead of seeking power at any cost, it now sought after the good of all world citizens at all cost. They used their influence and wealth to bring about the peace that the world now enjoyed. They also inadvertently set the stage that the Anti-Christ would use to fool people into following him. With a small twist here and a little misdirection there, he would turn some true believers into the mere shadow of their former selves and then he would convert the remainder of the world to his lie. This was the current mission of Captain Detestation.

Satan had tried many times to rid the world of Justin Johnson; a human he considered to be a trader.

He had been angry at first and had demoted many a demon for allowing the advancement of the enemy that had taken place over the past eight years of Justin's Presidency. Satan, however, is "The Father of Lies", and soon he conceived of a plan to turn what God had meant for good and twist it to Satan's own personal evil will.

*   *   *

Justin had just turned the Government over to new President Baxter Henderson who had handsomely defeated his opponent; the Senator from Texas, Fred Singerton. The Committee was meeting now to handle the transition from Justin's rule not only as President but also as the Chairman of the Committee.

Justin stood and spoke with a smile, "As you all know Amanda and I are resigning from the Committee as of today. You have all had an opportunity to bid on our shares of the organization and I want to announce the winner of that bid. As you know the winner of this bid will be the majority shareholder and therefore your new Committee Chairman. There is also the matter of filling our two seats on the Committee. This will entail allowing in a new family. To that end a select few of the wealthiest families were contacted from around the world and they were also allowed to bid for our shares and for a spot on the Committee.

The results are in and it is my pleasure to introduce to you, the two new members of the committee, and winner of the silent bid; David Whinestein and his son, Jesse C. Whinestein. Their family has been dealing in diamonds and other precious jewels for years and it is reported that they can trace their family line directly back to King David himself. They won the bid with an offer to pay Amanda and me thirty-six trillion dollars for our shares, which they have already deposited into our Swiss Accounts. Oh, here they are now."

As he was talking an older man walked in with a younger man following closely behind him; they were both dressed in traditional Jewish black, complete with the little black skull cap resting on the crown of their heads.

Mr. Whinestein walked up to Justin and said, "Thank you for the introduction, Mr. Johnson. You and your wife are now dismissed. I'll take it from here."

Justin was a bit surprised by this abrupt dismissal, but he smiled and said in farewell, "Well, gentlemen, he sounds like a Chairman already, so I'll leave you in his capable hands."

Justin and Amanda started for the door and they both felt the cold finger of fear as they passed the young man known as Jesse C. Whinestein. Justin hesitated for a moment but Amanda pushed him from behind and they were soon out of the Temple, the Illumin, Inc. nerve center, and then finally out of the building all together. Until they stepped out into the streets of Chicago, they both had the distinct feeling that they were being pursued by the hounds of hell. Sweat was beaded up on their foreheads, their hearts were beating a bit too rapidly and the knot in their stomachs threatened to gag them into a vomiting session.

Amanda said, "What in the world was that?"

Justin answered thoughtfully, "I'm not really sure Amanda, but it has something to do with that younger

Whinestein, I'm sure of it."

"I tend to agree with you, Justin. Just walking by that young man made me feel dirty somehow. It may have been a mistake to allow them to take over the Committee. I have a bad feeling about this."

"Amanda, I agree, but we had rules we had to follow. We did so and this is how the chips fell. We need to just leave this all behind us and move on with our own lives now."

Amanda looked back just once at the large building that had been so much a part of their lives and said, "You're right, of course, Justin, but I just can't shake the feeling of doom that has just come over me."

Justin smiled and said, "Well I know one way to rid you of this feeling of doom."

"What's that Justin?"

"We're going on vacation."

*   *   *

Agents JoHansen and Pickerton were transferred to the detail protecting President Baxter Henderson and his wife, Becky. Justin's Press Secretary, Patricia Perkins, went on to be the Press Secretary for the United Nations in New York.

Dr. Beatrice Moltice continued on as Surgeon General for President Henderson and young Peter Highston stayed on with President Henderson as his Political Advisor.

The world went on and over a rather short period of time, as with other high profile people, President Justin Johnson and his wife, Amanda, were delegated to a position in history and then for the most part forgotten; which fit nicely into Justin's plans to throw himself into his research project.

CHAPTER THIRTY-EIGHT

GATHERING THE TEAM

Amanda had been active all her life and she had insisted that she have a contributing role in the project. Justin, therefore, put her in charge of running the secret section of The Antidote. Kathy Saunders Peterson would of course remain the Director of the public research facility above them and her husband, Stan Peterson, would remain Chief of Security. They had done a wonderful job up to and including the past eight years. It was in the past eight years; however, that Justin and Amanda had witnessed firsthand their efficiency and professionalism.

Now, however they were activating the secret section as a research facility as it had originally been envisioned by Pastor Bob. Soon after Justin's tenure as President of the United States, Amanda had supervised the removal of all evidence of the facility serving for seven years as the substitute White House of the United States. Gone were the offices and personnel. Gone were the global defense war room, the world communication network, the press room, and the offices of the army of secretaries and staff that ran the government from this location. The entire operation had been transferred to the new offices the United Nations had graciously offered as the seat of the American government. Because of the nuclear fallout in and around Washington D.C., it had been decided to make New York the new Capital of the United States. Further, it was decided that the head of the U.S. Government and the leader of the U.N. could work more efficiently together if they were located in the same building. Therefore, new offices had been built with U.S. funds to house the U.S. Government. It had actually proven to be quit efficient and convenient for President Baxter Henderson and his new staff.

*   *   *

In the past year, Amanda had worked long hours in the supervision of the removal of one type of operational environment and the installation of another. Pastor Bob had arranged well for the original research facility but in the ensuing years great strides had been taken in research methods and the development of more advanced equipment therefore requiring a complete renovation of the lower level facility to remain on the cutting edge. So Justin and Amanda had moved into one of the upper level apartments while the renovation was completed. A botanical garden was added for Amanda. It had a domed ceiling which with new light weight construction materials and advanced lighting technics was made to resemble a spring time sky. The lighting and atmospheric conditions were computer controlled by accessing the over 300 sensors throughout the garden resulting in an environment that fostered plant viability and created Spring-like conditions year round.

Justin's home office had been moved out the apartment into the lab area so he could work while at work and then relax in his new den at home. In the den, mementos that had been collected from leaders around the world during his Presidency were displayed giving it a partial museum look. One wall was filled with Justin's favorite books and the room had thickly padded carpeting, with large stuffed leather chairs sitting in front of a gas fireplace giving it a partial library look.

In another section sat Justin's large desk facing what looked to be a blank wall, but in actuality was an O(rganic)L(light)E(mitting)D(iode) panel. With the touch of a button, the view could be switched from a scenic view to any video source desired from the comfort of Justin's large, heavily stuffed desk chair. The filing cabinet to the right of his desk was actually a refrigerator in which he kept his beverages and snack food. It was a man's room, made for a man's comforts and convenience.

The rest of the apartment was made up of a master bedroom, with its own private bathroom, walk-in closet, king-sized bed, dressing table, and a second closet which was filled from floor to ceiling with drawers. To finish off this room they had a round table with two arm chairs and a smaller OLED panel with various connections for entertainment, local and world news updates as well as research study.

Just down the hall was a fully furnished guest bath. Across from this was the guest bedroom, which would be occupied by Mr. Summons, when he wasn't occupied in his angelic form. This was a simple twelve foot by twelve foot room, with a Queen sized bed, dresser, closet and a smaller round table and two armchairs with a fully connected OLED panel (not that Kapre ever used it).

The hall then made entrance possible into the living room which was large and comfortable boasting of a couch, two recliner chairs, a love-seat, all made of mahogany with matching light-brown material on thick white carpeting. The coffee table was made of cherry wood, polished to a glass-like finish. The top had two square holes cut out and filled in with glass. All in all it was a very comfortable place to visit with friends and guests.

Just off of the living room was the dining room complete with a china cabinet (which was given to the couple by the Emperor of China) filled with authentic dining china. The dining table was a large oval table which could be expanded with two inserts. A crystal chandelier hung over the table and gave adequate light. Adjacent was the kitchen in which their cook would prepare their evening meal. Breakfast and lunch were taken at the cafeteria on the upper level. The laundry was sent out to the facilities dry cleaning and washing service. Scientists aren't much on domestic chores.

They had found that the new lab equipment was significantly smaller than the original equipment therefore requiring less lab space than originally planned; so the extra space was incorporated into the living quarters. Justin had explained that his work area, if properly equipped, didn't really need to be as large as it had been originally designed. Their living quarters on the other hand would have to serve them, probably the rest of their lives, so they didn't want to get miserly about the room they allowed themselves.

The facility had its own pool, gym, and spa, so they could use those when they desired. They financed the entire secret lab and the apartment themselves to save the upper facility from expending any further monies on this project. The facility could have afforded it but so could the former first couple, so why not. The upper facilities staff was the best paid in the nation and they knew it, earned it, and appreciated it. The staff that Amanda had hired for the secret facility would be small but they would be the best in their field and also well compensated. They would each get an apartment and permitted full use of the upper level recreation area. The secret lab wasn't after all really secret any longer but was still affectionately referred to that way in honor of Pastor Bob's memory.

The defenses of the Antidote were all still intact but all manned by civilian security personnel now. Once Justin left the Presidency then so did the army of Secret Service Agents and the staff of political personnel. He had refused to keep a personal Secret Service detail since he would be in the most secure facility available already. If he traveled outside, then a personal security detail would be provided by the facility. Justin knew that he still had many enemies that would love to take the credit for killing him, but he had stopped worrying about them long ago. He felt safe here and at peace. He was very content as well. Research had always been his first love and now after all these years of politics and administrative duties he could finally dedicate his time to that task.

He had given Amanda some guidelines as to what he needed in staff and few possible doctors to invite. From there, Amanda did it all. The many phone calls, interviews, criminal histories, medical check-ups, credit histories, and FBI clearances, Amanda was, in charge of it all. Justin in turn equipped the lab with what he wanted and needed. It became a researchers dream. Not hampered at all by finances, he obtained the finest and most up-to-date of everything he or his staff needed to the point of obtaining some items still in the development stage. Everything was the latest and best technology could provide.

Everything was set and today was to be final interview day and Justin had to join Amanda for the final say on who would actually get hired. This would take place in the conference room just off of the lab and would be decided more by attitude than qualifications. Everyone invited to the interview would be more than qualified for the research but that was not good enough. They would have to love the research as much as Justin. They would have to feel the need for speed, yet be accurate. They would have to be stable individuals and not some absentminded professor type. Finally, they would have to be team players. The ones, who would finally be hired for the task, would be well compensated for their efforts; just how much Justin had not yet determined. Kathy and Stan Peterson would also be present to ask questions or answer them as needed.

The lab was finished, cleaned, and shone and smelled of a newness that would be short-lived. It would seduce any researcher who knew what it contained and the availability of unlimited funding. Each candidate had to sign a loyalty and non-disclosure agreement. Immediately upon an individual leaving the facility all security measures would be modified to reflect the change in status. As part of the existing security measures, all codes were changed every forty-eight hours as well.

Justin found this life relaxing after the pressure

cooker life he had just left. He planned on having six researchers besides himself and they would each be allowed to pick four assistants. The assistants would undergo the same rigorous security scrutiny that their bosses had to pass.

No longer would Justin have to maintain the balance between the Committee and the United States government, let alone the United Nations. Gone was the responsibility of the world for he now only had to follow what God laid before him; finding a cure for all disease. He knew that God could just cure all disease but He didn't choose to do it that way. Like many times in our history, He would give the skill to men and women, who would then give Him the glory.

Justin was in the small conference room just off of the lab when Amanda walked in.

Justin looked up from a file he was reading, "Hi, Honey, are we about set?"

Amanda was all smiles, "The helicopter is just about here with the first four candidates Justin. Isn't this exciting? We are finally ready to get started. Kathy said that she would arrange to make our guests comfortable in a lounge upstairs while she brings them down here one at a time. Stan is taking care of security personally and will escort them from the heliport to that lounge and will join us when Kathy brings the first candidate down."

Justin smiled, "Stan takes all this security seriously doesn't he?"

"And well he might too, what with all the corporate espionage going on out there in the world. There is no reason to believe that your research wouldn't be very valuable to some corporation or another."

"Amanda, we are going to give this cure freely to the world, why would they try to steal it?"

"Oh Justin, how can you be so naive after all you've been through and done in the world?"

Justin smiled, "I guess I want to be. I thought we left all that cloak and dagger stuff behind with the Presidency."

"Afraid not Justin, just on a smaller scale is all, but the stakes are just as high. If you want to retain ownership of your research so you can later give it away, we will have to protect it first."

Justin held up his hands in mock defense and laughed,, "O.K. I surrender! You've made your point, honey. We'll follow all protocols and rules."

Just then the whine of the elevator warned them that at least one of their guests had arrived. They walked out of the conference room and into the hallway right where the elevator would unload its cargo. They would interview each person in the conference room first and then, if they decided to hire the person, they would be given a tour of the facilities. If not hired, they would be escorted upstairs again. No use showing them anymore than necessary. The door to the elevator opened and Operation Methuselah began.

CHAPTER THIRTY-NINE

PROJECT METHUSELAH

TWO MONTHS LATER:

In the two months since the search began Justin's administrative team had interviewed over fifty very qualified candidates and had finally decided on the six that would now work on the project. They had all arrived at The Antidote facility two days ago and had been settled into their apartments (which had just been completed). When they were hired, they had been given a tour of the lab which had been mostly finished except for the extra equipment each had requested. Now, they were given a tour of the practical facilities; gym, pool, laundry services, cafeteria, golf course (18 hole course complete with artificial grass; both rough and greens; and sand traps. No water traps, however.), tennis courts, and even a handball and racquetball court, and of course the movie theater; all of which they had been informed about but which had not been finished at the time of their hiring. The back wall of the stage area was one big OLED and could be used for screening a movie or provide a backdrop for the occasional live stage production. It was indicated Justin had plans for special performances of "A Christmas Carol" for the Christmas season as well as Broadway plays and various well known entertainers. The upper research facility had an extensive library of books and, of course, ninety percent of them could be accessed by the scientist's own computer terminal as needed.

Now, however, they all sat in their place around the conference table in the "secret" lab facility which most of the new arrivals called the lower facility. They had all met with Kathy and Stan and were now well versed in the security and administrative protocols of the upper facility. It was now time to acquaint them with the project at hand.

Amanda and Justin sat at the "head" of the oval table and Justin looked around the table for a moment. The scientists all looked apprehensive or excited, he wasn't sure which.

'Time to put them out of their misery', thought Justin.

"Amanda and I would like to officially welcome each of you to Project Methuselah. We will be trying to find out how Methuselah lived to be 969 years old and duplicate it to the best of our abilities. We are not looking for the fountain of youth, however, but rather a way to defeat disease, which may result in the same effect. Amanda will handle all requests for additional equipment and supplies that you may need. I will be the project director and coordinate our efforts. At this time I.
. ."

"Excuse me a moment, Mr. President."

"Yes, Dr. Glade?"

Dr. Glade was a tall, thin man as he proved when he stood and towered over them, "Not to put too fine a point on it sir, but you have spent your life as a politician, not a scientist. What qualifies you, sir, to be director of this type of scientific endeavor?" He sat down among whispers of agreement.

Justin smiled. He had expected this, "Yes, I have spent my life as a politician but my first love has been research. I may have neglected to tell you but I became a medical doctor at a very young age and have never stopped my education over the years. In each of the fields represented here today, I hold a Ph.D. degree. Oh I'm not the expert each of you are in your perspective fields but you won't have to talk baby talk around me. I will know enough of each of your research projects to allow me to see the overall picture and direct you in one direction or another. I also hold a Ph.D. in Computer Science and will work in the capacity of computer programmer, troubleshooter, and software expert."

Eyebrows shot up around the table, as if no one expected that answer, "I hope that will satisfy any further questions as to my qualifications. I have one further qualification not yet mentioned; Amanda and I are paying for all of this ourselves which should qualify us as your boss as well. While we are on the subject of money, this would be as good a time as any to finally tell you what you will be making. (All they had been told to this point is that they would make more than they do now). You are each considered equals in your expertise so you will all receive the same income. Your housing accommodations are free, including utilities, cafeteria, cleaning services; both clothing and apartments, and the recreational facilities at this research center. Travel arrangements; cars, helicopters, or airlines will all be arranged and paid for by Amanda. Dr. Howard Glade is the only married scientist here and I am sure that he will want to make weekly trips home, but these arrangements go for the rest of you as well. Medical, dental, eye exams and/or glasses will be provided here free of charge. In addition to all this, you will earn a salary of one million dollars per year; that's before taxes, of course."

The highest paid scientist at the table made two hundred thousand per year at their last job, so they were all pleasantly surprised. Justin was pleased that some of them were having trouble swallowing as he continued, "Amanda and I agreed that if a football player, baseball player and many other sports stars could make money in the millions then so should you. We will get account information from you later or you can open accounts in our own banking facility here at the center and we will transfer your first million this week. You'll be paid once per year in advance of the year in which you will be working for us; any questions about the financial arrangements?" Justin looked around the table and saw that look a person gets when they finally realize that they have made it.

He continued, "If there are no further objections, I would like to make the formal introductions so you will each be familiar with the other members of the team and what they bring to the table so to speak."

He opened the first folder and read, ' Dr. Angie Beasley, age 33, Vegetarian. Ph.D. in Nutrition - Specialty Biosystematics.'

Justin looked up and looked at Angie and said, "Would you please stand, Angie?"

She was fairly short but slim. Her short blonde hair was feathered back. Her blue eyes were magnified by black rim glasses which she apparently wore all the time. She had rather plain features but wasn't unpleasant to look at.

Justin said, "I would like to introduce to you, Dr. Angie Beasley, our team Nutritionist. I should add, so I won't have to repeat myself that you all have at least a Ph.D. in your perspective fields or you wouldn't be here. Angie specializes in Biosystematics."

"Oh, at this point I would like to ask that we get on a first name basis. We all know that we are doctors and I'm no longer President so just call me Justin. I do plan to call you by your first names."

Someone yelled out, "For a million dollars a year, you can call me anything you want." Justin saw that it had been Dr. Bruce Hamstring who had laughed after saying it. He seemed a happy type, one of the many reasons he was chosen.

Justin smiled, and then continued, "Angie will be collecting from her research biochemical, cytogenic, and other studies conducted to assess the taxonomic relationship of organisms or populations within a species framework. I was also very impressed with her work on the Appestat. As you all know, the Appestat is the area of the brain believed to regulate appetite and food intake. Welcome Angie."

Everyone applauded along with Justin and Amanda and then Angie sat down.

By then Justin had opened the next file and read 'Dr. Bruce Hamstring -age 48 - Biomedical Engineer. "Would you stand, Bruce?" As the man stood he still wore a broad smile and seemed to emit happiness from every pore. He was a short, rather over weight man. Bald except for brown and gray mix horseshoe shaped stubble around the edges and he had large brown eyes. He wore those little half glasses on a chain around his neck but they always seemed to be balanced on the tip of his nose, when he wasn't actually holding them in his right hand and chewing on the right stem of the glasses.

"This is Doctor Bruce Hamstring, our Biochemical Engineer"

Bruce smiled bigger and said, "Yes, it was hard to get through school with a name like Hamstring, but I managed."

Everyone laughed good naturedly and Justin continued, "Bruce specializes in biomechanics and biomedicine and will research the ability of a human being to tolerate environmental stresses and variances. He did similar research for NASA in the past for the Space Program, but will now concentrate on a more down to earth environment. He will also research the application of the principles of natural sciences to clinical medicine. Welcome Bruce."

More applause as Justin opened the next folder and read 'Dr. Cindy Lee - age 30 - Neuroanatomist and Neurobiologist.' "Would you please rise, Cindy?" As she stood Justin noticed that she was short, thin, and very pretty. She was American born but had oriental features. Her slanted green eyes sparkled with mischief and she would quickly become the group's resident practical joker, "This is Dr. Cindy Lee the team's Neuroanatomist and Neurobiologist. She will be researching the effects of your research on the nerves of the human body.

They were getting into a rhythm now of applause and introduction. The next file that Justin opened, 'Dr. Howard Glade - age 40 - Neurochemist. "Please stand, Dr. Glade." He was a tall thin man who carried himself sternly. He was all business with a no nonsense personality which almost got him eliminated. He is also the only married member of the team other than Justin and he was only saved there because his wife and children decided to remain at home to maintain the continuity of their lives. Howard had made arrangements to visit most weekends, holidays, and a vacation once a year.

Justin continued, "This is Dr. Howard Glade the team's Neurochemist. He'll be working closely with Cindy on the effects of chemicals on the human nervous system. Welcome Howard."

Justin was most nervous about this next one. He opened the folder which read, 'Dawn Delarenzo - age 38 - Neuroendocrinologist ' "Would you please stand, Dr. Delarenzo?"

She was an Italian woman who could have easily been a model for any magazine. Dawn was tall and sleek. She had olive skin with Italian features including full red lips, big hazel eyes with long eyelashes and long black hair which fell all around her shoulders. She was almost eliminated by Amanda but her credentials and Justin's promise to behave himself, helped Amanda overcome her jealousy; or at least he hoped she had.

"This is Dr. Dawn Delarenzo, the team's Neuroendocrinologist. Her research will involve the interaction between the nervous system and the endocrine glands and their secretions."

She sat down with the confidence of a woman that was used to being scrutinized closely by the men and women around her. She seemed to Justin to have a good personality and hadn't let her looks make her distant or

421

snobbish toward others. Actually, that was just another one of her charms.

Justin opened the last folder and read, 'Dr. Victor Vauhn - age 45 - Genetic Engineer.' Would you please rise, Victor?" Victor was born in Germany but was educated in the United States and he became a citizen about twenty years ago. He was a short thin man who sported a thin mustache over his even thinner lips. He had calm brown eyes which matched his laid-back personality and had short brown hair worn in a crew cut. When he spoke, a distinct German accent could still be heard in his English.

"This is Dr. Victor Vauhn the team's Genetic Engineer and he will be conducting research into how DNA sequencing or Cloning might help us."

As Victor sat down Justin concluded, "You have before you a packet of information compiled by Amanda and myself on the research we have already accomplished and where I would like to see this continued research go. Please take it to your office, study it, and prepare a preliminary but detailed synopsis of how you are going to conduct your own research. Please have that to me within a week, as no research can begin without it. Our normal work hours will be from eight in the morning to six in the evening. If you need access at times other than this, just make the proper arrangements with security. I know you have all been fully briefed on what's expected of you in that area. In other matters. . ."

Justin and the others were into their full scientific mode now and didn't notice Amanda stand up and quietly leave the conference room. She hadn't felt very well for about a week now and was beginning to think with the symptoms she was exhibiting, that she might be pregnant. She wasn't sure if she liked the idea of being pregnant but first things first.

She took the elevator up to the next level and entered the medical complex to keep her appointment with her doctor; Dr. Julia Lanchester. Amanda took a deep breath and entered the clinic with many mixed feelings bombarding her heart and mind.

CHAPTER FORTY

INTO THE VALLEY OF DEATH

Amanda had mixed feelings. It had been two months since she had walked into Dr. Julia Lanchester's office and found out immediately that she was not pregnant. She was at the same time relieved and saddened by the news, but that wasn't her biggest concern. If she wasn't pregnant, then what was zapping every ounce of her energy? She leaned against the wall of the hallway for a moment to catch her breath. She was panting like she had run a marathon when she had actually just walked a short distance. Amanda had never been sick before, not seriously anyway, and she already didn't like it. She had responsibilities and couldn't take all this time going to the doctor.

She had started walking again and felt a bit better. No, that's a lie, but she repeated it to herself trying to believe it. Amanda had never fainted before, but as she stumbled forward toward the doctor's office for her two-o-clock appointment she began to feel hot and tingly all over. Everything seemed to stretch sideways and she stepped off into oblivion. Her last conscious thought was, *'Oh Lord, into Your hands I commend my spirit!'*

*   *   *

Justin the researcher was a happy man. He felt

light as a feather and happy as a clam. He literally bounced around his lab and office up to his elbows in Petri dishes and bacterial cultures. He was happily losing himself in today's search for a way to kill bacteria sample 462. It had become a game (a very important game) but nonetheless a game, and one that brought joy to his heart.

He was looking into his microscope when his world crumbled around him. The phone rang and since she was closer, Dr. Dawn Delarenzo picked it up, "Yes? Lab, Dr. Delarenzo speaking." She looked toward Justin, covered the mouthpiece of the handset and yelled over the whir of the centrifugal separator, "Justin, Justin, it's for you."

She heard him sigh with irritation. He was like a boy with his favorite toy getting called for supper when all he wanted to do was continue playing. He took the handset from her and whispered, "Thank you, Dawn. This is Justin go ahead."

Dawn watched in fascination as all color drained from Justin's face. In the two months that she had worked with Justin, she had grown to like him very much. He was funny, very smart, and kind, yes, he had a kind and happy demeanor that was at the same time refreshing and disturbing. She often wondered how a man of his caliber could balance so many important responsibilities in his life and still come across as an innocent child sometimes. Amanda had told her that he was like that as President also. He could be in the middle of a serious situation and then suddenly get caught up in child-like awe when being briefed on a new jet fighter or a space transport and all he could say was, "Cool."

He could also throw his sense of humor around and keep people off guard at the most shocking moments. It both irritated and ingratiated people to him.

Dawn had seen all these things in him in the two months since the project started and more and she liked what she saw. Oh, they had been nothing but friends but it felt good to have a male friend of his caliber. Dawn liked Amanda also and wouldn't have done anything to hurt her, but what she saw transforming before her very eyes broke her heart.

Justin had not only turned white but he also dropped the phone and crumpled to the floor. Dawn instinctively reached out and caught him but his dead weight brought her to the floor with him. She suddenly found herself sitting on the floor holding a sobbing Justin in her lap. She didn't know what could affect a man this quickly but it felt good to hold him tightly and rock him in her arms. She immediately felt guilty for having these feelings but she just held on and tried to find out what was happening to Justin, "What's wrong, Justin? Speak to me, please."

All she heard was indecipherable gibberish from this grown man. He was angry and brokenhearted at the same time and it was tearing the man apart. She finally heard, "Amanda . . .cancer. . ." Then Dawn understood. Here was a man searching for a cure for all illness and his wife gets cancer and he already knew that he was helpless to help her. It would be years before they would have even a slight break-through, nothing that could help Amanda.

Dawn shook Justin slightly, "Where is she now, Justin?" No response. She shook him harder as she sat him up and yelled into his face, "Justin! Snap out of it! Where is Amanda now?"

He took a deep breath and said, "I love her so much Dawn. What am I going to do now?"

That made Dawn angry, "What are you going to do now? You're going to stop feeling sorry for yourself and get to wherever Amanda is and you're going to see what her needs are. Then fulfill them. Now get up!"

Dawn pulled him up and they eventually both made it to their feet. She straightened his coat and his hair and then said, "Now, Justin, where is Amanda now?"

He started walking and Dawn held his arm trying to steady him, "She's in the hospital. They found her lying on the hall floor in the medical wing. The nurse told me that I need to get there fast that they were about to lose her. I don't know what happened. Something inside me just snapped. I'm sorry for my display, Dawn, but I'm glad you were there with me. I don't know what would have happened if you had not been."

Dawn watched as Justin turned back into his more confident self and he had it together by the time they ran into the hospital and asked where Amanda was. They found out that she was in surgery and were shown to a waiting room. They didn't speak again. Justin was hardening himself to whatever news faced him and he looked as though he could handle just about anything now. Dawn picked up a magazine and started flipping through the pages not really seeing any of them.

Justin was aware of Dawn's presence and appreciated it but his thoughts were on Amanda. When death gets this close whether it's your own death or that of someone close to you, your life seems to flash before your eyes. It comes from the brain trying to recall every memory at once. He thought again of the old days before they were saved. He started telling Dawn stories about Amanda, stories that showed how ruthless she used to be, but also stories about the great changes in her since their conversion. He told her some things that he really shouldn't have for security purposes but he somehow trusted her.

Dawn for her part just listened; lost to the voice that washed over her very soul. It was about an hour later when Kathy and Stan literally ran in, "We just heard, Justin. How's Amanda?"

He told them what he knew and they comforted him the best they could. Dawn knew the moment of her usefulness had passed and she now felt awkward among these long-time friends. They did not notice her stand and walk out of the room and then the hospital. She would go back to her work and try to regain her own perspective. She was disturbed by the feelings that had stirred in her heart for Justin. She almost felt guilty but she kept saying to herself that they had just become friends is all and you, of course, feel empathy for a friend when they are hurting. It soothed her somewhat but she knew deep down that it was a lie. She just now came to the conscious realization that she had fallen in love with Dr. Justin Johnson. A love that she knew was out of place and inappropriate, especially now. The guilt that finally did get through wasn't from falling in love, however, but rather from the thought that just for a fleeting moment had crossed her mind, *'Maybe if Amanda dies. . .'* Tears welled up in Dawn's eyes. How could she think such a horrible thought? Instead of going back to the lab, she ran to her room and closed the door behind her. She slid down the door and wept bitter tears of pain and shame. She had nowhere to turn. She couldn't pray (she had never learned how) so she just wept and allowed her heart to break for Justin and for herself.

*   *   *

Amanda heard the voices first; distant voices that seemed strange and disembodied. What had she just heard herself say? There it was again, faint, weak, but determined, "Justin, I love you, Justin."

Then suddenly sound came roaring toward her jarring her to focus and she heard, "I love you to Amanda." She realized now that Justin was sitting by her bed holding her hand. He was squeezing too tight and it hurt but she loved the feeling all the same.

She looked up at Justin and whispered, "Justin, I have arranged for another companion for you. Don't you let me down with your usual stubbornness? Promise me, Justin."

Justin had no idea what she was talking about but he said, "I promise, honey, whatever you say."

She squeezed his hand weakly and smiled as darkness slipped back into her world. Her last thought was, *'Though I walk through the valley of the shadow of death, I will fear no evil. . .'*

*   *   *

Aegis touched Amanda's shoulder and whispered,

"It's time to go, Amanda." Amanda sat up and then stood. She suddenly felt great but what was this? She wasn't standing, she was floating. Her body lay below her and Justin knelt by her bed with his face buried in her chest, sobbing. Why was he so sad? She could no longer understand what sadness or pain was. These were things that belonged to that long ago life of the flesh, the memory of which was already slipping away. All she felt now was joy, peace, and a desire to move forward.

Amanda asked, "Aegis, will Justin be all right?"

Aegis smiled and said, "Of course, he will Amanda. Kapre will watch over him as I have you and he will find his way home in due time.

Her surroundings faded and she found herself standing before a Judge's desk. It was tall and three ancient men sat behind the desk. They were evil looking men; grumpy, withered, and mean spirited.

Aegis whispered, "Your accusers."

Before Aegis could explain the men opened a large book, on the cover of which were big gold letters; Amanda Dowling Johnson. They began to read from the book all the evil she had ever done to herself and to others. They drooled as they read of her evil works and yet she felt no fear.

She noticed that she floated in front of them. The room was incredibly plain. There was the Judge's desk in front of her. Behind and to the left was a door that on some conscious level she knew went to hell and there was a door behind and to the right that she knew went to heaven.

She whispered, "This can't be St. Peter at the

golden gate can it, Aegis?"

Aegis laughed and said, "No, as I said, these are your accusers."

Though she wasn't afraid she wondered how he could laugh in the face of their onslaught toward her and about to ask him that very question when the room suddenly filled with a warm, blinding, magnificent light. The very light itself was alive with love, peace, and harmony.

Amanda heard the men sigh with what? Disappointment?

The light dimmed slightly and it was then that Amanda realized that the light emitted from a man, yet He was more than a man. She knew him instantly. It was Jesus.

Jesus smiled at her and then turned his attention to the men and to the book they proudly held up for his study.

As they held it up they said, "Just read here, Lord, all the evil this child has done."

Jesus looked at the book and said, "What evil?"

They looked at the book and their faces turned red. They flipped through page after blank page and they began to turn pale. They yelled, "You can't do this to us, not again!"

Jesus looked angry for a moment and waved His hand over the men as He said, "I've told you before that I have no memory of evil that I have already paid the price for and neither does My Father." The men, the desk, everything was gone and Jesus stood alone facing Aegis and Amanda, "You have done another superb job, Aegis, now go and worship. Aegis smiled and immediately disappeared. There is nothing that honors an angel more than to be invited to worship at the very Throne of God.

That now left Amanda held in place by some unseen hand and Jesus her Savior. Jesus spoke first, "I have come for you as I promised, Amanda. Remember your lessons? Absent from the body present with the Lord?"

Amanda smiled, "Yes, I remember, Lord." The binding power holding her back was released and Amanda ran to the arms of Jesus and they hugged. He was real flesh and blood as she now was not. She knew this even though she looked the same as before, maybe younger even and definitely much more healthy.

Jesus could read her thoughts and laughed, "There is no sickness, pain, or evil of any kind here, Amanda. He held her to Him even tighter as tears of joy rolled down His cheeks.

Amanda spoke into His chest, which was crushed against her face, and she wished would never be removed, "I don't know what to do first, Lord. Do I kneel before you and beg for my life? Do I worship you now? I want to do those things but all I feel right now is joy, peace, and comfort."

Jesus said, "I already own your life, Amanda. I have paid the price for it and it need not be done again. As for worship, joy, peace, comfort and I might even add happiness; these are already yours to enjoy and they will never again be taken from you."

He held her hand; a Father leading a child. Jesus turned and opened the door behind him and they were facing pure light. In the light was the pure essence of God the Father. Amanda sighed, for she had no words for what she saw and felt. Jesus closed the door behind them and they were consumed by God's presence.

The flesh of her body did not melt away though His Glory would surely have done so to regular flesh and blood. She understood that the Light was the Holy Spirit as they passed through it toward the Throne.

Thousands of angels knelt in adoration of their God and He returned their love to them, purified, enhanced, and full of power. Amanda realized that the same was happening to her and she suddenly felt very ancient and wise. All the experiences of mankind rushed into her soul as did God's love for them. Magnificent creatures surrounded the Throne and cried praises constantly to their God. Jesus suddenly sat at the Fathers right hand and the love that passed between them was the Spirit of that love. It permeated all that was Heaven and all that it contained.

Amanda knelt with other immortal humans who she hadn't noticed before but yet she knew them all instantly. She heard a familiar voice, "What no hug for an old friend?"

She looked up and was shocked for some reason to see Pastor Bob standing there. On earth she had known little about him but now knew all that he had done and loved him for it. She jumped up and they hugged.

Jesus stood and said, "I would like you all to welcome Amanda. Well done my good and faithful servant."

To her surprise, everyone, including the angels and yes, even God the Father Himself began to applaud for her. Pastor Bob was suddenly holding a crown, embedded with countless and priceless gems and he placed this on Amanda's head. She also now wore a robe of pure white like the others.

Her joy was so immense that she was afraid that she wouldn't be able to contain it. She walked toward the Throne of God and climbed the steps to the Throne of Jesus the Christ and said as she removed the crown, "I owe all to You, Lord." and she knelt, placing the crown at the feet of Jesus. Suddenly behind Jesus the light split and parted. As it moved aside more and more of a glorious city became visible. It sparkled in the Light which was God and Pastor Bob took her arm and led her toward the city and her new home which had been prepared for her from before time. Yes, she was home and she knew that an eternity of adventure and pure uninterrupted life awaited her there.

As they walked forward, Amanda looked back and noticed that Jesus was gone. *'Off to meet another arrival no doubt,'* thought Amanda. As they passed through the Golden Gates of the New Jerusalem, Amanda's breath caught at what she saw. The first thing she noticed was that there was no Saint Peter at the gate. He was much too busy enjoying himself elsewhere. She knew why also, walking on a bit faster in order to embrace her new existence with open and loving arms. She laughed as she skipped. Spinning and laughing with the joy of her new knowledge. She yelled to no one in particular, "Oh, I had no clue!"

God smiled at her joy, increasing it with loving generosity, just as fast as she could absorb it. God whispered into her very soul, "This is what awaits all who love and honor My Son."

Amanda laughed and yelled, "Thank you, Father!"

CHAPTER FORTY-ONE

RISING FROM THE ASHES

Time didn't exist for Justin right now. He was holding Amanda in his arms. Kathy and Stan kept trying to get him to let go but he would not.

'*Amanda dead?*' thought Justin. He still hadn't had time to find out what had really happened. His heart broke with accusations that he made about himself, '*I should have noticed that something was wrong*', he thought as he rocked her back and forth praying for God to give her back.

Finally he stopped crying and rocking. He laid Amanda down gently and straitened her hair. Her mouth was open as well as her eyes and she had a bluish tint to her skin. She had lost most of her body heat and Justin could no longer deny that Amanda was gone.

He looked up at Kathy and Stan and whispered, "She's gone."

He looked so pathetically sad that Kathy's heart melted and she helped him to his feet and hugged him tightly to her. He hugged her back trying to remember Amanda's warmth. He kissed her on the forehead and whispered, "Thank you for being with me; you too Stan. Could you stay with me for a while in my apartment? I don't want to be alone just yet."

"Of course, they both said in unison," and they guided him out of the room and the hospital to his apartment. Dr. Lanchester had given Kathy a bottle and told her to give him two of these after they were back at the apartment.

Justin moved where they directed him without resistance. He took the offered pills and swallowed them and then at their direction lay down on his couch. No one spoke and soon the room began to spin and then darkness mercifully engulfed him.

*   *   *

There was a knock at the door and Stan answered it. Dawn Delarenzo stood there with a basket, "I thought you two could use a meal. I heard you came over with Justin over three hours ago."

Stan smiled, stepped aside, and said, "That's right, Dawn; and Justin has been asleep most of that time, mercifully." He closed the door behind her and said, "Smells good, what's in there?"

Dawn smiled, "Chicken, potato salad, slaw, and three pieces of apple pie."

She set it down on the dining room table and opened the basket. Kathy had gotten some plates and silverware and they had everything set out quick enough. They insisted that she join them, "Justin will be sleeping for hours according to the doctor who recommended a sedative." said Kathy as she filled her own plate.

They ate in silence for a moment and then Stan asked, "How is your work progressing?"

Dawn finished chewing a mouthful of food and then answered, "It has been slow going actually but we have a lot of preliminary tests to run before we can start with new theories. The facility is really first rate, though, and a wonderful change from the norm."

Kathy smiled, "I'm glad to hear it. A lot of planning went into that lab, not to mention the money it took to accomplish that caliber of a facility."

Stan looked and Kathy nodded. Stan stood and said, "Well, I have to get back to some important security matters if you ladies will excuse me?"

He bent down and kissed Kathy on the lips and threw a salute to Dawn and left the room, taking his apple pie with him. Kathy turned to Dawn with a serious expression on her face as she asked, "Dawn, I hope you don't mind this question but it was Amanda's dying wish that I talk to you about this. Do you love Justin?"

Dawn just about choked on the piece of apple pie she had just put into her mouth. She grabbed a napkin and spit the apple pie into it and coughed several times while Kathy apologized profusely, "It's O.K. Kathy you just surprised me. What makes you ask a question like that?"

Kathy was still patting Dawn's back when she whispered, "The day before Amanda died she came to my office and said, 'Kathy, I want you to know something.' I nodded and she continued, 'I am very sick; I believe it's cancer but all the tests aren't in yet, but that's not what I came to tell you."

"I got up and hugged her and she wept in my arms for some time before she continued. She was very pale and she whispered, 'I'm positive that Dawn Delarenzo is in love with my husband.' I must have looked shocked for she hurriedly continued with a laugh, 'Oh, I don't mean that they are having an affair or anything of that sort. She has been very careful not to act on her feelings and for that I'm very grateful, but she has the feelings nonetheless. I want you to help me with something.'

"Here she paused to catch her breath and then she continued, 'Justin is so caught up in his work that he hasn't noticed my illness and that's mostly my fault. I've hidden most of the symptoms from him. The point is that I don't think he has a clue how Dawn feels about him and I wouldn't have changed that for anything, except that things are different now. I've seen people suffer for years from guilt, and they live long lonely lives out of misplaced guilt or loyalty for their deceased spouse. Justin must not be allowed to suffer so. Do you understand?'

"Well, I told her that I didn't completely understand what she was asking me to do, so she said, 'Kathy, I want you to talk to Dawn immediately after my death and see if I'm right about her. If I am, and I believe I am, tell her she not only has my blessing but my request that she storm Justin's life immediately with that love. Justin can't be forced; he must be guided into what is best for him. Dawn will know how to do that. I don't want Justin to go through life alone and Dawn is a very nice person and a Christian; she will be good for him. They will have their work in common and I'm sure with her intelligence and charm she can win Justin over in time. I would go to her myself but I think it would embarrass her too much coming from me, so would you do it for me?'

"There, I got it all out. I told her that I would, never believing that her death would come so quickly, but there it is. It seemed to give her so much comfort that I had to follow through with her request. So, I ask you again, Dawn. Do you love Justin as Amanda thought?"

Dawn's eyes welled up with tears and she whispered, "Oh yes, Kathy, with all my heart and soul. I have felt so guilty for my feelings but maybe it was meant to be all along. Amanda was right when she said I never acted on my feelings and she was also right when she said that Justin hasn't a clue that I feel this way about him."

Kathy smiled at her, "I'm so happy you were honest with me and yourself, Dawn. You now know that you have Amanda's blessing to pursue those feelings and you also have mine. Guide him gently just by loving him and I'm sure that you will eventually win him over."

"But what will people think, Kathy? They'll think that I'm taking advantage of a new widower in his grief."

"Don't worry about what people think, Dawn. The Spirit of God has worked all this out with perfect timing and has even given you word from Amanda herself that it was all planned from the beginning. She would never have said those things if she didn't believe them herself. Amanda was never shy about telling people what she thought, so take it at face value."

"I feel happy that you told me but at the same time I feel guilty. I'm also a bit afraid that Justin will reject me. How could he believe me when I tell him that Amanda arranged for us to get together?"

Both women jumped when Justin said, "She told me herself Dawn."

They looked at him as he leaned against the door frame. They hadn't heard him get off of the couch and enter the room. He said, "Amanda told me right before she died that she had arranged for a companion for me and that I was not to reject her. She didn't tell me who but I guess I know who it is now. You were both right about me. I was too involved in my work to notice either her illness or your love for me, Dawn, but that will never happen again. Not after this.

Dawn jumped up and ran to Justin and hugged him desperately and he hugged her back just as desperately. Kathy got up and made a discreet exit.

*   *   *

Kapre smiled at the new couple and felt joy as Amanda laughed with glee as she stood at his right side. Her plan had worked and now she felt free to enjoy her own new existence. They faded back into heaven and Amanda was completely and permanently absorbed into God's presence.

CHAPTER FORTY-TWO

BACK ON TRACK

FOUR YEARS LATER:

Justin had learned his lessons well over these last four years; spending several hours per day in his lab doing his very important research, while at the same time showering Dawn with the attention their new relationship deserved. They did this by having supper every night; they tried to watch a movie a couple times a week and they were a sickeningly romantic couple. So for the most part, one wonderful day ran into another until four years had passed and Justin found himself sitting across from Dawn in the privacy of their living room.

Dawn looked at Justin very seriously and said, "Justin, I hate to add even more pressure to your already pressured life but I just found out today that I'm pregnant."

Justin stared at her for a moment and then they jumped up simultaneously, hugged tightly, and then jumped up and down like giddy children. The next nine months sped by and before they knew it they had a new little boy in their lives.

This was a different experience for Justin. He was fifty one years old and when most men were becoming grandparents, Justin became a father. The squirmy, wrinkled, whimpering newborn infant brought a new importance for human life to Justin's mind and heart.

On this day, he had fully reentered the world of the fully conscious parent. His hard heart, which was slowly thawing over the last almost five years had, at the instant his newborn was placed in his arms, completed the transformation and his life, mind, heart, and yes, even his soul, were all pure again as they had been when he was a young boy. Just by coming into this world and dropping into Justin's arms, this little boy had done what no other could. He had allowed his father's love to grow even more and perhaps soften a bit.

Mr. Summons came over and took charge of the boy while Justin turned his attention back to his wife. She lay on the very same hall floor where Amanda had collapsed. Dawn had been a week late delivering but when she did; it happened too fast for them to even make it to the hospital. One minute she was in a contraction, the next she grabbed Justin's arm and yelled, "He's coming do something!"

He had been literally running down the hall pushing her in a wheel chair but when she turned, grabbed his arm and yelled; Justin had stopped, gotten down in front of her and delivered his own son into the world. Mr. Summons had called for help but the boy had entered the world by the time he had delivered their location over the center's internal communication system.

Dawn was smiling despite the pain she had just endured and the sweat which caused her hair to stick to her forehead. Just when Justin was wondering how to handle the mess; hospital orderlies, doctors, nurses and even house cleaning all rushed onto the scene like the proverbial cavalry arriving at just the right moment. They politely, but firmly, pushed him aside and the floor was cleaned, Dawn was being pushed along toward the hospital on a proper gurney, and Mr. Summons was relieved of his little burden as well. With nothing else to do, Mr. Summons grabbed Justin by the arm and propelled him back toward their apartment, to get him cleaned up and calmed down. It was true; he had turned into a bundle of nerves once the duty was performed and the baby and mother were safely receiving loving treatment from others. Within a half hour, they were on their way to the O. B. Ward of the facility hospital.

Little Robert (Bobby) Johnson was snuggled up close to his mother, nursing at her breast contentedly, when Justin arrived. Dawn was aglow with the euphoria that comes with nursing your own child in the safety and comfort of a warm bed. They made quite the picture as Justin smiled down at them, not saying anything; neither of them wanted to spoil the moment with words.

Justin's communicator vibrated alerting him that his attention was required in the lab. He bent down and kissed Dawn on the forehead and whispered, "You two take care and I'll see you soon."

Dawn just smiled up at him and nodded as he left the room.

*　　　*　　　*

When Justin arrived at the lab the rest of the team was gathered in a group facing the door. They all yelled, "Congratulations, Daddy." Angie Beasley ran up and kissed him on the cheek. Bruce and Howard came over and pounded his back. Next, Cindy Lee planted another kiss on his other cheek and finally Victor came over and said, "On behalf of the team, I want to say," he stopped, looked at the others and nodded and they all sang, "For he's a jolly good fellow, for he's a jolly good fellow, for he's a jolly good fellow, that nobody can deny!" They all laughed and asked how Dawn and the baby were and just had an all-around good time. A cake was cut and devoured. Punch was served and downed and when things started to wind down some, Victor made the announcement, "Justin, while you were off delivering your son into the world, your team was following up on the research that you had assigned us some time back. We are proud to announce that you were right."

Justin had to stop and think for a moment and then his face brightened, "You mean?"

Victor said, "Yes, the appendix angle just might be the key. At first when you presented the idea, well, most of us thought you were nuts, but keeping an open mind as we all do," he smiled at the obvious over exaggeration of that point, "We went to work on the hypothesis as if it really had validity. You told us that you believed that the useless little organ may have had a purpose back in Biblical times and that it may even be linked to the reason why people lived so long back then. Well, we have proven at least that the appendix was just part of an organ which had long since disappeared."

"With computer probabilities and a little genetic investigation, we have formed a new hypothesis that we may be able to force the growth of the original organ as originally designed by our Lord all those many years before. It also appears that the organ was tied into the human immune system in some yet undiscovered way. I, or I should say, we, believe that if we can successfully regenerate that organ using the DNA pattern already existing in each person's appendix that it will naturally filter out all disease before it has a chance to grow and harm the body in any way. We now feel, as you proposed, that this organ was responsible for the long life of humans a millennia ago.

"We, of course, have years to go yet but we feel that we are back on the right track."

Within minutes they were all lost in the world of research and nothing else mattered in their small universe but finding the answers to their many new questions.

CHAPTER FORTY-THREE

BREAKTHROUGH

Justin sat in his wheelchair in the middle of the Botanical Garden that Amanda had created and that Dawn had loved and enjoyed so much. It had brought them hours of pleasure. He thought about the two women he had loved in his lifetime. He had been enriched by their love and care. Amanda was just a memory after being dead these past forty-eight years. Dawn, however, had just passed two years ago and he still had clear feelings and memories of their years together. His mind was still clear as a bell which he thought was a great accomplishment for a man of his age. Ninety-nine years today. He still couldn't believe it. He had been in a wheelchair just since Dawn's funeral when he tripped and fell. He had twisted his ankle, wrenched his knee, and broken his hip, all in a matter of seconds. He never recovered full use of it since and wouldn't take the time or the risk for surgery.

His son, Bobby, had grown into a fine man and was a Captain in the new Space Program. He was on his way to the new Mars Colony. He was Captain of his own L(unar)M(ars)C(olonization)T(ransport) and was taking the first "civilian group" of married couples and their children (1289 souls) to the new Mars Colony. The Colony consisted of a Domed City, quite the site from the pictures he'd seen. They would live, work, and grow in their new environment and build other Domed Cities and populate them as well. It was quite an ostentatious project.

Justin could marvel at the work and dreams of others but never thought of his own work as anything out of the ordinary. To the rest of the world his research was nothing less than miraculous. The members of his original team were all dead now, he was the last. The Antidote facility was filled with new faces, young faces, but they still held Justin in the highest esteem. What he and his original team had accomplished was nothing short of amazing and Justin was still right in the middle of the research. He had learned and adapted over the years and could keep up with the brightest minds of this new age of accomplishment. Just last night they had found the breakthrough that was needed to make the "Antidote" to all disease work. He had gotten away from the bustle so he could think about and absorb what they had actually accomplished. Mr. Summons stood tall behind him. He, of course, had aged only slightly over the years which surprised everyone but Justin, who knew all too well what and who Mr. Summons really was.

It was to Mr. Summons that he addressed the problem, "The fight will now begin you know?"

Mr. Summons simply stated, "Yes."

They both knew that Justin's time on earth was drawing to a close but that didn't worry either of them.

Mr. Summons said thoughtfully, "It's probably not too late to use this new discovery on yourself and prolong your life here a bit."

Justin just cackled a hoarse laugh and said, "Why would I want to do that? I think I've been around quite long enough, Kapre." When they were alone Justin always used the angel's real name. "This discovery was never meant for me and you know it. It's for the young people who have the hope of building a better world than their ancestors."

Kapre smiled and said, "They'll have a chance at that now that they have turned more fully toward the Lord. You have done much through your generosity to world charities and telling people when asked, 'Why do you support the feed the world charity?' or 'Why help the homeless with extensive housing projects which you allow them to live in for the work they do maintaining them?' and you always answer the same." Now here they both said in unison, "I'm just sharing the love that the Lord Jesus has given so freely to me." They both laughed. Kapre continued, "That has done much more for furthering the Kingdom than all the sermons that have ever been preached about it. You don't even realize that there are millions of young people taking up your charities as their life's work and it has gone far to make the world a safer and better place in which to live."

Justin looked up into Kapre's face and said, "Not bad for a man who hasn't left this building in over fifty years I suppose."

The room they were in was very beautiful with blooming flowers and flowering trees and humming birds flitting here and there. As relaxing as it was, Justin could wait no longer. He asked, "Have the arrangements been made to meet with Jennifer?"

Jennifer Saxon was now President of the United States and would soon be part of the new World Governing Panel which would replace the old United Nations and have far more actual power. By this move, they had stripped the Committee of much of its power. However, its influence would still be felt in many of the decisions that were still left to be made. Jesse C. Whinestein, the new Chairman of the Committee, was actually a pretty good sport about the whole thing and by playing along had landed himself a powerful role in the new government as Ambassador for the United States. As such he would spearhead negotiations with many other countries making sure that the interests of the United States of America were always looked after; and of course making millions of dollars for himself in the process. He had a son; a very bright lad, if only half of what Justin had heard was true. What was his name? Oh yes, Christian Whinestein, only twelve years old but bright. (His mother and father had him late in life).

Justin's mind snapped back to the present moment and he had to stop to think what he was going to say. His mind, he had noticed lately, wondered like that from time to time, flooded as it was with information all at once and he had to forcefully sort through the onslaught of information in order to carry on a simple conversation.

Kapre helped him out by answering, "Yes, she is coming here this afternoon."

Justin thought, *'She? Oh yes, Jennifer. Nice woman. Smart too."*

However, he said, "So soon? I'm not ready yet. There is so much to do."

Kapre smiled, "It's being seen to as we speak, Justin. Don't worry about it now just relax."

Justin's head leaned forward as he slipped into one of his many daily naps.

Kapre smiled at his charge and prayed for peace and health to see Justin through what would most likely be his final tasks here on earth.

CHAPTER FORTY-FOUR

HIGH PRAISE

"Lord Satan!" Captain Detestation entered Satan's presence and immediately bent down on his right knee, bowed his head and slapped his right fist against his own left shoulder.

Satan, who was sitting high on his elaborate dais, looked down on his Captain and smiled; Captain Detestation held his position and would hold it until given permission to rise by Satan himself. The Captain was an impressively large Demon and he held about as much power as Satan had allowed any of his Demons. Detestation had the distinction of being the "Spirit Guide" of the father of the Anti-Christ himself. Of course to that man he was known as "Grandeur the Great". His new charge was seventy-one years old and had a son who was only twelve years old at this time. Into this boy Satan had poured much of his power and he, Satan, would at the right time, personally possess this boy's body. Satan intended to become the leader of this world, in human form, much as Jesus Christ could have, had he listened to simple reason and logic. Instead he had rejected Satan's offer and had paid the price for that refusal.

Satan came out of his reverie and commanded, "You may rise, Captain."

Captain Detestation rose and awaited questioning, hoping desperately that he had all the answers.

Satan smiled at the Captain's nervousness and

after a moment of enjoyment asked, "Is the boy progressing as planned?"

The Captain smiled and said, "Way ahead of schedule, sire. I trained his father well in all of our methods and have helped him to pass it all on to his son. At age twelve, the boy's powers are already surpassing those of his father. In just six more years, he will have doubled his capacity to receive your gifts, sire, and will be ready to rule the world."

"The people of the world have been prepared for the inevitability of a world leader. Over the years with improvements in communications and travel, the world has been made compact enough to control. The people have been desensitized from individualism to the preferable 'For the good of all' mentality. Science has replaced religion, comfort and convenience have replaced duty and responsibility, and a vast majority of humans are feeling lost and alone. Fewer and fewer of them are turning to well, you know who." Here Captain Detestation pointed a finger upward.

Satan said, "It is all right to just say the enemy. We'll both know to whom you are referring, Captain."

"Yes sir!"

"Speaking of the enemy, Captain, what are they up to lately?"

"Well sir, you know how hard it is to keep track of all their plots, but one really big one is the creation of some kind of antidote against all disease. I have tried to stop it but they seem to be keeping just one step ahead of me, sir." Sweat began to bead up on the Captains forehead.

Satan didn't miss the response but he said, "You

have done quite well, Captain so relax just a little will you. I didn't call you here to punish you. On the contrary, I have called you here to give you the highest praise that I can. I am promoting you to General from this moment on. Congratulations."

Captain, now, General Detestation smiled and looked down on each shoulder and sure enough the insignia of a General had appeared on each shoulder. His entire stature, had in fact, been altered to match that of a great warrior and leader of Satan's Army. Satan had very few Generals and that was indeed the highest praise that he could heap upon Detestation.

Satan stood and announced, "Guard, open the gates and let the army in. The celebration of General Detestation will now begin."

The gates opened, the feast was set and the lengthy celebration began.

*　　*　　*

General Logos couldn't believe what he had seen, Satan rewarding Detestation after losing a man like Justin Johnson to the enemy. Satan had something up his sleeve and Logos didn't like it. No, he didn't like it at all. He had a feeling that he better prepare his men for action. A celebration dinner like the one Satan was throwing could only mean one thing. War! Well if they attack Justin, they will have to come through Logos and his army first.

THE ANTIDOTE

*   *   *

President Jennifer Saxon liked Justin Schaefer Johnson; partly because he made her feel young again and partly because he was always so positive. She was sixty-two now but still carried herself well and was still beautiful. Her long chestnut hair, which had a few streaks of gray, that Jennifer wisely left alone, flowed down over the shoulders of her dark blue business suit. It was a dress suit as opposed to a pants suit because Jennifer was all woman. She accomplished a perfect mixture of the effeminate with the power and strength of her office.

She stood patiently, waiting in the conference room, when the door opened and the low smooth humming sound of his wheelchair announced the arrival of President Johnson. She turned and walked toward him raising her hand as she approached.

Justin stopped his chair and took her hand in his and kissed it and then looked up into her blue eyes which sparkled with intelligence and humor, "It is such a delight to see you again, Madame President."

"And you, Mr. President."

"Ah if I were only thirty years younger, Jennifer, I'd be after you full time."

"What a nice compliment, Justin. Coming from you, I would have to let myself be caught. Age never has really mattered to me, though. If we weren't so busy, I might just let you catch me now. You could probably out run me in your new chair I'm sure."

"Ah, you do an old man's heart good, Madame President. You're right; however, we are too busy for

456

personal enjoyments aren't we?"

"I'm afraid so, Justin. Much the pity, isn't it?"

"Yes, yes, too bad for sure. I suppose you have read over all the material I sent you, Madame President."

"Jennifer, please, Justin. All that formality we can save for the public. Let's enjoy a little intimacy at least shall we?"

"Of course, you are right Jennifer. We are good friends after all. Come now, time is of the essence for a man my age. Tell me what you thought, what your scientists thought, and what your advisors thought."

"The scientists found it all very interesting and they all agree that it will probably work. My advisors are also afraid that it will work. They say that it will be the ruin of the economy. The price of medicine and health care has always been a sore spot with them, but now faced with the elimination of all need for health care; well it scares them to death. What will we do with all the doctors, nurses, hospitals, etc. etc."

"I took that into account you know?"

"I hoped you had, Justin. What would you tell them?"

"People will still need vitamins, they will still need to be attended for emergencies; accidents, old age, cosmetic surgery etc. This will take care of all disease but they will still need to monitor patients for complications and simple ailments that will still most likely arise.

"We will still need research into feeding the world and healing the atmosphere etc. so they change their majors and take on new challenges. Besides this procedure won't work on the elderly, most of whom have had their appendix out already, so they will have plenty of time for the changes that will need to be made. We will need surgeons to perform the procedure on the young so the transition will occur over a period of years. This procedure will be rather expensive, but the various governments will be able to pick up the balance of the cost from the money they will save in other areas of research. Funded research in areas such as diabetes, heart disease, cancer, and many more, none of which will be needed any longer.

"I'm going to patent the discovery in the name of humanity, so it will belong to all governments. The only rights I will hold on it is that it must be given freely to all peoples of each country. That's where you come in, Jennifer. I need your help to sell this to the other nations as well as our own. They must see the importance of giving this to all classes of people freely and it must be done worldwide or else wars will be fought to get at it."

Jennifer whistled, "Well you don't think small do you, Justin?"

"I was hoping that this new World Governing Panel would take this on as their first assignment. It is a gift to be shared, it's the only way; you do see that don't you, Jennifer?"

"Yes, I'm afraid I agree with you. It won't be easy though."

"No but it is possible if the information is shipped to all governments at once and explained well and we give them the means to do it. Their technologies will need to be advanced enough to carry it out, which means that we must give them equipment and technicians that will be able to train their staff where needed. We can do this."

"What about the Committee, Justin?"

"To my surprise, Jesse C. Whinestein has agreed to help enforce this, if we will give his son, Christian Whinestein, a large role to play in its distribution and enforcement."

"His son is only twelve years old, Justin."

"I know that but I was a doctor at fourteen and Christian is already a doctor at twelve. I understand that he is very bright and energetic and unusually mature for his age."

Jennifer shivered, "I met him once, Justin, and he gives me the creeps."

Justin smiled, "Very new age oriented and has his own Spirit Guide I understand. Unfortunately, we need him to pull this off. One more thing, Jesse Whinestein wants Christian to take over his spot on the WGP when this is over. He hopes the boy will prove his worth by then and make it easier for you to appoint him. He will also help you when re-election rolls around and you know how helpful that can be."

"I just don't like owing that man." Jennifer shivered again.

Justin smiled and said, "Don't worry about it. You know that the Lord has your back, right?"

Jennifer smiled back and nodded.

Justin's smile broadened, "Then we are agreed?"

Jennifer smiled and said, "I agree fully. Now let's look at the particulars. . ."

Their meeting lasted another two hours as they hammered out the details and preparations were made to distribute Justin's discovery worldwide. A discovery that once found turned out to be quite simple really. A liquid formula would be injected into each participant and an electrode stimulator would be surgically attached to the appendix. The combination would stimulate the natural growth of the gland that in Biblical times had existed in humans. That gland (known as the 'Justin' gland), would now, as then, keep the body free of all diseases and would allow people to stop aging quickly. As a matter of fact, they would again live to be perhaps eight or nine hundred years old, just as our ancestors had. Only people, who still had their appendix, could be treated and the very young would receive this procedure as easily as they had gotten vaccinations for childhood diseases. The surgery would be done laparascopically and the infinitesimal scar would be as accepted as the navel.

Justin sat back satisfied that they had finally thought of everything and when Jennifer agreed they smiled, shook hands and she said, "Well Justin, I'll see you in about six months if everything goes well for us. I really think that we can pull this off."

"I do too, Jennifer, and I'll be looking forward to finally getting the project from theory to practical application as soon after that as possible."

"You should be very proud of what you have accomplished, Justin. It may be the biggest step forward that the human race has taken in years. You will, in effect, be creating an entirely new race."

"Thank you, Jennifer, but all the glory must go to our God, who is really just giving us the gift of long life back, a gift that He had given us long ago and one that we abused. I hope that we can use it this time to trust our God and to give our lives and our service back to Him as a gift".

They shook hands and then Jennifer leaned in and kissed Justin on the cheek and whispered, "By the way, happy birthday, Justin." She kissed his cheek again and said, "Until then?"

"Yes, till then and thank you." He said to her back as she walked out of the room. He touched his cheek and smiled, thinking, *'What a nice birthday present; she gave me a kiss for each wife.'* A tear of joy rolled down the old man's cheek.

CHAPTER FORTY-FIVE

THE SYMPOSIUM

General Logos had been correct to be alert. As the day of the Symposium, dawned General Logos of the Nostrum, found himself in the enemy's lair. It was a large cavern which served as General Detestation's base of command. The enemy had decided to remove President Johnson once and for all. They had cooperated out of their own greed to help Justin's project on the one hand but had decided that they would kill the inventor on the eve of his greatest success. To do this, Satan had enlisted the help of a man who hated Justin with all of his being, a cunning and patient man and one who even now was being directed by the forces of evil under General Detestation's control.

'What we need is a distraction.' thought General Logos.

*   *   *

The man, disguised as a camera man, climbed the back of the large screen which was located about one half mile from the lectern where President Johnson would deliver his speech. His camera was in reality a very high-powered rifle which would deliver a deadly hollow-pointed bullet to its intended target with an accuracy that had been practiced for months now. The man's life had been consumed with preparation for this one last act of violence toward a man he had grown to hate more than he did life itself.

He strapped himself into position, raised the camera/rifle and looked through the scope. The podium zoomed toward him like he could reach out and touch it. It was a special podium, designed for a man in a wheelchair. It was low and would not block his shot.

He smiled as he thought, *'Finally, Mr. President, we will meet on the field of battle and you will die.'*

*   *   *

Logos screamed his battle cry, "For My Lord GOD Almighty!" as his bright, pure white blade sliced effortlessly through Detestation directly to his heart. He stood frozen for what seemed an eternity, years of effort flashed before his eyes. He knew what horrors awaited his failure and tears formed in his eyes. The mighty demon of Satan, Detestation, cried one last desperate, "Nooo!" as he puffed out of existence, losing everything he had fought so hard for. His long reign of terror was over, as was disease; a cure had been found at last. The earth year 2099 was just passing as the large and final puff of reddish brown smoke filled the now empty chamber, all other demons having wisely fled the premises.

Logos, dropped his sword, collapsed to his knees in exhaustion, and ignored the blood oozing from the open wound in his chest. Never had he fought so hard, or found it so difficult to defeat a foe. He decided that he was badly in need of a vacation, perhaps even retirement. *'The cabin?'*, the thought brought a smile to his face and he ignored his wounds while he prayed his prayer of thanksgiving.

*   *   *

The sniper had waited patiently for the words that were his cue to act.

Justin raised his old, shaky hands to the sky and yelled, "Praise and honor be to our Lord and Savior, Jesus Christ. . ."

On the backside of one of the large screens, the side facing the speaker, a man was strapped into position. He raised the high powered rifle and looked through the scope once again. Needles pointed from all directions to the center of the scope's sight and centered in that sight was President Justin Schaefer Johnson. The sniper's breathing was smooth and even. The ever increasing pressure that he now applied to the trigger was patient and ever so smooth. The sniper whispered to himself, "Good night, Mr. President."

The silenced explosion released the hollow-pointed bullet at an unbelievable velocity and it raced toward its intended target; the heart of President Justin Schaefer Johnson.

Before any human could have acted, computer sensors detected the bullet and activated a transparent bullet-proof shield that shot into position just a fraction of a second before the bullet arrived at its intended target.

President Johnson jumped involuntarily as the almost invisible shield shot up in front of him and just a fraction of a second later the bullet hit, severely cracking the shield but it held. Security rushed to both Presidents and surrounded them as they were both rushed from the stage. Jennifer running and Justin wheeling as fast as his chair would go. Other snipers found their target and opened fire snuffing out the life of the would-be assassin. The crowd screamed as they hit the ground and fell on one another. Panic reigned for a few seconds as alarms blared, people screamed and orders were given. Then just as quickly it was over.

*   *   *

Four hours later and safely back in his office deep in The Antidote; Justin read the report that had been handed to him by security. As he read the security Chief said, "The sniper was an Alverez Lopez; a cousin to one Scotty Lopez. I believe you worked with him at one time in your youth, Mr. President."

Justin turned pale and whispered, "Our sins do indeed come back to haunt us, don't they?"

"What was that, Mr. President?"

Jennifer stepped up and said, "Nothing! Now leave us won't you?"

Once they were alone, Jennifer came over to Justin and said, "We mustn't bring up the past, Justin."

Justin smiled weakly and whispered, "I know that I have been forgiven for all the lives I have taken, but it still breaks my heart and weighs heavily on me even today. I only hope that the work God has done through me will make up for it in some small way."

Jennifer was about to reassure him when President Justin Johnson turned pale and slumped to one side. His work here was finished.

*   *   *

Jesus finished reading General Logos' report and smiled. Well written, Logos. I have reached a decision about you. You have had some time off to relax and reflect and I must agree that Kapre has shown himself to be worthy of My Nostrum. I have a special assignment for Michael, my Archangel, and he will no longer have time to run the Nostrum. I would like you, Logos, to take over those duties. Will You?"

Logos didn't hesitate, "You know best, Lord. It would be my honor."

Jesus smiled and said, "That will, of course, leave your spot empty and you will of course get to choose your own replacement. Do you still stand behind Kapre as your choice?"

Logos smiled, "Yes, Lord, I do."

Just then a beam of light flashed and standing before them were Kapre and a young and healthy Justin Johnson. Jesus stood and said, "Welcome home, Justin."

The Savior and the saved hugged and Justin felt a love that could never have been described to him. Kapre had been right about that. Amanda and Dawn ran up and greeted Justin as did Pastor Bob and many others.

As they basked in the joy of reunion, Jesus turned to Kapre and asked, "How do you like your new armor?"

Kapre looked confused, and then looking down noticed that he was now wearing the gleaming armor of the Nostrum. He looked up in surprise and before he could say anything Tutor came up and slapped him on the back and said, "I knew you could do it boy! I always knew you could do it!"

THE ANTIDOTE

Other angels congratulated Kapre and he soon fell into his new role and his new duties. Many things were left to be done before the end of the world would come and the new life promised by the Lord could begin.

This has been just one story of a human and an angel. There are many more in the process of being written even as you read these words. Yours, my dear friend, is one of them. Make it a good story won't you? Make it count. Join Jesus in His mission to save the world and do it while there is still time.

THE END